W9-BWQ-440

# SECONDS
## TO
# MIDNIGHT

## Also by Philip Donlay

# SECONDS

## TO

# MIDNIGHT

### A DONOVAN NASH NOVEL

## PHILIP
## DONLAY

OCEANVIEW

PUBLISHING

LONGBOAT KEY, FLORIDA

ISBN  978-1-60809-228-4

Published in the United States of America by Oceanview Publishing

Longboat Key, Florida

www.oceanviewpub.com

10 9 8 7 6 5 4 3 2 1

PRINTED IN THE UNITED STATES OF AMERICA

To the memory of Gary Shulze

Consummate bookseller and friend

You will be missed

# ACKNOWLEDGMENTS

WRITING BOOKS IS for the most part a solitary process, though I've grown to respect as well as appreciate the fact that success hinges on dear friends, colleagues, and experts. Without them, I have no doubt that my efforts would be futile, so I want to offer my deepest thanks to those who never fail to keep me pointed in the right direction. To my parents, Cliff and Janet, as well as my brother, Chris, and son, Patrick—thank you. To Scott Erickson, Bo Lewis, Pamela Sue Martin, Kerry Leep, Nancy Gilson, Thomas Brandau, Darcy Eggeman, Tex and Heidi Irwin, Philip Marks Jr., and Brian Bellmont, you've all played a bigger part in the completion of this book than you'll ever know.

I'd also like to thank my agent, Kimberley Cameron, and her team of talented professionals. Then of course there are the people who shed light on a myriad of subjects well beyond my expertise. Dr. Philip Sidell and Dr. D.P. Lyle, thanks for all that you do, both medically and literarily. Victoria Dilliott, Mark Hurwitz, David Ivester, Jeff Frye, Samantha Fischer, and Maddee James, you're all amazing, and I'm the first to admit that I couldn't do what I do without your efforts. To Oceanview Publishing, the people who turn my words into books—thank you.

And finally, heartfelt well-wishes go out to all of my brothers and sisters around the world, who, like me, battle Ankylosing Spondylitis and the associated nightmares that come with this fearsome disease. You inspire me each and every day to keep fighting and move forward.

# SECONDS
## TO
# MIDNIGHT

# CHAPTER ONE

WHEELING IN THE rarified air at thirty-nine thousand feet, Donovan Nash and his entire four-person crew aboard the *Galileo* marveled at the spectacular brilliance of the Northern Lights. Sitting next to him in the cockpit was Michael Ross, flying their precise track in the empty airspace miles above Northern Manitoba, less than five hundred miles south of the Arctic Circle. In the eastern sky, the sun was only minutes from rising above the horizon, yet the remnants of the Northern Lights continued to swirl and dance with ethereal green and red tendrils. The largest solar storm ever recorded was in progress, bombarding Earth with massive solar radiation, and those aboard the *Galileo*, Eco-Watch's highly modified Gulfstream IV, observed the celestial extravaganza from the front row.

From the right seat, Donovan caught a momentary flash from far away. He squinted into the sun, a narrow sliver peeking above the eastern horizon, and saw nothing. Then it blinked again, a brief point of light in his peripheral vision. He turned to find what looked like a solitary contrail that blended perfectly with the snow-covered ground. Donovan followed the unfurling vapor trail until he found its source. What seconds ago was a glimmer on the horizon, quickly became a Boeing 737 closing in on them at nearly the speed of sound.

"Climb, Michael! Climb!" Donovan yelled.

Without hesitation, Michael pulled hard on the controls and simultaneously pushed up both throttles. They hurtled upward out of thirty-nine thousand feet, and Michael banked the *Galileo* to the left just as the Boeing flashed beneath them.

The sound of the stick shaker reverberated through the cockpit, warning of an imminent stall. Michael lowered the nose, trying to gain the speed he'd lost avoiding the Boeing. In one violent action, the Gulfstream descended into the Boeing's wake turbulence. The two horizontal tornadoes that streamed back from the 737's wingtips enveloped the *Galileo*, and the powerful vortex flipped the Gulfstream upside down before the inertia just as quickly flung them free. Michael kept the Gulfstream rolling all the way around until they were once again wings level.

Donovan watched the Boeing angle away from them holding a northwest heading. Behind them, in the back of the *Galileo*, were two scientists using the Gulfstream's complex sensors and optics array to record as much data about the solar storm as possible. A glance over his shoulder told Donovan that both men were still at their stations.

"Dear God, that was close," Michael said. "Do you still have him? What in the world is he doing out here?"

"What in hell is that guy doing?" Rick Mathews, the third Eco-Watch pilot, said as he rushed from the cabin into the cockpit. "It happened fast, but that looked like a private 737."

The severe atmospheric conditions prevented any communication with air traffic control. "They're descending. Follow him," Donovan said, his fear tapering off, his adrenaline mixed with anger.

Michael added power and brought the speed of the Gulfstream up to redline. Traveling over five hundred miles per hour, the *Galileo* closed on the Boeing. "I think it's best if we come at him from above and behind," he said. "There's something really off about all of this. I want to get a good look without him knowing we're here."

"I like that plan, Michael," Donovan said. "Rick, did you get a look at his registration? Do we know what country he's from?"

"No, all I saw was a 737 with what looked like green and gold stripes."

Donovan picked up a telephone that served as an intercom to communicate with the two researchers seated in the back. "Dr. Samuels, is everyone still in one piece back there?"

"Captain Nash, what in the hell was that all about?" Dr. Samuels asked. "Is everything okay?"

"Everything's fine, we had to take evasive action to avoid a midair collision with another airplane."

"I thought Canadian air traffic control said there would be no traffic for the entire time we were on station?"

"That's what they told us, which is why we're following this guy. He's flying without a working transponder, which is why there was no collision warning. With the sun coming up, I was wondering if you could use some of our optical equipment to help us identify them."

"Let me see what I can do," Samuels replied. "Exactly where is he right now?"

Donovan looked up and spotted the 737 just as it vanished into a deck of clouds below them. "He just went into the clouds. I'll get back to you."

"I'm going to offset our course a few degrees so we don't run into this guy if he slows down," Michael said as he swung the *Galileo* to the left to parallel the Boeing.

"I know we can't communicate with the outside world via radio right now," Donovan said to Rick. "But how far south do we need to be, to get someone via satellite connection?"

"On our way north out of Minneapolis last night, we lost all communication about an hour's flying time south of here," Rick said. "Though, from what Dr. Samuels was saying about the storm, communication access could continue to fluctuate."

When the *Galileo* burst out of the bottom of the cloud deck, all eyes searched the sky for the 737. All that lay below them was the frigid snow-covered ground of Northern Manitoba.

"I've got him," Michael called out, his eyes fixed low and to their left. He immediately throttled back and deployed the speed brakes to get the *Galileo* lower. "He's slowed way down and is descending fast. I'm going to make a three-sixty to the left and come in behind him."

"Are they in trouble?" Rick asked. "Is that smoke coming from somewhere in the rear fuselage?"

"Could be," Michael said.

Donovan checked to make sure he had the emergency frequency dialed in the backup radio. "If he's having a problem, the short-range transmissions should work, and we haven't heard any kind of a distress call." He dropped his eyes to the flight management display. The closest airport was Churchill, Manitoba, and it lay 140 miles east of them. He looked out and once again located the 737. With Michael's massive descent and tight turn, they were quickly closing the gap.

The intercom to the back pinged. Donovan brought the phone to his ear without taking his eyes from the Boeing. "Doctor, what do you have?"

"We've got the camera array locked on to the Boeing. We have no Internet to gather more information, but from the onboard database I can tell you it's a Boeing Business Jet, based on a 737-800. We captured the registration. It's HZ-NCT."

"That's a Saudi Arabian aircraft," Donovan said. "Any owner listed in our database?"

"No," Dr. Samuels said. "From what we can see, smoke appears to be coming from the very aft part of the fuselage."

"Got it, thanks," Donovan said.

"Captain, wait! One of the over wing exits was just opened. There's smoke pouring out of the fuselage. Oh Jesus, something just fell from the aircraft!"

"Track it!" Donovan could see the increase in smoke from the 737. Michael was coming in high and fast and gaining, but whatever was happening, the *Galileo*'s optics still gave them the best view.

"We have the coordinates of the object plotted," Samuels said.

"Any clue what it was?" Donovan asked.

"I don't know yet; we'll have to enhance it later. It fell like something solid, but there was also fluttering, like cloth. I hate to speculate, maybe a body? Whatever it is came down in the forest."

"Lock onto the 737 and keep recording."

"He's putting down flaps," Michael said as the *Galileo* drew up less than a quarter of a mile behind the stricken Boeing. "Dear God, he's going to try and put it down."

"All of these lakes are frozen," Donovan said as he studied the terrain below, then turned to Michael. "Could he pull this off?"

"I don't have a clue how much snow is on top of the ice, but it looks like we're about to find out," Michael said. "Give me twenty degrees of flaps. I want to slow down to stay behind him."

"He just put his landing gear down," Donovan said. "He's picked his spot, the lake three miles dead ahead. It looks long enough."

"This is crazy. No distress call, no nothing," Michael said.

Donovan found himself holding his breath as the Boeing, still trailing smoke, cleared the tops of the snow-covered trees along the shore. Then, in a blur of billowing snow, everything vanished from his view. Michael swung the *Galileo* into a left turn as they flew over the top of the Boeing. All Donovan could see was a rising cloud of snow that completely obscured everything but the top of the tail.

The second they raced beyond the 737, Michael added power and cranked the Gulfstream around to the right to bring them back around for another look.

The Gs from the steep turn pushed Donovan down into his seat as Michael expertly maneuvered the *Galileo* only a hundred feet above the trees. As the Gulfstream swung around, Donovan strained to catch sight of the Boeing. It took him a moment to find the jet. The blizzard it had created on landing was still gently floating down onto the 737. As Michael flew back across the Boeing, the 737's wings rocked as bluish fissures raced out in all directions from the ice cracking beneath them. The Boeing lurched and then bucked sideways as the once solid surface of the lake collapsed and gave way. The entire airplane dropped straight down through the ice and splashed into the lake, geysers of water exploding upwards. As Michael flew closer, Donovan spotted a figure stagger from the smoking cabin through the emergency exit and fall, landing hard on the wing. As the *Galileo* drew closer, Donovan saw the person stand up and run unsteadily toward the wingtip as the Boeing began sinking, tail first.

As the Gulfstream flew low and raced straight for the sinking Boeing, the person on the wing stopped and looked upward, and Donovan could see it was a woman. Thrown off-balance by the abrupt motion of the metal shifting beneath her feet, she slipped, careened sideways, and then jumped in an effort to clear the open water and make it to the ice.

"Michael, did you see that?" Donovan said as his friend pulled the *Galileo* into another steep turn to bring them back around. In the turn, Donovan saw the swath that the Boeing had made in the snow, the soft blue coloring from the ice just visible in the morning light. "Did she make it?"

"I see her, she's in the water." Michael swiveled his head to keep the sinking Boeing in sight as he flew. He made the turn toward the 737. Only the cockpit of the Boeing was still above the water.

Craning his neck, Donovan spotted the woman. She was clutching the edge of the ice trying to pull herself out of the water.

"I don't see anyone else in the water," Michael said as he banked for another low pass. "Are you thinking what I'm thinking?"

"I say we do it."

Michael's eyes narrowed as he looked out the window at the lake. "The Boeing cleared a long enough swath of loose snow on the lake to use as a runway. My concern is stopping on the ice."

"If the reverse thrust isn't enough, you can edge the landing gear into the snow and slow us down that way," Donovan said. "The ice will hold. We're a good thirty thousand pounds lighter."

"The 737 has underwing engines, and they're hanging down by the main gear only a couple of feet above the ice. I think that's why they broke through the ice," Michael said as he started to slow the Gulfstream. "Our engines are up on the tail far above the ice. My concern is our brakes melting the ice and then freezing. If that happens, we'll be stuck here. The key is to keep the wheels turning, so I'm not shutting down the engines, or stopping this thing for more than a few seconds. The moment we're stopped, the airstair goes down, you jump off, and I keep us moving."

"Rick, take my place." Donovan threw off his harness. He gave Michael a nod of understanding and slapped his shoulder as he exited the cockpit. His trust in Michael was complete, forged in the cockpits of Eco-Watch jets over the years.

"I'm not wasting any time," Michael called over his shoulder. "Be ready to go."

Donovan stopped at the crew closet just behind the cockpit. He pulled out heavy boots, and as he laced them up, he called to Dr. Samuels and Dr. Yates. "Strap in, we're going to land, and once we land, stay seated. You'll understand when we get there."

"We saw everything. She managed to pull herself out of the water, but she collapsed running for the shore," Dr. Samuels said. "We'll have blankets ready."

Donovan threw on his heavy parka and made sure his gloves were in the pocket. He'd already heard Michael lower the landing gear and felt him maneuver the Gulfstream around to land. Ready to go, Donovan moved forward and sat in the jump seat between Michael and Rick.

When the tires kissed the ice, the aircraft began shaking violently from the imperfections in the ice. Instantly, Michael yanked on the reverse thrust handles and pulled them to maximum. The *Galileo* shuddered under the onslaught of the reversers and the uneven surface. Donovan was forced to use both hands to brace himself as Michael slowed the Gulfstream down to the speed of a brisk walk. He retracted the flaps and stowed the reversers and spoilers in preparation for a quick departure.

"This is about as close as I dare get us to the hole in the ice," Michael said. "When you open the door, she'll be fifty yards directly off the left wing."

Donovan slipped on his sunglasses to face the harsh morning sunlight, pulled on his gloves, donned his watch cap low on his head, and stood ready. The moment the *Galileo* lurched to a stop, he lowered the airstair, raced to the bottom, and hit the ground moving. Standing in the doorway, Rick began to raise the airstair so Michael could keep the Gulfstream rolling and the brakes warm.

Donovan's first breath of cold air was painful enough to bring tears that immediately froze on his cheek. When he exhaled, condensation billowed and clung to his skin. The snow made the going slow, but he followed Michael's directions and spotted the woman. Above the dull roar from the *Galileo's* engines, he could still hear the ominous sound of cracking ice spread out in all directions. He ran faster toward his target.

Once there, Donovan slid to a stop, dropped to one knee, dug his arms into the snow, clutched her body firmly, and lifted. He was surprised when she didn't budge. He dropped to both knees and rocked her back and forth in order to pry her frozen clothes free from the ice. The instant she was free, Donovan rolled her on her back and gathered her up. He was startled that her eyes were open. For a moment he thought she might be dead. Then she blinked.

"Don't—"

"Who are you, where were you going?" Donovan asked as he lifted her up off the ice and cradled her in his arms.

"Don't let anyone know about me," she said, her voice weak and fading. "They'll kill us all, even our families. Don't tell—"

"Who are you?" Donovan asked. All around them he could hear the ice pop and screech as broken sections rubbed together. She closed her eyes and her head slumped sideways. Donovan made sure he had a firm grip on her and began to run.

As Michael spotted him, he swung the slowly moving Gulfstream around so the cabin door would face Donovan's side. Moving as fast as he could, each breath a dagger in his chest, Donovan continued to trudge toward the *Galileo*. He could hardly see through the ice that had built on the lenses of his glasses as he intercepted the Gulfstream and reached the first step. He staggered briefly and felt Rick reach down and take part of his load. Together they lifted the woman up the stairs and into the warmth of the cabin.

Donovan turned and took one last look at the open water where the Boeing had slipped beneath the surface. He spotted no other survivors. In the frigid air, the water was already skimming over with ice. He turned away as Rick moved past him to close the door.

"Rick, tell Michael to crank up the heat," Donovan said over his shoulder as he hurried to where the woman lay in the aisle. He ripped off his gloves and peeled off his useless glasses. He saw her face clearly for the first time. Even with her eyes closed, and her face nearly drained of color, soaking wet and half frozen, she was hauntingly beautiful. She was maybe in her mid-twenties, with jet black hair, long enough to reach her shoulders, high cheekbones, and a distinct jawline. As he crouched and searched her neck for a pulse, the *Galileo* lurched forward and began to trundle down the rough makeshift runway. Once again, Donovan had to hold on to steady himself as Michael guided the powerful Gulfstream back the way they'd come. The engines spooled up to maximum thrust, and they accelerated away from the hole in the ice. The airframe shook and the wingtips rocked and flexed as the Gulfstream powered through the ridges in the ice and raced across the lake until the pounding stopped. The *Galileo* lifted free and climbed steeply into the frigid Canadian morning.

Airborne, and with the help of the two other men in the cabin, they began peeling off the woman's wet half-frozen clothes. They used towels to dry her skin and then wrapped her tightly in blankets. As they worked, Donovan gathered her clothes and quickly checked the pockets, finding nothing. All he had was an unknown woman and her solemn warning.

# CHAPTER TWO

DONOVAN STRIPPED OFF his coat and boots and stuffed everything in the closet. He fished in his briefcase until he found his phone and then went back and stood over the woman. He took numerous pictures of her face, turned her head gently to the side, and snapped several profile shots. He asked Dr. Samuels for a sheet of white paper and unwrapped the blanket around her just enough to extract her right hand. He couldn't help but notice that her skin was cooler than his own. He turned to the side, ran his index finger in the recessed seat track until it came out black from the dry graphite they used as a lubricant. He smoothed it uniformly onto her thumb and forefinger and then pressed each one against the sheet of paper. He blew the excess powder away and examined the makeshift prints.

He tucked her hand back inside the blanket and then turned to Dr. Samuels. "There are some hand towels in the lavatory. Can you dampen them and heat them in the microwave? We'll wrap them around her neck and wrists to try to heat the blood traveling through her arteries and veins." Donovan thumbed through the images he'd shot and then pocketed the phone and went forward and sat in the cockpit jump seat.

Michael turned to face him. "Is she going to survive?"

"I'm not sure," Donovan said, scanning the instrument panel and spotting the airport code Michael had programmed as their new destination. "CYWG. Is that where we're headed?"

"It's Winnipeg," Michael said. "We're still too far north to talk to anyone, so I chose the closest city with first-class medical facilities. As soon as we can talk to air traffic control, we'll report the crash and give them the coordinates."

"I need to let you guys in on something," Donovan said. "As I carried her to the plane, she whispered for me not to tell anyone about her, or 'they'll kill all of us, and our families.'"

Michael turned in his seat to look at Donovan over the tops of his sunglasses. "That's a hell of thing to say to someone trying to save your life."

"She might not survive," Rick said. "If that's the case, then those were her final words, a little disconcerting to say the least."

"We all agree that the Boeing 737 was not supposed to be in this airspace, it acted erratically, and minutes later it crash-landed. She's the lone survivor, and neither she, nor the wreck, is going anyplace soon," Donovan said. "I have pictures and fingerprints that I'm going to send to Montero the second we can reach the outside world. What do you two think about waiting for some further information before we turn this into an international incident?"

"I hear what you're saying, and it's a fine line," Michael said. "At the moment, we've broken no laws. The solar storm won't let us talk to anyone, so we're doing what any Good Samaritan would do, which is to get the survivor to a medical facility."

"Exactly. Let's find out more about her and the 737 before we elect to land in Winnipeg. The last thing I want to do is end up in the middle of a crashed airplane media storm—or worse."

"We'll have a satellite window in ten or fifteen minutes," Rick said. "Radio communication in maybe another hour."

Donovan glanced at the display. Winnipeg was only an hour and a half away. He needed to work fast.

"One more thing," Michael said. "We know nothing about what happened back there. In fact, she could be the one who caused the Boeing to crash in the first place. I'm just saying, keep an eye on her."

"Got it." Donovan hurried to the back of the plane and found Dr. Samuels sitting cross-legged next to the woman, taking her pulse. Hot air was pouring from the *Galileo*'s vents and warm towels were wrapped around her neck.

"Any improvement?" Donovan asked as he sat down at one of the science stations.

"Hard to say. Her pulse is a little stronger, but not by much. I'm not sure why she's unconscious, unless she was injured when she was thrown into the water or she's been drugged."

"Do we have Internet connectivity yet?" Donovan asked Dr. Yates who sat at the adjoining workstation.

"Not yet," Dr. Yates said, swiveling one of the larger monitors turned toward Donovan. "I thought you should see this. I went back and reviewed the telemetry we recorded of the Boeing. It's impossible to identify the object that was thrown from the emergency exit, but I do think it's a body. I also noticed this."

"What am I seeing?" Donovan said as he leaned closer to the monitor.

"It's only there for a moment, but as the camera follows the object, it briefly pans across the registration number of the Boeing. It looks like something has come loose or peeled back slightly. I'm thinking it looks like a decal, or adhesive of some sort, and just underneath there is something that looks to me like black paint."

"We don't know what it says, but we know what it is—the actual registration number." Donovan leaned back in the seat. "The

Saudi identification is bogus. Someone has slapped it over the real registration."

"We're showing a green light for Internet connectivity," Dr. Samuels announced.

Donovan connected his phone to the computer terminal and began uploading the pictures he'd taken. He pulled down an e-mail screen and began to type. Once finished, he attached all of the images to his message and hit send. The second he confirmed it had gone out, he leaned back and hoped that, half a world away, Eco-Watch's new Director of Security would be looking at her e-mail.

Former FBI Special Agent Veronica Montero was not only a good friend, but she had been at one time one of the most complex, intelligent, and formidable opponents he'd ever come up against. Years earlier, while she was with the FBI, she'd put him in the crosshairs of an investigation, and even though he was innocent, it had threatened to destroy everything he had built over the last twenty-five years. Ultimately, they reached an uneasy peace and ended up bringing down a man who would have been one of the deadliest terrorists in history. Since then, she'd become close with not just Donovan, but with his wife, Lauren, and their daughter, Abigail. Over the last year, Montero had demonstrated her loyalty and her superb investigative skills, and as long as no one called her Veronica, she was happy. If anyone could get a jump on the identity of the unknown woman, and who owned the Boeing, it was Montero.

He thought of his wife, Lauren, and their six-year-old daughter, Abigail. With Donovan immersed in studying the massive solar flares, Lauren had taken Abigail to Innsbruck to visit their dear friend Kristof and his daughter, Marta.

Donovan missed his family but knew Abigail would have a wonderful time at the chalet. Rumor had it Kristof had brought in horses for her to ride, Abigail's current obsession. The other Eco-Watch jet, the *Spirit of da Vinci,* was in Savannah, Georgia, home to Gulfstream, for maintenance and upgrades. Until a few minutes ago, it had been a fairly quiet week at Eco-Watch.

"I just scanned several Internet news outlets," Dr. Yates said. "There's no mention of a missing airplane anywhere in the world."

"There will be shortly," Dr. Samuels said. "I see on the inflight display that we're headed to Winnipeg?"

"That's the closest major city with first-rate medical facilities," Donovan said, repeating Michael's reasoning.

"You know the Canadians will question us for hours, maybe days." Samuels pressed on his temples as if enduring a great pressure. "This solar event isn't going to wait for the slow wheels of bureaucracy to run its course. I'd like to be back up here tonight if at all possible."

"We will if we can," Donovan said. "I'm waiting on some information I just requested from Eco-Watch's Director of Security."

"Are you talking about Ms. Montero?" Dr. Yates asked.

"Yes," Donovan said. "You both met her in Virginia."

"I know that Eco-Watch has the well-deserved reputation of being the preeminent privately funded research organization in the world, but how did you hire her? She's famous," Dr. Yates said. "She's the FBI agent that took out the terrorist trying to attack Washington, D.C. She was even on the cover of *Time* magazine."

Donovan shrugged. Though the actual story regarding the terrorist had been altered at the highest levels of the FBI, Eco-Watch, Donovan, Lauren, and Montero had all been at the center of the attack. Stopping it had been a team effort, but he'd gladly pushed the spotlight onto Montero so his family could be left out of the media frenzy. "I hired her because she's very good at what she does. I'm glad you two understand her capabilities. Hopefully we'll hear back soon and make a decision."

"What kind of a decision? What are the other options?" Samuels asked.

"This is probably as good a time as any to tell you what I know. When I got to the woman, she was still conscious. She whispered for me not to tell anyone about her. She said they'll kill all of us, and our families."

"That's messed up," Samuels said as his face turned red. "I mean, we saved her. How could she say something like that?"

"That's what I'm trying to find out," Donovan replied. "I thought you two should know."

"To hell with her," Samuels blustered. "I say we fly straight to the United States and turn her over to the FBI."

Donovan held up his hands in a calming gesture just as he spotted the arrival of an e-mail from Montero. "Gentlemen, Ms. Montero just replied; let me see what she has to say, and we'll proceed from there."

With a click of the mouse, Donovan opened the e-mail and was surprised by its brevity.

*This woman is listed by Interpol as a Jane Doe, a woman who was possibly abducted three years ago in Krakow. A year ago, a German diplomat was murdered in Berlin and she may be connected with that homicide. Nothing but unanswered questions. Do not land anywhere until we can talk. I'll call as soon as you're in range.*

*—Montero*

# CHAPTER THREE

LAUREN AND MARTA sipped afternoon tea in the sunroom and admired the towering snow-covered Austrian Alps filling the expansive windows. Kristof Szanto and his daughter Marta's gorgeous chalet outside of Innsbruck was like a bit of heaven. They'd all stayed up late last night to witness the spectacular Northern Lights. Abigail had been excited by the Aurora Borealis, or rainbow clouds, as she called them. After Kristof told her that unicorns and leprechauns had made them just for her, she'd danced with the unbridled joy of a six-year-old. Now, jet lag and the late night had taken its toll, and she had agreed to take a rare afternoon nap. Kristof also needed his rest as he endured the latest round of treatments for his prostate cancer.

Kristof and Donovan, friends since childhood, had grown up together, both the firstborn sons of families with great wealth. They'd traveled and caused mischief on four continents until they'd had a massive falling out over what they referred to as their philosophical differences. Not long ago, they'd reconnected after nearly thirty years. Donovan and Kristof, despite vast differences, shared a past that was essential for not only them, but for their families. To Donovan and Lauren's surprise, they discovered that Kristof had a daughter, Marta, who was now in her mid-twenties. Highly intelligent, Marta had been groomed to take over her father's business since she was a teenager. Despite years of separation, the two men had discovered that the time apart, and their prior differences, mattered little. For Lauren, Kristof was a link to her husband's past, just as Marta needed Donovan and marveled at the stories that only he could tell.

"I love this place," Lauren said. "The peace and quiet is so wonderful, and I can't get over the horses."

"It was Dad's idea," Marta said. "He never did get to spoil me as a little girl, so I think he's making up for that now with Abigail."

"She does love to ride," Lauren said. "When I was her age it was sailing. My dad would take me out on the Chesapeake Bay, and we'd sail on this little wooden boat he'd built. We also had an antique wooden motorboat, a Chris-Craft that we would go out in, but I loved to sail. I was fascinated by using the wind to propel us through the water. I was going to be the youngest girl to sail around the world and be famous. I think that idea lasted for one whole summer."

"Sailing, being out on the water and in the weather, is that where your interest in Earth Science began?" Marta asked.

"Probably," Lauren said. "Though it wasn't until a grade school science fair that I became enamored with how everything worked. Dad wanted me to be an engineer, but I wanted to be outside, living and working in the thick of it, solving problems."

"So, a science fair sprouts a girl who graduates with a PhD in Earth Science from MIT? Who then becomes a senior analyst with the Defense Intelligence Agency?"

"Technically, I'm just a consultant," Lauren said, though everything Marta had said was true.

Marta's phone buzzed to life, and as she glanced at the screen, a quizzical look spread across her face.

"I'll give you some privacy," Lauren said as she pushed back her chair.

"No, stay. It's Montero." Marta picked her phone up from the table and answered. "Hello. Yes, she's here with me. Okay, you're on speaker."

"Sorry to bother the two of you," Montero said, dispensing with any niceties. "I just got an e-mail from Donovan aboard the *Galileo*, which I am forwarding to you as we speak. The short version is that Donovan and Michael rescued a lone female survivor from a plane crash in Northern Manitoba. He sent me her fingerprints and photographs to try and determine who she might be."

"Why would he do that?" Marta asked as she downloaded the first image on her phone, viewed the picture. "What's going on? They're still airborne, right? Why is he in such a hurry to identify her?"

"You'll read all the details, but when he reached her in the snow, she warned him not to tell anyone about her, or they would all be killed, along with their families. I made a few discreet inquiries and the first pop came from my source at Interpol."

"Interpol?" Marta said as her brow furrowed. "Do tell."

Lauren studied the image of the unknown woman. Her face looked colorless, giving her the illusion of a nearly flawless porcelain doll. Tiny lines around her eyes told Lauren she was probably in her early to mid-twenties. But with the woman wrapped in blankets on the floor of the *Galileo*, Lauren couldn't discern anything further. She set the phone back down on the table, trying to fit together the pieces of how such a woman could have ended up on board the *Galileo* with her husband.

"According to my source, using the images Donovan sent, this woman is a Jane Doe thought to be abducted in Krakow three years ago," Montero said. "She's also a person of interest in a homicide last year in Berlin. The victim was a German diplomat."

Lauren saw a rare flash of unease cross Marta's face, and a second later, it was gone. Over thirty years ago, Kristof had sold his inherited fortune and built a bigger one in the black market arms business, rising to near legendary status as the criminal known as Archangel. In certain circles, the whispered name represented one of the most feared entities in the world of organized crime. In Marta's world, unknown people were always a concern.

"Do you know the name of the German who was killed?" Marta asked.

"No, my source didn't have immediate access to that file," Montero said. "We don't know anything for sure, except that we have a possible threat on our hands."

"This is not good," Marta said.

Lauren felt the first unmistakable chill of vulnerability race up and down her spine. "Montero, what do you think?" Lauren asked, hoping the perceived threat was an overreaction to the ramblings of a woman traumatized by a plane crash. Montero was the Director of Security for Eco-Watch, and her responsibilities included the protection of the families of Eco-Watch employees.

"I think this could end up being nothing," Montero said. "We'll know more in a few hours, but in the meantime I say we play it safe. Lauren, I need to put you on alert. I've already initiated the appropriate protocols. An hour from now, a private jet will be in position at Innsbruck airport, and it will be placed on twenty-four-hour standby to take you out of Europe if needed. I've also left a message for our former SAS friends in London. I may bring them into the picture as the situation gels."

"You called Reggie?" Lauren asked. She and Donovan, as well as Montero, had sat down months ago and implemented a series of measured reactions to certain events that might threaten Eco-Watch or its people. Reggie was the man who led a highly capable group of former SAS soldiers that had been brought in from time to time to help with security. Lauren thought highly of them, and two in particular, Reggie and Trevor, she considered friends.

"I can promise security here at the chalet," Marta said. "Dad and I of course have considerable resources toward that end."

"I was hoping you'd say that," Montero answered. "I'll keep you both in the loop as best I can. Due to the communication problems from the solar storm, I haven't been able to talk to Donovan directly. Our immediate issue is to try and identify the woman. Once that's accomplished, we'll know what to do."

"Thanks. Tell Donovan to call me when he can," Lauren said.

Marta severed the connection and leaned back in her chair and rubbed her temples. "Wow, that's a lot to take in. Do you think Montero's overreacting?"

"No, I don't," Lauren said as her phone chimed, announcing that she had a new message. A glance told her it was from Donovan.

"What?" Marta asked. "Is there something else?"

"Yes, an e-mail from Donovan."

"Open it."

"It's a video file from the *Galileo*'s onboard mainframe, recorded earlier today." Lauren selected play, and the image of a Boeing 737 filled the screen. Viewed on her phone, it was too small to make out all the details. With Marta peering over her shoulder, they watched as the airliner jettisoned something unidentifiable and then moments later landed on a frozen lake. The camera zoomed in on a person rushing out of a smoke-filled over-wing exit, and then falling into the water as the Boeing broke through the ice. That was where the loop ended.

"We have to watch that again on a bigger screen," Marta said.

Lauren nodded. She pieced together what she knew so far, and became more confused, a sensation she didn't relish. What the loop didn't show was Donovan and Michael landing the *Galileo* on the ice to save that woman—a woman who then warned Donovan of a threat to them and their families.

# CHAPTER FOUR

THE SATELLITE PHONE buzzed in the cabin of the *Galileo*. Donovan had been expecting the call. He picked it up before the second ring and moved to the rear of the cabin, out of earshot from Samuels and Yates. "Montero, it's me. What have you got?"

"I don't know much," Montero said. "This woman has no name, no history at all. It's believed she was abducted from Krakow, Poland, three years ago. A security camera witnessed the abduction, the kidnappers were never identified. A file was opened, and Interpol entered her picture into their database. This morning, facial recognition from your image tagged her as the woman from Krakow, the same woman who was classified as a person of interest in the death of a German diplomat a year ago."

"What about the fingerprints?" Donovan asked.

"Her prints are not in anyone's system."

"This seems so disconnected," Donovan said. "Do we have any idea why she was aboard that jet?"

"She's only part of this mystery. There is no record of that 737's existence, at least with a Saudi Arabian registration. There are no reports of a missing airplane, anywhere. At this point I don't know what to think."

"What you're telling me is that if we land and start telling people what we saw, it'll be breaking news within the hour. The last thing I want to do is end up in the middle of an international spectacle that may or may not make all of us targets," Donovan said. "I need more information about what we're dealing with before I'm forced to sit down with the authorities and explain what happened."

"I've already spoken to Lauren and Marta. They're up to speed. I'm hoping between my Interpol connection and Marta's network, we can solve this fairly fast. Do you want me to alert William and Stephanie?"

"Yes, William needs to be aware of this." Donovan thought of William, his oldest friend and the man who raised him after Donovan's parents died. As a senior member of the State Department, given the title of Diplomat-at-Large, William was in a unique position to advise him on this situation and perhaps even run some interference. Stephanie was William's niece, like a sister to Donovan. As far as Donovan knew, Stephanie was home in England preparing for everyone's arrival for New Year celebrations. Donovan assumed William was at his home in Washington.

"The way I see it, you've got two options," Montero said. "Divert to Winnipeg, tell them what happened, and you'll probably be on your way home in a day or two, but the media exposure will be intense, and if there is a threat out there, they'll know exactly where to find you. The other option is to land in Minneapolis as planned, and contact the FBI later, after we know more and can assess the threat. At least we'll be on our side of the border. We can always admit to poor judgment, and we can use our connections to mitigate any legal fallout. If needed, you can pull William into the mix to help apply the correct amount of pressure in Washington to keep you and Eco-Watch out of trouble."

"I like that option. We land in Minneapolis and say nothing. I'll see to this woman's medical needs. But she issued her warning, and I want to know why. If Homeland Security, the FBI, and the Canadian authorities all get involved, it'll end up a bureaucratic mess."

"A word of warning—don't underestimate the woman," Montero said. "After all, she could have been the one who brought down the Boeing."

"I understand." Donovan recalled Michael's identical warning and knew they were both right. For the moment though, he doubted that the woman lying on the floor of the *Galileo* posed much of a threat. "Here's what I'm going to need inside the next hour. Pick a hospital in Minneapolis that will serve her medical needs, as well as our requirements for staying out of the spotlight—I'm thinking a nice, suburban hospital. Then we'll need to create a credible story about why I'm bringing an unconscious woman to the emergency room instead of calling for an ambulance. She has no ID, no name. They're going to ask questions—I need good answers that won't set off alarms. The kind a former FBI agent knows about."

"Use the one story everyone in the emergency room hears all the time," Montero said. "You're a married, fifty-two-year-old businessman from Virginia. You're in Minneapolis for a few days, you met an attractive woman, and the two of you hit it off. Tell them she was conscious in the car, but not feeling very well. You, being her concerned friend, brought her to the emergency room. Work out a brief, simple backstory you can repeat under stress. Tell the nurses she lost her purse. Make up a name for her, offer to pay the bills, and they'll be bored with your story before you finish talking."

"Anything else?"

"I'll do some research, and once I find the right hospital, I'll text you some geographical points to use, so it'll all make sense to the staff. Memorize what I send, and then delete it all. You've ignored some threats in the past—and paid dearly," Montero said. "I think this is the best move."

"I agree. I want you to charter a jet and get to Minneapolis as fast as you can. Wait. On second thought, stop in Norfolk first and pick up some equipment that will be waiting for you at the airport. It'll be from Eco-Watch Marine. Bring everything to Minneapolis."

"The *Atlantic Titan* is out to sea, steaming towards Monserrat," Montero said as a reminder. "Are you sure what you need is going to be in port?"

"Positive," Donovan said and pictured the *Atlantic Titan*. She was one of two ocean-capable research vessels operated by Eco-Watch. A third was under construction, only months away from being launched. The equipment he had in mind would be in storage at Eco-Watch Marine headquarters. "Oh, and you'll have an additional passenger from Norfolk to Minneapolis."

"Who else are you bringing into this?"

"Jesse Burke; you remember him, right?"

"Yes, and I recommended to you that his employment be reassessed," Montero said. "Jesse Burke has problems, which make him unpredictable. It wasn't me, but someone at Eco-Watch finally had the good sense to place Jesse on leave after he was arrested for another DUI."

"I'm the one who did that," Donovan said. "But Jesse has useful skills. We'll talk about all of this when you arrive. Send me the information you promised, as well as your ETA. I'm going to call Jesse, and I intend to give him one more chance. I'll talk to you soon. Right now I have a crew to brief."

Donovan stowed the phone, stood, and stretched, ignoring Samuels' and Yates' questioning expressions as he walked past, motioning for them to follow him toward the cockpit.

"What's going on?" Michael asked as Donovan sat down in the jump seat.

"Can everyone hear me?" Donovan asked. Surrounded by his crew to his left and the science team to his right, he only wanted to say this once. He was met with four solemn nods. "I have some information, and it's not good. Bear with me while I try to explain. The woman in the back is a mystery, a Jane Doe possibly abducted three years ago. In some circles she's thought to be a person of interest in a homicide a year ago. So, her warning could be real. I'm not willing to risk our lives, as well as the lives of our families, by turning this situation over to the Canadian authorities, or even the American authorities. In either case we immediately lose containment, and the last thing I want is for my people to become visible targets."

"I agree." Samuels broke the silence. "What about the Boeing? Does it just stay hidden forever?"

"It's not going anywhere," Donovan said. "This is what I need to happen. When we land, I'll drive the woman to the hospital. The four of you act as if nothing has happened, and prepare the plane for the next mission north. Then go to the Marriott and get some sleep. I'll continue to chase down the situation. If I have any information you need to know, I'll call no earlier than six o'clock this evening."

"What if we don't hear from you?" Michael asked.

"Fly the scheduled mission. Do the job we're here to do. Be sure to pass over the lake again and gather as much information as you can. Get images of the crash site and the area where we think the jettisoned object came down."

"But at some point, we will turn this over to the FAA or the FBI?" Yates asked.

"Of course," Donovan said. "Montero is on her way to Minneapolis, and once we know for sure we're not targets, she'll use her connections to orchestrate a very quiet handoff of information. At that point, the authorities will move in and take over."

"Are you sure we shouldn't just turn everything over to the FBI when we land?" Samuels asked.

"The time frame immediately points to us," Donovan said. "It wouldn't take the media very long to find out we were the only airplane in the area where the 737 went down. In fact, my guess is that CNN would have that information within hours and we become the targets we're trying to avoid. What I'm hoping is with some answers in hand, days from now, those questions about Eco-Watch are far less pertinent. Ultimately, we need the woman to explain this threat. In the meantime, we need to keep her a secret. If there are no other questions, Rick, once her clothes are dry, check all of her pockets again for anything of interest. Look for labels, scars, tattoos, or any other mark that might help us identify her. Then get her dressed.

"Rick," Michael said. "Do what you need to do, but get her ready before we start our descent into Minneapolis. I'll need you in the cockpit."

"Mr. Nash, what are you going to do?" Samuels asked.

"I've got more phone calls to make." Donovan grabbed his briefcase from the closet and excused himself once again, stepping over their mysterious survivor. When he reached the rear of the Gulfstream, he opened his directory, found Jesse Burke's contact information, and dialed.

"Jesse here, go."

"Mr. Burke," Donovan said. "This is Donovan Nash."

"Mr. Nash," Jesse said. "Yes, sir. I, uh, wasn't expecting a call from you."

"Listen carefully. When you and I last spoke, I put you on leave for your second DUI in three years. Tell me honestly, what have you done with your time off?"

"I'll be honest, sir. For the first week I drank, and in the ten weeks since, I haven't had a drop. I run, I go to the gym, I'm in the best shape I've ever been in my life. I owe you, sir."

"Yes, you do," Donovan said. "And I'm calling in that favor. I'm willing to take you off suspension effective immediately, but I need you to travel to Minneapolis."

"Yes, sir, I'll catch the next flight out."

"A chartered jet is being arranged. You'll be flying from Norfolk to Minneapolis with Montero. She'll be in touch with the details. Before you head to the airport, I need you to go to the Eco-Watch facility and put together some equipment for the trip." Donovan rattled off what he wanted Jesse to secure.

"I have it, sir," Jesse said. "This will be ready to go as soon as possible."

"Are you comfortable using all of this equipment?"

"I don't see anything particularly dangerous on the list, but I do have a question. I heard that Ms. Montero wanted to fire me after I was arrested, but that you overruled her. Is that true? And if so, has her opinion changed?"

"Looks like you're about to find out. See you this afternoon."

# CHAPTER FIVE

"WHAT ARE YOU ladies doing?" Kristof stood in the doorway, cane in one hand, and a cell phone in the other. He looked thin, but handsome, in gray slacks, a black pullover, and a casual dinner jacket.

"Come." Marta gestured for him to sit at the table. "We're looking at something from Donovan that I think will interest you."

Lauren marveled at the love, closeness, and genuine mutual respect that existed between Marta and her father. Marta had been born in Warsaw and raised by her single mother, who slowly deteriorated, eventually losing her battle with drug addiction. As a teenager, before her mother passed away, Marta learned that her father was a man called Archangel. Familiar with the stories behind the man, Marta made a desperate move. She'd found a picture of her and her mother taken years before. She gave the photograph to a criminal she knew who was rumored to have ties with Archangel. She had no idea how such a move might play out. One day while cleaning tables in a bar, the place suddenly cleared out, and Archangel himself walked in and introduced himself. After they talked, he asked for a saliva sample to run a DNA test. Archangel said he'd be in touch. He left her some money in an envelope and walked out.

Ten days later he showed up again, and just like that, she went from living in a run-down apartment to a penthouse. Her indoctrination into a completely new world was rapid. Marta was sent to Cambridge, where she studied social and political sciences, as well as psychology. In the summers, Kristof took her to Scotland, where, under his watchful eyes, a former Mossad agent tutored his daughter until she mastered weaponry and tactics, martial arts, and poker. When Kristof became ill, Marta gradually took over the family business. Even though Archangel was now a twenty-seven-year-old woman, the name still carried the same frightening weight; only the voice running the organization had changed.

"What's Donovan up to now?" Kristof pulled out a chair and sat next to his daughter.

"As you know, he's studying the solar storm, flying scientists up near the Arctic Circle to collect data, all very routine for Eco-Watch—until this morning," Marta said. "A private Boeing 737 nearly collided with them and eventually crash-landed on a frozen lake. Donovan managed to land on the ice and rescue the sole survivor."

"Sounds like something he'd do," Kristof said. "With him, it's never simple. What else?"

"The survivor is a woman," Marta continued. "As Donovan reached her, she warned him not to tell anyone about her, or everyone and their families will be killed. Then she lost consciousness."

"What else do we know?" Kristof asked.

"Pictures." Lauren slid the several pages of images they'd printed across the table toward Kristof. There was no text, nothing but the various angles that Donovan had shot of the woman.

As Kristof picked up the first one, his eyes narrowed. He silently studied each page and then set them down.

"Do you recognize her?" Marta asked. "Interpol says she's a Jane Doe, possibly abducted from Krakow three years ago, and then a year ago was labeled a person of interest in the murder of a German diplomat."

Kristof carefully inspected each image one more time until he finally shook his head and slid the photos back to Lauren. "I don't know this person. What do you know of the diplomat who was killed? Did it happen in Berlin?"

"Yes," Lauren said.

"I think I remember the event," Kristof said. "The victim, if I remember correctly, was driving home late at night. There was a car accident, a hit and run. His neck was broken. Forensics later determined that the force of the wreck wasn't sufficient to inflict such an injury. There was traffic camera footage showing a woman reaching the man first. Authorities confirmed that she snapped his neck."

"We also have the video of the other plane taken from the *Galileo*'s optics array." Marta slid her laptop toward her father.

When the video ended, Kristof looked up at Lauren and then over at his daughter. "Play it again."

After the second viewing, Kristof leaned back. "Do we know what was jettisoned from the Boeing's exit? Was it a person?"

"Not yet," Lauren said. "Though, from the data they collected, we can come very close to pinpointing where it landed."

"Who knows about this?" Kristof asked.

"As far as I know, just the *Galileo* flight crew, the scientists on board, Montero, and the three of us," Lauren said.

"What's Donovan going to do?" Kristof asked as he pushed away from the table and stood. Using his cane, he went to the credenza, selected a crystal decanter, and poured himself a drink.

"Montero is on top of this, but as it stands, he has several options. Dad, do you know something you're not telling us?"

"I'm just thinking," Kristof said as he took a small sip of his drink.

"What do you think?" Lauren asked. "Is this woman's warning credible?"

"I think Donovan needs to treat it as such," Kristof said. "Abductions are a nasty business; there are so many variables in play.

She could be anyone by now. Three years is a long time—people change, or can be changed. She could be a call girl, a spy for either a government or a corporation. She could be a professional killer, a con artist, or simply someone being blackmailed. Whatever the case, Donovan needs to be very careful."

"I say we do two things at once," Lauren said. "Let's see if we can track the airplane. We certainly have the resources to start that process, but what if we also do some digging in Krakow?"

"That's not impossible," Marta said. "We could pull in some contacts in Poland. We have people who go back far longer than three years."

"Leave it to me," Kristof said, looking over his shoulder toward the doorway. "There are still some things an old man can do. I'll make some calls."

Abigail, her long, reddish-blond hair still tousled from her nap, rounded the corner, heading straight for Lauren.

"Hello, sweetheart." Lauren pulled her daughter onto her lap and hugged her. "How do you feel, honey?"

"Okay." Abigail brushed her hair away from her eyes. "Mom, can I go help Hannah feed the horses and say goodnight to them?"

"Of course." Hannah was a wonderfully sweet girl from a nearby equestrian center. She was the trainer Kristof had arranged to tutor Abigail. He'd also made arrangements to temporarily board two Austrian Haflingers, Gemini and Zephyr, for the duration of Abigail's stay. The horses reminded Lauren of a Palomino, but the Haflingers were shorter and stockier, bred for the rugged terrain in the Alps. Hannah was knowledgeable and very careful with both horse and rider. Abigail had immediately fallen in love with Zephyr. With renewed energy, Abigail flung herself off of Lauren's lap and headed for the back door of the chalet.

"Go," Kristof urged Lauren. "We'll start digging into some of these issues. It'll be dark soon, and then we'll have dinner."

Lauren followed Abigail and helped her with her boots and cap, made sure she had her gloves, and then threw on her own coat and followed her daughter out the door. Hannah waved as Abigail ran toward the stable, swerving back and forth to travel from the sidewalk through the unbroken snow covering the lawn. Lauren loved watching her daughter enjoy the snow, the mountains, and especially the horses. At six, Abigail's rapidly expanding world mostly revolved around horses, her friends at school, and her parents. She had her own horse, Halley, stabled near their home in Centreville, Virginia. Lauren sometimes rode with her daughter, but most of the time she was just an enthusiastic spectator, amazed at Abigail's constant improvement as a rider.

Behind the chalet, the terrain rose gently, and snow-covered trees surrounded several beautiful meadows. Ultimately the rolling hills gave way to the mountains that jutted skyward into the magnificent Austrian Alps surrounding Innsbruck. The sunshine mixed with the brisk late-afternoon air seemed like a kiss from the heavens, and Lauren breathed deeply as she heard her daughter's laughter roll from the stable. The peaceful moment was interrupted by the chime of her phone—a text from Donovan. She quickly thumbed to the page.

*I'll call as soon as I can. We're about to land in Minneapolis.*
*Love, Donovan*

# CHAPTER SIX

WITH DONOVAN WATCHING over his shoulder, Michael taxied slowly, glancing back at the *Galileo*'s wingtips as he followed the lineman's directions until they were parked next to the hangar. Though Donovan knew it was only twenty-five degrees Fahrenheit outside, it was going to feel warm after Northern Manitoba.

Michael shut down the engines, and Donovan checked the cabin to make sure everyone was ready. As far as customs knew, they'd departed Minneapolis the night before and hadn't landed anywhere else, so technically they'd done nothing more than over-fly Canada. No inbound clearance or inspection was required. Donovan lowered the airstair down to the ramp. He motioned for Samuels and Yates to deplane ahead of him. They'd all made their plans on the flight. Samuels was going to the Marriott to sleep. Yates would be staying with friends. They all agreed to meet in the lobby of the Marriott that evening prior to going to the airport.

After the science team departed, Donovan motioned for one of the linemen to join him at the top of the stairs.

"Yes, sir, what can I do?" the young man asked.

"Would it be possible for you to bring my rental car around to the plane? It's a black sedan parked in one of the crew slots just to the left of the main lobby." Donovan handed him the keys. "We had a passenger get pretty airsick today. She took some Dramamine and she's been out since."

"Sure, no problem." The young man grabbed the keys and hurried off.

"Are you sure you have this?" Michael asked as he climbed out of the cockpit.

"Yes. I have all the instructions from Montero and she's on her way here. You and Rick get some rest. I won't bother you before five o'clock. If anything urgent comes up, you'll be the first to know."

Donovan heard a car door slam. His rental car was now sitting, running, at the bottom of the stairs. He went back to where the woman lay in the cabin. He lifted her and carried her through the cabin and down the stairs. As the lineman opened the passenger door, Donovan placed her into the front seat of the car. He fastened her seat belt and closed the door. He handed the lineman a twenty-dollar bill, thanked him, slid behind the wheel, and slowly eased the car away from the *Galileo* toward the gate.

Donovan had memorized the directions Montero sent, and minutes later, he merged into traffic on Interstate 94 west. He followed the blue signs off the highway and finally wheeled past the emergency entrance of Methodist Hospital, coming to a stop in an empty parking space. He ran around to the passenger door, slid the woman from the car, and raced through the sliding doors, cradling her in his arms.

"Through here!" A man in scrubs opened a door and motioned toward a gurney.

"She said she wasn't feeling well," Donovan said in a rush as he laid her down. "I'm not sure what happened. She just blacked out. Please help her."

Another man in scrubs and a nurse wheeled the gurney into the emergency room and into a stall. They immediately drew the long curtains to block the view. Moments later, a woman rushed toward the room, but not before she shot Donovan a curious once-over look.

"Excuse me," a woman's voice said from behind him. "I need you to follow me, please. There's paperwork we need to get started. Have a seat in here and someone will be with you shortly. May I have your name please?"

"Mr. Gregory," Donovan said as he gave her the name of an alias.

As Donovan sat in the waiting room, he tried to guess how many of those in the circle of chairs were patients and how many were friends or loved ones. He was too amped up to sit and read a magazine so he pulled out his phone and started sifting through e-mails and checking the latest news.

He looked up when a different woman walked in and called his name. She led him to an open cubicle. He took a seat across from her desk and pulled out his wallet.

"My name is Francie and I'm with admissions," she said as she slid on reading glasses that had been hanging around her neck on a gold chain. She nudged her mouse to bring her computer screen to life and then looked up at him. "Okay, first, I need the patient's name."

"Diane," Donovan said, and Francie looked at him, waiting for more. "That's all I know."

"What is your relationship to the patient?"

"We're friends," Donovan said.

"I see," Francie said as she let her glasses drop. "Do you know where the patient lives? Did she have a purse?"

"I'm not sure where she lives. St. Louis Park? Does that sound familiar?" Donovan stuck with the script Montero had provided.

"I'm going to need to see your ID."

Donovan had switched wallets in the plane. At Montero's insistence, he always traveled with a separate identification, complete with driver's license, credit cards, insurance and prescription cards, as well as pictures of a wife and child that bore no resemblance to the ones he actually had. He slid his driver's license out of its slot and handed it across.

"Mr. Gregory, is this your current address?"

"Yes," Donovan said, though the address didn't actually exist.

Francie made a copy of the license and handed it back to Donovan. "Will you be taking care of the patient's medical expenses?"

"I'm happy to cover the costs." Donovan glanced down at his hands and then back up at Francie. "Not through insurance, though. Is there a way to keep all of this quiet?"

"I see," Francie said.

A door opened behind him and he heard footsteps coming his way and turned. It was the woman he'd seen earlier, the one he assumed was a doctor.

"Francie, I need to ask this gentleman some questions."

"Of course, Dr. West. Mr. Gregory and I can finish when you're done with him."

"Mr. Gregory, come with me, please." The doctor turned and walked down the tiled hallway.

Donovan followed, noting that not once did the doctor check behind her to see if he was still in trail. Donovan guessed she was in her early to mid-forties, attractive, slender. She moved quickly, the purposeful stride of someone who was comfortable and in charge. Her straight brunette hair was pulled back into a pony tail that swung back and forth as she pushed through a set of doors and kept walking.

"Where are we going?" Donovan asked as they went through another set of doors that led into the emergency room. She remained silent and continued until they came to the bay where they'd taken the woman. She opened the drapes and held them open for Donovan, then slid the drapes closed behind them.

Donovan saw the bed was empty and turned to face the doctor. "Where did you take her? Is she going to be okay?"

"I've seen a hundred men your age bring in their young unconscious girlfriends. What drugs did you give her?"

"I didn't drug her," Donovan said. "She'll confirm that. Where is she?"

"All of her symptoms point to a dose of some type of narcotic. I sent her for an MRI to rule out any head injuries," she said as she pulled out her buzzing phone, clearly annoyed at the intrusion and brought it to her ear. "Yes?"

Donovan watched her frown get deeper as she turned and made eye contact with him.

"Seal off the hospital," she said. "Find her, we can't let her leave."

Moments later, the overhead speaker announced a code green in radiology. "What's happening?" Donovan asked.

"An emergency in radiology." Dr. West yanked the curtain open. "It's where I sent your friend."

"Which way?" Donovan asked.

"You need to stay here."

Donovan ignored the doctor and rushed from the room. He spotted a sign that pointed toward radiology and began running. He charged through the double doors and found himself in a small seating area. Just beyond, a group of people were leaning over a figure on the floor. Through the gaps, Donovan caught sight of the patient, a woman with a similar frame as the woman he'd brought to the hospital. He could tell from the movements they were attending to the woman's head, applying a compress. Donovan finally glimpsed the woman's face, and despite a large bandage on her forehead, he realized she wasn't the woman from the lake. He heard a woman in scrubs describing what happened to another nurse.

"There was a commotion in the unit; I saw a panicked woman in a hospital gown run from the room. No one saw where she went after that. One of the techs found this woman lying half naked outside the changing room."

Donovan turned away and stepped out into the hallway. If the woman had fled, she'd need a place to change from her hospital gown before she could get out of the hospital. He spotted a set of restrooms and moved toward them. As he approached, he heard a noise from the women's room, and when he reached for the handle, the door to the men's room opened behind him and something solid slammed into the back of his head. Donovan dropped to his knees as he felt another blow. He fought for control of his thoughts and his body, but in the end, he collapsed facedown on the floor and closed his eyes.

# CHAPTER SEVEN

DONOVAN'S HEAD ACHED. He opened his eyes and looked at his watch, surprised to find he must have dozed off. Two hours had passed since they'd escorted him to the emergency room and given him a bed as they examined the bump on the back of his head. Beyond the curtain, he heard Montero's voice. Her tone told him she was angry, and making no effort to hide the fact.

"We're leaving," Montero said as she threw open the curtain and breezed into the space. She motioned for him to get up and follow her.

"Thanks," Donovan said as he gathered himself and they walked out. There were three security guards posted in the outer room, which was most likely the audience that Montero had just addressed. One guy in particular caught Donovan's eye. He appeared smitten by Montero, and his eyes followed her as she left the room.

"Don't say a word until we're outside," Montero said as she led the way to the elevator. Donovan could tell she was fully focused on their problems. In this state, she was all about results, and her determination was one of the traits that he respected most about her.

They burst out of the hospital into the brisk late-afternoon air. A breeze whipped through the parking garage, and Montero hurried toward her rental car, unlocked the doors, and got behind the wheel. Donovan lowered his still throbbing head to brace himself against the chill and slid into the passenger seat. She cranked the engine and turned up the heat, but made no move to put the car into gear.

"Thanks for getting me out of there," Donovan said. "Did you find out anything at all about the woman?"

"I didn't see any of this coming. I anticipated some momentary suspicion with you bringing a Jane Doe into the emergency room, but I fully expected the woman to wake up and at least recognize you as the man who saved her," Montero said. "No one saw who hit you, so it could have been the very woman you saved. Who is now missing, along with any details of her threat. Turns out, as we feared, she's a total mystery with a serious set of escape and evade skills."

"The hospital's security tapes," Donovan asked. "Did she leave alone, or did she have help?"

"I don't know what the tapes show. All they told me was that you were no longer a suspect in any crime. I did talk to Dr. West. She is certain that the woman was drugged and thinks her meds wore off. When she woke up in the MRI, she freaked out. She assaulted the woman who was changing clothes and fled in her clothes and stole her purse. By now, she's somewhere in the Upper Midwest with at least an hour and a half head start."

"We need to see their security footage."

"To them, we're strangers off the street. They're not going to share."

Donovan waited, sensing that Montero probably wasn't finished.

"Everyone's attention was fixed on the poor woman on the floor. I think our woman from the lake is a pro. You don't needlessly kill people or make a bunch of noise unless you have to. Confusion and misdirection are the earmarks of someone who knows what they're doing. Think about it. In a matter of minutes, she woke up in a strange place, a different country no less, and found clothes, an ID, perhaps cash, credit cards, and access to a car. I'd call that pretty damn resourceful."

"Is there a way to piggyback off of the hospital's search? Maybe play nice with the security guy who has a crush on you?"

"I figured you'd notice that." Montero pursed her lips. "He was cute, very knowledgeable, and impressed by my taking down a terrorist organization."

"Ancient history," Donovan said. "I believe the question was, can you use him for information?"

"Probably," Montero said. "I already have my guy in Florida running down everything there is on the woman who was attacked: address, credit cards, phone, you name it. We'll have it as fast as the police can get it, maybe sooner, since we operate without red tape."

"That's a start," Donovan said. "How was Jesse?"

"Whatever you said to him seemed to make a difference. He was uncomfortable, but all business. He carried himself well and looks like he's in good shape. Let's say I'm cautiously optimistic. When we were at the Minneapolis airport, he stowed the equipment he brought from Norfolk aboard the *Galileo*. We can talk about all of that later. I did grab your briefcase and suitcase. They're in the trunk. Your Sig is there as well."

Montero's phone buzzed in her pocket. In one fluid motion, she glanced at the screen then slid it to her ear. She mouthed to Donovan that it was her guy in Florida. "What do you have?"

Donovan watched Montero's face fall and her expression crumble. She squeezed her eyes closed as she listened. It seemed to take all of her effort to control her emotions as she acknowledged to the caller that she understood. When she ended the call, her hand dropped in her lap and she sat motionless.

Donovan waited. He'd seen Montero endure a great deal in the years he'd known her. He knew her to be a woman of tremendous determination, drive, courage, and strength. He was also one of the few who knew her human side. With Montero's strength came considerable passion, and whatever she'd just heard was so bad she had to struggle to keep herself together.

"Talk to me," Donovan said quietly. "I'm here."

"My contact at Interpol, Anna. You've heard me talk of her?"

"Of course. She's the woman whose life you saved years ago, who then started to help you."

"I spoke with her this morning after I heard from you. Since we initially thought the jet was registered in Saudi Arabia, I sent her the photographs and prints you sent." Montero didn't make any effort to avoid the first tear that escaped and trickled unchecked down her cheek. Her voice wavered as she continued, "She was just found dead in Prague. She'd been tortured before she was killed."

Donovan understood that this was one of the worst things that could happen to Montero. She'd had a rough upbringing, and her life could have taken many wrong turns, but she was lucky, she had options and ended up on the right path. When she was still with the FBI, she began working with battered women's shelters in South Florida. Once she left the Bureau, she expanded full-time into helping at-risk women, as well as missing and exploited children. For Montero to lose someone she'd helped was devastating.

Montero blinked and more tears rolled down her face, but then she sniffed and popped the trunk release. "Get your gun, we're leaving."

"What are we doing?" Donovan asked, unprepared for her sudden change in behavior. "I have a rental car in the emergency lot."

"Leave it, we'll call them later," Montero said. "We need to get to work. If Anna is dead, we have to assume that whoever killed her knows about the woman who was rescued by Eco-Watch, and they also know we're in Minneapolis. They may even know we're in the hospital parking lot. We need to go. Now."

Donovan wasted no more time. He ran to the rear of the car, collected his briefcase, and slammed the lid closed. He slid back into the passenger side, and Montero pulled out of the lot. Moments later, they were speeding toward the hospital exit.

"We're in trouble," Montero said. "The woman's warning is real, and we can assume they'll come for us, all of us."

# CHAPTER EIGHT

"So, what do we think about these developments out of Minneapolis?" Kristof asked as he took a sip of his red wine and selected a tool to poke the last of a dying fire.

They'd finished a late dinner when Lauren had gotten a phone call from Donovan. She could hear and feel the frustration in her husband's voice as he described the woman escaping. What she couldn't gauge was Donovan's reaction to the news about the murder of Montero's source inside of Interpol. The three of them gathered in the great room, and she shared what she'd just learned.

"She certainly has some skills to make her escape the way she did," Marta said. "But honestly, anyone with even the most basic military training could have pulled that off. It wasn't all that impressive."

"I agree," Kristof said. "Though I find the fact that her first instinct was to flee, and use brute force in the effort, more telling. She woke up in a hospital, in a country she couldn't have expected, and didn't ask a single question before deciding to run."

"It sounds to me like someone who is clearly terrified, which coincides with the warning she gave Donovan from the very beginning," Lauren said. "When you connect her actions with the murdered informant in Prague, perhaps she has every reason to be scared."

"We certainly have to tie the two together," Marta said. "What is the media in Minneapolis reporting?"

"Donovan said it's somewhat contained," Lauren said. "They're saying that a person was assaulted at a local hospital. No mention if the assailant was an employee, a patient, or a visitor. It's vague enough at this point that we can be cautiously optimistic that it doesn't point a finger directly at anyone."

"We need to look at the broader picture," Marta said. "Someone, somewhere, has an overdue jet on their hands. What's aboard the jet? Is it people? Cargo? Who are they, where are they, and what are the people at either end going to do about it?"

"What are you suggesting?" Kristof asked, prodding the logs again, causing a shower of sparks to float upwards.

"Is there anything in the Eco-Watch arsenal that would allow us to watch the lake?"

"No, not really," Lauren said. "That part of the world isn't a threat, so to task a satellite is out of the question, and even if we planted surveillance gear, the solar storm has already disrupted communications that far north."

"What have you heard from William?" Kristof asked. "Has he gotten back with you yet? I'll feel better when he's in the loop about recent events."

"No, and I'm not sure why," Lauren said with a shrug. "He's usually so good at returning calls. I'll try again later. I have another question, and I don't mean to pry, but one of the subjects that Donovan brought up was the status of our security here?"

"You're not prying, and I understand his concern. His wife and daughter are here, and he wants to make sure you're safe," Kristof said. "The chalet is protected by a total of twelve armed men. You'd never know, or suspect, but I own the house next door, which is actually my security headquarters. It's specially outfitted with state-of-the-art surveillance systems, and at any given moment there are four men on duty, twenty-four hours a day. There are no other properties on the street, and as you know, it dead-ends up the hill. I own the property behind the chalet all the way to the foot of the mountain and for three miles in every other direction. Any vehicle traffic is monitored far in advance of arrival at the chalet. You've already seen the safe room downstairs. There is also a tunnel that leads to a similar space next door. So, as you can see, I believe we're well protected. My men have orders to stay out of sight, especially with you and Abigail here, but they're there, and ready to protect all of us."

"Thank you," Lauren said. "I had no idea. I lived with round-the-clock protection for a time, and I grew to hate it."

"When was this?" Marta asked, leaning closer, curious.

"I don't talk about it often, but three years ago, Donovan and I were separated for a while. I took Abigail and moved to Paris. I had friends within Mossad that provided twenty-four-hour security."

"Ah, yes." Kristof nodded. "Donovan explained to me about the events that brought Montero into your lives. There was all of that ugliness with the attempted terrorist attack on Washington. I can see how you garnered your ties to Mossad. I'm sorry, continue."

"Abigail and I were in France, Donovan was in Virginia working. Yes, after the failed terrorist attack, Mossad decided that we needed their protection. It all went fine until we were attacked in Paris. Stephanie VanGelder, one of my closest friends, was visiting from London. Kristof, you know Stephanie, right?"

"Of course, William's niece—she's like a sister to Donovan. When he was at Oxford, I saw her often and I even had a momentary crush on her. She had the good sense to avoid me and all of Donovan's other unruly friends."

"So, Stephanie and I were in Paris, and Donovan was getting threats, so we were at least warned that we might not be safe. I had a bad feeling, and we were in the process of leaving when the attack came. It started in a department store, and after a running gun battle, we escaped by car to a rooftop pickup point. We barely got out via helicopter. It was the first time I met our friends, Trevor and Reggie; they're both former SAS. In the end, my entire security detail was killed protecting us—it still haunts me to this day."

"I had no idea that was you," Marta said, wide-eyed. "I know of that attack. We all read of the chase through the streets of Paris and the daring helicopter escape. You're one of the few who ever survived being targeted by Nikolett Kovarik. I met her once, years ago in Budapest. She didn't know who I was, but she was clearly a dangerous psychopath. Wait, did you kill her?"

"No, someone else did." Lauren shook her head and immediately changed the subject. "My point to all of this is that I don't want anyone else sacrificing their lives to protect Abigail and me, and I don't want to make the two of you a target of any kind. Maybe I should think about leaving?"

"Nonsense, you're not going anywhere," Kristof said. "This threat affects us as well. Marta and I both know Trevor, and we think highly of the man. As for Reggie and his team, docs Abigail know these men?"

"She knows Reggie." Lauren dabbed at the unexpected tears that had formed from her telling of the events in Paris. "After the firefight and we were safely aboard the helicopter headed low and fast out of Paris, Reggie calmly produced a red lollipop and gave it to Abigail. That single act of foresight and tenderness helped Abigail, at least for a moment, put aside the trauma she'd witnessed, and it won me over forever."

"I'll make you a promise," Kristof said. "If we have to leave, or if the threats escalate, we'll reach out to these men for additional help."

"I couldn't agree more," Marta said as she got to her feet to give Lauren a comforting hug.

"Thank you," Lauren whispered.

"I'm off to bed," Kristof announced, and clutched his cane for support as he rose. "You ladies sleep well, and we'll talk at breakfast. Goodnight."

"Goodnight, Dad," Marta said.

Lauren got to her feet and gave Kristof a hug. He patted her affectionately on the back and then limped out of the room. Lauren turned to Marta. "I didn't upset him by bringing up Trevor and Reggie, did I?"

"No." Marta shook her head. "Quite the opposite, not that you needed to, but I think you earned a great deal more respect with him this evening. I know you did with me."

"That wasn't my intention." Lauren sat down and reached for her wineglass. "Being married to Donovan Nash came with a steep learning curve, and most of the time I'm still working to catch up. I've been in situations I never expected, or could even have imagined. I mean, I'm a scientist, a housewife, not a spy. The most thrilling thing in my life before meeting Donovan was riding through hurricanes in airplanes."

"That sounds pretty thrilling—and now?"

"There doesn't seem to be a limit. I've had to learn how to defend myself with a gun. I've killed people. I've lived through two airplane crashes, as well as a helicopter crash. Like we talked about earlier, I survived the assassin Nikolett Kovarik, and it never seems to end. I keep thinking that somehow things will settle down, go back to some semblance of normal. Whatever I thought my life was going to be has changed completely. Even I don't recognize it sometimes. My worst fear is that Donovan and I will finally get everything figured out, we'll get to this place we both talk and dream about, and the moment we do, something will change, and it'll vanish."

"Tell me about that place."

"I don't know how to explain it, but there's a distant future where Abigail's grown up, she's found and hopefully accepted her unique place in the world, she's surrounded with people who love her, and maybe she has children of her own one day. We'll lose William eventually, as well as my mother, and I dread when that happens. But someday, Donovan and I will retire, and be together all the time, and hopefully be content. I want us to look back and feel that we did the best we could. I guess it's the thought that one day, short of death, there can be peace."

"Let's hope that happens, but until then, don't forget that you're one of the most capable women I've ever met." Marta raised her glass toward Lauren. "If you want something, you'll find a way to make it happen."

"Thank you." Lauren smiled. "I'm very lucky to be surrounded by good people."

"Some incredible people. I mean, Donovan is fearless, and Montero is a force to be reckoned with. I sometimes can't believe that I know her, that she's a friend," Marta said. "What she did to stop one of the boldest terrorist attempts in history is legend. I know Donovan played a huge part as well, but Montero became famous after what she did—she's amazing."

"Montero is one of a kind, and I know she thinks highly of you, which is significant, coming from her. Marta, I can't tell you how nice it is to be able to talk freely to another woman, especially one who found herself in a situation completely beyond her making, and then thrived."

"Thank you, I feel exactly the same way about you. As you can see, there's a considerable lack of female friends in my life."

"But not a lack of male company, I gather."

"What are you talking about?" Marta said.

"It's just a hunch, women's intuition," Lauren said, sensing she was right.

"I don't want to talk about it," Marta said. "Not yet at least."

"He's not married—is he?" Lauren decided to press. "Do I know him?"

"It's been a long day," Marta said. "I think I'll turn in."

"Very well," Lauren said. "So much for getting Archangel to reveal a secret. Just remember, I'm your friend. You can trust me, and I'm here if you need to talk."

# CHAPTER NINE

"How did she sound?" Montero asked, the moment Donovan got off the phone with Lauren.

"She's good, concerned, but good. The thing about my wife is that she needs a little time to process all of the data before she formulates a final opinion. We both know how smart she is, so this processing doesn't take very long, but it needs to take place. It's then that I fully understand what she's thinking. It's frustrating at times, but always worth the wait."

"That's a perfect thumbnail summation of one of the most complicated women I know," Montero said.

Donovan watched Montero take the exit off of Excelsior Boulevard and loop onto the expressway that would take them toward downtown Minneapolis. She was in her zone, her eyes shifting to each car that she passed and then darting to the rearview mirror. He knew that if you asked her to close her eyes and describe the vehicles in play around them, she could not only recite the make, model, and color, but also the number and gender of the occupants, plus the license number of any she was concerned about. She had decided to head downtown so they could quickly respond in any direction if they heard anything about the location of the mystery woman.

Montero's phone rang and she glanced at the screen. "My guy in Florida. I'm going to put it on speaker."

"Hello, are you there?" a male voice asked.

"I'm here," Montero said. "I've got you on speaker. I'm with my boss. What's up?"

"I was able to access the hospital security system. I have all of their video files. I'm sending you two of the screen captures. The woman in question left in the company of two men, and they departed the hospital parking lot in a black Chevy Suburban."

"Did she leave voluntarily or by force?" Montero asked.

"It's impossible to tell for sure, but I think one of the men is armed. Based on body language alone, my hunch is she was taken against her will."

"Thanks," Montero said. "Anything else?"

"I'm still working on Prague. I have all available sources scouring the world for any leads. You'll be the first to know if I find something."

"Thanks." Montero disconnected the call without taking her eyes from the road.

Donovan didn't miss the fact that Montero had winced at the mention of Prague. "Are you okay?"

"Quit asking me that." Montero handed her phone to Donovan. "Take a look at the security camera shots he sent and tell me what you see."

Donovan took the phone and brought up the first attachment. He studied the image; it was taken from high up in the hallway with the field of view aimed at a doorway.

"What is it?"

"Part of the woman's face is visible, turned upward toward the camera. If she's such a professional, why look up at the camera? There are two men, medium to large build, one on either side of her. The guy on the right is wearing a coat that seems at least a size too large, and I can see what looks like the barrel of a pistol poking down from his sleeve. There's no way to know if she's being kid-napped, or walking away with friends."

"Her looking at the camera is the tip-off," Montero said. "I think she's being kidnapped. I wonder if the reason she went off at the hospital was that she realized she was in danger, and then maybe these guys showed up. What's the second picture show?"

"It's the parking lot. The Suburban doesn't have any stickers or markings that I can see. There is a partial license number, it's a Minnesota plate, but another car is blocking the view. We've got nothing. How did they get so far ahead of us on this one?"

"Prague," Montero said. "Whoever killed Anna knows who this girl is and wants her. They had several hours to put something in motion. They could have been waiting for you when you landed, followed you from the airport to the hospital, and then grabbed the girl."

Donovan's phone rang. He saw it was Michael.

"Donovan, I know it's not quite six o'clock, but I'm awake and wondering what you had in mind for tonight?"

"I lost the woman," Donovan said. "We think someone forcibly took her from the hospital."

"So, she's on the loose?" Michael said. "I say you and Montero get to the airport, and we get out of this place as fast as possible. Let's go somewhere and regroup."

"You get to the airport and start getting the *Galileo* ready to fly. Montero and I will be there as fast as we can."

"Where are we going?"

"Put on enough fuel to fly us back up north. We still need more reconnaissance. We can talk about the rest when we get there." When Donovan glanced at Montero, he saw a new look of concern in her eyes. He disconnected the call.

"We have a problem," Montero said. "I just picked up a black Suburban about eight cars behind us. They're keeping up with us, not trying to catch us, just following."

Donovan was watching them in the side mirror when Montero braked hard to avoid a white Mercedes sedan that pulled out right in front of them. Montero swerved and then passed it. In the rear seat of the Mercedes, Donovan caught sight of a man watching them intently just as he spotted what looked like the twin barrels of a sawed-off shotgun. Before Donovan could shout a warning, Montero cut across traffic, turned hard, and then accelerated.

"The guy in the back of that car has a shotgun," Donovan said. "The photo from the hospital parking lot—a white Mercedes was blocking the plate of the Suburban."

"We need to gain the advantage. I'd really like to talk to these guys," Montero said, once again changing lanes.

Donovan watched as, behind them, the Mercedes held steady and the SUV hung a little further back, clearly content to watch and follow. The sun had finally set, and now, in the headlights, Donovan could see that it was starting to snow.

"Call Michael and tell him to leave without us," Montero said.

Donovan kept his eyes on the two trailing vehicles as he speed-dialed Michael. "Michael, it's me. Where are you?"

"We have a problem. Dr. Samuels wouldn't answer his phone, so we called security, and when they finally opened his room, they found him gagged and taped to a chair. It's bad," Michael said, his voice strained and hushed. "He's been tortured but he's still alive."

"What about Dr. Yates?" Donovan asked.

"He's fine," Michael said. "He's staying behind to go with Dr. Samuels to the hospital. He said he'd tell the police nothing about Canada. Jesse is on the phone arranging round-the-clock private security for them both. We're leaving for the airport shortly. Where are you?"

"We're not coming. We've had some complications of our own. We're being tailed and we've elected not to bring them your way."

"I understand. Where are you going?"

"It's a moment-by-moment itinerary," Donovan said. "We still need you to fly up and collect as much information as you can about where the Boeing went down. Call me when you're ready to taxi out for takeoff."

"You got it," Michael replied. "You know, I've been thinking about everything that's gone down since we landed, and I don't see how any of this happens unless we were followed from the moment we arrived in Minneapolis. Otherwise there's no other explanation."

"That's exactly what we think happened. Montero's Interpol contact, Anna, was found murdered. She knew the details of what took place in Canada, she had the pictures, everything. They had a several-hour head start to get their people into position. We were outplayed, badly. You better get airborne."

"Donovan, this situation sucks, you be careful. I'll call you when we're starting engines."

"Will do." Donovan ended the call as the illuminated skyline of downtown Minneapolis became visible through the falling snow. With a glance in the mirror, he discovered the Mercedes accelerating, quickly closing the distance.

"The Mercedes is coming fast." Donovan rested his finger on the button that would power down the window and allow him to open fire.

"I see him," Montero said as she accelerated to match his speed and keep their distance from the powerful Mercedes. "We're almost to the highway."

Donovan kept an eye on the rearview mirror as Montero glanced over her left shoulder, yanked the wheel, and crossed over two lanes amid the angry honking of horns. She tucked against a retaining wall and pressed the gas pedal. They roared into a tunnel, the overhead lights casting an orange glow against the concrete. A road sign advertised multiple exits.

"Shit," Montero whispered as her eyes locked on the mirror.

Donovan, too, saw the white Mercedes round the corner behind them.

"I want to lose this guy," Montero called out. "We need a major misdirection."

Donovan braced himself as Montero made the exit onto Washington, which fed them off the highway and into the north side of downtown Minneapolis. The rental car's tires screeched as she accelerated and then turned hard.

Montero made two more right turns. Dead ahead, Donovan saw they had two choices, 394 West, or 94 West. An instant later in the mirror, he caught sight of the speeding Mercedes as it overshot the turn and vanished. Montero took the 94 West ramp and pushed the sedan as hard as she could. Donovan once again spotted the Mercedes as the driver recklessly backed into the intersection in an effort to follow. An instant later, the cab of an eighteen-wheeler sailed into view and smashed into the Mercedes, spinning it sideways, pushing it over the curb, and then crushing it against the brick wall of a twenty-story building. Through the curtain of now densely falling snow, Donovan caught the flash and glow of what could only be a post-crash fire.

"Did you see that?" Montero said.

Donovan felt his phone ringing. A quick glance confirmed the caller. "Michael, are you ready to go?"

"We have our clearance, but it started snowing pretty heavily, and we're going to have to shut down and de-ice. Where are you?"

"We're traveling west out of town. Call me when you're airborne." Donovan ended the call and noticed that the snow was starting to stick to the pavement.

"Uh-oh," Montero said as her eyes darted from the mirror to Donovan. "The black Suburban is still back there."

Donovan looked in the side mirror and spotted the SUV at the same time a red dot from a laser sight bounced through the interior of the rental car.

# CHAPTER TEN

THE MIRROR ON Donovan's side of the car exploded and was swept away in the car's slipstream, leaving only a shattered stub. Montero, in the fast lane, pushed their speed toward eighty. Donovan felt and heard the steady hum from the rubber tires on the concrete change pitch as they hydroplaned over the accumulating snow. Montero pushed the rental faster.

The two vehicles were jockeying for position. Every now and then, the red dot swept across the interior and then vanished. Donovan pictured the shooter, whose only option was to stick the weapon outside the window into the freezing blast of air and try to hold it steady enough to get off an accurate shot. Almost impossible, except that the SUV was closing the distance.

As they passed a truck, Montero swung into the right-hand lane to block the SUV's line of sight. Her eyes were locked on the road. Donovan glanced at the speedometer: ninety miles per hour. He sensed the rear-end getting a little light, but Montero kept them tracking straight ahead.

"What happens if we get off the highway?" Donovan asked. "Could we lose them on the back roads?"

"No," she answered. "Too much snow on the roads. The Suburban may have four-wheel drive. We'll lose our advantage completely. We have to stay on the Interstate as long as we can."

Donovan's phone rang. It was Michael.

"Donovan, we're airborne, just climbing through ten thousand feet, heading north."

"They found us and they're shooting. We need your help."

"Where are you?"

"We're on Interstate 94, headed northwest. We just passed a town named Rogers."

"I'm on it," Michael said. "Here's Jesse."

"I'm here, Mr. Nash," Jesse said.

Donovan let a small grin come to his face. When Michael Ross swung into action, there would be results. In the background, Donovan could hear Michael reel off a series of instructions to Rick. The next thing Donovan heard was Michael transmitting an urgent call to Minneapolis departure control. Reporting they had a baggage door warning light and needed to descend and turn toward St. Cloud airport.

"I don't know how much you can hear, Mr. Nash," Jesse said. "We're turning and descending. Michael says we're headed in your direction. We need to know which car is yours."

"We're in a white four-door sedan, going ninety miles per hour. We're being followed by a black Chevy Suburban. We just went past the exit for a town named Albertville. Monticello is next."

"Michael is flying via the heads-up display infrared interface. He's says we're coming up fast behind you," Jesse said. "Michael wants you to flash your bright lights twice."

Donovan relayed the instructions to Montero. Cycling the lights heightened their ability to see how hard it was snowing.

"We have you in sight," Jesse announced triumphantly. "Mr. Nash, Michael says to stay in your lane, and try to increase the distance between you and the SUV. We're going dark."

Donovan heard Michael telling Rick to turn off all the external lights as well as the altitude reporting connected to the transponder.

No one would know the Gulfstream's altitude except Michael. He'd be flying using the infrared imaging of the *Galileo* to turn the nighttime blizzard into a sharp black-and-white image.

"Donovan, it's Michael. Hey, I just came over the top of you guys. I saw two occupants in the front seat of the SUV, but I also caught another heat source. In the very back, there's someone lying on their side, as if they were tied up and thrown in the rear door."

"The woman?"

"That's what I'm thinking."

"If you don't stop the people shooting at us, or at least slow them down, then it won't matter who it is."

"Got it," Michael replied. "Tell Montero to go faster and not to flinch."

"What's going to happen?" Montero asked.

"Focus on the road. The *Galileo* is running without lights and Michael is going to come in low and fast. He'll illuminate all the lights at the last second, and it should be enough to scare the crap out of the guys in the SUV. He said not to flinch."

Montero didn't say a word, just pushed the car faster.

Donovan strained to see in the darkness. They and the SUV were the only vehicles speeding down this section of the Interstate. The darkened *Galileo*, visible for only an instant in the headlights of the rental car, passed less than twenty feet above them, and as it did, all of the high-intensity lights came on at once and lit up the SUV. The roar from the twin jet engines penetrated through Donovan's entire body, and Montero flinched and ducked, but held the steering wheel steady as they blew through the snow thrown up by the Gulfstream's wake.

Donovan snapped around to watch out the back. Michael had the Gulfstream down on the deck. The *Galileo*'s brilliant lights no doubt giving the driver of the SUV the impression of an impending head-on collision. Then the Gulfstream pulled up steeply and vanished into the blizzard. The SUV momentarily disappeared in the swirling snow from the *Galileo's* turbulence, and when Donovan spotted it again, it was starting to slide sideways.

The Suburban jerked to the right. The driver tried to correct and began to lose it the other way. Donovan held his breath as the SUV threatened to roll, but the driver caught it, and the vehicle spun completely around before tipping up on two wheels, going over, and landing on the driver's side. In a shower of sparks, the Suburban rotated until the headlights careened off into the darkness as the heavy vehicle finally came to a stop in the ditch.

"Stop, go back!" Donovan yelled.

"Why in the hell would we do that?" Montero said, while at the same time, easing off the gas.

"The *Galileo's* infrared," Donovan said as he found his gloves. "Michael saw what might be the woman lying in the back of the SUV."

Montero slowed, did a skidding U-turn, and raced down the shoulder toward the SUV. As they drew closer, Donovan could see either smoke or steam billowing from under the hood. Montero pulled over and aimed the sedan's headlights at the scene. She lit up the emergency flashers, pulled her Glock, and jumped out the door. Donovan was right beside her as they surrounded the SUV. Both men were still inside the car amidst deflated airbags and shattered safety glass. They were unconscious, or worse.

Donovan raced to the shattered rear window and looked inside. In the lights from their rental he could see her. It was the woman, with tie-wraps around her ankles and wrists. He yanked on the handle, but the rear door wouldn't move. Without hesitating, Donovan went headfirst into the rear compartment and crawled to her. He grabbed her under the arms and pulled her toward the opening where Montero waited.

"Hurry, cars are coming."

Donovan jumped to the ground and eased the woman out. He was about to gather her in his arms when she kicked out with both legs and caught him in the shoulder, then she threw a wild head butt toward Montero. Donovan staggered sideways as Montero slammed the barrel of her Glock under the girl's chin and used her other hand to punch her hard in the solar plexus. The blow took the fight out of her, and with her hands and feet still bound, Donovan lifted her in his arms. They ran as fast as they could to the rental. Montero held the rear door open, and Donovan eased the woman inside. Then, sliding the seat belt through the tie-wrap on her wrists, he snapped it into place. Montero climbed behind the wheel and killed the lights. Donovan piled in on the passenger side and slammed the door as Montero spun the car around and sped off. Grabbing his phone, Donovan did a quick check to confirm he was still connected to the *Galileo*.

"Jesse?"

"No, it's Michael. Is everyone okay?"

"Yeah, we're good. We have her."

"The *Galileo* is full of fuel," Michael said. "We're too heavy to land. What's the plan?"

Donovan thought for a moment and then turned to Montero. "They can't land. Are we good without them until tomorrow?"

"Ask him if they're going to the lake," Montero said.

"Yes," Michael said. "We'll do as much reconnaissance as possible and then land somewhere safe."

"Works for me," Montero said. "We've got a lot to do between now and tomorrow morning, anyway."

"Fly safe," Donovan said to Michael. "Let us know where you spend the night. And, Michael—thanks."

"No problem. Just try and stay out of trouble until I get back."

# CHAPTER ELEVEN

"CAN YOU HEAR me?" Donovan said as he clicked on the dome light and leaned into the backseat. He brushed the hair from the woman's face, but made no effort to free her. The woman, who had been nothing but a wild card from the start, was awake, and no doubt angry. He had no idea what to expect. "Who are you? Can you tell me your name?"

"You're him," she said as she focused on his face in the dim light.

"Where do you remember me from?"

"The hospital."

"Do you know where you are?" Montero asked.

The woman acted like she was going to answer, but no words came. She lowered her head as if thinking, but produced nothing more than a look of complete confusion. To Donovan, she said, "Those men, they took me and drugged me. Are they gone?"

"Yes," Donovan said. "Do you know who they were?"

"No."

"What questions did they ask you?" Donovan asked. "Did they tell you anything?"

"They asked me how many people were on the airplane. They kept asking me about Eco-Watch."

"Was it one of them who hit me?"

"No, I hit you. I thought you were a threat."

"*Oni govoryat po-russki?*" Montero asked in Russian.

"*Da ya russkiy.*"

"What was that?" Donovan asked.

"I asked if the men spoke to her in Russian. She replied yes, and said that she's Russian." Montero paused until she made eye contact with the woman in the mirror. "*Yest' li u vas russkoye imya?*"

"Sofya," she said with a nod and a tiny smile of victory.

"Sofya? My name is Donovan, and this is Montero. We just rescued you, so you understand we're not going to hurt you."

"The hospital—why was I there? What happened to me?"

"You were in a plane crash. Do you remember?"

Her eyes filled with fear and confusion, "I don't understand what you're telling me. How can any of this be happening? Where are we?"

Donovan saw an emergency vehicle speeding in the opposite direction, lights flashing. He glanced at Montero. "How long are we going to be safe in this car?"

"Not much longer. St. Cloud is up ahead; I thought we'd find some new wheels there."

"Are we not safe? You told me those men were gone. Are we still in danger?"

Donovan could see the alarm in her eyes. "None of us have been safe since we landed in Minneapolis and I took you to the hospital. The further we travel, the safer we'll be."

"Donovan, use your GPS and help me navigate to the airport," Montero interrupted. "And call ahead to see if you can rent us a car."

Donovan turned his back on Sofya and found a rental car at the general aviation terminal in St. Cloud. The rest of the drive went by in silence as he and Montero navigated to the airport through the snow.

When they reached the airport, Montero said, "Go ahead, I'll drop you off. No reason for anyone but you to go inside."

Donovan stepped through the accumulating snow and into the warmth of St. Cloud Aviation. Handing over his alternate identification and credit card, he explained to the young woman behind the counter that he'd be returning the vehicle in a week. He selected a Lincoln Navigator, and as she filled out the paperwork, Donovan remembered that he still had a rental car sitting in the Methodist Hospital parking lot in Minneapolis. He'd take care of that tomorrow.

"Space four is out the door and to your right, along the fence."

Donovan thanked her and hurried back out into the cold. He started the Lincoln and cranked up the heat, using the windshield wipers to push the snow from the windshield. He found a brush in the backseat and cleared the side and back windows of snow, then slid behind the wheel and drove across the lot to where Montero and Sofya waited. He jumped out and draped his coat around Sofya. He saw that Montero had freed her ankles, but her wrists remained bound. He escorted Sofya to the Navigator. Montero lagged behind, loaded her bag into the back, and then climbed into the front passenger seat. As before, Donovan latched the seat belt through the zip tie securing Sofya's wrists before climbing behind the wheel.

Montero studied the screen on her phone. "Fargo is a two-hour drive, and it looks like there's a mall there that's open until nine. Since Sofya has no clothes, we could still take care of that when we get there."

"Who are you people?" Sofya said in a whisper that sounded like either fear or rage. "What are you going to do to me?"

"Donovan, let's sit here for a minute so the three of us can talk," Montero said and got out so she could slide into the back next to Sofya. "Now is as good a time as any to explain to you what's happened. I'll let Donovan describe how he found you."

Donovan turned to face them. "Early this morning, I was in Canada, flying over Northern Manitoba. My crew and I witnessed an airplane in distress, a Boeing 737. The 737 made an emergency landing on a frozen lake. We saw one survivor climb out of the Boeing before it broke through the ice. You're that survivor. We got there just after you collapsed in the snow."

Sofya recoiled, her eyes wide with confusion and disbelief.

"When I reached you, you were still conscious. What you said to me set off a series of events that has brought us all here. You told me not to tell anyone you were alive—or they would kill us and our families."

Sofya lowered her head. The tears came, followed by shaking sobs.

Donovan continued, "We treated you for hypothermia and flew to Minneapolis. I took you to the hospital. There is security footage that shows you leaving the hospital. We think you were taken by the individuals who were chasing us on the highway."

"How did they find me?" Sofya asked.

"I have a background in law enforcement; I know a great many people," Montero said. "In an effort to identify you, Donovan sent me your photograph after he'd saved you. I, in turn, sent them to one of my contacts in Europe, and the initial finding suggests you were a missing person. Do you remember being in Europe?"

"No."

"It's believed that you were in Krakow at one point. My contact, who was working to identify you, was murdered not long after she started her inquiry. I can only assume she was compromised, and that the information on you was released. We know very little, though, thanks to you, we do know the men in Minneapolis spoke to you in Russian. It's a start."

"We're maybe the only friends you have right now," Donovan said. "We need to put some distance between the three of us and what happened back there on the highway. We're going to work our way toward the Canadian border, which should put a blizzard between us and Minneapolis. That should give us time to regroup, sleep, and be ready to leave in the morning."

"We are going to Canada?" Sofya asked.

"We need to discuss logistics and make some arrangements," Donovan said. "But my plan is to go back to where the airplane crashed. It's my hope that once we're there, we'll be able to find the answers to our questions."

"Sofya, does anything we've said sound familiar?" Montero asked. "The smallest fragment might help us help you."

Sofya shook her head. "I still can't believe I was in a plane crash and that I made threats."

"Not a threat, more like a warning," Donovan said. "We'll work on this together, and hopefully, we'll find the answers in Canada."

"Am I your prisoner? Is that why my hands are still bound?"

"You're in protective custody. I'll remove them when we're both ready," Montero said. "I know it's difficult. You've been through a great deal of trauma. We just want everyone to stay safe, including you. Right now, I want you to try to relax. I'd like to ask you some questions."

Donovan listened as Montero spoke soothingly to Sofya. It was clear that she had experience dealing with traumatized and terrified women, and Donovan was seeing a side of Montero that he hadn't expected.

He put the car into gear and used the GPS to guide them back out to the highway. As he drove, he thought of Lauren and Abigail, confident that Kristof would keep them safe. The *Galileo* was enroute to the lake where they found Sofya, and using the aircraft's sophisticated onboard optics, they'd be able to map the entire area. Knowing Michael, he'd have all of their options figured out by morning. His best guess was that everyone connected to the woman was, for the moment, safe—except for him and Montero.

# CHAPTER TWELVE

"Good morning, Kristof," Lauren said as she breezed into the kitchen. "Where's Marta? She's usually up by now."

"She left to run errands," Kristof said as he sipped his cup of tea.

"Oh," Lauren said, pouring herself coffee from the maker. "I didn't know she was going anywhere today."

"She'll be back before lunch."

"Okay." In the short time Lauren had known Kristof, she'd seen a range of emotions, though when he seemed distracted, which he did now, she was always reminded that he was ill.

"It sounds like Abigail is up," Kristof said. "Have the two of you made any plans for the day?"

"She'll be down in a minute. I promised her I'd go for a ride with her this morning. Other than that, we have nothing planned."

Kristof attended to his teabag and added more hot water to his cup. "Can I ask you a question? It's about Marta."

"You can ask me anything," Lauren said.

"One of the things I most admire about you is your relationship with Abigail. You're a wonderful mother, and Abigail is a treasure. I especially marvel at the boundaries you set for her without damping any of her youthful enthusiasm. You and Donovan allow Abigail to explore so many things, which is wonderful to watch."

"Why, thank you. That's so kind of you to say, but how does that relate to Marta?"

"You don't love horses, do you?"

"It doesn't matter," Lauren said. "As long as my daughter loves them, then I do, too. I think as a parent, it's my job to adapt to her interests and passions, or it's unlikely she'll be able to develop them fully."

"That's my point. Do you think I've made the wrong decision bringing Marta into my business? I've always insisted that it be her choice, but at times I wonder if I made that clear, or if she felt the choice was there at all. I worry that she would be happier doing something else. And my bigger fear is what I may have done to her future. A husband, and children—how does any of that fit with what she and I do?"

"I think you're worrying about nothing, though I know it's hard as a parent. As long as kids know they're loved, that they have that anchor, they'll reach out and test the world. Marta is one of the brightest, most balanced and confident women I know. The best thing you could have possibly done was send her to school in England. She learned, participated, and looked at everything as a possible life path. You also left the door open for the family business, and she walked in of her own volition. She'll be fine."

"I hope so. Yet, I wonder, how do you bring a young man home to meet your father when he happens to be me?" Kristof said as he shook his head as if to ward off the thought.

"If said young man has the bravery to get himself in the position to meet Archangel, my advice for you is to make him feel welcome. Marta is a pretty good judge of character. She'll weed them out as they come along. She'll be fine, Kristof, trust me."

"Thank you," he said as he reached out and took her hand.

Abigail blew into the room, all energy and smiles. "Good morning, Uncle Kristof. Mom, can I have cereal with a sliced banana for breakfast?" She was dressed for riding, her hair tied in a ponytail.

"Yes, I think we can manage that." Lauren rose from the table, set out a bowl, and began slicing a banana.

"Hannah's already here!" Abigail said excitedly as she heard the sound of the stable door opening. "Mom, I have to go tell her we're both riding today."

"Put on your boots and coat and then hurry back. You have to have breakfast before we go anywhere."

"I know." Abigail ran from the kitchen toward the back door.

"The energy," Kristof said as he went back to his tea. "She's such a joy. Makes me imagine Marta at that age."

"They're wonderful at all ages," Lauren said. "Though some days you have to look really hard for it, but it's there."

An explosion shattered the morning peace, shaking the house. Lauren felt her ears pop. She dropped the knife and banana in the sink and bolted for Abigail. Grabbing her coat, she flew out the door just as a large plume of dark smoke climbed above the trees. The house next door was burning—the one Kristof said was his security headquarters. From what Lauren could see, it was completely leveled. She heard the staccato sound of automatic weapons fire as she threw open the door to the stable.

Abigail and Hannah both turned as she entered.

"What's happening?" Hannah's voice wavered with fear.

"We need to go back to the house. Now." Lauren grabbed her daughter's hand and turned to find Kristof at the stable door.

"It's bad," he said, the small radio in his hand crackling with static. "There's been a total breach of security, and intruders are coming down the road. Most of my men are out of commission. Get on the horses and ride toward the mountain. Circle down to the village but avoid the main road. Go!"

Lauren nodded, and Kristof pressed a Glock into her hand. Then he turned and headed for the house. She put the pistol in her pocket, knowing it was fully loaded, and all she had to do was pull the trigger. Hannah had both horses saddled and ready. Lauren swung her daughter up into the saddle atop Zephyr. The horse snorted and sidestepped, skittish from the gunfire. Lauren jumped on behind Abigail, reached around her daughter, grabbed the horn, and used her knees to hold on. The stirrups were already adjusted for Abigail's legs and her daughter held the reins.

"Abigail, just let Zephyr follow me and hang on," Hannah said in German-accented English as she kicked open the larger doors that would free the horses. She jumped up on top of Gemini and nudged the horse out into the morning, calling out softly so that Zephyr stayed close. A burst of gunfire rattled nearby, and Hannah urged Gemini up the path, then kicked hard. Both horses began to run, quickly reaching full speed through the snow.

Lauren was terrified for Abigail. She didn't think her daughter had ever ridden this fast. She took a quick look behind them and found the powerful hooves throwing snow high in their wake. Lauren spotted what was left of the house next door—smaller wisps of smoke were starting to rise from the chalet. Lauren was still looking behind them, trying to spot Kristof, when the first tree flashed past on their left, then more trees, and the two horses plunged into the forest, racing up the snow-covered trail as fast as they could travel.

"Hang on, Mom!" Abigail cried out as Gemini, and then Zephyr, jumped a fallen log.

Lauren winced as she rose and then came down hard, but Abigail rode perfectly, standing in the saddle's stirrups, urging Zephyr faster. Lauren followed Abigail's lead as they reached a fork in the trail and leaned with the horse as the trail broke right. When they reached a clearing, Abigail swung out and quartered Gemini as Hannah eased up and brought both horses to a halt.

"Great job, honey." Lauren hugged Abigail and silently hoped that Kristof made it to his safe room, out of harm's way.

"Abigail, very good riding," Hannah said.

Lauren saw Gemini's ears pivot as the horse picked up a sound in the distance. Lauren cocked her head and listened. She, too, could hear something, but she wasn't sure what it was.

"It's a snowmobile. We need to go," Hannah said, turning Gemini. "Abigail, we need to cut through those trees to stay ahead of whoever is coming. Give Gemini and me a four-second head start so Zephyr doesn't get blinded by the snow we kick up. Let him run, he'll follow just fine, but stay low. Do you understand?"

"I understand." Abigail nodded and then turned to look back at Lauren. "Mom, you need to lean forward until you're below Zephyr's head or else you could get hit by a branch."

Hannah kicked Gemini and they immediately took off for the trees. Abigail waited, holding the reins firmly, until she nudged the horse and Zephyr bolted. Lauren leaned as far forward as she could, feeling more than slightly troubled that her six-year-old daughter was giving her orders.

Zephyr pounded down the trail into the forest. Ahead, Gemini swept past snow-covered boughs, creating a miniature blizzard of ultra-fine snow. The spacing worked perfectly; by the time Zephyr arrived, the worst of the disturbed snow was settling. As they wound through the trails, the sound of the snowmobile drew closer. Abigail leaned forward, shifting her weight to help Zephyr with the turns, and Lauren mimicked her daughter's motions. Lauren turned and spotted a flash from the low-slung snowmobile, followed by a sharp crack. There were two riders, and one had a pistol.

"Mom, hang on!" Abigail cried out as Zephyr jumped another log. Lauren was ready and braced herself better this time. She turned to watch as the snowmobile swerved to miss the obstruction and tipped over, throwing both riders into the snow, and then the motor died.

"They crashed," Lauren said, hugging her daughter tighter. "Go, sweetie, go!"

Zephyr blew out of the stand of trees and raced after Gemini, pounding through a huge open pasture covered with pristine snow. Up ahead, Lauren saw a long row of trees with only one opening and the horses were slowing, laboring as the snow deepened. Hannah had them running toward the gap in the trees when Lauren heard the high-pitched sound of the snowmobile as it erupted from the trees behind them and accelerated quickly in the open field. Lauren did the calculations and could see there would be no place to hide once they rode beyond the row of trees.

"Abigail, the second we're through the gap in the trees, can you make a hard right turn?"

"Mom, what are you doing, what's going to happen?"

"I'm going to jump off, but I want you to keep riding with Hannah. You two get to town and go to the police. Okay?"

"I'm scared," Abigail said.

Lauren wished she had time to ask her little girl what scared her most, but they were almost to the trees. "Don't be frightened, sweetheart. Stay with Hannah, and I'll see you in a little while."

Abigail ducked and Lauren followed her lead as they blew through the gap. Abigail hauled hard on the reins and Zephyr dug in, turned sharply, and continued running. Lauren released her grip and rolled to the side, the momentum of the turn throwing her free, and she landed hard, rolling in the powdery snow. She raised her head and saw that Abigail had found snow that wasn't as deep, and Zephyr was thundering hard across the field. Lauren snapped her head around. As she'd hoped, the trees had blocked the men on the snowmobile from seeing what she'd done. As fast as she could, she scrambled to her feet and hid behind the trunk of a tree and waited. She peeled off her right glove, unzipped her coat pocket, and pulled out the Glock. She let the sound of the speeding snowmobile guide her aim. When the machine was within twenty paces of the opening in the trees, Lauren swung out, put the driver in her sights, and started pulling the trigger. Keeping the barrel level, she tracked the snowmobile's occupants and fired eight shots until the man driving slumped, and the snowmobile jerked to the side, slammed into the trunks of some smaller trees, and then went quiet. Snow poured down from the limbs above and covered the men and their stalled machine. She turned and fled on instinct, paralleling the trees.

A bullet sizzled through the air next to her ear at the same time she heard the report from the pistol. In the distance she saw Hannah and Abigail crest a hill, still riding fast, and then they disappeared. Lauren ducked and slid into the snow-covered brush, trying not to jostle a tree and give away her position.

"Don't move," a male voice called out from the other side of the trees.

Lauren hadn't expected him to cover so much ground unseen. He'd come up behind her, and now she was going to die. She had to get off a shot. She gripped the Glock firmly, and tried to gauge his position. She was about to spin and start shooting when she heard him abruptly exhale. She turned and brought the Glock up to fire, just as his knees buckled and he collapsed. The solitary crack of a high-caliber gunshot echoed throughout the quiet valley. Lauren lowered her pistol. The man had toppled face-first into the snow, so she could see the entry wound the high-velocity bullet had made between his shoulder blades. He was dead before he hit the ground.

She crouched, trying to find the source of the shot. She finally heard an engine and in the distance, spotted a familiar gray Range Rover plowing through the snow-covered pasture. The driver stopped where the snowmobile had crashed. Lauren kept her Glock ready, and inched toward the figure who stepped from the vehicle. She saw a scoped rifle slung over a shoulder and a pistol in a gloved hand. The driver wore a fur hat, a leather jacket, and sunglasses. When the scarf was lowered and the figure turned, Lauren discovered it was Marta.

"Are you okay?" Marta asked.

Lauren closed the distance, astonished that Marta had come to her rescue, and gave her a hug. "Oh my God, how did you—what hap—?" Relief overwhelmed Lauren and she couldn't talk, so she just held on.

"Get in. I passed three vehicles I didn't recognize when I was leaving the chalet and decided something wasn't right, so I turned around. I heard the explosions from the rocket attack and arrived at the chalet in perfect position to take out the unsuspecting attackers from the rear. Dad was in the safe room, and he told me where you'd gone. Here I am. Dad is headed for the airport. We need to keep moving. Where are Abigail and Hannah?"

Lauren pointed to the top of the ridge where she'd last seen the girls. "I never got a chance to talk to Hannah, but I told Abigail to get to the police." Lauren swallowed hard as thoughts of Abigail pressed in on her. She slid into the Rover and checked the Glock. She had four bullets remaining.

Marta threw the SUV into gear and with wheels spinning, they paralleled the tree line until they came to the main route into town. Marta plowed through a snowbank and was forced to brake heavily to stay on the roadway, but once stabilized, she stepped hard on the gas and they sped downhill.

Marta swerved to pass a slower car, and they rounded a turn just before the ground dropped off dramatically all the way to the valley floor.

"I see them!" Lauren said as she pointed to her right. "Two figures on horseback, they're down there in the field, paralleling the road."

As Marta floored the Range Rover, Lauren's eyes darted back and forth between her daughter and the road behind them, unsure who else might be in pursuit. They closed the distance, and as Marta rounded another curve, Lauren could see that Hannah had them headed toward what looked to be a trail leading into a grove of trees.

"We're not going to be able to catch them," Marta said as the road swerved the other way, taking them away from the girls. "I know where that trail leads. They'll be safe. We'll meet them on the other side of the trees."

Lauren spotted the emergency vehicles at nearly the same time as Marta. They were racing up the hill in the opposite direction. Marta slowed and pulled to the side as the official cars roared past, lights flashing and sirens wailing. The moment they were clear, Marta once again floored the Range Rover. Two more turns and she slowed, took a right turn off the road, and they bounced and rumbled across a snow-covered field.

"Jump out, let the girls see you!" Marta said as she brought the vehicle up a small crest and came to a sliding stop.

Lauren climbed down into the calf-deep snow and began running toward where the trail emerged from the woods. The instant Hannah and Gemini burst from the shadows, Lauren began waving her arms and yelling for them to stop. Several seconds later, Abigail and Zephyr were out into the open. Abigail began to rein in her horse, and Hannah, seemingly startled by the scene, at first turned away, and then circled back to join Abigail.

"Mom!" Abigail cried out as she slid off the horse and ran.

Lauren crouched, wrapped up her daughter and held her close, feeling Abigail's cold cheeks pressing into her neck. The moment was broken by the crunching snow under the Range Rover's tires as Marta wheeled in next to them.

"Girls, get in the back," Lauren said as she pulled away from Abigail. "We have to go."

"What about the horses?" Abigail asked.

"They'll be fine," Hannah said. "They'll find their way back home, it's not too far."

With the girls inside the SUV, Marta drove the Rover back across the field until they popped onto the road and were once again speeding toward town. "Hannah, are you okay?"

"Yes, I'm fine. Who were those men?" Hannah asked as she peeled off her hat against the warmth inside the vehicle.

"I'm not sure," Marta said. "Which is why I need to take you somewhere safe. What about your uncle, the one who is a constable in Zirl? If I take you to the police station, will that be okay?"

"Yes, I'll be safe there."

"Hannah, I'm so sorry all of this happened, but what you and Abigail did was remarkable," Marta said. "Tell your uncle exactly what happened, and that we're all okay. Someone representing my father and I will be in touch with him later."

"Mom, where are we going?" Abigail asked.

"I'm not sure." Lauren caught a subtle shake of the head from Marta, telling her to be cautious. Hannah didn't need to know any more than she already did.

"We're going to meet up with Uncle Kristof," Marta said as she slowed the Range Rover, entered the village limits of Zirl, and drove straight to the police station. She parked in front of the main door and then turned toward the girls in the backseat. "Hannah, again, thank you so much. I don't want you to be afraid. I think those men were looking for my father, so they don't have any idea who you are—you're not involved in this at all. Your uncle will be able to protect you. Tell him hello, and I'll talk to you in a few days."

The moment Hannah hurried across the sidewalk and pushed through the door into the station, Marta gunned the Range Rover in the direction of Innsbruck.

"Are we headed to the airport?" Lauren asked

"The jet should be waiting," Marta said, checking her rearview mirrors.

"Abigail and I don't have our passports."

"I grabbed your bag on my way out, it's in the back." Marta said.

The drive down the valley, across the river, and to the airport took only minutes. Marta parked the Rover, opened the rear hatch, and handed Lauren her bag, then the three of them hurried toward the general aviation lounge. Lauren pushed through the doors to find Kristof waiting. The four of them walked across the ramp and boarded the Gulfstream. The flight attendant introduced herself and took their coats. Lauren held Abigail's hand and they went down the aisle to the four club seats near the rear of the jet. The door was closed and Lauren listened to the familiar sounds of both engines being started.

"Where are we going?" Lauren asked.

"We're flying to Luton, north of London," Kristof said. "We're going to Stephanie VanGelder's country home."

Abigail's face lit up at the prospect of seeing her aunt Stephanie. "I can't wait to tell Aunt Stephanie that I rode a horse faster than a bullet!"

"Honey," Lauren said as the Gulfstream swung out onto the taxiway. "What do you say we tell Aunt Stephanie together, so she can hear both sides of our adventure? Maybe tonight, after we get settled?"

"Okay." Abigail shrugged and turned to the window to watch the takeoff.

"What about your treatments, your doctors?" Lauren asked Kristof. "Will you be okay?"

"I'm fine for a few days. After the events in Minnesota last night, and now this, the doctors can wait. Stephanie is waiting for us, and as promised, I already made a phone call to Trevor. Our SAS friends are on their way to her home as well."

"What events in Minneapolis?" Lauren tilted her head as if she hadn't heard correctly.

"Check your phone," Kristof said. "I'm sure you were copied on Montero's e-mail."

Lauren found her phone. There was a message from Montero and one from Donovan. She clicked on her husband's first. The moment she saw it was sent on his phone, she knew it would be brief. He hated typing on the small keyboard.

*Change of plans. Departed Minneapolis. Girl's name is Sofya, she's Russian. Everyone is okay, but we're on the move. Tomorrow we go north to salvage the Boeing. Be safe. Love, Donovan.*

Lauren opened Montero's e-mail and found a three-paragraph after-action report written in the crisp, concise manner she'd been taught while at the FBI. Lauren read through the recent events and lowered her phone. "Today, the men at the chalet—were they Russian?"

"Yes," Marta said. "As close as we could tell, they were mercenaries, freelancers, not part of any organized group we're familiar with. Though I'm completely convinced that everything that has happened leads back to that plane, and to that woman."

"We don't know anything," Kristof whispered, his eyes narrowed into slits. The lines etched into his face conveyed a mixture of physical pain and barely contained outrage. "Except for the fact that they tried to harm the four of us in my home, and I promise, they'll pay dearly for that mistake."

\* \* \*

The flight to the Luton airport took a little over an hour, and as the chartered Gulfstream broke out of the low clouds, Lauren took in the familiar countryside north of London. Stephanie's country home was a stark contrast to her modern apartment near St. James Park. Lauren loved the stately, five-bedroom Tudor, surrounded by expansive gardens and trees. Stephanie, an award-winning photojournalist, had exquisite taste and a great eye for detail.

"How long since you've seen Stephanie?" Marta asked her father.

"It has to be back when Donovan lived in Los Angeles. I'd flown over for a party, and Stephanie was there—maybe twenty-seven, twenty-eight years ago."

The main wheels touched down and the Gulfstream came to a gentle stop. Once they'd cleared the runway, Lauren began the delicate task of waking Abigail. The instant her daughter realized they'd arrived, she began searching out the window for Stephanie. When the jet swung around on the general aviation ramp, Abigail spotted her. The door swung open and the flight attendant requested that everyone remain seated for a quick customs inspection. A uniformed man climbed the airstair, greeted the crew, and was given everyone's passport. He scanned the declarations and walked back into the cabin.

"Welcome to England," he said without smiling. "What's the nature of your trip?"

"Pleasure," Lauren said. "We're here to visit friends for a New Year's Eve get-together."

"Sounds rather pleasant." He opened up the first passport. He matched the photo with the person and then handed it to Marta. He repeated the process with Lauren and Abigail, and then finished with Kristof. "How long will you be in England?"

"I suspect we'll depart on New Year's Day," Kristof said. "Or the day after, depending on how everyone feels."

"Very well then." The man handed Kristof his passport, turned smartly, and walked off the Gulfstream, giving a wave to the flight attendant.

"We're all set. You're free to deplane," the flight attendant said. "Your vehicles are being brought around."

With a firm grip on her daughter's hand, Lauren went down the airstair to where Stephanie stood. Abigail broke from her mother and leapt into Stephanie's waiting arms. Lauren reached around her daughter and managed to hug her dear friend. Two Range Rovers pulled up. Trevor stepped out of the first one and immediately went to Marta, then to Kristof, exchanging greetings. Lauren turned toward Reggie as he appeared from behind the wheel of the second Rover and waved. It was the first time she'd seen the man since he'd saved her and Abigail in Paris.

"Hello again," Reggie said.

Lauren smiled and gave him a heartfelt hug. Over his shoulder, she spotted Stephanie meeting Trevor and Marta, and then giving Kristof a kiss. Lauren broke away as Trevor came toward her. He kissed Lauren on both cheeks. Reggie introduced himself to Kristof and Marta, and then Lauren noticed Reggie slip Abigail a red lollipop before suggesting they all get into the vehicles and be on their way.

"Shall we ride with Reggie?" Lauren asked Abigail.

"We've actually arranged for Abigail to ride in Trevor's Rover," Reggie said. "I was hoping we could use the drive to chat."

"Come on, Abigail," Marta said. "Looks like we get to ride with Trevor, Stephanie, and Uncle Kristof."

Abigail promptly pivoted and followed Marta.

"Thank you for calling us," Reggie said as they settled into the plush front seats. "I would hate to think you were in trouble and we weren't there to lend a hand."

"I remember it was Buck who called you the first time," Lauren said, feeling the familiar twinge of sorrow at the mention of his name. Former Navy SEAL Howard "Buck" Buckley was an Eco-Watch employee and dear friend. He'd been dead for two years, but the thought of his death was still painful.

"I'm sorry I couldn't make it to the funeral," Reggie said. "We were helping another old friend, and in our line of work, the first priority is to the living."

"You sound like him." Lauren tried to smile, to focus on all that was good about Buck. "He thought very highly of you."

"And we of him. He was one of the good ones," Reggie said. "Abigail seems her usual resilient self. How are you holding up?"

"The lollipop was sweet." Lauren set her jaw against the tears.

"It wasn't intended to be sweet," Reggie said. "It's important to build a bond with younger principals. I need her to recognize and trust me. Now, how are you doing?"

"People tried to kill my daughter this morning. I was forced to shoot a man, and all I can think about is how everything could have gone wrong. I'm scared, angry, and I don't know when my life reached a point that I need professional soldiers to keep me and my daughter alive. How do I deal with all of this?"

"Exactly as you are." Reggie reached across and took Lauren's hand. "You did what any mother would do. You protected your child. Relish that part. You're strong, smart, and resourceful, and you have a great many people who care about you. We'll figure it out. I promise."

"I hope so."

"I've already been to Stephanie's house and some of my other lads have gone over the layout and it's good. Obviously, you'll never see anyone but Trevor and me. We're houseguests, same as you. That should minimize Abigail's perception of living among armed bodyguards."

"Thank you for that. You must have spoken to Kristof?"

"Yes, nice guy actually," Reggie said. "I'm not quite sure how an analyst with the Defense Intelligence Agency and her six-year-old daughter have fallen in with the family I believe is known in some circles as Archangel, the long-time arms dealers, but I'm sure stranger things have happened. I just can't think of anything offhand."

"Archangel is a secret that needs to stay between you and me," Lauren said. "What isn't going to be a secret much longer is Trevor and Marta."

"What do you mean?"

"I can't be the only one to notice the crush they have on each other."

"Bloody hell." Reggie shook his head. "I thought I was crazy. That thing is real?"

"Very."

# CHAPTER THIRTEEN

"ARE YOU SURE you're both okay?" Donovan asked as he paced back and forth in an empty portion of the lobby of the Grand Forks executive flight support facility.

"Yes, we're all fine," Lauren said. "Your daughter was remarkable. The way she rode that horse in the snow and through the trees—it was amazing."

The fact that Abigail was remarkable was something he already knew. Though the image of his six-year-old daughter, fleeing for her life on horseback, caused a tightness in his stomach and throat, and tears threatened to form in his eyes. Even though everyone was now safe at Stephanie's, and the country house was being guarded by Reggie, Trevor, and other former SAS Special Forces personnel, it did nothing to erase his shock of hearing about the attack in Innsbruck.

"When are you leaving?" Lauren asked.

"Shortly," Donovan said. "Last night Montero took some pictures of Sofya, and sent them to her guy in Florida. If everything goes as planned, FedEx should deliver a package this morning with Sofya's new passport and other identification."

"Then where do you go?" Lauren asked.

"After last night's mission, Michael landed and spent the night in Minot, North Dakota, well to the west of the snowstorm that moved down from Canada into Minnesota. I talked to him a little while ago. He's on his way to Winnipeg. Montero and I will drive north with Sofya and clear customs at the border. Montero didn't want to risk putting Sofya through the anxiety of an airplane flight along with subjecting her to the stress of passing through customs."

"Overall, how do you think she's doing?"

"Which one?"

"Start with Sofya."

"Montero has been working with her, and Sofya seems convinced that we're on her side and want to help. Montero talked with her the entire time we were driving to Grand Forks, soothing her, and telling her over and over she wasn't a victim, and that we were her friends. Montero finally released Sofya's bound hands in a production that was both touching and highly calculated. I can't tell how much Montero really cares, or if she's intentionally inducing the Stockholm syndrome. Either way, it's fascinating to watch. I've never really seen this side of Montero."

"I doubt many have, but take into consideration everything else she's good at, and it would follow that she takes her commitment to victimized women seriously. For all we know, it's what she does best."

"Maybe, but I also think it's hard on her, harder than hiding everything behind her toughness."

"I'm sure. Keep in mind that Montero also just lost her source in Prague. If I remember correctly, she came to that girl's rescue once upon a time. We both know Montero feels deeply responsible for the people she tries to help, especially the disenfranchised. Give her some space, but make sure she has what she needs. More than anything, Montero wants to solve problems, but try not to let her get overwhelmed. It sounds like you're going to be with Sofya for a while."

Donovan looked up as Montero stuck her head around the corner, a FedEx envelope in her hand. "Our package just arrived. We need to go. Tell Abigail Daddy says hello, that I love her, and I'm really proud of her. You have a good evening with everyone, and I'll let you know what's happening at this end."

"I will. Be careful," Lauren said. "I love you."

"I love you, too." Donovan ended the call and went to find Montero and Sofya.

Montero was in a conference room, and as Donovan entered, he closed and locked the door. She ripped open the package, and three envelopes slid out onto the polished tabletop.

Montero opened the first one and pulled out a passport. "We need a pen."

Donovan handed his to Sofya, and Montero showed her where to sign.

When Sofya was finished, Montero thumbed through the pages and worked the spine back and forth to loosen it up and then handed it to Sofya. "Memorize all the information inside. Know it backwards and forwards. We'll all work on our cover story while we make the drive."

"What's her name?" Donovan asked.

"Sofya Wilkins. She's twenty-five years old." Montero opened the next envelope and out tumbled a driver's license as well as several other cards. "She lives in Melbourne, Florida."

"What else did she get?" Donovan asked.

"The details that sell the whole thing." Montero emptied the contents. "We have a student identification card for the Florida Institute of Technology, a gym membership, three credit cards, several receipts, a picture of a cat, and an assortment of coupons."

"Nice touches," Donovan said as Sofya opened her new purse and removed the wallet that still had the tags attached. "What's in the third envelope?"

"Cash. I didn't want to resort to using an ATM," Montero said as she presented Sofya with a rather worn billfold that she'd already emptied. "Here, Sofya, use my old one."

"Why?" Sofya asked.

"Law enforcement can get suspicious when everything looks brand new. We'll swap. Give me the one you bought. If anyone asks, you're an intern working for Eco-Watch, studying solar storms."

"Montero, I've cleared customs with you before," Donovan said. "All they do is focus on you. It seems like every single person in law enforcement knows who you are."

"Well, I *was* on the cover of *TIME* magazine." Montero shrugged as if it were no big deal.

"What did you do?" Sofya asked, looking expectantly at Montero.

"Long story," Montero said, as she collected the empty envelopes and began ripping them into pieces. "Oh, I found an article in this morning's *Minneapolis Star Tribune* about some of the car accidents last night in and around the metro area. Most are being blamed on the weather. One accident killed three people in downtown Minneapolis after their car was hit by a truck as they traveled the wrong way down a one-way street. Out on the interstate, two occupants received medical care for non–life threatening injuries after the driver lost control of their SUV while traveling at high speed. Both men were turned over to the St. Cloud County Sheriff to face outstanding warrants in Minneapolis, as well as St. Paul. I have their names; they're both Russian nationals in the country on student visas."

"What's your name?" Donovan said as he turned to Sofya in an effort to catch her off-guard.

"Sofya Wilkins," she replied evenly. "I live at nine fifty-six University Boulevard, apartment three-twenty, in Melbourne, Florida."

Donovan's phone buzzed and he recognized the caller. "Thank God," he said, enormously relieved that William was returning his calls.

"Come on, Sofya," Montero said. "We'll give Donovan some privacy."

"I was starting to worry about you," Donovan said as he answered the call. "Where are you?"

"I'm in Washington," William said. "Working long hours on State Department business."

"Have you spoken to Lauren or Stephanie? Are you up to speed about current events?"

"I was going to call Lauren and Stephanie next, but I wanted to talk to you first. I received a detailed assessment from Montero a few hours ago. You landed a Gulfstream on a frozen lake?"

"It sounds riskier than it was." Donovan knew it was a weak deflection, and that, as usual, William was worried for his safety. "It was no big deal, and we did save the woman. We're about to go back up there and see if we can uncover some answers."

"Montero suspects that the woman, as well as her adversaries, might have ties to Russia. At the moment, watching from the sideline, everything that's happening seems reactive and dangerous."

"We're taking precautions; Montero is involved, and we think we can be in and out of Manitoba before anyone knows we're there."

"Are you sure that's the best play?" William said.

"What's going on?" Donovan asked.

"You know you've had the Russians' respect for years, going back to when you and Michael saved one of their submarines. That, coupled with your recent accomplishments in Eastern Europe, and I've been able to leverage your actions to create some meaningful discussions with senior members of the Politburo. These are delicate negotiations—we're pushing aside generations of distrust, so all I'm asking is for you not to be in the line of fire."

Donovan frowned; the request from William had suddenly expanded beyond normal proportions. In the nearly four decades that

William had been a father figure, mentor, and business partner, Donovan wasn't sure that he'd ever heard William directly wave him off. If anything, William was usually Donovan's greatest supporter. The elder statesman was always the cool and calm one, the unwavering voice urging Donovan forward.

"Am I asking too much?" William asked.

"I hear you, I really do, but I'm trying to find out who's threatening my loved ones. There is no force on earth that would allow me to stand aside and let anything happen to the people I care about. You know the list of people I'd take a bullet for, you're on it. Don't slow me down with politics on this."

"Walk away and let me handle this. I'm in a far better position to handle the Russians than you are."

"We're dealing with different Russians then. So far we've encountered what Montero describes as gang members. They're punks sent to do grunt work. If I pull on this particular piece of string and it unravels to the point that there are confirmed Russian political implications, I will bring it to you, and defer to your assessment."

"If that's the best you can do, I understand."

Donovan knew he'd drawn a line in the sand that William didn't like. "I'll see you for New Year's Eve, and we'll talk—everything will be fine."

"Think back, son, and tell me if everything always turned out fine."

"That's a low blow, and you know it." Donovan disconnected the phone and felt like he'd been blindsided. No, everything hadn't always turned out fine, but it was unlike William to use that fact as a bludgeon. With frayed and conflicting emotions, Donovan exited the conference room and walked down the hall toward the lobby. The first person he spotted was Montero, and he thought of her loss, the woman in Prague. He thought of the men shooting at his wife and daughter in Austria. William had asked him to back off—but he couldn't. Too much had already happened, and to walk away now would put everyone at greater risk.

"Donovan," Montero called out and motioned for him to join her.

"Are we ready?"

"Sofya is in the bathroom, and I haven't really had a chance to talk to you without her listening. I want you to know that we're taking a hell of a risk bringing her through Canadian customs. I'm not a doctor, but I've seen this more than once. My guess is she has what's called dissociative amnesia, meaning that all of her memories are in there, somewhere, but something like PTSD cuts them off and blocks the information. She's traumatized, and I agree with the doctor in the emergency room who believed Sofya had been drugged. One wrong nudge by anyone, a customs official, a waitress, anyone with a uniform, hell it could be someone's dog that sets her off. It's rarely a full cognitive recovery; the memories come in clusters and are highly confusing. Or she could implode, have a psychotic break, and we have no real way to explain her presence, or her behavior."

"You've been amazing with her," Donovan said, not completely surprised by Montero's warning. "At least for the moment, Sofya seems stable. Do you think she can hold it together for an hour or two?"

"That's the thing. We are not going to know until it's too late."

"We can't leave her here, and we really need to get inside that airplane. I don't think we have a choice, for us or her."

"I agree," Montero said as she started for the door. "It's my job to assess the risks, and right now, she's a big one."

Donovan nodded as Sofya walked toward them. He really had no idea if she were friend or foe, only that for now she trusted them, and that she was a very lost soul. He collected Sofya and followed

Montero out of the lobby, across the snow-packed parking lot to the Lincoln Navigator for the two-hour drive to Winnipeg. As he settled behind the wheel, he turned and found Montero with her hand out.

"Give me your gun. I think I should hold the weapons through customs."

Donovan handed over his Sig.

"Okay, here's our story," Montero began as they headed the seventy miles that would take them to the Canadian border. "Donovan, you're my boss, head of Eco-Watch, and we've all taken time off from our scientific mission to escort Sofya, who is an intern, to her grandmother's funeral in Fargo, and we're scheduled to rendezvous with the Eco-Watch jet in Winnipeg."

"That's the story?" Donovan asked.

"Yes. I knew a guy in border protection. He told me once that sick kids and funerals are almost an automatic wave-through. I say we use it. I pulled up some obituaries and I think I have a candidate."

Donovan listened to Montero and memorized the details, but as the miles rolled past, he kept thinking of William's words, and he became even angrier at what had been said. He had no doubt that William was fuming as well, and the exchange began to swirl in his mind as he drove. William had swung below the belt in what was clearly a lack of confidence. Donovan's ghosts were his, and never all that far away, and William knew that fact, thus amplifying the transgression. The bigger question was—what was behind William's verbal attack? The elder statesman was a consummate diplomat and never lost his temper or flew off the handle. There had to be something specific behind the words, and Donovan found himself wondering if William's loss of faith in him was an isolated event or if it was a long-held belief that had finally been brought into the light of day. Either way, Donovan couldn't shake his apprehension of the next confrontation with William.

# CHAPTER FOURTEEN

LAUREN HAD SLIPPED away to the upstairs parlor to call Donovan, and as she said good-bye to him, she spotted Stephanie walking down the hallway toward her.

"I'm not intruding, am I?" Stephanie asked from the doorway.

"No, not at all." Lauren shook her head. "I just finished."

"How did he take the news?"

"He was a little freaked out at first. What father wouldn't be? I calmed him down, and he felt better when he understood where we were, and who we were with. The connection wasn't very good, but I'm sure he'll be okay," Lauren said, but made no move to leave the room and join the others. Over the years, she and Stephanie had grown close and she always loved her compassion and insight.

Stephanie entered the room and closed the door behind her, as if sensing Lauren's need to talk. "What's wrong?"

"I'm just stressed about what happened at Kristof's, and then we all barge in here, complete with armed guards. The house is beautiful—all the work you must have done in preparation for New Year's—and now this."

Stephanie stepped in to hug Lauren. "I love having everyone here, even if it is a few days early. As for Kristof, he's an old friend, and though I just met Marta, she's an absolute delight. If you'll remember, I was there in Paris with you when Trevor and Reggie swooped in and pulled us off the roof of that building. Class act, that Reggie; Trevor as well. They can stop by anytime."

Lauren looked up at the ceiling and fought back her tears. "Abigail was so magnificent today. She was in control and coaching me on what to do. I can promise that comes as a shock when it's from your six-year-old."

"Let's not forget who her father is." Stephanie led them to a sofa and they both sat. "I don't know what you were like when you were six, but I was always scaring my parents to death. It's in the job description, I suppose. How you react will shape her perceptions of fear and danger. I'd say you've done a brilliant job of being a mom."

"Thank you, but can you imagine her at twelve if she's like this at six?"

"By then she'll have an even larger village looking out for her, just like Uncle William did for Donovan and me when we were growing up. She'll be fine."

"Have you heard from Uncle William?" Lauren asked, remembering her unreturned calls.

"I did, but the phone reception was terrible. The effects of the solar storm are starting to hit. I heard there were blackouts in the north, complete electrical grids shutting down."

"It's likely to get worse before it gets better. What did William say?"

"He's working on some high-level diplomatic meeting. He couldn't talk about any of the particulars, but he says he's safe, and that he was happy we were as well. He did say that he and Donovan had spoken, but that he didn't want to discuss it. Did Donovan say anything?"

"No, why?" Lauren's concern was immediate.

"I don't know, something seemed off." Stephanie shrugged. "It could be nothing, just my imagination."

Lauren decided she couldn't worry about Donovan and William; there were more pressing matters at hand. She looked up as someone tapped on the door.

"Come in," Stephanie called.

Lauren smiled as Abigail walked in and she made room for her to climb up beside her.

After a deliberate breath, Abigail began, "Aunt Stephanie, Uncle Kristof told me that you might have some pictures you took of wild horses, and I wondered if maybe you could show them to me?"

"Uncle Kristof has a good memory," Stephanie said. "I do have a photo album of wild horses that I took near Yellowstone Park. I'd love to show them to you."

Abigail's eyes grew wide and she began bouncing up and down, unable to contain her excitement. "Mom, can I have a cookie, no wait, two cookies since I've been good. Please?"

"Just one," Lauren said.

"That particular album is downstairs. Help me get up." Stephanie held out her arm, and Abigail slid off the couch. Hand in hand, Abigail led the way out the door, nearly running into Marta who was coming down the hall balancing a tray with tea service.

"Would you care for some tea?" Marta said to Lauren after she sidestepped Stephanie and Abigail. "It's one of the things I learned to enjoy while at school in England."

"How nice. Sure."

Lauren's phone buzzed and she saw the number belonged to Deputy Director Calvin Reynolds from the Defense Intelligence Agency, her supervisor, and long-time friend. "It's Calvin, I need to take this. Please sit, this shouldn't take long."

Marta nodded.

"Calvin, good afternoon." Lauren was surprised by the amount of audio distortion on the line. Waves of static rose and fell in uneven succession.

"Lauren, can you hear me?"

"Just barely. What's up?"

"I know you're with family, and I hate to interrupt you, but we've been closely monitoring the geomagnetic situation associated with the current solar storm. I was alerted by NASA's Solar Dynamics Observatory that they just recorded five powerful solar flares, as well as a high-volume coronal mass ejection. They're saying that this is bigger than anything we've seen—ever."

"How fast is the shock wave coming?"

"They estimate it at three million miles per hour," Calvin said. "It'll be here in roughly thirty-five hours, with a duration of three to four days."

Lauren processed what Calvin was saying. The most famous storm occurred in March of 1989, when the sun disgorged a huge cloud of super-heated gas. Three days later the Northern Lights were visible as far south as Cuba, and a power grid failure in the Northeast United States plunged over six million people into darkness as their electricity failed. In 2003, a giant solar flare reached Earth in a record nineteen hours and wreaked havoc with dozens of satellites, even destroying Midori-2, a $450 million research platform. If an even larger event hit Earth full force, it could be devastating. Global Positioning Satellites, power grids, as well as radio and satellite communication in the entire Northern Hemisphere, could be compromised.

"Did you hear me?" Calvin asked through the static.

"Yes, I heard you," Lauren said. "This is a little out of my area of expertise. What is it you want me to do?"

"The Pentagon is worried about the storm. They're requesting that all senior-level analysts be recalled."

"You're breaking up," Lauren said even though she heard Calvin issuing orders that would bring her back to Washington, D.C., and isolate her in a control room at DIA headquarters.

"I said you need to return immediately. Can you catch the next available—"

"I can't hear you," Lauren said louder. "The power has been fluctuating, and the Internet is currently down. Calvin? Calvin?" Lauren severed the connection and placed the phone on the table and then looked at Marta.

"You just lied to your boss, didn't you?"

"Yes. They want to bring me home because the solar storm is getting worse." Lauren dismissed the idea that she could be of any service to the DIA. The sun was going to do what it was going to do, and the DIA had a room full of astronomers and astrophysicists to advise the Pentagon. Any guilt she had evaporated. "I'm sorry for the interruption. The tea is a nice diversion. Now, what's up?"

"You don't miss much do you?"

"You never need to engineer an excuse to talk to me, though I'm assuming this was more to excuse yourself from your dad."

"Yes. Dad and I were discussing all of the recent events, and I want to run something past you." Marta paused as if she were collecting her thoughts, and then continued, "I know we're also invited guests of Stephanie's, and my God, this house is amazing, but I think Dad and I might leave."

"And go where?" Lauren asked point blank.

"As you can imagine, Dad is still incensed that someone would attack us at our home in Innsbruck. He's put out the word through our organization to find those responsible. We have several leads, with one in particular that needs to be investigated."

"What did you find?"

"We think we found one of the men involved in the death of Montero's friend inside Interpol. He came to us for help, terrified, after two of his accomplices were killed."

"Is he still in Prague?"

"No, we've had him moved to a safe house across the border in Poland, to a city named Wroclaw. We have a tactical and political advantage in Poland. Lauren, the sooner we can debrief this guy, the better. If we can find out who gave the orders, or better yet, who ended up with the information, we'll be one step closer to understanding who's behind all of this. The murder of the Interpol source, the attack on Donovan in Minnesota, Innsbruck, everything starts and ends with this woman Sofya. The man in Wroclaw may hold the answers. As we're the only ones with the entire picture, Dad and I think we should be there to ask the questions."

"What does Reggie think?" Lauren asked as she imagined and then processed a dozen scenarios, each one leading her to believe Marta was right.

"I haven't talked with anyone except Trevor. He says, and I agree with him, if we make a bit of a production leaving England, sort of advertise that Archangel is on the move, then it would make you, Abigail, and Stephanie safer, less of a target. Right now we're all bunched together, and sooner or later, we'll be found. Trevor says if we split up, he wants to go with us to Poland to act as backup."

Lauren noticed that Marta's eyes lowered for an instant at the mention of Trevor. "I'm inclined to agree with that assessment. At best, it's going to take Donovan until tomorrow to reach the sunken plane, and even longer to get to a place where he can tell anyone what he's discovered. I think you and Kristof should go to Wroclaw, and I'm coming as well."

"What about Abigail?"

"I go on business trips all the time. She'll be fine here with her aunt Stephanie and Reggie."

"Okay." Marta tilted her head as if unsure of Lauren's motives. "This isn't because you don't think Dad and I can handle this, is it?"

"That's the last thing that crossed my mind. Do you remember last night when we were talking about how lucky we both were to call Montero a friend? Right now she's hurting because of the woman who was killed in Prague. If Montero weren't overseeing the safety of my husband, and the others within Eco-Watch, including Sofya, she'd be here, and if the positions were reversed, you know she'd be doing the same thing for us. I think we owe Montero that much."

# CHAPTER FIFTEEN

DONOVAN STOPPED THE Lincoln when prompted by the customs agent. He rolled down the window and handed over all three passports. Montero's was on top. Icy air poured into the Navigator's interior, stinging Donovan's cheek.

"Ms. Montero?" The agent leaned down to get a better look. "Are you *the* former FBI Special Agent, Veronica Montero?"

Donovan knew she hated the name Veronica with a passion, yet she smiled, and her face lit up as if pleased to be recognized. "That's me."

"What brings you to Canada?"

"We've been to a funeral in Fargo, and now we're meeting up with the Eco-Watch jet in Winnipeg."

"I read about that. Studying the solar storms, are you?"

"Yes, haven't the Northern Lights been incredible?"

"Yes, ma'am." The agent handed over all three passports without bothering to look at Sofya's or Donovan's. "It's a pleasure to welcome you to Canada and a personal highlight to meet you in person."

"Thank you, you've made my day," Montero said.

"My pleasure, ma'am." He stepped back and motioned Donovan to proceed into Canada.

Before Donovan could say a word, Montero cut him off. "I don't want any flak from you. I got us through, okay? It was overplayed, but we're in Canada."

"Yes, ma'am," Donovan said. "It was a pleasure to see you in action, ma'am."

"Keep in mind I've still got all the guns."

"If you were going to shoot me, you'd have done it a long time ago." Donovan smiled and glanced in the mirror, hoping to find Sofya amused as well. What he found was a silently sobbing, frightened girl, her arms wrapped tightly across her chest. "Sofya, what's wrong?"

The girl gulped and her silent sobs became wails, as if she were in physical pain. Montero threw off her seat belt, climbed over the seat to sit next to Sofya, and wrapped the traumatized woman in her arms.

Donovan listened to the jumbled words as Sofya tried to talk through her gasps. None of it made sense, though what registered in his mind was that Montero had been right. She'd warned him that Sofya could unravel, and Donovan had no idea if this was an isolated event—or the beginning of something they couldn't control. As he drove, he wondered if the uniformed customs officer had triggered Sofya's meltdown—or if it had been the fear of being discovered.

The remaining sixty miles passed slowly as Montero calmed Sofya down until she fell asleep with her face buried into Montero's shoulder. Donovan and Montero shared guarded looks in the mirror, and Montero simply shook her head. The overcast had finally broken up, giving way to clear skies as Donovan followed the signs to the Winnipeg airport. He turned onto Hangar Line Road when he spotted the private aviation facility he and Michael had discussed earlier. The *Galileo* was sitting on the ramp.

When Donovan parked the Navigator, Sofya snapped awake, her bloodshot eyes full of uncertainty.

"You're fine," Montero said as she swept Sofya's hair away from her eyes. "We're at the Winnipeg airport. Let's go inside and freshen up. Then we'll introduce you to the rest of the team. Okay?"

Sofya took a deep breath and nodded.

Once inside, Donovan found the lobby, where a receptionist spotted them and signaled for someone from the line staff to take care of the luggage. Moments later, Montero and Sofya emerged from the ladies room. Sofya looked better, though her eyes were still red and puffy.

"The luggage has already gone out," Donovan said. "Are we ready?"

"Let's go," Montero said.

Donovan led Sofya out the automatic doors, into the frigid air, and the three of them hurried across the ramp and up the steps into the *Galileo*. Just inside the jet, Michael waited.

"Hi guys, hello, Sofya, I'm Michael. It's nice to see you again."

"I'm sorry, I don't remember meeting you." Sofya looked at Donovan for help.

"It's okay," Donovan said. "Michael knows you might have a few gaps in your memory. I thought we might have a meeting before we take off. Are we taking on fuel here?"

"Already taken care of," Michael said, and then shot a distressed look toward Donovan. "Wait, we're having a real meeting? Like one of those staff meetings everyone in the free world hates?"

"Yes, and no one hates these more than I do. Get everyone together in the back, and we'll get this thing started."

"But there's no donuts," Michael mumbled as he winked at Sofya. "Staff meetings require donuts. It's a rule."

Donovan caught the lines of amusement pass briefly across Sofya's face, and he silently thanked his friend for recognizing her stress and making her smile.

"Where should I sit?" Sofya asked.

"Right here." Donovan motioned to a seat that would place her between him and Montero. "As you can see, this airplane is designed for scientific research. The usual plush interior has been replaced with work stations. Typically, we fly with a small group of scientists and study natural events such as hurricanes, volcanoes, high-altitude winds, and weather. We can design the equipment for the mission."

"Like solar storms?" Sofya asked.

"Exactly." Donovan smiled, and then it dawned on him that despite all of the equipment, there wasn't a single scientist in the group this trip. Montero squeezed past him and sat in the seat he'd saved for her, close enough to react to Sofya if needed. Michael, Rick, and Jesse joined the group and they all looked toward Donovan. "Okay, I'm going to make this quick, I want to be airborne as soon as possible. Everyone, this is Sofya."

"You've already met Michael," Montero said to Sofya in a soothing, nonthreatening voice. "Next to him is Rick, another pilot, and then there's Jesse. We're all with Eco-Watch."

Sofya nodded.

"Jesse, as you know, we have a Boeing 737 sitting at the bottom of a lake. You and I spoke on the phone about all of this, but I need to hear it from you again, in person. Can we do this? Can we get inside this airplane?"

"Yes," Jesse said, confident at first, but with a bit of a shrug thrown in as if to hedge his bet. "I mean, it will all depend on how deep the lake is, and if the aircraft is in a position that allows access. If it's flipped over on its back, we may have to cut our way inside. There can also be issues with the condition of the ice. Will I be going straight down from above the wreck, or will I have to make my way from the shore? More swimming eats up the downtime, as well as my endurance. We have dry suits, but the water temperature is still a significant issue. I won't be able to stay down for extended times. But, yeah, I've done cold-water salvage before. It's doable if all of the variables are in place."

"Michael," Donovan said. "Did you find anything new last night as you surveyed the area?"

"Overall, the area is flat, though the terrain rises slightly between the lakes, but no more than a hundred feet, so it's of no concern flying in visually. We did spot what looks like a fishing or trapper's cabin on a lake not far from the crash site. It's in the woods and covered with snow. The only reason we spotted it are the boats stacked near what appears to be a removable dock stored near the shore. There looks to be a channel or river that connects the two bodies of water, so we should plan to try and utilize the cabin. With the extreme temperatures, the hole in the ice where the Boeing broke through has already frozen over. Based on the current temperatures, we don't think there can be more than three or four inches of new ice. We didn't see any evidence of footprints or tracks of any kind, unless you count the caribou. As to the object that fell from the plane, we conducted an intense search where we calculated it came down. We found snow and limbs knocked from some treetops, but we couldn't confirm the object's presence."

"How far is the object from the plane?" Montero asked.

"Exactly 10.2 miles."

"How are we going to get from the cabin, overland, to conduct the search?" Montero said.

"Hold that thought," Michael said. "Rick and I have drawn up the logistics and we'll get to that in a minute. Our cover story is as follows: with the solar storm as our backdrop, we're going to set up some stationary monitoring equipment to measure the radiation levels aboveground, as well as below the water. This will explain the diving gear, but again, we're Eco-Watch, everyone knows what we do. Rick, why don't you walk us through the logistics. You used to fly in Alaska, so that makes you our expert."

"Yeah." Rick cleared his throat. "I spent three years flying back and forth to the oil fields on the North Slope, so I know a little

bit about cold weather. Mainly that I don't recommend it to anyone. The closest airport that can handle the *Galileo* is Churchill,
Manitoba. As a former military base, they also have hangar space
for the Gulfstream, which we'll need. The current daytime high
temperature in the area is running steady at minus twenty degrees
Fahrenheit. It's clear and cold, and expected to stay that way due
to a big dome of high pressure parked over Northern Manitoba—
which is why we chose the area to study the solar storm in the first
place. As long as the high-pressure area remains, there won't be any
snow, though with the extreme cold, we all need to be aware of hypothermia as well as frostbite. One of our first priorities is to make
the fishing cabin a suitable base camp. We ordered some equipment
from an outfitter here in Winnipeg that was delivered just before
you arrived. It's already been stowed on board—basic winter survival gear. Snowshoes, snow suits, goggles, boots, gloves, all the
same equipment that climbers wear when they ascend a mountain."

"How far is the lake from Churchill?" Montero asked.

"It's one hundred and fifty nautical miles," Rick said. "We were
able to charter a plane out of Thompson, Manitoba, that will serve
our needs nicely. It's a de Havilland Twin Otter on skis. Based on our
estimates of the full weight of gear and personnel, we'll all fit into
the Twin Otter with room to spare. They're flying it to Churchill as
we speak, and it should be there by the time we arrive."

"Here's where it gets a little tricky," Michael said. "Under no cir-
cumstances do we want the Twin Otter pilots to know what we're
doing. When we set up the charter, we gave them coordinates for a
different lake, west of Churchill. We'll change that destination once
we're airborne. The distance is the same, so it won't affect the fuel
situation on the Twin Otter, it just keeps our actual destination a
secret. By having the Twin Otter land at the lake with the cabin,
they'll have no idea what we're actually doing on the neighboring
lake."

"How do we get the diving gear from the airplane to the crash site?" Montero asked.

"Part of the cold-water equipment from Norfolk is an inflatable sled—it also doubles as a litter if we have an injury," Jesse said. "It's designed to ride up on top of the ice and therefore is easy to pull. With snowshoes, it will take us a little while to get everything from the cabin to the dive site. Think of it this way, the jog will help keep us warm."

"Once we arrive at the cabin," Rick continued, "we'll offload the diving gear and other supplies, and then the Twin Otter will fly to a lake ten miles away, where the distance from the shore to the unknown object looks to be about a hundred yards. According to the meteorological data, there's been roughly two feet of snowfall so far this season. The hike through the forest will be tough enough, but to find whatever it is under all that snow is going to be especially challenging."

"Is this the airplane we've chartered?" Montero looked up from her phone and held it out for Donovan to see.

Donovan leaned over and saw a Twin Otter. "Yep, a rugged twin turboprop with a fat high wing. It offers slow speed in return for large payloads and high lift capability. It's been around forever, it's a proven workhorse and one of de Havilland's most successful designs. It's a good choice."

"It looks like the box some other plane came in," Montero said. "When are we leaving Churchill to fly to the lake? And more importantly, since we're splitting up, who's going where?"

"We'll fly to Churchill today and plan to be wheels up tomorrow at first light, which this time of year is nine o'clock in the morning," Michael said. "The sun sets at three thirty, so we'll have about six hours of useful daylight. We may very well have to spend the night at the cabin, and while it's going to be rustic, we'll all survive. As far as duties once we land, the plan is for me to go with Montero and

Sofya, to search for the object that was dropped from the plane. That leaves Donovan, Jesse, and Rick to get to where the Boeing went down."

"Most of all, I want to impress on everyone that the charter pilots see and hear nothing," Montero said. "We've broken a law or two over the last few days, and while we'll make everything right in due time, having our actions revealed to the authorities ahead of schedule does not work in our favor. Is that clear?"

Donovan waited until everyone nodded. "Very good. Are there any other questions?"

"Won't we be leading the men trying to kill us straight to the crashed airplane?" Sofya asked. "They could kill us all out in the middle of nowhere and no one would ever know."

"The way they've been able to follow us is through public flight-tracking websites," Michael said. "The sites typically get their information from the government database that generates all of the instrument flight plans. With the weather being as clear as it is over Canada, we're not going to file a flight plan. We'll simply fly using visual flight rules; we'll be at a scenic seventeen thousand five hundred feet for the trip to Churchill. If someone is watching the flight-tracking data, it will show that we haven't departed Winnipeg. That and the remote location will help make it practically impossible for anyone to know where we are. From a logistical standpoint, my guess is we have a good twenty-four hours until we could expect company."

"I agree," Donovan said. "Sofya, I hope that answers your question. If we didn't think we could do this and stay safe, I promise, we'd look for a different way."

"I believe you."

"Is there anything else?" Donovan asked as he looked into the determined faces of his small team, happy to find nothing but resolute expressions. "Okay, let's get out of here."

# CHAPTER SIXTEEN

As LAUREN HAD suspected, Abigail wasn't the least bit upset when she explained that she was leaving on a short business trip and that Aunt Stephanie and Reggie would take care of her. Her daughter had shrugged it off, and as was her style, exacted a promise ensuring that Lauren was going to be back for New Year's Eve when Daddy and Grandpa William arrived. Lauren had agreed to the terms, and satisfied, Abigail immediately held up the book she'd selected. As it had for months, tonight's story revolved around Princess Noel and a faithful pony named Skyler. Abigail pulled her covers up to her chin, wiggled into the mattress, and nodded that Lauren could begin.

It was late, but even so, Lauren was worried that Abigail would be too revved up from the day's events in Innsbruck, the plane ride to London, and yet another extraordinary display of the Northern Lights for her daughter to fall asleep easily. She was relieved, as she lay on the bed reading to her, to see Abigail's eyelids begin to droop. Lauren always loved putting her daughter to bed. They'd always talk about the next day, and then Lauren would read a book that Abigail picked out. When Abigail's eyelids stayed closed and her breathing slowed into the rhythmic cadence of sleep, Lauren leaned down and kissed her on the cheek. She switched off the light and went down to join the others.

"Any problems?" Kristof asked.

"No, she seems to be fine," Lauren said. She took the glass of wine Stephanie offered and sat on the sofa between Marta and Kristof. "Today wasn't the first time she's been in that situation, and her response has always been pretty much the same. She recovers quickly and seems to gain confidence from the experience."

"Does that sound like anyone we know?" Stephanie said.

"He's always been that way. I remember Donovan when he was maybe ten or eleven." Kristof said the words as if he'd somehow drifted into the past and could picture every detail. "It was summer vacation, and he and I were in Virginia, and it was a really windy day. We'd decided to sneak off to where they were building a neighboring house. Since it was a Sunday, there were no workers around, and Donovan found this big section of cardboard that had been removed from a furnace or a hot water heater or something. The second he saw it, he had this idea, and as he surveyed the site, he explained to me that if we cut handholds into the cardboard, he'd be able to hold on and jump from the top of one of the dirt piles into the howling wind, and fly."

"Oh God, I remember this story," Stephanie said and then put her hand up to her mouth to hide her mirth.

"In theory, it wasn't a bad idea." Kristof grinned. "Though, the fierce gusts kept ripping the cardboard from Donovan's little hands. Although once we found the ball of heavy twine, all of our engineering problems were solved."

As Kristof spoke, Reggie's and Trevor's phones vibrated at the same time. They reacted instantly. Weapons drawn, Reggie turned out the lights, plunging the house into darkness. Trevor and Marta bolted for the back door, Kristof following them. Reggie grabbed Lauren and Stephanie, and the three of them raced upstairs to the corner bedroom where Abigail lay sleeping. They eased themselves into her room, Reggie closed the door, and Lauren hurried to her daughter. A quick check told her Abigail was fine, her breathing slow and steady. Lauren gathered her sleeping daughter into her arms without waking her. Reggie eased Lauren away from the bed, making sure she stayed down as they moved past the windows, and motioned for her and Stephanie to sit together against the wall.

"What's happening?" Lauren whispered as Reggie knelt near a window and stole a quick look outside.

"My men discovered an intruder," Reggie replied as he uncoiled an earpiece, plugged it into a small tactical radio, and listened.

Lauren sat in the darkness and mentally raced through their options, processing her fight or flight response, until she realized that waking Abigail and plunging her into an unknown situation would only make things worse.

"There were two of them," Reggie whispered. "One is down; the other has been apprehended and is being taken to the van for questioning. We've swept the area, and we're all clear. They seem to have been conducting reconnaissance."

Lauren felt her fear begin to manifest into something else, something harder. She made no effort to reign in the anger fueled by a mother's protective fury. She got to her feet and gently tucked the still-sleeping Abigail back into bed, turned, and without waiting for Reggie, marched down the stairs through the darkened house, and into the kitchen. With no hesitation, she snatched a large chef's knife from the butcher block and barged out the kitchen door into the cold night air.

The sky still glowed from the undulating tendrils of the Northern Lights, and Lauren spotted Marta and Trevor standing outside the oversized van that served as the command post for Reggie and his team. Not bothering to ask any questions, Lauren shouldered her way past Trevor and slid open the side door and climbed inside. One of Reggie's men was inside, and he turned and stepped back in surprise as he recognized one of the principals he was protecting. Lauren's eyes went straight to the man tie-wrapped to a chair. The man had a shaved head, his arms were heavily tattooed, and he was bleeding from the nose and mouth. He looked up at her, unconcerned, until he saw the flash of a knife arc toward his face as Lauren used her fist, weighted by the hilt of the knife, to hit the man just above his eye.

Stunned, the intruder recoiled as the fresh cut along his eyebrow began to bleed.

"We've got this," Trevor said. He and Marta moved in, grabbed Lauren's arms, and held her firmly.

"Who is this son of a bitch?" Lauren strained against her friends. "How dare he sneak in here and try to harm us! Let me go, I'm going to carve those goddamned tattoos off one by one until he talks."

"Have it your way." Trevor released his grip, as did Marta.

Lauren, too, had seen the fear on the man's face as she'd threatened to carve him up into little pieces. Leading with the razor-sharp eight-inch blade, she stepped closer and slid the knife between his heaving chest and the already ripped fabric of his shirt. She pulled, parting the fabric, exposing all of his bare skin from the waist up. She studied his tattoos until she found the one she thought she could best use to her advantage. Over his heart was an intricately inked image of an angelic young woman.

"No," the intruder muttered and shook his head as he seemingly read Lauren's intent. Lauren pictured Abigail sleeping upstairs and her rage grew exponentially. She threw another punch and hit the intruder in the same spot, producing more blood and a moan of pain.

Lauren pressed the edge of the knife against the skin at the top of the woman's image and began to press. "She's someone you care about, isn't she? That's why you keep her close to your heart. Start talking or I'll remove this picture and destroy her image while you sit there and scream."

"No, please." The man tried to shrink from the blade. "Stop, please stop. I was sent to watch the house. I was ordered to count how many people, and to report when everyone was asleep."

"Who do you report to?" Lauren pressed harder with the knife.

"I don't know. A man gave me five hundred pounds, a phone programmed with a single number, and the directions. That's all I know, please stop."

"Is this the phone?" Trevor stepped forward.

"Yes, that's the one," he said, grimacing against the knife pressing his flesh. "There's only one number."

"Call them," Trevor said to the man as he pulled Lauren's hand away and produced an ominous curved blade of his own. "Call them, or I let my friend begin again, and then I'll pick a tattoo to remove, myself."

The sight of the second knife unhinged the intruder even more. He panicked and fought furiously to free himself until he felt the point of a blade press against his Adam's apple and he froze, wide-eyed.

"I'm going to dial this number," Marta said. "You tell whoever answers that the house is dark, there are no more than five people inside, and that the perimeter is clear. Is there a code word?"

The man was rigid, his breathing quick and shallow, his eyes filled with terror as each nervous swallow served to further jab the knife point into the tender skin of his neck. Trevor eased the pressure slightly, and Marta received an immediate nod to confirm her question.

"What's the code word?"

"Archangel."

"Interesting," Marta said as she looked to Trevor, who nodded his approval, and then she hit the send button and put the phone on speaker as it rang.

"Report," a gruff voice answered.

Lauren listened as the prisoner repeated word for word what Marta had ordered him to say.

"Be ready, we'll be there in fifteen minutes," the voice replied.

Marta switched off the phone and handed it to Trevor, who slid it into his pocket. He produced a square of cloth and doused it with a clear liquid from a plastic bottle.

"Wait," Lauren said.

"What?" Trevor asked.

Lauren waited until the man's eyes shifted from Trevor back to her, and she swung a roundhouse punch that connected above his eye for a third straight time, and he cried out in agony.

Trevor pressed the cloth against the prisoner's mouth and nose. The man struggled briefly until the chloroform took effect and he went limp.

Lauren jumped to the ground, and as she walked away, she felt her entire body begin to shake from the adrenaline pumping through her system. As she made her way into the still-darkened house, she placed the knife in the sink and stood for a moment. She knew she'd never been out of control like that in her life—and it scared her.

# CHAPTER SEVENTEEN

THE SUN HAD set in Churchill hours earlier, though with the undulating ribbons from the glowing Northern Lights, it seemed as if twilight had never ended. The Twin Otter had arrived before the Gulfstream and was sitting in the warm hangar when they landed. The *Galileo* was pushed back into the same hangar, and Donovan was the first to meet the Twin Otter pilots. Paul, the captain, was in his early thirties, intelligent and likeable, as well as tall and muscular. Lonny was younger, a smiling dark-haired woman in her mid-twenties. She was short, a little plump, seemingly full of energy. Working with Rick and Jesse, the two charter pilots made quick work of transferring the equipment from the Gulfstream to the Twin Otter. Paul and Lonny often conferred with each other on the details of the weight and balance, arranging everything to keep the center of gravity where it needed to be. Once everything was loaded, Donovan was pleasantly surprised with how much room was left in the Twin Otter's cabin.

"How much under gross weight are we?" Donovan asked Paul as they were finishing.

"We're in good shape," Paul replied. "We've probably got close to eight hundred pounds to play with. Why, what did you forget?"

"I was thinking about a snowmobile," Donovan said. "If I found one we could borrow, or even buy, would we be able to get it aboard without rearranging everything?"

"Sure," Paul said. "It's Canada. We fly those things around all the time. They usually weigh somewhere around six hundred pounds, the same as three people. We've got seats for twenty, and only six passengers. You find it, we'll load it."

Donovan grabbed his hat and briefcase and went straight to the airport office to find Russell, the airport manager he'd met when they landed.

"Mr. Nash, what can I do for you?" the man, coffee cup in hand, called out from behind his desk.

"You told me if there was anything I needed, to come see you," Donovan said. "Well, I need something."

"I'll do what I can to help, but keep in mind we're in Churchill, Manitoba."

"I want to rent, or buy, a snowmobile, something less than six hundred pounds that can be loaded in a Twin Otter."

Russell laughed deep from his ample belly and set his cup down on the desk to keep from spilling the contents. "Other than snow, a snowmobile is the next easiest request I can fulfill. I've got one I can rent you for a hundred bucks a day."

"Throw in fuel for three full days, and you've got a deal," Donovan said.

"Done," he said. "If you wreck it, you bought it at ten thousand bucks."

"Works for me." Donovan reached across the desk and the two men shook hands. "Where is this machine, and how do I get it to the hangar?"

"It's in our shop, which is the building next door. I'll have the guys bring it over and help you load it onto the plane."

Donovan hurried back outside, put his head down against the cold, and let himself into the side door of the hangar. He pulled off his hat and joined Paul and Michael.

"That was fast," Paul said.

"What was fast?" Michael said. "What did I miss?"

Donovan caught the sound of a two-stroke engine as it pulled up somewhere in back. A man in a snowsuit came in through a side door and raised a garage door while another guy drove the snowmobile over to the Twin Otter. It was black and yellow, like a giant wasp on skis. It looked new, the engine purred smoothly, and the fiberglass nose cone gleamed with fresh wax.

"I missed the part where you got us a snowmobile," Michael said. "I grew up at the beach. Do we have anyone who knows how to drive one of these things without killing people?"

Donovan turned as Rick raced down the steps of the *Galileo*, drawn by the sound of the snowmobile. "I bet he does."

"We're about to find out." Michael stood back to watch this unfold.

"The extra fuel and the helmets are on their way," the man on the snowmobile said after he shut down the engine.

"Rick, can you drive one of these?" Donovan called out to the young man as he approached.

"Hell, yes," Rick replied, his eyes running eagerly back and forth over the snowmobile.

"The five of us can probably lift this through the cargo door right now if you want," the man said as he dismounted the snowmobile and pulled off his gloves.

Donovan was surprised at how light the machine actually was. They were easily able to position it where Paul directed, and then Lonny secured it to the floor with heavy nylon straps.

With everything set at the airport, they'd gotten a lift to the hotel Montero had found. The sea ice on Hudson Bay had formed early and the polar bears were far out to sea by now, prompting Churchill's tourists to flee south, leaving the one thousand permanent residents to settle in for the winter. All eight members of the expedition had a relaxed dinner, and then as the Eco-Watch group moved to the bar, Paul and Lonny had excused themselves. Jesse, who wasn't drinking, and then Rick, bowed out next. Montero, Sofya, Donovan, and Michael were left at the bar. There was no one else in the place except for the owner, a sweet woman named Ingrid, who brought the drinks and then moved into the dining room to finish cleaning for the night.

"I think I'm about done," Montero announced as she finished the last of her whiskey and stood. "I'm going to see if there's any way to connect to the Internet or maybe make a phone call. Sofya, shall we? We'll see both of you at seven o'clock for breakfast."

"Goodnight," Donovan said as both women went off in the direction of their rooms. The remoteness of being in Churchill seemed a little like being at the edge of the world. It was a sensation Donovan always enjoyed.

Michael took a drink of his beer and then spent a moment studying the label before he asked, "Did something happen between you and William? Montero seems to think there was some sort of a disagreement. I told her to leave it alone and that I'd ask."

"The conversation with William was not what I expected. In no uncertain terms, he told me he was in a better position to deal with the Russians and to back off. I told him I could never sit idle and ignore a threat to the people I care about. I told him everything would be fine. Then he asked me if everything I'd done in the past had turned out fine, and then we hung up."

"Ouch," Michael said. "There has to be something else going on then, something we don't know about. That just doesn't sound like William."

"I don't have the answers." Donovan shrugged.

"We have plausible deniability," Michael said. "If we find anything that points farther up the Russian food chain than the people we've encountered already, we pause, walk away, and then maybe

put Reggie and his SAS guys on the hunt, or even your friend
Kristof and his Archangel group. You and I are someplace far away
if anything happens. We're loyal to William, and we still get the situation remedied. Did I mention this plan works better if we're on a
beach, someplace warm?"

Donovan felt a warning shiver start in the pit of his stomach
and push up his spine until his brain felt the jolt. There was no way
Michael, who had only met him twice, was supposed to have any
idea that Kristof was Archangel.

"From the look on your face, I'm assuming you must be wondering how I know for a fact that your friend Kristof is Archangel?"
Michael said, a superior look etched on his face as he laced his
fingers together and put them behind his head and smiled. "I'm
more than just a pretty face around here; I figured things out after
Budapest. It took me all of about ten minutes on the computer to
trace down some of the equipment Kristof had provided. It was all
stolen from various military installations, and according to an investigative report on BBC, Russia and other former Soviet satellite
countries have a terrible time with their own soldiers selling military equipment to arms dealers. The largest and most feared being
the organization run by a person called Archangel. Or as we know
him, Kristof, and his beautiful and very lethal daughter, Marta."

"I don't know what I'd do without you." Donovan laughed out
loud for the first time in what seemed like days. "Your imagination
is certainly a source of constant amusement. I met Kristof years
ago when I was in Africa. He's a nice guy, a terrible poker player,
and I can't believe he could be this Archangel character. And really,
Marta, do you think she's part of this arms business as well?"

"That's the interesting part." Michael leaned in as if someone could overhear. "With Kristof sick, Marta might actually *be*
Archangel. After all, it is a family business. You saw her in a firefight.

I mean, who would you pick first to be on your team, Montero or Marta?"

"I'd pick you." Donovan slapped his friend on the shoulder. "Then I'd let your imagination run wild and we'd win, hands down, regardless of whoever else was on the team."

"I think I'd pick Montero," Michael said, still locked in his mental picture. "Based only on her advanced skills of cunning and pure guile. Plus, she's just so damn mysterious. I mean you and I, we're both an open book, but Montero is practically an enigma. Has she ever told you the reason why she hates her first name so much? It's Veronica; it's a nice name."

"I was named after my aunt, who turned out to be a major bitch, so I decided I didn't care for the name," Montero said, standing directly behind Michael.

Michael ducked in surprise at the sound of her voice.

"That was a short phone call," Donovan said, having watched her enter the room. "Did you get through?"

"No such luck; either the lines are all tied up or the storm is causing problems. The Internet is down as well. What did I miss?"

"How long were you standing there, listening?" Michael asked.

"Long enough to hear that Kristof is Archangel and you were setting up your fantasy army. Is that like fantasy football?"

Michael turned and smiled sheepishly and kicked out a chair for her to join them. "I was just explaining to Donovan that his friend Kristof is actually the criminal Archangel. Have you ever heard of him? Anyway, I think that's why Marta is so good in a firefight, it's a family business requirement, right? Though as you no doubt overheard, I'd choose you to be on my team before Marta. I want that out there for the record."

Michael was spot on in his assessment of Kristof. Montero also knew the story of Kristof, aka Archangel, and Donovan being boyhood friends, a fact that best remained a secret. Donovan sat back to watch her go to work.

"I saw the BBC report about arms dealers, as well, and made some inquiries. As it's my job to look into all matters of security, I checked them both out, Kristof and Marta, and, Michael, you couldn't be more wrong. Archangel is actually a myth, a totem if you will, created by three powerful arms dealers who have long since been killed or imprisoned. Archangel might as well be a unicorn, but because of the fear the name invokes, it's thrown around by any criminal who wants to try to amp up his street cred. Kristof made his fortune importing building supplies into famine-plagued Africa. Which is where Donovan met him. Pretoria, right?"

"It was," Donovan replied, impressed with Montero's fabrication.

"I also heard you talking about William. I understand it's a slippery slope, but from where I sit, we're too far down the rabbit hole to turn back, or even slow down now. It's not far-fetched to use the communication issues in our favor, and we can deflect or negate any connection to all things Russian, long before they become a factor in William's world."

"The communication problems will buy us some time," Donovan said. "Though, I'm more concerned with the bigger picture as it pertains to William. We also have custody of Sofya, a Russian, and we have no idea who she is."

"That's a problem I'm not sure how to fix," Montero said. "I have no idea if Sofya will ever get her memory back, nor does she, a question that's at the root of a great deal of her fear. Considering everything she may have been through, that might not necessarily be a bad thing, though she may always have a bull's-eye on her back. The problem is—what becomes of her when all this is over?"

"I've been wondering the same thing," Donovan said. "The best I can come up with is we find some sort of international witness protection that would keep her safe."

"There is one other possibility we have to consider, and then I'm going to bed," Montero said. "Sofya could get her memory back, and we might not like who she really is, and then, all of a sudden, we have an enemy inside the gate."

# CHAPTER EIGHTEEN

LAUREN SAT IN the rocking chair in Abigail's darkened bedroom, silently propelling it back and forth, waiting. In her left hand she held a cup of tea, long since gone cold. In her other hand was a Glock. Stephanie lay on the double bed next to Abigail. Lauren had come down off her earlier rage. The combination of the day's events had reached a violent crescendo with the tattooed thug who would bring harm to Abigail. Lauren wasn't proud of what she'd done, though she wasn't ashamed either; her sins had been reactive, not proactive. The slender difference seemed important, though her earlier surprise at her own behavior lingered.

Everyone was in position and the waiting had begun. Reggie explained to Lauren that it didn't matter who might be coming, having an SAS team in place essentially made any attack a non-event. Lauren had no idea what time it was. Through a tiny opening in the drapes, she could see the iridescent greens and blues from the Northern Lights, which gave a false promise of the coming dawn. She let the rhythmic motion of the chair distract her from the world outside.

A knock was followed by Marta slipping inside the bedroom and silently closing the door behind her.

"Is it over?" Lauren asked, still rocking.

"Yes, none of our people were hurt."

"Were they Russian?"

"Yes, all were unknowns except one. His name is Alexy Stanislav, he's Sluzhba Vneshney Razvedki."

Lauren stopped rocking. "The men who came to kill us included a member of the SVR, Russia's foreign intelligence service?"

"Yes," Marta said. "We should think about leaving."

"And go where?"

"Reggie thinks these people are after you, me, and Dad. If you want to come with us to Wroclaw, we think everyone in England will be safer."

"Part of me wants to take Abigail home, deal with this on my turf."

"I'm not a parent, so I won't stand here and tell you I understand how you feel, I don't. However, judging by what happened in Minnesota, if you went to Virginia, they'd find you. With Reggie taking care of Abigail and Stephanie, you'd have more peace of mind than you have now."

"Is there an endgame to all of this?"

"Yes. We know that someone with considerable political clout in Russia is trying to silence anyone with knowledge of the woman. If we can pull enough information together, we'll be able to determine who and why. From there, a solution will present itself."

"More killing?"

"Probably. With people like this, that's typically necessary."

"How can you be so . . . unattached?"

"Who says I am?" Marta replied, her voice softer, less militaristic. "We all deal with things differently. Right now I feel like I'm fighting for more than just my friends and family. These people are threatening my very future, and I need to stay focused."

"Because of how you feel about Trevor?"

"I figured you knew. Yes, I have feelings for Trevor."

"Does your Dad know?"

"Oh, hell no."

"He asked me something yesterday morning when we were still in Innsbruck. It was the morning you'd gone to town. He was concerned that you'd never find anyone, that being his daughter had robbed that from you."

"He said that?"

"I explained that you would find someone and that person would accept who you are, and who your family is, as well. I reminded him that anyone you brought home had already passed a great many tests, and that he should try to relax and enjoy your happiness."

"That might be the nicest thing anyone has ever said to me."

"How long have the two of you been . . . romantic?" Lauren asked.

"About five months—not long after we met. After he went back to England, we started talking on the phone, then it seemed like we were calling almost every day. We started meeting in Innsbruck or Vienna. Sometimes I'd sneak away, and we'd rendezvous in London."

"He knows about the family business?" Lauren asked.

"He suspected and wasn't at all surprised when I confirmed his suspicions." Marta shrugged. "He's a former SAS operative turned mercenary, so it's kind of perfect."

"How does Trevor feel?"

"He'd sit down and talk to my father right now if I gave him the go-ahead."

"From everything I've seen, Trevor is a good guy. If he's not intimidated by you, he has nothing to fear from your father." Lauren stood and smoothed her clothes.

"You're probably right," Marta said, and stood as well. "Let's go talk to Reggie."

Lauren and Marta slipped out of the bedroom into the dimly lit house. Downstairs in the parlor sat Kristof, his face pale in the firelight. He was stocking-footed, which meant he'd probably taken part in the defense of the house, and had muddied and then removed his shoes. The evening's exertion seemed to have swallowed both his energy and color.

"Dad, are you feeling okay?"

"Not really." Kristof shook his head. "I must have overdone it, and now I'm paying the price."

"What can we do?" Lauren asked.

"I want to get you to a doctor," Marta said as she went to her father and put her palm on his forehead. "Trevor, Reggie!"

"Right here," Trevor said, hurrying into the parlor and going to Kristof the moment he saw him. He knelt and took Kristof's pulse. "What is it I can do for you? What do you need?"

"Is there a doctor on call?" Marta asked.

"I just need a minute," Kristof said. "I'm a little light-headed . . . I feel washed out."

"What happened?" Reggie asked as he hurried into the room.

"Marta thinks we should get Kristof to a doctor," Lauren said.

Reggie nodded, pushed a button on the phone in his hand, and swept it to his ear. "Doc, it's me. Yeah, we need you here. Fast. Five minutes? Good, one of the lads will be waiting at the main entrance."

"Five minutes?" Lauren asked, confused.

"Before any action, especially here in England, we put the doc on standby. He and his team are waiting nearby," Reggie said. "We'll get Kristof checked out in no time."

"You know he has cancer, right?" Lauren asked.

"Yes," Reggie said. "I also know that to be safe, I'd like us out of this house before sunrise."

"You can take Abigail and Stephanie someplace secure?"

"Of course," Reggie said.

"I need to know that at the first sign of trouble, you'll get them in the hands of the State Department. You're well aware that Stephanie's uncle is Ambassador William VanGelder, and wherever he is, he'll move the universe to protect his family. It'll bring the United States government into our business, which is not ideal, but we can deal with them. Do I have your word that you'll do this?"

"Yes, I swear that I'll abide by your wishes."

"Thank you," Lauren said. "In that case, I think I'll go to Poland."

"One moment, please," Reggie said. "I'm not sure who is going where at this point. I do know you're not going anywhere by yourself."

"I can hear both of you," Kristof bellowed. "I'm a little winded, not on my deathbed. We'll all go as planned."

"No," Marta said. "You're going to get a full workup, and I'm not leaving your side until you do. I'm going to sit right here until you agree with what I say. Do you understand me?"

"I'll get the checkup, but only if you and Trevor get to Wroclaw and find out who's doing this," Kristof said. "Reggie, I've chartered a plane for the flight to Wroclaw—a Hawker 800—and it's waiting at Luton. That leaves Lauren's Gulfstream on twenty-four-hour standby for you if you need to leave England. Trevor, I've arranged to have some additional inventory made available to you upon your arrival. Marta knows the details."

Reggie cocked his head as a transmission came through his headset. He said something in return and then gestured to Trevor. "The doc is here. Can you help the men get Kristof ready for transport? I'll start making the arrangements for the rest of us to move out."

"I agree we need to leave the house, but I think we all need to make sure that Kristof is doing okay before we leave England for Poland," Lauren said, happy that Marta and Trevor both nodded in agreement. "We'll get everyone where they're supposed to be, then we'll leave."

# CHAPTER NINETEEN

INSIDE THE TWIN Otter, a row of single seats ran down the left side, double seats on the right, and a narrow aisle in the center. Donovan sat in one of the single front seats; Michael plopped down across from him. Although the airplane had been in the heated hangar all night, the walk from the lounge to the flight line was brutal. There was little to no wind, but the air was frigid. Warming from an overnight low of twenty-eight below zero, the daytime high wouldn't reach ten below, and then the temperature would plunge again. Donovan, like the others, wore layers of fleece covered by a heavy insulated snowmobile suit. Gloves and wool watch caps were standard, as the cold immediately assaulted any exposed skin. Each painful inhalation was followed by clouds of condensation upon exhaling.

Donovan fought off an involuntary shiver and wondered why anything or anyone would live in this extreme climate. When the passenger door latched shut, he watched as Paul and Lonny donned headsets and quickly went through a checklist, culminating in the right engine spooling up to start. The Twin Otter was a high-wing design, which kept the engines and propellers well above the ground, an added plus for off-airport operations. With unobstructed visibility below, Donovan studied the landing gear. Attached to each strut was a tire and an adjustable ski. With the ski retracted, they would roll smoothly on the concrete. When they were ready to land on the snow and ice of the lake, Paul would lower the skis and the airplane would touch down on what amounted to three sleds.

Once the right engine revved up to speed, immediately the left engine began its start cycle. Once both engines and propellers were checked, the Twin Otter pivoted and moved across the ramp to the taxiway. In a nontypical arrangement, both throttles hung from the overhead panel, and Donovan watched as Paul, seemingly relaxed and in control, casually reached up and manipulated them as they maneuvered toward the active runway.

Across the aisle, Michael was trying to sift through a large envelope while still wearing his gloves. Donovan turned and looked down the aisle. Montero was seated behind Michael, and across from her sat Sofya, a worried expression on what little of her face he could see. Rick and Jesse sat in the next row, and both were looking out their windows. Their gear, secured by heavy cargo webbing, was stacked in the rear of the plane.

"We've been cleared for takeoff," Lonny's voiced sounded over the cabin speakers. "Everyone double-check that your seat belts are fastened."

The Twin Otter made two quick turns, and Paul reached up and gripped the throttles in the unmistakable way a pilot does when it's time to advance them for takeoff. The twin turboprops roared to full power, and the Twin Otter rumbled down the runway. The high-lift wings coupled with the dense arctic air served to shorten the takeoff roll, and the Twin Otter lifted free from the runway and climbed out steeply. The morning sun cast its orange light in the Canadian sky, and as far as Donovan could see, the ground was covered with snow. He caught a glimpse of Hudson Bay and saw no open water, just a solid sheet of ice that fanned out until it touched the horizon.

The Twin Otter, while efficient, wasn't particularly fast. Paul leveled the unpressurized airplane at 4500 feet, and Donovan could see over Lonny's shoulder that their speed was right at 140 knots, which made it about an hour's flying time to the lake. Once they'd put Churchill well behind them, they'd inform the crew of the new destination. Donovan surveyed the view out the window and found he was enjoying the low-altitude vista. The Gulfstream typically cruised seven or eight miles above the ground at speeds approaching 600 miles per hour, and the sensation of speed was muted. Below him he could see individual trees, lakes, details of the frozen terrain. Mostly, Donovan realized, it felt good to finally be traveling to the lake.

"Here's the best angle," Michael said as he finally wrestled the contents out of the envelope and handed Donovan a high-resolution image taken from the *Galileo*. Though shot in the dead of night, the synthetic aperture camera had captured and constructed a detailed black-and-white image of the lake. Donovan glanced at the data block to find true north and immediately began to identify separate features. The surface where the 737 had broken through was a slightly different shade of white compared to the surrounding ice. The only evidence of anything amiss was the tire tracks from both the Boeing and the Gulfstream still clearly visible in the snow. Confirmation that no snow had fallen since they'd left. He studied the neighboring lake and the cabin they'd discovered, as well as the frozen river that separated the two. Donovan pictured the different approach paths the Twin Otter would probably fly, and he decided that it would be unlikely for the charter crew to notice anything.

"I'm going up front," Michael said as he finished jotting some coordinates on a piece of paper and glanced at his watch.

"Break a leg," Donovan said as Michael unbuckled his seat belt to go to the cockpit. Donovan was confident that Michael would sell the change of destination to the pilots without raising any suspicion. He gave a quick backwards glance at Montero, and she, too, was watching what was happening. Donovan saw Lonny laugh, and Michael shrugged and was smiling as he turned to return to his seat. A few seconds later, the Twin Otter banked to the right.

"Just for the record, I am a highly trained Gulfstream captain, but I may have made a small error." Michael spoke loud enough for everyone to hear, as he held up both hands in surrender. "My bad. It turns out I may have transposed some numbers when I initially gave the coordinates to the crew. I promise we're headed in the right direction now."

Donovan smiled. Leave it to Michael to make a calculated course change into a joke that had everyone laughing. Michael had once explained that no one feels manipulated or deceived when they're laughing. As they traveled the corrected course, Donovan turned his attention to the images taken from the *Galileo*. Each time he thought through the events of their first rendezvous with the Boeing, he tried to picture what had really happened inside the 737. Each time, he imagined a different scenario. He ended up staring at the discolored ice where the Boeing sank and realized that anything could have happened.

Mild turbulence shook the Twin Otter, followed by a shift in the sound of the engines. Donovan looked up and a quick glance outside told him that Paul was starting a gentle descent. Donovan turned his attention back to the image that perplexed him most. It was where they'd tracked the object that fell from the Boeing. He could see where some snow had been knocked from the tops of the trees, but in no way was it conclusive. From what he gathered, trying to see through the treetops, the forest floor seemed littered with deadfall. He spotted what looked like large tree trunks as well as an assortment of limbs scattered on top of each other and then covered with snow. It would be hard going to get to where the object had come to a rest, though if anyone could power through that mess, it was Michael and Montero.

The propellers changed pitch and the Twin Otter banked left. Donovan watched as Paul's hands went to the overhead panel, pushing the propeller controls forward in preparation for landing. Another sound reached Donovan's ears, and he looked down and realized that the landing gear had been configured for the snow; the tires were up and out of the way so that the skis would touch first. Lonny was reading from a laminated checklist when Donovan felt the gentle rise as the flaps were lowered. The cold morning air seemed to mute the sound of the engines, and Donovan cinched his seat belt tighter as they descended closer to the tops of the trees. They flashed over the forest that bordered the frozen lake, and the Twin Otter descended until the main skis lightly touched down in the snow, followed by the nose. The Twin Otter shook and rattled as Paul used the power to keep the airplane moving along the frozen surface until Donovan spotted the cabin tucked back in the trees. Paul allowed the Twin Otter to settle in the snow until he and Lonny finally brought the airplane to a stop. Moments later, both engines were shut down, and the propellers slowed and gradually stopped spinning.

Donovan worked his way down the aisle, and as he reached the door and stepped down to the frozen lake, the outside air hit him hard. He lowered his goggles over his watering eyes and pulled up his scarf to try to breathe through the wool and reduce the pain of the frigid air flowing straight into his lungs.

The baggage door was opened, and Paul, Lonny, and Rick slid the cargo ramp into place. They unloaded the snowmobile, and once it was out of the way, they piled the other equipment at the edge of the door, where Michael and Jesse began to make separate stacks.

Diving gear in one pile, the duffel bags of personal gear in another. Donovan slung a heavy pack over his shoulder, snatched a duffel bag in each hand, and started the uphill trudge toward the cabin. Montero and Sofya grabbed what they could and followed.

The cabin sat beneath a canopy of trees about thirty yards from shore and was larger than he'd guessed. Feeling the hill, Donovan registered the burn in his legs and shoulders as the skin of his exposed cheeks grew numb from the cold. The three of them did their best to make a pathway through the knee-deep snow to the porch. Donovan turned the simple wooden lock, built to keep animals out, and pushed the door open.

He stopped as his eyes adjusted. It was dark inside, the only light from the open door. The windows had been boarded over for the winter. The walls were pressed particleboard nailed to the studs, and a picnic table sat in one corner. There was a cast-iron stove and a kitchen cupboard over a wooden counter and sink. Donovan sat his load down and took a quick glance into the first open door. The bedroom held two sets of bunk beds, with four yellowed foam rubber mattresses rolled up on the two top bunks. A quick check into the next room revealed the same setup. One other small door opened into a bathroom, complete with primitive shower, sink, and toilet. All the amenities were useless without liquid water.

Montero was examining the stove, and Sofya was gathering kindling from a wooden box.

"I'm going back down for more bags," Donovan said and hurried outside and down the path toward the Twin Otter. The plane was already unpacked and Jesse was inflating the sled with a foot pump. Michael had bags in both hands and was coming up the path. They passed wordlessly, and Donovan slid on another backpack, picked up a box of rations, and spun to start the trek back up the hill.

"Mr. Nash!" Jesse called out as he continued to step on the pump. "We'll be ready to go in about twenty minutes."

"Okay," Donovan replied and headed toward the cabin. As he climbed, he spotted the first wisp of smoke escaping from the steel chimney, and the unmistakable aroma of burning wood filled the air. He came through the door and found Montero kneeling in front of the stove, blowing on the flames of a small fire.

"Wow, this sucks," Michael said as he slapped Donovan on the shoulder, then brushed away the ice that had formed on the wool mask protecting his mouth and nose. "I'm going to go see if there's any more firewood."

Donovan heard the engine of the snowmobile sputter to life and grinned beneath the layers of wool. At least they wouldn't have to walk to where the 737 waited.

# CHAPTER TWENTY

LAUREN DIDN'T OPEN her eyes until the chartered jet's main gear touched down in Wroclaw. After a sleepless night in London, it had taken several hours to transport Kristof to a private hospital and then there were the good-byes to Abigail and Stephanie as they drove off with Reggie. The traffic to Luton had been brutal, especially with the detours Trevor threw in to make sure they weren't being followed. The hour-and-a-half nap was exactly what she had needed. She looked out the window and found reduced visibility with low ceilings and fog, a dreary winter afternoon in Central Europe. Across the aisle, she saw that Marta had opened her eyes but not yet moved.

Trevor was sitting up straight, alert. "Marta, wake up. We're here."

Marta yawned and begrudgingly sat up in her seat.

"You wanted to call Tomasz the moment we landed, to make sure he got the message to meet us when we arrived."

Marta found her phone, turned it on, and thumbed it to life. "How strange, I have part of a text message from Tomasz. It makes no sense."

"Call him," Lauren said as she powered up her phone as well. As soon as it cycled on, Lauren's phone beeped, then flashed that she had no signal.

"Anything?" Lauren asked.

"It's ringing," Marta said. Then the expression on her face plummeted. "Voice mail. Okay, we're going to have to go in and clear customs. They know me, so it's no big deal. The second we're cleared, they'll send us out a door into the old terminal and we'll be on our own, Tomasz or no Tomasz."

As the Hawker came to a stop, the copilot came out of the cockpit to open the cabin door. Lauren grabbed her bag, descended the stairs, and waited for Marta to lead the way. Trevor brought up the rear. An agent escorted them across the chilly ramp, leading them toward a door being held open by an armed guard. The air inside the building was over-warm and Lauren immediately shed her coat and draped it over her arm. Standing several steps in front of Marta, a man in a suit and tie opened a door and in English asked for all three passports. He flipped through them, and said a few words in Polish to Marta. They both laughed, and he waved all three of them through a door.

The old terminal was quiet and their footsteps echoed in the empty space as they walked toward the glass doors that would take them outside.

"No one is here," Marta said as she turned up the collar on her coat to ward off the damp chill. "Trevor, there's a parking lot just around the corner to the right. We'll need to find something to drive."

As they walked, Lauren's phone beeped, announcing the arrival of both voice- and e-mail messages. She opened the menu and found a message from Montero's contact in Florida. She opened the first e-mail and began reading.

*Situation urgent:*

*You were tagged leaving Innsbruck after an armed attack on the residence of an unknown occupant(s). The Austrian authorities*

*have classified you as a person of interest in connection to the at-*
*tack. Law enforcement agencies in Europe are being advised to*
*detain you on sight. Call as soon as possible.*

"You look worried," Trevor asked. "What is it?"

"Trouble," Lauren said as her phone began to ring. She answered before the second ring.

"It's Florida calling. Did you get my messages?"

"Yes." Lauren could sense the urgency in the man's voice. "We just landed and cleared customs. How bad is this?"

"I'm relieved you made it through customs. I wasn't sure you would. Don't have any interaction with police. If you plan on leaving the city, avoid public transportation."

"Do you have any idea where my husband might be?"

"His last known position was Northern Manitoba. As of a few hours ago, the entire country of Canada became a communication nightmare. Rolling electrical disruptions are the rule. They're effectively cut off from the rest of the world."

"Thanks. I have to go. I'll call you back." Lauren ended the call. She announced to Trevor and Marta, "I'm wanted in connection with the attack in Innsbruck. I'm to be arrested on sight."

"Who exactly sent you this warning?" Marta asked.

"Montero's source in Florida." Lauren reopened the e-mail and handed the phone to Marta so she could read the text. She, in turn, handed it to Trevor.

"Good God," Trevor said as he read the e-mail and handed the phone back to Lauren.

Lauren opened the attachment and saw it was a picture taken of her in the parking lot of the Innsbruck airport. Marta was there, as well, but her hat, scarf, and dark glasses would preclude any identification. Lauren handed her phone to Marta and scanned the parking lot and beyond. Her world had just tilted on its axis. A single atten-tive policeman, and she could be arrested.

"Let's get out of here. This truck should work nicely." Trevor opened the door and leaned inside.

Lauren quickly transferred her Glock from her overnight bag to her coat pocket, and leaned into the truck just as Trevor ripped a handful of wires out from under the dash.

"I don't like this," Marta said as she once again tried to reach Tomasz. "Now all I get is a busy signal."

"Ladies, let's go." Trevor cranked the engine until it started, then jumped behind the wheel.

Marta slid into the middle and Lauren climbed in and closed the door.

"Make a left and follow this road into town," Marta said. "Our destination is a commercial garage we use as a safe house."

As they drove in silence, Lauren glanced into the side mirror for anyone following them. Trevor and Marta sat close and scanned ahead for suspicious vehicles.

"Take the next exit and then exit the roundabout heading south," Marta said. "It's the second building on the right, the gray one."

Lauren spotted what looked like any other single-level industrial building in the area. A sliding chain-link gate matched the fencing around the entire property with strands of barbed wire laced into the top rungs of the fence.

Marta's brow furrowed as she scanned the building. "The gate is open, which is unusual. Trevor, drive past, and we'll turn around. When we come back, pull up to the front door, and Lauren and I will jump out. You head for the side of the building where the cars are parked. There's a side door there."

Trevor pulled through the gate and stopped in front of double steel doors. A sign written in Polish hung above.

"Let's go." Marta stepped to the ground, gun at her side.

Lauren followed as Marta pushed through the door, and they found themselves in a small foyer behind a wooden counter. The building felt deserted, and Marta motioned for Lauren to follow. They moved through another door into the main workspace, and Marta brought up her gun, sweeping her weapon back and forth as they moved across the shop floor.

Marta went to the side door and with her hip, pushed the bar to let Trevor inside. She pointed up at a walled-off section built against the back wall. A set of stairs led up to a closed door. Moving silently, they headed for the stairs and quietly climbed to the door. Marta tested the knob and then with both hands on the butt of her pistol, she used her shoulder to charge into the room. She found the switch that would turn on the lights, and a single overhead fixture jumped to life, illuminating an empty chair in the middle of the room. Lauren scanned the room and spotted several spent shell casings along the baseboard, as well as an empty hypodermic needle.

"Is this where your people brought the man captured in Prague?" Lauren asked.

Trevor followed them in and left the door open behind him. She saw him reach down and pick up a hypodermic needle. "Sodium thiopental I'm guessing?"

The drug known as *truth serum*, though Lauren realized its reliability remained in question.

"Partly," Marta said. "It's a cutting-edge cocktail formulated by scientists in Israel." She went to a cabinet and removed a slender cloth-wrapped container, checked the contents, and stuffed it into her pocket. "It has a complicated scientific name, but the latest recipe involves MDMA, or Ecstasy, as it's commonly known. This mixture keeps the subjects calmer, and they're less likely to become overwhelmed as the interrogation escalates. The Israelis have had astounding success. They're letting us test a small batch before we put it in the inventory."

"What do you think happened here?" Lauren asked. "Would they have already interrogated the man about Anna's death?"

"I doubt it. I think they'd just administered the drugs when this place came under attack." Marta went to a solitary window with a view of the floor of the shop. "There would have only been one person, Tomasz, up here with the prisoner, prepping him for our arrival. I'm guessing the shell casings are from Tomasz returning fire."

"There's no blood," Lauren said. "Do you record the interrogations?"

"Tomasz probably used his phone to record the dialogue. There are security cameras outside the building," Marta said. "To be honest, I'm not sure how we access them. I don't think the data is stored on premises."

Lauren took out her phone and within ninety seconds was connected with the man in Florida. "It's me, I have a favor to ask."

"Go."

"If it's okay, I'm going to put a friend of mine on the line about some video footage that might be stored on a remote server."

"We need to do it fast, I know you've been busy, but the initial surge from a coronal mass ejection is reaching our upper atmosphere. The geomagnetic storms are topping anything NASA has ever recorded. There are predictions from astrophysicists at the leading think tanks that suggest countries above forty-five degrees north will all have serious power outages over the next seventy-two hours."

"Thanks for the update. Here's my friend. She'll tell you what she knows about the digital setup we're looking to retrieve." Lauren handed her phone to Marta and walked over to Trevor.

"So we have no idea if this guy talked, or if he's dead, or alive?" Trevor asked.

"We don't know anything yet," Lauren said, taking a quick look at her watch. She couldn't stop thinking about the news: she was a wanted woman, and had just cleared passport control when they entered Poland. What she didn't know was if the authorities were going to wait for her to surface again—or start hunting her.

# CHAPTER TWENTY-ONE

DONOVAN WAS WITH Jesse in one of the bedrooms, far from the warmth of the stove. He was consumed by the frigid air as he stripped down to his underwear and pulled on the first pair of thermal underwear. He followed with a layer of polypropylene designed to wick away body moisture and capture body heat. The specially designed under-suit system was rated for water as cold as twenty-eight degrees Fahrenheit.

"We'll put on our snowmobile suits before we leave." Jesse zipped the heavy insulated garment up to the middle of his chest before sliding on his boots. "The dry suits are far too bulky for the trip. We'll suit up for the dive once we get out there."

Donovan nodded and threw his snowsuit over his shoulder.

"Ready?" Jesse asked as he adjusted his heavy stocking cap.

"Right behind you." Donovan followed Jesse out of the bedroom into the main room, appreciating the warmth from the fire crackling in the cast-iron stove.

"Whoa," Montero said when she saw them. "I thought Jesse and Rick were diving."

"I'm the safety diver," Donovan replied and waited for Montero to start in on him.

Michael preempted Montero's response. "You don't even like the water."

"I don't like the ocean," Donovan said. "A lake is different; it's just like a giant swimming pool."

"Jesse," Montero said. "Are you okay with Donovan being your safety diver?"

"Absolutely," he said. "When Donovan first called me, we talked about what I needed, and the first thing I told him was a dive buddy. I'll admit, I was a bit skeptical until I looked at the list of qualified divers on the Eco-Watch master list. His name is there, signed off by my dad, as well as Mr. Buckley."

"I didn't know you learned to dive! Buck signed you off?" Michael said. "Where was I when all of this happened?"

"When I first learned to dive, you were most likely in preschool," said Donovan. "I was twelve when my dad wanted me to learn. Then I didn't dive for a long time. Years later when I was working with Jesse's father setting up Eco-Watch Marine, he suggested I requalify so I'd understand the latest technology. I did, and then Buck, being the Navy SEAL he was, put me through the wringer when we were together in Norfolk, and my name was kept on the active list."

"What about when it comes time to climb into a pressurized Gulfstream and leave Churchill?" Michael asked Donovan. "I've heard the bends aren't pleasant."

"He'll be good to fly," Jesse said. "If the submerged Boeing is in less than fifty feet of water, Donovan can dive to that depth and still be safe to act as flight crew. If the dive needs to go deeper than fifty feet, I'll be the only one who goes there. We'll worry about the flying part when the time comes. Donovan will hover at a safe depth and observe, fifty feet, no deeper. In my experience, these northern lakes have good visibility, so we'll be able to see each other. Plus, we'll have Rick topside at the end of the tether; it'll be fine."

From outside, Donovan heard the snowmobile once again sputter to life, the signal that Rick was ready to leave.

"I think our ride is waiting," Jesse said, as he pulled on his goggles and gloves. "Once I double-check the sled, we'll be ready to go."

As Jesse opened the door to leave, Paul and Lonny paused to allow him to pass, then stomped the snow off their boots and came into the cabin.

"Nice," Paul said as he went toward the fire and started peeling off layers.

Lonny followed suit and sat down at the picnic table. She unfolded an aeronautical chart and spread it out.

"How soon can we leave to fly to the other lake?" Michael asked. He walked over to Lonny and leaned over her shoulder to study the chart.

"I'll leave this part to you guys," Donovan said as he finished donning his snowsuit. "We're all to be back here an hour before sunset, which doesn't give us much time. If we haven't finished our work, we'll spend the night and start again in the morning."

Donovan stepped off the porch, adjusting his woolen face protector and lowering his goggles on the way to the lake. The tinted plastic eased the brilliant white reflection of the sun off the snow. Rick was seated on the snowmobile. The sled was attached to the back, and Jesse had made a place to sit amongst the duffel bags. Donovan swung a leg up and over, straddling the seat behind Rick.

"Everyone ready?" Rick glanced back over his shoulder.

"Let's do this," Donovan confirmed.

Rick started slow, and as the snowmobile plowed through the snow, he watched the sled and then gunned the throttle. The machine and its cargo picked up speed and sped over the wind-driven drifts toward the far side of the lake. Within moments, they were racing across the ice.

Rick slowed the snowmobile as they neared the shoreline, looking for the inlet into the river channel that would take them to the other lake. Scanning the expansive white snow on the lake, Donovan spotted what looked like a small break of the brown and green that marked the trees. With a gloved hand, he pointed in that direction, and Rick swung the snowmobile into the mouth of the frozen river.

Donovan judged the channel at perhaps forty or fifty feet across. Snow-covered boulders and fallen trees were scattered down each bank, and Rick maneuvered around the obstacles, plowing a serpentine course down the river. The channel opened into the adjoining lake, and Donovan pictured the images taken from the *Galileo*. It didn't take long before they found the aircraft tire marks in the snow, and, as planned, Rick paralleled the ruts and followed them toward where the Boeing had sunk.

"This is good!" Jesse shouted from the sled. "Stop here and let me out."

Rick nodded and shut down the engine. Donovan swung himself off the snowmobile and removed his helmet. He expected complete quiet, but instead he heard creaks and a groaning sound from beneath his feet.

"Weird, isn't it? I've heard it said that the ice never sleeps," Jesse said as he hauled himself out of the sled, stomping on the ice to knock the snow from his clothes. He leaned into the sled, brushed the snow from a duffel, and unzipped the opening. He removed a chainsaw as well as a collapsible walking stick. "Rick, I want you to find the safety lines. They're in this red bag. Get them rigged and ready to use. If we fall through the ice, get us a line and then use the snowmobile to pull us out."

"Will do." Rick swept away more snow from their cargo, pulled the bag from the sled, and began setting out the neatly bundled lines.

"Donovan, let's go figure out a safe place to make a hole." Pleased that Jesse had taken charge and in a controlled, concise way, Donovan trudged toward him.

"You can see the heavier furrows," Jesse pointed out. "I'm guessing those are from the Boeing's landing gear. I'm thinking we follow them until they end, and then we should be standing at the edge of where the ice buckled."

"Judging from the tracks showing where Michael turned the *Galileo*, it's not far."

"Unbelievable," Jesse said as he surveyed the scene. "It sounded pretty amazing when you explained about landing the *Galileo* on the ice, but now, to be standing here, it sinks in just how intense it must have been."

"It was. Now, let's go find the Boeing."

Jesse led the way, driving the sharp end of his walking stick into the ice ahead of him. As they continued, Donovan spotted where the tire marks ended. Jesse slowed and methodically probed with his stick until it finally pierced the ice. Jesse repeated the process and continued to test the ice. Once he was confident he knew where the new ice bordered the thicker ice, he handed Donovan the stick and began the process of cutting the dive hole.

The roar from the chainsaw was harsh, and Donovan stood back as snow and ice were thrown in the air when Jesse began cutting. He worked quickly, and when he finally shut off the noisy engine, there were large chucks of ice floating inside a six-by-six-foot square of open water. Jesse set the chainsaw down and motioned for Rick to bring the snowmobile closer.

"How long do you think it'll take us to get set up to dive?" Donovan said, cognizant that the sun was already headed toward the horizon.

"We'll see how fast it goes." Jesse, too, glanced at the angle of the sun. "First, we'll suit up, and then try to get the hole clear of ice." Jesse took his walking stick from Donovan and used it to point at the field of thin ice. "Try to keep in mind that ten feet out that way, the ice isn't strong enough to hold your weight."

Rick situated the snowmobile as Jesse instructed. The three of them began to unload the sled, lining up the duffel bags on the snow. Jesse got Rick started on assembling a tent and then fired up a propane burner that would eventually create a small haven of warmth. Jesse pulled out the dry suits, hoods, gloves, masks, and fins. From another bag he removed the weight belts, personal floatation devices, and two air tanks. From inside a cushioned hard plastic container, Jesse gently handled the twin regulators and assembled the first tank. He repeated the process until the second tank was ready. Next came the tools common for salvage diving, a waterproof camera, as well as several assorted mesh bags that could be filled with items from the Boeing. Once attached to an inflatable balloon, they'd float to the surface.

"What's next?" Donovan asked when Jesse stepped back from the assembled equipment.

"The painful part," Jesse said. "We're running out of time, so there's no use waiting for the shelter to heat up. We'll do this quick and dirty; the tent should be heated when we get out. I'll suit up first, so you can watch and learn. Speed is important. We do as much as we can while we're wearing our snowmobile suits. Here, put on your neoprene neck collar, and then you can help me into my suit."

Donovan watched as Jesse shed his snowmobile suit and quickly stepped into his dry suit. The heavy black skin zipped in the back, and Donovan watched carefully as Jesse pulled and dipped his shoulders to maneuver into the thick material, his breath condensing in great clouds as he exhaled. Once the suit covered his frame, Donovan held it steady as Jesse pushed his head through the neck opening, and then Donovan pulled the zipper up all the way. Next there were integrated gloves that connected to the suit as well as a hood that protected most of Jesse's face.

"Good, okay, Donovan, your turn. Rick, can you hand me his dry suit and be ready to take his snowmobile suit and set it next to mine in the tent?"

Donovan slid out of his insulated snowmobile suit and stepped into the dry suit. Each exhale blinded him and he held his breath so he could see through the frozen vapor. He felt ice collect in his nasal passages and on his exposed eyebrows. Following Jesse's instructions, Donovan dipped and struggled to get his shoulders encased in the heavy material. Jesse zipped him almost all the way up, then had Donovan squat, to burp the air out of the suit before easing the zipper all the way to the stop. Donovan slid on his hood and gloves, and finally exhaled, his chest tight against the frigid air.

"The dry suits are very buoyant, so we need weight," Jesse said as he fastened his own belt and then helped Donovan with his. "Now, I'm going to lift up your tank. Put out your right arm."

Donovan anxiously eyed the water, knowing that it was forty degrees warmer than the air. Once again, he blinked away at the ice that formed on his eyelashes as Jesse lifted the tank into place and adjusted the straps.

"Everything looks good," Jesse said as he moved around Donovan, double-checking his equipment. "Here's your mask, your snorkel, and fins. There's also a mesh sleeve and a lift bag—anything we collect from the plane we'll float to the surface. Okay, let's move to the opening, and get the chunks of ice out of the hole so we can get into the water."

There were two regulators per tank, and Donovan was mindful to keep them out of the snow. Frozen regulators were a hazard in the frigid temperatures, which was why cold-water divers always had a backup. He carefully lowered himself down to the edge of the ice, used his heels to crack through the thin film of fresh ice, sat, and dangled his feet into the water. Jesse lowered himself down next to him and together they lifted the first chunk of ice from the hole and set it next to them for Rick to toss aside. The three of them cleared the ice to open a six-foot patch of water. Donovan and Jesse, with Rick's help, slid on their flippers and then kicked gently to keep the water moving so fresh ice wouldn't form.

"Here goes the guide line, our pathway back to the hole in the ice," Jesse said as he tossed a weighted line into the water and payed it out until it stopped. "It's deep, maybe sixty feet. Rick, check the shelter and make sure the burner stays lit, and don't forget to keep the hole from freezing over. Donovan, once we're under, I want you to go down ten feet or so and stop. Grab the guide line if you want. We'll check everything over before we go down any further."

Donovan nodded that he understood. He slid his mask into place and found his mouthpiece, bit down on the rubber, then pushed off the edge and slipped beneath the surface. He breathed in and heard the regulator functioning normally and felt the air filling his lungs. In his head he heard Buck's words as he focused on breathing slowly and evenly as he descended. Above him, in a blur of bubbles, Jesse entered the water as Donovan continued down. At ten feet, he grabbed the guide line and stopped his descent. Waiting for Jesse to join him, Donovan glanced below him and was met with the eerie sight of the submerged Boeing 737. Twenty feet below him, on a steeply sloped sand bottom was the nose and cockpit of the Boeing. The fuselage tilted away from him and he could make out the wings and the engines, then the remainder of the Boeing dropped off into deeper water, the tail fading from view in the depths of the lake.

# CHAPTER TWENTY-TWO

"I KNOW THE storm is interfering with communications, but is there any way to ping someone's phone and see where they might be?" Marta continued to pace while talking with the man in Florida.

Lauren heard Marta rattle off the European phone number she guessed belonged to Tomasz.

"You know, don't you?" Trevor asked without warning.

"I know a great many things," Lauren said. "Can you narrow it down for me?"

"About Marta and me," Trevor said.

"Oh that." Lauren allowed herself a small smile. "Everyone knows."

"Who's everyone?"

"Reggie knows, and I'm assuming other members of your team. Then there's myself, the charter pilots from earlier today, and probably Kristof."

"Bloody hell," Trevor said, his face contorted as if he'd just bit into a lemon. "Reggie *and* Kristof."

"I'd guess that Stephanie and Abigail know by now as well."

Trevor blew out a long breath as if to steady himself. "Do you think I should I have said something to Kristof already? Did I muck this up?"

Lauren had seen Trevor fly a burning helicopter into a firefight without this much second-guessing and anxiety. She found it charming. "Can I offer you some advice?"

"Please."

"There is a particular mind-set a man needs if he's involved with a strong, intelligent woman. Do you agree that Marta is strong and intelligent?"

"Of course," Trevor agreed.

"You can't always be the one in charge," Lauren said. "Unless it's a situation for which you're hands down more qualified than Marta. Be a team. Ask her for her help and advice, respect her thoughts, and by all means, listen to her. I promise you'll get the same in return, and one day you'll know when it's time to talk to Kristof."

"Thank you," Trevor said, and there was no mistaking the earnestness in his tone.

"We found the footage of the raid on this place, but it doesn't tell us much," Marta called out. She'd ended her call and started toward them. "The men were professional—they wore masks and disconnected the feed to the surveillance equipment. And we found Tomasz's phone. He's in the hospital."

"Does Tomasz have any immediate family?" Lauren asked.

"No." Marta shook her head.

"He does now," Lauren said. "Let's go to the hospital and assess Tomasz's condition, see if he can talk, maybe tell us what happened."

"We can do that," Marta said. "You back me up, and Trevor can wait in the car."

"This could be a trap," Trevor warned. "Leaving Tomasz's phone on as a beacon, to lure us to the hospital. Well, it's something I'd do."

"Marta," Lauren said. "Your dad told us he had some inventory moved into the area. What exactly did he mean by that?"

A knowing smile came to Marta's face, and she turned to Trevor. "Dad had a helicopter brought in, just in case. Can you fly a Eurocopter AS-365? I think it's also called a Dauphin?"

Trevor rubbed his palms together in anticipation. "Yeah, I can fly a Dauphin."

"Where is this helicopter?" Lauren asked. "Is it military?"

"No, it's a civilian model. We just bought it from the owner in Germany. I do know we haven't started any modifications yet."

"So, no guns?" Trevor asked.

"No guns, strictly civilian. Dad had it brought to a small farm we control about fifteen minutes south of here," Marta said. "We'll take the van parked outside. We should also drop the stolen truck somewhere."

Lauren turned and followed Trevor down the steps. As they reached the main floor, Marta headed straight for the main door. Trevor gave Marta a quick kiss, then split off and pushed through a side door and headed for the truck. Marta went to what sufficed for a secretary's desk situated behind the counter. Seconds later, she held up a key ring.

Marta drove the van, and Trevor followed in the stolen truck. She led them to an apartment complex not far from a large shopping area. They pulled in to a half-filled parking lot where Marta pointed toward a parking space marked for visitors. Trevor used his handkerchief to wipe the steering wheel free of prints and then jumped into the van.

They watched the traffic behind them as they swung out of the apartment complex and headed toward the main road that would take them south.

Marta traveled the speed limit, and fifteen minutes later, they exited the highway. At different intervals, Lauren tried to make a phone call, but each time, it went straight to voice mail.

"There's a phone and computer in the hangar," Marta said. "Who are you trying to call?"

"I wanted to reach Reggie or Stephanie," Lauren said. "I wanted to talk to Abigail."

"Save your battery. My guess is Reggie will have taken all the phones offline," Trevor said. "They're fine. He'll initiate untraceable phones, and we'll hear from him when he's settled."

"I don't like not knowing," Lauren said.

"I agree," Marta said.

"Kristof, as well as the others, are fine," Trevor said. "Reggie is as good as they come, so let's focus on our jobs here tonight. We need to get inside the hospital, find out what happened to Tomasz, and if we're a bit lucky, we'll find someone else who has an interest in Tomasz."

"What if he's under police guard?" Marta said to Lauren. "You'll be at risk of being identified. I'm the only one who speaks Polish. You won't be able to talk your way out of anything. Maybe we need to rethink this?"

"You'll need backup," Lauren said. "I'll be fine."

"Let's slow down and give this operation a little time to breathe." Trevor held up his hands to signal a time-out. "Once we get to the hangar, let's all have some tea, and we can sit down and discuss this properly to come up with a solid plan."

Marta snapped a glance at Trevor and then turned to Lauren. A curious frown crossed her face, yet instead of saying anything, she accelerated the van. They were soon traveling on a tree-lined dirt road. When Marta slowed, she made a left turn and stopped abruptly. In front of them was a heavy metal gate that was nearly invisible between the tree trunks and hanging limbs.

"Is there a lock?" Trevor asked, poised to jump out and open the gate.

Marta lowered the sun visor and pushed a simple garage door opener, the gate swung inward, and they pulled up to what looked like an old barn with a small farmhouse attached by a breezeway.

"There shouldn't be anyone here." Marta shut off the engine, drew her Glock, and stepped out of the van.

Lauren followed as Marta punched in a code on a keypad mounted near the door. Moments later, Marta had the lights on. In the center of the barn, Lauren saw a bright yellow helicopter with blue trim around the windows. From what she knew about helicopters, this was the same model still in use by the United States Coast Guard. It even had a similar external hoist mounted on the right side just above the door. She and Donovan had ridden in one once, and she remembered it was both fast and maneuverable. As she walked around the machine, she saw it was registered in Germany.

Trevor headed straight to the cockpit, opened the door, and climbed inside.

Marta and Lauren walked toward the tail of the helicopter. "Tea and a chat," Marta said. "What was that about?"

"It's cute, is what it is." Lauren tried to disarm her friend with a smile. "I may have given Trevor some advice about dating a strong and intelligent woman. Just a few things about working together that I've learned the hard way from being married to Donovan."

"Tea?"

"No. The tea is because Trevor's British. He wants to slow the two of us down, to sit and work out a proper strategy. He's the professional soldier, but he cares about what you think," Lauren said. "You're welcome."

"Oh, well, that puts a different slant on things, doesn't it?" Marta said with a smile.

"The fact that this is a civilian helicopter gives us a great many options," Trevor called out as he leaned out the door. "Where are you two?"

"We're back here," Marta replied.

"It's perfect. You two walk into the hospital, find Tomasz, and I'll hover nearby to back you up." Trevor got out of the helicopter. "Let's go iron out the details, but I'm thinking a quick in and out. Where better to fly a bright yellow helicopter than to a hospital?"

"Before we get too far into this plan, what happens if it doesn't work?" Lauren said. "What if we leave the hospital with nothing? We need to discuss our next step."

"We fly to Prague and keep digging," Marta said.

"That could work." Trevor began to scan the exterior of the helicopter. "Though investigating a case that Interpol is no doubt actively pursuing could be risky, especially if they're also looking for Lauren."

"You being on a watch list is a concern," Marta said to Lauren, "but for now, let's go and get some water started for tea."

"I'll be in shortly," Trevor called as he hoisted himself back into the cockpit.

"I was wondering . . . earlier when I was on the phone," Marta whispered to Lauren. "I couldn't help but notice you and Trevor talking. What does he think about the mission? Does he have another plan in mind?"

"No," Lauren said. "When Trevor and I were talking, for the most part we were talking about you."

# CHAPTER TWENTY-THREE

DONOVAN FLOATED ABOVE the ghostlike Boeing. The 737 looked intact, but completely out of its element. It was resting on the sharply sloped lake bottom, about eighteen degrees nose up. Playing the beam of his dive light around the nose gear, he found that the tires had settled down into the sandy bottom. The light illuminated the windshield and reflected back into his eyes. He needed to adjust his angle to see inside the flight deck.

A flash illuminated next to him. Donovan turned to find Jesse taking photographs. After he shot several, he motioned for Donovan to descend with him. Except for the rhythmic hiss of the regulator, and an occasional sharp report from the shifting ice, there was no other sound.

Together, they swam down the side of the plane until they reached the point where the right wing joined the fuselage. As they'd planned, Donovan wouldn't go below fifty feet, so he stopped and hovered on the wing, next to the open emergency exit. First he trained the beam of his flashlight onto his depth gauge, steady at forty feet. He then moved the beam into the interior of the jet. Jesse, however, continued down to the tail to find the actual registration number on the side of the plane.

Donovan's flashlight illuminated sofa cushions and other floating debris trapped against the ceiling. He could see that the beige carpet was littered with glass.

Rising bubbles alerted Donovan to Jesse's ascent, and moments later, Jesse was kneeling on the wing next to him. With his flashlight, Jesse surveyed the interior, then stowed his light and began to shed his air tank. With the regulator in his mouth, Jesse pushed his tank through the narrow emergency exit ahead of him and swam into the interior.

Donovan did the same, swinging the tank up and over his head, careful not to clip the valve or the regulator on the edge of the opening. With his tank secure in his arms, Donovan kicked through the opening into the 737. With the airplane on a slope, Jesse took the deeper tail section, and Donovan slid his tank back into place and slowly worked his way toward the cockpit. As the reality of being inside the wrecked plane began to sink in, Donovan found that his breathing rate had increased. The bubbles from his regulator floated to the ceiling, flattened out, and worked their way forward, rising with the angle of the jet.

Kicking gently, Donovan pushed cushions aside and scanned back and forth below him in an effort to spot anything out of the ordinary. The lush interior was a blend of leather-covered chairs and sofas, mixed with polished wooden tables and credenzas. Numerous personal flat-screen televisions were mounted seat-side, all standard fare for a private Boeing 737. The cup holders, seat belts, and overhead air vents appeared to be gold plated. As Donovan inched his way forward, he spotted a sturdy leather briefcase sitting on the floor between two seats. This was the first clue as to who may have been on board. He swam down, grabbed the handles, and lifted. It was much heavier than he'd expected. He swung it up onto a table and with his heavy gloves, he fumbled at the latches until they snapped open and he could lift the lid. Normally he'd try to bring up the entire case unopened, but he wasn't an archaeologist on this trip, he was looking for answers. On top were soaked papers in file folders, the notations written in what Donovan recognized as the Cyrillic alphabet. He pushed the files into his mesh dive bag, and then discovered several canvas bags were under the folders, nestled in the bottom of the case. He removed the knife from his ankle sheath and slit the material of each bag. He watched in dismay as gold coins spilled out of the openings. All three bags contained investment-grade coins, a mixture of South African Krugerrands, Turkish Republic gold coins, American Eagles, as well as gold coins from Canada and Australia.

Donovan left the case open and pushed on toward the cockpit. The sweeping beam of his flashlight revealed fire-damaged carpet, sidewalls, and charred furniture. As he swam forward, he spotted two bodies floating near the ceiling. He drew closer and discovered the first corpse, a male, had burns on the hands, legs, and arms. His face seemed undamaged, except for a bullet hole in the forehead. The dead man had thinning blond hair and blue eyes. Donovan patted down the dead man's clothes, feeling for a wallet.

He found an object in an inside jacket pocket, but his thick dive gloves made it impossible to grasp anything. He finally ripped the entire pocket apart, and a phone, not a wallet, sank to the floor. Donovan maneuvered it into the bag and continued to the next corpse. The man was in his thirties, bald, and also had burned hands and a bullet wound, this time behind his left ear. After a quick pat-down, nothing registered, and Donovan continued toward the front of the plane. The passageway narrowed and he came to a lavatory, the lock indicating it was unoccupied. The galley was next, where he found aluminum tins on the floor, as well as plates, some broken some intact, and scattered utensils. Shattered glass covered the floor. He swam to a door that he assumed led to the crew's rest area and managed to negotiate the latch with his gloves. When he opened the door, he found two empty bunks. He closed the door and continued toward the cockpit door where he found the next body. This one was an older woman, maybe late fifties, thin, with wrinkles, jewelry, and very long fingernails. She, too, had been shot in the head. Donovan floated her away from the door and pushed into the cockpit.

Light filtered down through the ice above and illuminated the cockpit. The captain sat in the left seat, still strapped in, and wearing his oxygen mask. The first officer was out of his seat, floating freely. Donovan estimated he was probably mid-thirties with curly brown hair and a mustache. He'd been shot in the chest. Another look at the captain told Donovan he'd been shot from behind.

Donovan backed out of the cockpit into the entry space and pulled himself to the base of the main entry door. Using his sturdy dive knife, he pried up the heavy bar that was attached to the emergency slide and freed it from the floor. He swung the locking mechanism of the main door and pushed against the solid frame until it swung open. When he spotted Jesse swimming toward him through the cabin, he pointed to the briefcase on the table.

Jesse stopped and photographed the coins, collected an assortment, and dropped them in his own bag. As Donovan hovered near the main door, Jesse took pictures of each corpse in the cabin, moving to different angles to get pictures of faces as well as the burns. Donovan moved aside to allow Jesse to continue to document the scene, both in the cabin and the cockpit. Once he was finished, Jesse checked his watch and motioned to Donovan that they needed to start up.

Donovan and Jesse moved through the main cabin door, then connected their mesh bags together. Once both were attached to a bright orange lift bag, Jesse squeezed off several bursts of oxygen from his spare regulator, which quickly filled the lift bag and it climbed toward the surface. Together they modulated their personal flotation devices to slowly ascend toward the surface. Jesse stopped them at ten feet for a cautionary decompression stop, to purge their blood of any nitrogen bubbles.

Waiting seemed like an eternity until Jesse signaled Donovan he could continue to the surface. In that time, he started to feel the effects of the cold in his hands and feet. When he started kicking for the top, he could also feel the stiffness in his knees and hips. When he broke the surface of the water, he squinted against the sunlight to see Rick perched on the edge of the opening. Donovan spit out the regulator and immediately felt the stab of the brutally cold air torture his lungs. As fast as he could, he separated himself from the tank, which Rick lifted up onto the ice. Then he handed up his weight belt, the mesh container, and deflated lift bag. With Rick pulling, Donovan kicked hard to get out of the water. As he sat on the edge of the ice, Rick unstrapped his flippers, then pulled him to his feet.

"Your snowmobile suit is inside the tent; the small gas furnace has been working hard," Rick said. "It's nearly forty degrees inside. Or as I call it, Paradise."

Donovan hobbled to the shelter, stopping just outside for Rick to pull off his gloves. Then in one quick motion, Rick unzipped the dry suit and helped peel it off Donovan's body. Once free, Donovan stepped into the enclosure and closed his eyes as he soaked up the warmer air. He toweled off and then put on his snowmobile suit, dried his face and hair, and slid on his wool head protection, boots, and gloves. He stood near the stove for one more moment and began to think he might survive.

"Are you okay in there?" Jesse yelled from outside.

"I'm fine," Donovan said as he left the warmth of the enclosure and hurried to the hole in the ice.

"How was it?" Jesse asked as he treaded water. "You did great. How do you feel? Did you stay warm?"

"I'm good. I felt fine."

Jesse shrugged off his tank. "Cool, how about a hand getting me up and out of the water?"

Donovan and Rick pulled Jesse up and out of the frigid water and repeated the same process Donovan had just gone through. When Jesse slipped into the tent, Donovan noticed how low the sun had sunk in the west. They would need to leave soon. He went straight to the mesh bags they'd floated up from the plane. The contents had already frozen into a clump of ice, and Donovan knelt and dipped it into the lake water to momentarily thaw it out. He clenched his teeth against the cold, removed his glove, and fished out a water-logged passport. Inside was a photograph of Sofya, who now had a last name—Baronovsky. She'd just had her twenty-sixth birthday. Donovan risked trying to turn to one of the sodden pages to see where Sofya had traveled, but couldn't; ice was already freezing the paper together, and he was forced to stop.

"That feels better." Jesse stepped from the tent dressed as he was before, in his heavy snowsuit, hat, and gloves. "That was incredible. I've never dived on what amounts to a crime scene. I can't show you any of the pictures until we get back and the equipment warms up, but this 737 has a VR registration. VR-CSB, to be exact, and in the back of the plane were bags of gold coins, as well as several cases filled with automatic weapons, AK-47s I think, and boxes of ammunition."

"Cayman Islands," Rick said. "VR-C registered planes are a familiar tax and identity dodge. It wouldn't surprise me if there were a trail of fake names and shell companies attached to this plane."

"From what I saw, the people on board were doing business in Russian," Donovan said. "We need to get back to the cabin, stow all of this, and make sure the charter pilots don't find out what we're doing. It's going to be difficult to get any of the papers or electronics dried out. Depending on what the other team found, I say we come back in the morning and make another dive."

"I agree," Jesse said as he began to carefully fold the dry suits for transport. "I didn't have a chance to open all of the closets and storage areas. I mean, this is still nothing but a mystery."

"What else did you find?" Rick asked Jesse.

"It wasn't pretty, but there was a woman and man near the aft stateroom," Jesse said. "It looked like the man had been shot twice, once in the stomach and again in the throat. He also had a deep cut on his forearm. The woman looked to be in her mid-thirties. She was shot as well. I'm no forensic expert, but I watch enough television to know that burns around the hole in her blouse meant she was probably shot at point-blank range."

"So, the total body count is two women and three men, plus the two pilots," Donovan said. "Everyone I saw had a gunshot wound, plus two of the men had serious burns."

"What in the hell," Rick said. "Sofya didn't have a mark on her when we rescued her."

"Maybe she's the one who inflicted the damage?" Jesse said.

"Or," Donovan said solemnly, "they hadn't gotten to her yet. You didn't by chance see a gun, did you?"

"I didn't, but to be honest, I wasn't really looking."

Donovan tried to connect the chain of events that still made no sense. "It could have been thrown around as the plane sank. We'll look for it tomorrow."

It took them another half hour to pack the sled and begin their journey back to the cabin. The trip went faster, as they could retrace their own distinct tracks in the snow. Rick navigated the snowmobile back through the frozen river with more speed than before. When they burst out of the narrow confines onto the first lake, Donovan spotted the Twin Otter in the distance, parked near the cabin. A solitary column of smoke rose from the chimney and mixed with the tops of the trees. It looked as if the airplane had just arrived and they were still unloading.

Rick slowed as they neared the camp and guided the snowmobile as close to the cabin as he could. As he shut it down, Montero stepped from the cabin as did Michael, and walked toward them.

Donovan pulled off his helmet. "Any luck?"

"No," Montero said. "You?"

"Some, but I'd like to spend the night and go back down in the morning."

"We need to get back out there tomorrow, as well, and cover more ground," Michael said as they headed toward the snowmobile to help Jesse and Rick unload the gear.

Montero signaled Donovan to join her, and together they moved off the main pathway where they could talk in private.

"You first," Montero said. "Did you make it inside the plane?"

"It was a mess. We found seven bodies. The two pilots had clearly been shot shortly after they landed. There were three other men and two women; they'd all been shot as well. Some of them were burned. We also discovered a great number of gold coins, and Jesse found crates of assault rifles, complete with ammunition. It looked to me like someone was running. We salvaged some laptops, a number of documents, and a phone or two. Everything I saw was written in Russian. Once everything dries, perhaps we can translate them?"

"Were you able to find out where the jet is registered?" Montero asked.

"Cayman Islands."

"That figures. Nothing about this case has been easy."

"What is it you wanted to talk to me about?"

"It's Sofya," Montero said. "She's becoming more unstable. I was with her as we were out there searching, and the longer we walked, the harder she began to cry. She spoke aloud, became unfocused, disoriented, as if reliving past events."

"We're at ground zero of a plane crash that probably initiated her PTSD and associated amnesia. Isn't her starting to remember a good thing?"

"I don't know." Montero shoved her gloved hands into the pockets of her parka. "With the traumatized women I've worked with before, we had a fair idea from social workers, family members, or police reports to understand what was buried. The doctors could eventually coax it out into the light with the appropriate safety nets in place. With Sofya, we have no idea. Imagine having amnesia, and then without warning, horrible realities came flooding back all at once."

"We found her passport. It's Russian. Sofya Yvette Baronovsky. She's twenty-six years old."

"That's interesting," Montero said. "I wonder if it's really her name."

"I don't know, but after what you've said, let's keep that information to ourselves for now. Do you think Sofya can make it through one more day?"

"I think so, but what if she went with you to the airplane? From the surface of the ice, she wouldn't be able to see the 737. It might be easier than the anxiety of searching for an unknown object. Besides, I think Michael and I can cover more ground if it's just the two of us."

"She can go with me." Donovan was about to turn away when he caught a glimmer of motion to the east and stopped. The first twilight dance of the Aurora Borealis was making its appearance. The shimmering colors of green and pink danced upward, seeming to leap from the tops of the snow-covered trees and pulse straight up into the purple sky, where the energy would fade and then it all began again. Donovan felt as if he were standing on another planet, and for a moment, it was as if he were a million miles away from everything he knew. In that instant, he felt a sting of regret about the argument with William, and he missed his wife and daughter almost more than he could endure.

# CHAPTER TWENTY-FOUR

MARTA STOPPED, SPOKE to the woman seated behind the information desk, and was directed to an elevator bank. Lauren, in turn, her hair in a ponytail, wearing a scarf and reading glasses low on her nose, walked past the information desk like she knew exactly where she was headed.

They ignored each other as Marta pushed the button that would take them to the third floor.

"He's in room 347," Marta said once they were alone in the elevator.

When the doors opened, they each headed in a different direction. Lauren knew from studying the hospital layout that each floor was a rectangle, so if she kept walking, she'd eventually rendezvous with Marta at Tomasz's room. As Lauren came around the last corner, she spotted a wooden chair about halfway down the hallway. A check of the room numbers confirmed that this was Tomasz's room.

Lauren walked past 347, slowed briefly, and heard nothing out of the ordinary. She continued to walk, but before she came to the end of the hallway, a uniformed guard sauntered around the corner toward her. He was a big man, his bottle of water was nearly invisible in his huge hand, his jowls oozed over his collar, and his thighs rubbed as he walked.

He said something in Polish, and Lauren smiled as they passed. He continued down the hallway and eased into the chair outside room 347. Lauren continued walking, with no idea if Marta was inside the room or if she knew that the guard had returned. The moment she rounded the corner, she reached into her pocket for a scrap of paper.

Then she spun, rounded the corner, and walked back to the guard. He looked up and kept his eyes on her as she held the scrap of paper, going from room to room as if lost. As she neared him, she smiled again, shrugged, and held out the paper as if asking for help.

In the instant before he realized there was nothing written on the paper, Lauren, in a move Montero taught her, put her hand on his face, and with leverage generated from her core, she popped the back of his head against the wall. She coiled herself for another strike, but his arms dropped to his side, telling her he was out. She crossed his thick arms across his chest and then steadied him from falling from the chair. For the moment, he appeared to be asleep. When Lauren pushed inside, she found Marta going through the drawers in a small dresser. The room held two beds. One was empty; the other held a heavily bandaged man. He lay under the covers with a monitor, as well as IV bags, nearby.

"What was the noise I heard?" Marta whispered.

"The guard," Lauren said. "I don't know how long he'll be out."

"Shit," Marta said. "Tomasz is badly beaten. I don't know if he's been able to talk to anyone. I can't find his phone."

Both women heard a new sound from the hallway before two men, guns drawn, pushed into the room. Lauren reached up as if adjusting one of the monitors and then turned and smiled.

That single act slowed the men down long enough for Marta, whom they hadn't seen, to spring into action. The first man took Marta's boot to the face, dropped his gun, and collapsed into his comrade, throwing him off balance as they both crashed into the wall. Marta kicked the gun across the floor toward Lauren. Then she stepped forward, grabbed the second man's gun, and with one hand pressed over his mouth, she bent his wrist back until something snapped. He was leaning against the wall in shock and pain when Marta slammed her knee into the side of his head. Then he was out.

"Hurry, we need to lift both of these men onto the empty bed," Lauren said as she peeled back the blanket and sheet. "Lay them side by side."

Marta and Lauren both strained to lift the first man up far enough for Marta to crouch and use her legs and shoulder to propel the man up onto the bed. Together, they wasted no time moving the second man. Lauren arranged the unconscious men's arms and legs. Once the two men were positioned to her liking, Lauren stood back.

"Now what?" Marta asked.

Lauren took two pillows and tucked them between the two men on the bed. When she was finished, she threw the sheet and blanket back over them until all that showed was one head. She smoothed the pillows until they were contoured to look like one large body. Lauren found and released the bed brake and began to swing it away from the wall.

Marta opened the door while pulling the bed. Together they eased it out into the hallway. Marta pulled out her radio and transmitted that they were on their way.

They passed a woman and a man dressed in civilian clothes, and neither one paid any attention to Lauren and Marta.

Over Marta's shoulder, Lauren spotted the elevator, the doors opened, and someone stepped off and walked the other way. Lauren pushed faster and Marta caught the elevator and they rolled the bed into the car and pressed the button for the first floor. They waited several agonizing seconds for the door to finally shut.

Lauren looked under the blanket to check the men. "They're not going to wake up and cause a problem, are they?"

"If they do, I'll take care of them. Plus, we don't have far to go. Once the elevator opens, we go to the right and follow the signs. The exit leading to the helipad will be marked."

Lauren took a deep breath as the doors opened, and they began rolling their prize down the tiled floor toward their destination. After the right turn, as promised, Lauren spotted the exit that signaled their destination. Marta pushed a red button and as the doors parted, they were met with bracing cold air and the sound of a helicopter. They hurried down the long sidewalk toward the helipad just as Trevor descended into view in the bright yellow Dauphin. He lowered the landing gear, slowed his descent, and touched down lightly.

Marta unlatched the door and slid it back on its tracks. They maneuvered the bed until the side was flush with the helicopter. Buffeted by the rotor wash, Lauren threw back the covers. She and Marta quickly rolled both men from the bed until they dropped onto the floor of the helicopter. Lauren turned and spotted a uniformed security man trying to push past a group of onlookers gathering near the doors. Lauren shoved the bed away from the helicopter, jumped in after Marta, and latched the door. Trevor powered into the air, raised the wheels, shut off all the lights, and with one graceful pivot climbed away from the building and vanished in the darkness.

# CHAPTER TWENTY-FIVE

"ARE YOU COMFORTABLE?" Donovan yelled above the roar of the snowmobile engine. As they'd packed the sled earlier, Donovan had asked Jesse if he could stack the bags to allow for two people to ride amongst the bags holding the diving equipment. He'd come up with a rearward facing arrangement that blocked most of the wind and snow. Jesse and Rick sat on the snowmobile itself, and Donovan was in the sled with Sofya. So far, she'd seemed normal, doing her best to help, staying focused on the task at hand.

"Yes," she said. "How much longer?"

"Not long. How are you feeling?"

"I'm fine, though I never had a chance to ask you what you found out here yesterday."

"We found some papers and a laptop, but nothing else really." Donovan was ready for her questions; the last thing they wanted to do was upset her. Montero had told him this morning that the papers they'd recovered yesterday were still soggy and unreadable, and would stay that way until they were thoroughly dried. The solitary laptop computer and phone were still soaked, and with no way to charge the batteries, it might take a return to civilization to uncover the data stored within.

"It's really beautiful out here," Sofya said. "I feel better today."

Donovan had no idea how anyone could feel better today. Wrapped in a sleeping bag, trying to stay asleep in the frigid cabin on an aged foam rubber pad on a wooden bunk, he'd had one of the worst nights he'd ever endured. The torture from the freezing bedroom was only surpassed by the bitter cold of the unheated outhouse. Whatever the day held, it had to be an improvement on last night.

Rick slowed the snowmobile and brought them to a stop a safe distance from the red flag that Jesse had left to mark the edge of the hole they'd made the day before. Donovan climbed off the sled, then helped Sofya up. Using the chainsaw, Jesse made short work of the fresh ice. With four people working, the job of unloading and preparing for their dive went quickly. Jesse got into his dry suit first, before helping Donovan with his.

Once ready, Donovan grabbed the last chunk of ice bobbing in the water and lifted it to the pile. Rick dropped the weighted tether line into the water, payed it out, and then secured it to the snowmobile. Jesse slipped into the water. Donovan followed, taking his first breath through the regulator, testing that it was working correctly. Below him, Jesse watched to make sure everything was okay, tucked, and began to swim down toward the plane.

Donovan kicked after him, and they both arrived at the open main door. Like the day before, Jesse would go deep toward the tail section, while Donovan spent more time in the cockpit. Jesse pulled himself into the Boeing and swam down the main aisle. Donovan went in next, and after maneuvering past the older woman's body, he pulled himself into the cockpit. He did his best to ignore the bodies of the crew. Instead, he was focused on finding any type of paper, a chart, a flight plan, anything that would tell him where this plane came from, and where it was headed. It wasn't until he searched behind the seats that he found the airworthiness certificate as well as the registration. Using his flashlight, he read in English that the airplane belonged to CSB Enterprises. He cursed into his regulator. They were the same letters painted on the tail. The airplane was its own entity and offered absolutely no information as to its actual owner.

Donovan began to search the copilot for a wallet or phone. He cut away the material of a back pocket and found a thin trifold wallet. Inside, he could see the edges of several plastic cards. He used the tip of his rubber glove to move the first card out far enough to understand it was a laminated identification of some kind, and he assumed the text was Russian. The second card was an American Express card with the words CSB Enterprises in raised letters. The name on the card was Vladimir Krishenko. Donovan secured the wallet in the mesh bag. Perhaps Montero could track the company through charges made on the card. He was about to search a narrow crew closet, when he caught sight of the tether line bouncing wildly just outside the cockpit. Looking up toward the surface, Donovan could see that Rick was pulling on the line and letting it drop, trying to get someone's attention. Donovan pulled himself from the cockpit and spotted Jesse, who was on his way up as well. Donovan swam out of the Boeing and waited for Jesse to join him. They followed the line and reached the surface together.

The first thing Donovan heard was the beating of rotor blades.

"A helicopter," Rick yelled. "They already flew over once, and they're swinging back around."

Donovan spit out his regulator. "Were there any markings? Could you tell who they were?"

"No, it's a Bell 212, orange with black stripes."

Donovan felt helpless as the helicopter made a sweeping left turn and headed back toward them. He saw the side door slide back and a gun barrel jut from the opening. Without a word, Jesse vanished underwater.

"Oh shit!" Rick saw the gun and immediately turned toward Sofya. The machine gun erupted and a barrage of bullets threw up explosions of snow all around them. Sofya dove for cover behind the snowmobile, and Rick was caught off balance in the open as the trail of bullet impacts kicked up more snow.

As the gunner walked the stream of bullets toward Rick, Donovan reached up and grabbed Rick by the wrist, pulling him down into the frigid water just as the heavy slugs tore up the snow and ice where he'd been standing. Donovan found his regulator, took a breath, and pushed it toward a struggling Rick, who took a quick breath, then another, then relinquished it, and passed it back to Donovan.

The helicopter swept overhead. The silhouette flashed over the opening above them and bullets exploded into the open water, the slugs darting from the surface, slowing rapidly, and then sinking. Donovan looked into Rick's terrified face as he handed him the regulator. He could already see that the ice-cold water was slowing Rick's motor functions. He calculated how fast he could get to his snowmobile suit and his Sig, but as he hung underwater, buddy breathing with Rick, his pistol seemed a million miles away.

The noise below the ice changed. There was a repetitive thumping noise, followed by piercing snaps like the ice cracking. Then a deep vibration resonated from above. It took a moment for Donovan to realize that the helicopter had landed. He reached to take the regulator from Rick when a lift bag rushed past him rising toward the surface trailing a line that was tied to one of the AK-47 assault rifles. Another bag followed close behind, and inside the mesh container were magazines of ammunition.

As fast as he could move, Donovan slipped out of his tank, draped it over Rick's shoulder, and then looped the tether line around the tank as well, so Rick wouldn't drift away. Donovan took one last breath. He placed the regulator in Rick's mouth, relieved that Rick was still awake. Donovan shed his weight belt and floated upward. He snatched the rifle, and using his knife, separated the netting that allowed him to free a fully loaded magazine. Despite his cumbersome gloves, he was able to insert the magazine and pull the bolt, but he knew they would make it impossible to pull the trigger. Donovan used his knife to make a slice in the tip of his glove, then kicked toward the opening in the ice as hard as he could. He ignored the cold water that rushed down his arm as he continued holding his breath and raced the last few feet to the surface.

He erupted from the hole in the ice and came down firmly on his elbows. He ripped off his mask, tilted the gun to drain the barrel of water, and then brought the AK-47 to his shoulder. He ignored the bitterly cold air that froze the stock to his cheek. Thirty yards away the 212 idled on the snow, and trudging toward him were two men in white snowsuits. Donovan, anchored by his elbows, squeezed the trigger on the AK-47. The first man crumpled. The second man, caught by surprise and with nowhere to run or hide, was an easy target. Donovan dropped him with one shot. Then he swung the barrel toward the pilot. With his finger solidly frozen to the steel trigger, Donovan held the sight steady and sent two bullets through the side window. The pilot slumped forward, held only by his harness.

To his left, Donovan caught sight of another white-suited man as he stepped from behind the tent. The intruder had been out of Donovan's view and had snuck up unobserved. He was bringing a small compact machine gun to his shoulder. Donovan was helpless as he tried to pivot the heavy AK-47 around in time. When he heard the first gunshot, he knew he was a dead man. Four quick shots followed, and the man in white dropped his gun and staggered backwards, splotches of blood forming on his chest. Sofya emerged from behind the snowmobile, holding Donovan's Sig with both hands. She fired one last shot and the man dropped in a heap.

"Sofya!" Donovan yelled above the whine of the helicopter's engine.

Covered in snow, she turned her head and then pointed the pistol straight at Donovan.

"Sofya, it's Donovan. Put the gun down."

She looked at him, and then at the weapon she held, and then back at him, seemingly unsure as to what had happened.

"Sofya, hurry," Donovan said. "I need you to help me save Rick."

The words finally seemed to reach her. She lowered the weapon to her side, shook it from her gloved hand, and dropped it into the snow.

Donovan pulled the ice-cold AK-47 down into the lake to allow the warmer water to unfreeze his skin from the gun, and tossed the weapon up on the snow. He struggled to get his mask secured, took a deep breath, and submerged. Below him, in a maze of bubbles, he spotted Jesse with Rick in his arms, and he was bringing him up in a hurry. Donovan used his knife and freed the mesh bag holding the extra ammo and wrapped the cord around his wrist. He turned and kicked hard for the surface. He came up out of the water as far as he could and jabbed his knife into the ice to keep from sliding back into the water.

Hands reached down under his arms and began pulling. Donovan kicked and twisted until he was out of the water. Sofya yanked off his flippers and helped him to his feet. Turning, he dropped the bag of ammunition, went down on one knee, and grabbed Rick just as Jesse pushed him up to the surface. Donovan struggled to hold him in place. His waterlogged snowmobile suit made him far too heavy to lift. Beside Rick, Jesse jettisoned both tanks, and with Sofya's help, slithered up onto the ice like a seal. He dropped down next to Donovan, and together they pulled Rick's exhausted body up on the ice.

Rick turned on his side, vomited up water, and then curled up and began to shiver uncontrollably in the subzero air.

Sofya jumped up. "I'll get the survival blankets."

"Hang in there, Rick." Donovan unzipped Rick's snowmobile suit and began to free him from the sodden garment, while Jesse pulled away his gloves and boots. Sofya ripped the first blanket from its packaging and handed it to Jesse.

"Sofya, how warm is the shelter?" Donovan asked.

"It's not," she said. "We were trying to get the burner lit when we heard the helicopter."

"We have to get him to shore and build a fire," Jesse said. "Or he'll die. Jesus, we can't do anything in these suits. Help me get out of this thing."

Jesse turned so Sofya could unzip his dry suit. She helped him take off the gloves and boots. Jesse stepped out and let the suit crumple in the snow. He grabbed his snowmobile suit, yanked it on, pulled on his boots and hat, then he got down and helped Donovan wrap the blanket completely underneath Rick.

With Sofya's help, Donovan shed his dive suit and scrambled against the cold to get changed. In a movement that Jesse didn't see, Sofya slid Donovan's Sig back into the snowmobile pocket where she'd found it earlier

Jesse reached down, gripped Rick under his neck, and pulled him up and over his shoulder, and carried him to the snowmobile and placed him in the sled. Jesse jumped on the snowmobile, pressed the button, and the engine fired to life.

"Hurry, get on," Jesse yelled to both Donovan and Sofya. "It's going to take us a while to build a fire, and I don't know how long he has."

Donovan looked into Jesse's fear-filled eyes as Rick shivered uncontrollably. He turned his attention toward the idling helicopter. "Forget building a fire onshore. Get him to the helicopter."

Jesse snapped his head over his shoulder in a questioning look.

"There's heat inside the helicopter, and the stove is going at the cabin. Go! We're right behind you."

Jesse gunned the throttle and covered the distance in seconds.

Donovan turned to a trembling Sofya. "Help me gather Rick's clothes, he'll need them." Then he added, "When did you get my gun?"

"When you pulled Rick into the water. I was all alone, and the helicopter was turning to land."

"I was coming back," Donovan said as they ran toward the helicopter. "Could you have taken all of them out?"

"I don't know," she said. "Maybe."

When they reached the cabin of the helicopter, Donovan lifted the frozen clothes inside. Jesse was working to wrap the emergency blanket more tightly around Rick. Sofya climbed in to help, and Donovan closed the door and ran toward the cockpit.

Donovan processed his history involving helicopters. He'd hated them most of his adult life. Not that he avoided them, he just hated the things. With over ten thousand hours as a fixed wing pilot, there was very little about flying helicopters that translated to flying an airplane. Eco-Watch had owned and operated helicopters for years, mainly operating off of their oceangoing ships. Donovan had tolerated the flights he'd been forced to take with open disdain. Then one night over drinks, Janie Kinkaid, one of Eco-Watch's helicopter pilots, had issued a challenge. She'd called him out on his aversion to helicopters. Much bar-talk had ensued as the night continued, until Donovan accepted her challenge and they made a wager. The next afternoon, he found himself at the controls of one of Eco-Watch's Bell 412s. Janie was patient and helpful, though flying the machine was difficult and unnatural. Although Donovan did manage to safely take off and land and thus satisfy the challenge— he walked away still hating helicopters.

Donovan opened the cockpit door, found the quick release for the harness, and rolled the dead pilot out onto the snow. He brushed the shattered Plexiglas off the seat, climbed up, and settled behind the controls. He was well aware of Janie's glaring absence as he strapped in and adjusted the seat. Nevertheless, he reached down toward his knee and gripped the collective. It was the control that doubled as the throttle to both engines and also controlled the vertical component. No airplane had such a setup. Donovan clicked the setting that commanded the computer to spool up the engines from ground idle to flight mode. Above him the rotor began to spin faster, the engines built up speed and reached a steady whine. Donovan placed his feet on the pedals, which were used to keep the nose pointed in the direction they were flying. Between his legs was the cyclic control, or the stick, as Donovan called it, much to Janie's exasperation. It was the one aspect of flying a helicopter that might have evolved from an airplane.

Donovan searched for and found the instrument that Janie had told him always dictated if the thing would fly or not. The rotor speed gauge was in the green. Donovan put his cold, numb right hand on the rubber grip, took a deep breath, and pulled up on the collective.

The lightly loaded 212 lifted quickly off the ice. Donovan over-controlled, and the helicopter immediately began to descend and wobble. He pulled again, this time more carefully, and at the same time, he eased forward on the stick, and the 212, twenty feet above the lake, began to slowly drift forward.

Donovan's eyes were locked on the trees ahead. He added more pressure to the collective and used a combination of tension and fear to coax the helicopter higher. Hot air flooded the interior, yet the frigid wind pouring in from the shattered window was hugely distracting. Nothing felt natural, and Donovan reminded himself to keep forward pressure on the stick, that the helicopter would fly one hundred and forty knots if he let it. Donovan flew the oscillating 212 up and over the trees before he relaxed, and then by trial and error, managed to get the helicopter to fly straight and level. He made a slight turn in each direction, and then made a small climb followed by a descent in an effort to get a feel for the machine. Up ahead, across the ice and snow, he spotted the cabin. Thankfully, the Twin Otter was gone. He had the lake to himself for landing. His right hand was white and still partially numb. He was pretty sure the lack of blood flow was partly a result of the death grip he had on the controls.

Fixed on the smudge of smoke rising from the distant chimney, Donovan lowered the nose and began a gentle descent. The speed increased, and he, once again, over-controlled and was forced to react. His muscles tightened as he eased off of the collective. The helicopter dropped, and he raised the nose. They slowed, but were still a hundred yards from shore. As Donovan worked to nudge the 212 in the direction he wanted, he flew low enough to kick up a massive cloud of snow from the lake, which obscured his view and blew in through the broken window, dusting his legs.

Blinded, Donovan pushed the stick forward and the helicopter lurched. He accelerated out of the self-created snowstorm only to find the trees dangerously close. He stepped on the right pedal and eased the stick in the same direction, and the 212 thundered around in a sweeping turn to the right. Donovan slowly dropped the collective and raised the nose as the helicopter slowed and he began another approach. As the 212 came around, Donovan again caught sight of the trees, and fought the stick and collective until he had the machine traveling forward just above the lake, the storm of blowing snow behind them. The trees were visible straight ahead, and looming larger. He pulled back on the stick and dropped the collective. The second he did so, he knew he'd been too quick. The skids hit hard and he was pushed down in his seat. He dumped the collective and brought the engines back to idle.

Sliding forward with the remaining momentum, the 212's skids bounced through the drifts until the helicopter came to a stop not far from the shore. Donovan released his grip on the controls and with a sense of relief found the helicopter was sitting stationary on the ice, engines at idle, rotor spinning lazily—which was exactly how they'd started.

The rear door slid open, and Donovan twisted in his seat as Jesse jumped to the ground. The heat inside the helicopter had helped dramatically, and Jesse eased Rick, now dressed in Jesse's snowmobile suit, feetfirst to the ground. Rick draped his arm around Jesse's shoulder. In the same moment, they both shot Donovan a guarded glance that left no doubt that both men were eternally thankful to still be alive. They knew full well that Donovan was in no way an actual helicopter pilot.

"Have you got this?" Donovan yelled through the broken window.

"Yes. Why? What are you doing?" Jesse yelled, starting to shiver, wearing only his long underwear.

Sofya jumped down and slammed the helicopter's cabin door closed. She took Rick's other arm, put it across her shoulder, and slid in to support him. She looked at Donovan. "What's going on?"

"I'm taking this thing back to where we found it. I'll be back with the snowmobile and the equipment. Hopefully I'm back before the Twin Otter. Not a word about the helicopter to the charter pilots."

Jesse nodded his understanding, and with Rick sandwiched between them, he and Sofya made it up the hill and into the cabin.

Donovan took two quick breaths to steady himself. He put his left hand on the collective, flipped the switch, the engines spooled up from ground idle, and the rotor blades whipped through the air as they accelerated. A quick check of the rotor rpm, and Donovan once again lifted the 212 into the air. He used the torque from the tail rotor to rotate the helicopter a hundred and eighty degrees, and then nudged the stick forward. The helicopter wavered and pitched up and down slightly as Donovan gained altitude and flew out across the frozen lake. Safely airborne for the moment, he relaxed, and was surprised to find that despite the frigid north, he was sweating underneath his snowmobile suit.

# CHAPTER TWENTY-SIX

TREVOR WAS STILL wearing night-vision goggles when he called from the cockpit, "We've got company." The whine from the engines had just died and the rotor had nearly stopped spinning. "Someone walking this way."

Lauren had no way to see what was happening. She was sitting in the back of the helicopter between the two men they'd kidnapped. Marta, gun in one hand, put her other hand on the lever that would open the door.

"Wait. He's waving," Trevor said. "I can see what looks like a shotgun in one hand and a dog on a leash in the other."

"What kind of dog?" Marta asked.

"A German Shepherd," Trevor said. "Use the flashlight fastened to the bulkhead. Figure out if this guy is a threat or not."

Marta snatched the flashlight from its bracket. She leaned into the door latch and slid it open. Shining the light as an extension of her gun barrel, she illuminated the man and recognized him as he shielded his eyes. "Henryk!"

Lauren turned her head against the cold air rushing into the cabin. She released her seat belt, jumped down to the ground, and followed Marta into the hangar. She found the older man hugging Marta, and the German Shepherd wagging his tail as if waiting for his turn.

"Lauren," Marta said as she waved her closer. "This is Henryk. He and Dad go way back. Henryk, this is Lauren, one of my dear friends. And this is Baca. You're a good boy, Baca. Sit."

Marta knelt and hugged Baca as Lauren and Henryk shook hands. Lauren could tell from the firm grip and calloused fingers that Henryk was strong and wiry. He had a tall lanky frame, pleasant open features topped with thick gray hair, but his best feature were his intelligent blue eyes.

"I figured it was you that took the helicopter earlier," Henryk said. "I was only a few miles down the road helping my son with his tractor. I wish you'd have called. Where's Kristof?"

"He wasn't feeling well. He sends his best. It's just the three of us. Trevor is in the helicopter. We should probably go help him."

"I'm assuming Tomasz brought you up to date?" Henryk said as he waved his hand and Baca immediately laid down, his nose between his front paws.

"No," Marta said. "The building in town was raided, and Tomasz was beaten. He's in the hospital. Two of the men responsible are in the helicopter."

"The man from Prague?" Henryk asked.

"Gone."

"You got two of them? Good work." Henryk pursed his lips and shook his head in anger at the news. "Let's drag them inside where we can do this properly."

"We need information," Marta said. "Not revenge."

"Okay. Revenge can wait." Henryk's blue eyes narrowed into dark slits. "Sometimes it's better that way."

They pushed through the door that led back outside and found Trevor in the passenger compartment with a flashlight.

"Trevor," Marta called. "What are you doing?"

"Working," Trevor said as he jumped down to the ground and handed Marta three cell phones and two wallets. "I tie-wrapped both guys around the wrists and ankles, then I searched them. The smaller guy had two phones. This one is different than the other two, so I thought it might be Tomasz's."

Marta handed Lauren the phones.

"Trevor, I'm Henryk." The older man held out his hand. "Do you need any help getting those men inside?"

"It's nice to meet you, Henryk. Kristof spoke highly of you," Trevor said as they shook hands. "I think we're good. I want to leave them in the helicopter for now. They're strapped in nice and tight and aren't going anywhere."

"As long as they can't escape," Marta said, "let them lie in the back of the helicopter and think about what's going to happen to them."

"What else can I do for you, then?" Henryk asked.

"Do you have any fuel?" Trevor gestured at the Dauphin. "I'd like to top off the tanks on this thing so we're in a position to leave in a hurry if we need to."

"I'll bring the truck around," Henryk said, and whistled for Baca to follow as he hurried into the shadows.

"Marta," Trevor said. "You do what you need to do, but keep in mind the police are probably looking for us."

"Got it," Lauren said as she broke the first phone's security code and began pushing buttons until she found the call log. She held the screen so Marta could see. "Isn't that your number?"

"How did you get in so fast?" Trevor asked. "I looked, and they were all locked."

"It's a little trick Montero learned from the FBI. Depending on the model, if you push certain buttons at the same time, the code resets. Okay, there's a video here. It starts with a man in a chair." Lauren waited for Marta and Trevor to gather around, then she hit play.

"Who gave you the order to kidnap Anna, the woman from Interpol?"

"That's Tomasz's voice," Marta said in rush. "In the chair is the man we brought from Prague."

"I already told you, we didn't know she was Interpol. Tatiana Reznik told us to bring the woman, Anna, to her."

"Stop," Marta said. "I know of Tatiana Reznik. She's involved with gambling, drugs, and prostitution in the Czech Republic and other countries as well. She's probably in her late fifties, maybe even early sixties. Her methods are ruthless—she's a true throwback to the former communist rulers."

Lauren hit play. The rest of the recording cemented the fact that Tatiana Reznik was behind the murder. Lauren turned to Marta. "I know the security tape didn't show much, but what time was it taken?"

"Almost three hours before we arrived. Why?"

"The guys in the helicopter," Trevor said. "We have their phones and hopefully a list of who they called after they beat and no doubt interrogated Tomasz."

"Exactly," Lauren said. "What we need to know is what Tomasz gave up, and more importantly, who was given that information? I'll start trying to mesh the incoming and outgoing call logs from all three phones."

Henryk pulled up in a truck with a fuel tank fixed to the bed, and Trevor turned to talk to him. "I'll be right back," he said.

As Trevor and Henryk spoke, Marta climbed back into the helicopter. Lauren started to walk to the hangar and the promise of warmth to get started on her task. Once inside, she went to what passed for an office, which reeked of ancient coffee and cigarettes. She shed her coat, sat down at a small desk, and began working on the next phone.

Twenty minutes later, she had a list of the called and received phone numbers, the times, and the names or initials associated with each number. Marta and Trevor had given her space to work as they waited together. Lauren grabbed her coat and let herself out of the office and realized how nice it was to once again breathe fresh air. She rounded a corner, came to a door, and looked through the dirty window only to find Marta pressed against a wall, locked in a passionate embrace with Trevor. Without hesitation, Lauren opened the door and breezed into the room. Trevor, startled, jumped backwards, and dropped his arms to his side. Marta turned away and used her hands to quickly smooth her hair.

"Sorry to interrupt," Lauren said as she waved her sheet of paper. "I have the information we need. I think we need to get airborne."

"All right then." Trevor hurried to open the door that would lead them out to the hangar.

"Trevor, you don't mind flying us around for a little bit, do you?" Lauren asked. "It shouldn't take us long to get our answers."

"Where is it we're going?" Marta said before her eyes flew wide open as she realized what Lauren was saying. "That'll be effective."

"I think we have effective covered," Lauren said. "I'm concerned about how fast we can get this done."

"On my end, five minutes, and we'll be airborne," Trevor said as he opened the cockpit door.

"I'll go tell Henryk what we're doing," Marta said. "Don't start without me."

Lauren opened the door to the Dauphin's cabin. In the dim lights from the cockpit she could see both men. The larger of the two looked up with wide-eyed apprehension. The other turned his head as Lauren stepped aboard. Above them, the first engine turned over, and Lauren could feel the helicopter vibrate as both the main and tail rotors began to spin.

Marta stepped in the cabin and slid the door shut behind her. She slid on a headset, said something to Trevor, and then replaced it on the hook. From under her coat, she drew a sizable knife, the curved blade gleaming in what little light there was in the cabin. As the second engine spooled up, the man on the floor began to struggle against his bonds. His breath came in panicked gasps, and Marta placed her boot against his neck to persuade him to be still.

Lauren watched as Trevor slid on the night-vision goggles, and as soon as he adjusted to the different light level, the helicopter lifted free of the ground, thundering upward in the night sky. She felt the first of several turns before they seemed to level off.

Marta pulled out a Czech passport, opening it to show the man on the floor that it was his. "Do you speak English?"

"Yes," he said.

"I won't bother myself learning your name. When I speak to you, you'll know it. Do you understand?"

"Yes."

"Where is Tatiana Reznik?"

"I don't know who that is."

Marta knelt and placed the edge of her knife against the skin just under his earlobe. She pressed the blade with just enough force for him to feel the first sting.

"I don't know who she is!" His eyes bulged in their sockets.

Marta stood and went to the smaller man. "Viktor, I will remember your name. I'm sure you speak English as well; am I correct?"

"Yes," Viktor said.

"Viktor, I asked your friend a question, and he didn't answer. I'm going to ask you the same question. Where can I find Tatiana Reznik?"

Viktor shook his head. "I don't know her."

"Oh, but you do. You beat our friend Tomasz and waited at the hospital for his friends to show up, and here we are." Marta stepped away and raised her voice so both men could hear her. "If you don't tell me what I want to know, then your friend is going to die. You have ten seconds, and then I'm going to throw him out of this helicopter."

Lauren popped the latch and slid the door open. Viktor's expression turned into a mixture of confusion and surprise. The man on the floor began to scream in a language that Lauren didn't understand. With a tilt of her head, Marta gave Lauren the signal. Lauren moved to the center of the cabin, sat on the floor, and used both feet to push the horrified man closer to the blackness beyond.

"Tatiana is in Berlin," Viktor cried out, helpless as his friend slid nearer the edge. "She owns a club there, it's called Adrenaline. Now please, stop!"

Lauren caught Marta's final signal. She rolled the screaming man past the edge and in an instant, he was gone. Lauren slammed the door shut.

Marta turned to Viktor who had closed his eyes as if trying not to imagine his friend's freefall to earth. When he exhaled, all resistance had left his body.

Marta pressed the razor-sharp blade against Viktor's neck. "Talk."

"We silenced the man from Prague and interrogated the one you call Tomasz. We spoke to Fraulein Reznik and were instructed to allow Tomasz to be taken to the hospital. We were also sent to the hospital to set up and wait for whoever came."

"What did Reznik tell you to do?"

"She said to kill everyone."

"Is she the only person you report to?"

"Yes."

"How long is Tatiana going to be in Berlin?"

"I have no idea."

"So, the hospital here in Wroclaw was supposed to be a trap?"

"Yes. Fraulein Reznik said Archangel was coming from London, and that if we could kill him, she would make us very rich men."

"Tatiana used the name Archangel?"

"Yes. She hates him."

"Why?"

"Archangel supplies weapons to the people that keep Mother Russia from being great again."

"Did Tatiana tell you what Archangel looked like? Or his name?"

"Yes. She said his name was Kristof, that he was old and sick, and should be easy to kill."

"She was wrong, wasn't she?" A flash of anger crossed Marta's face as she said the words.

"Yes."

"I have a surprise for you, Viktor." Marta picked up a headset and said something to Trevor.

Lauren heard the distinctive sound of the Dauphin's landing gear being lowered, and an instant later they touched down. Even though Lauren knew the plan, she was momentarily disoriented by the sensation. In reality, Trevor had taken off, flown once around the property, and returned to hover only a few feet off the ground in the complete darkness. He had executed it all flawlessly with the help of his night-vision goggles. Lauren slid the door open and found Henryk and Baca standing over the man she'd kicked out of the helicopter. His nose was bleeding and it appeared as if he'd wet himself. She glanced at her watch. The entire interrogation had taken less than ten minutes.

Marta jerked Viktor out of the chopper and tossed him to the ground next to his colleague. She turned to Henryk, raising her voice to be heard above the idling rotor blades. "Both of these men beat Tomasz under orders from Tatiana Reznik."

"I know of Tatiana." Henryk shook his head in disgust. "I hear she is protected by the Russians."

"Why would she need to be protected?" Lauren asked.

"I've heard rumors that she deals in trafficking, mostly young girls from poor areas of Eastern Europe. The Russians turn a blind eye."

"Really?" Marta said. "Reznik is in Berlin. We're going there now. Bring these two to the rendezvous point near Brody, and we'll be there when we can."

Henryk's expression turned grim. "Are you sure you want me to bring them? I can easily take care of them here."

"I think we may still have use for them," Marta said. "And when we arrive at the Brody house, we'll want to refuel again."

"I'll make it happen," Henryk said. "Don't worry. I'll bring everything we'll need."

Marta kissed Henryk on each cheek, then turned and climbed back into the helicopter.

"Ready?" Trevor asked above the whine of the idling engines.

"How long is the flight to Berlin?" Marta asked.

"We have to do a little low-level trickery near the border, but no problem really," Trevor said. "It'll take a little over an hour."

Lauren strapped in and pulled out her phone. Just as before, there were no messages, only a wildly fluctuating signal. She thought of Calvin's earlier situation report on the solar storm. She calculated that the onslaught of radiation and supercharged particles should be relentlessly bombarding Earth's atmosphere by now and would rage for hours, if not days. Unseen above them, in the air above the heavy overcast, the Aurora Borealis was without doubt putting on another astounding display. As the rotor spun up to speed, Trevor eased the helicopter off the ground and switched off all the external lights as he accelerated the Dauphin toward the German border.

# CHAPTER TWENTY-SEVEN

HIS FEAR OF breaking through the already cracked ice played a large part in how delicately Donovan set the helicopter down. He was momentarily surprised when the skids touched gently, and he carefully allowed the full weight of the 212 to settle, fully prepared to climb away at the first hint of trouble. Convinced he was safe, he brought the engines to idle and sat inside the empty helicopter and tried to remember the shutdown procedure. While scanning the panel, he had another thought and began to scroll through the flight management system, trying to determine the 212's point of origin. As he clicked through the electronic pages, he found what he wanted. The 212 had departed from Thompson, Manitoba, and flown north. Donovan wondered how the pilot had obtained the coordinates, and as he scrolled, he found what he wanted, the full list of waypoints.

The first fix after leaving Thompson was the coordinates Michael had used when he was shopping for charters, a latitude and longitude that should have taken them to a lake twenty-five miles away. The second fix listed was the exact coordinates they'd given the pilots of the Twin Otter after they'd departed Churchill.

He thought for a moment. Then he spotted something that looked out of place. A frequency, 131.75, didn't fit the typical visual flight rules radio frequencies. He then searched until he found a chart of the area. Of all the posted frequencies, 131.75 wasn't one of them.

Donovan felt his anger rise. Their exact coordinates had been provided by talking with someone on the discreet frequency. Suddenly annoyed by the whining engines, he simply reached up and pulled both fire emergency "T" handles and the engines promptly shut down from lack of fuel. He found both battery switches on the overhead panel and switched them off, too. The only sound came from the gyros spinning down and the ticking from the engines as they rapidly cooled off.

Donovan searched the cockpit for any other paperwork. Other than a checklist, he found very little of interest. He bundled up, slid on his goggles, and let himself down from the cockpit. He memorized the registration number, went to where the pilot lay in the snow, searched him for any identification, and found nothing. He repeated the process on the other three corpses and came away empty-handed. He had no idea if the attackers were Russian, or what events had transpired for them to have traveled this far north only to lose their lives on this desolate lake.

As he pondered all the seemingly disconnected threads, Donovan began collecting the diving equipment and carefully packing it in the duffel bags. He was halfway through when he remembered the mesh bag with the pilot's identification that he'd collected inside the 737. In all of the chaos, he'd left it behind. Angry at his mental lapse, he finished packing the sled, making sure the AK-47 and extra ammunition went with him back to the camp, and as he cinched down the last strap, he had one more thought.

He stood for a moment, piecing together all of the events. That's when he spotted old tracks in the snow. On impulse, he retraced the footprints that Sofya had left as she fled the wrecked and sinking

Boeing. With the lack of any new snow since the crash, he followed her path until he stood where she'd collapsed. He began kicking through the snow until his boot connected with something solid. He kicked the object free of the ice and then knelt and lifted a Glock from the snow. He swept away the ice, pulled back the action, and found a bullet in the chamber. Sofya had a loaded gun when she fled the sinking Boeing.

Donovan stuffed the Glock in a pocket and hurried to the snowmobile. He cranked the engine, and took one last look around the frozen lake. Everything Eco-Watch had brought in was leaving with him. The next blizzard would cover the bodies and maybe even eventually the helicopter. He pictured the Boeing that lay beneath the frigid water, resting on the sandy bottom like an aluminum tomb. One day, those people would be found, still preserved in the icy water, and they could be given a proper funeral. The men on the surface of the lake would be found by wolves. There would be no ceremony for them.

Donovan nudged the snowmobile's throttle and maneuvered around the helicopter, and then gradually increased his speed until he was roaring across the lake toward the mouth of the river. He navigated through the river channel, but instead of speeding toward the cabin, he stopped and scanned the lake to see if the Twin Otter had returned. The airplane was nowhere to be seen, and he accelerated across the lake toward the cabin.

Jesse came running out of the cabin at the sound of Donovan's approach, slipping on his gloves and hat as he hurried down to the lake to meet him.

Donovan stopped at the shore but left the engine idling. He removed his helmet and peeled the ice away from his face mask. "How is he?"

"He's good. The cabin is nice and toasty. We filled him with hot liquid. He seems alert and functioning."

"That's good news. Look, Jesse, we've had a change of plans. I'm going to pull this snowmobile up behind the cabin, and then we need to obscure the tracks. I don't want the Twin Otter crew to know we're here when they get back."

"Uh-oh, what did you find?"

Donovan explained his theory about the coordinates he'd discovered aboard the 212, and the odd frequency. Jesse nodded as Donovan connected all of the pieces.

"I'm with you." Jesse rubbed his temples as Donovan finished. "I don't see how anything could have happened any other way. I was there when Michael made the phone calls. The only charter operator that asked for the coordinates was the one in Thompson. No one else had airplanes available, so they never asked where."

"There's some connection between the attack today and our charter crew," Donovan said. "We just need to find out what it is."

"What about Montero, is she armed?" Jesse asked.

"Yes. I'm not worried about her and Michael," Donovan said. "If this goes the way I hope it will, once the Twin Otter lands, either Michael or Montero will be the first off the plane and will head toward the cabin. The charter pilots will stay behind to secure the aircraft, and that's the separation we need. When they arrive, this is going to happen fast, so I'm not sure what to expect. I need you to watch over Sofya, try to keep her calm."

"You bet," Jesse said.

"I didn't have time to say anything earlier," Donovan said. "But you saved all of us out there, and I want to thank you. Your idea of floating up the AK-47 made the difference. What made you think to do that?"

"When I saw the chopper was coming in armed and all we had to fight with were knives, I thought of something Montero said to me on the charter flight. We were talking about preparation. She said something about never taking a knife to a gunfight. So I put a gun into the mix to change the odds."

"That you did, and then you kept your head, and without hesitation, did everything you could for Rick. I'm impressed."

"Don't be too impressed," Jesse said lowering his head. "I dove down to nearly seventy feet, twice, without any decompression stops. I may have screwed up."

"It wasn't a screw-up," Donovan said. "It was an act of bravery, and I can't tell you how happy I am that you did what you did. How do you feel?"

"I feel fine," Jesse said. "And I may be fine, but I needed my dive buddy to know what took place, just in case I start having problems."

"You tell me the second you have any symptoms of the bends. I mean it, and we'll abort this mission and get you to Churchill for medical attention."

"Thanks, I'm good for now." Jesse smiled and gestured to the snowmobile. "Lead the way. I'll start covering the tread marks."

Donovan went slow, easing the snowmobile up the hill and around to the back of the cabin. He shut off the engine, dismounted, and began to trudge through the snow, obliterating the telltale snowmobile tracks. He and Jesse walked up and down several times until all the signs were gone, and as they finished, Donovan heard a familiar drone. He scanned the sky until he spotted the Twin Otter low on the horizon.

"I see them," Jesse said, turning to Donovan. "That is them, right?"

"It's them. Let's go inside and get ready."

Donovan stomped the snow off his boots and suit as best as he could, and then pushed into the cabin. The air inside, heated by the glowing coals inside the stove, immediately fogged his goggles, and he slid them up on his forehead and unzipped his suit halfway so he wouldn't overheat. "Rick, how are you doing?"

"I'm still alive, thanks to you," Rick said, sitting in street clothes and stockinged feet, sipping from a mug.

"What's going on?" Sofya asked.

"I think the charter pilots sold us out," Donovan said, noticing that Jesse had removed one of the sheets of particleboard that had been nailed over the window, and now sunlight filled the cabin. Donovan found a pair of binoculars on the table and positioned himself to observe the approaching plane. He found a blurred shape, and he drew the Twin Otter into crisp focus just as the high-winged twin turboprop touched down. He could see the struts flex on the uneven surface and hear the propellers as they moved from forward thrust into reverse pitch to slow the plane. The Twin Otter reached trodden snow near the shore, and Paul turned the aircraft until it was pointed out across the makeshift runway on the frozen lake. The Twin Otter continued to sit there, both propellers idling.

"Why doesn't he shut it down?" Jesse asked.

"I'm not sure. He's got them throttled back to idle, so the blades aren't producing any thrust. I wonder if there's a problem." Donovan swept the binoculars forward and spotted Lonny still in the cockpit.

When the double cargo doors aft of the wing swung open, Donovan readjusted the binoculars to focus on Montero as she lowered the steel ladder into place, and then climbed down the four rungs from the airplane to the snow. Michael was right behind her. As they walked toward the cabin, Michael looked off to his left and then up at the cabin before he said something to Montero. She nodded as she slid her pistol from under her parka, keeping it partially hidden within her sleeve.

"Michael spotted the skid marks from the helicopter," Jesse whispered. "Montero's going to come in here with her gun drawn."

Donovan put down the binoculars and moved so he'd be the first person Montero saw when she burst through the door. He held his hands up in the air just as she rushed through the opening, the barrel of her Glock pointed at his chest.

"Please don't shoot me," Donovan said.

"Jesus!" Montero lowered the gun. "What are you doing here? Where's the snowmobile? Whose clothes got wet? What in the hell is going on?"

"How'd you get here?" Michael said from behind Montero. "I saw tracks in the snow. Was there a helicopter?"

"I'll explain later, we don't have much time," Donovan said. "Montero, I need you to go back out to the plane with me. Act like you forgot something, but keep an eye on Paul and Lonny. Michael, trade parkas with me. Do you have any idea why they're still running the engines?"

"It was a short flight," Michael said as he peeled off his heavy coat. "Paul wants to make sure the batteries are fully charged before he shuts everything down."

"We had company at the dive site—some guys in a helicopter started shooting at us." Donovan spoke as he zipped up Michael's coat and then handed Michael his Sig. "I think either Paul or Lonny radioed the helicopter pilots our coordinates. Michael, you're the last line of defense—there's an AK-47 in the sled out back if you need it. Montero, you're with me. I've already been shot at once today, so I'd appreciate it if you could keep that from happening again."

"What are we looking for?" Montero asked as she adjusted her face mask and goggles, leaving her gloves in her pocket so she could better handle her Glock.

"I'll explain on the way," Donovan said as he opened the door and allowed her to pass through first. "Okay, in the helicopter that attacked us, there was an out of place frequency set into the primary VHF radio, 131.75. I have a feeling one of our Twin Otter pilots was communicating with the helicopter, giving them our position."

"What if they simply changed the frequency when they were finished?" Montero asked.

"My guess is they're still using the frequency," Donovan said. "They might even be trying to reach the helicopter right now."

"Is anyone going to answer?"

"No," Donovan said as they reached the Twin Otter.

Montero climbed the ladder and bolted into the cabin. Donovan followed as fast as he could. As his eyes adjusted to the semi-darkness, he found Montero mid-cabin, holding a portable radio arm's length from a startled Paul. Donovan saw Lonny sitting in the cockpit, eyes forward, still monitoring the engines.

Donovan took the radio from Montero's hand and saw the numbers dialed in the active window were 131.75. Donovan yanked his hood back, peeled off his goggles and face mask, and glared at Paul. The expression of wide-eyed disbelief on the young pilot's face spoke volumes about his guilt.

"Why?" Montero asked.

In his peripheral vision, Donovan spotted Lonny in the cockpit taking in the scene unfolding in the cabin. The moment she locked eyes with him, the startled copilot erupted into action and pointed a pistol at Donovan.

Montero was quicker. She raised her Glock. Paul lunged at her, knocking her against the seats on the other side of the aisle. Lonny fired twice before Montero, off balance, put a bullet into Lonny's right shoulder. She twisted away and cried out in pain but managed to slam the propeller controls and throttles all the way to the stops before turning to start shooting again.

Donovan drew the Glock that Sofya had dropped in the snow. He fired twice, forcing Lonny to duck back behind the bulkhead. Donovan started forward, but stumbled over Paul's body in the aisle, a crimson pool already gathering on the floor surrounding his head. One of Lonny's errant shots had struck Paul, and he was down. As Donovan stopped to step over the body, the twin turboprop engines finally surged to full power and threw him backwards against Montero. As the plane accelerated, the skis beat roughly against the uneven snow. Montero tried to steady herself as she squeezed off three more shots.

Lonny ducked to avoid them.

Without hesitation, Donovan grabbed Montero around the waist and charged toward the open cargo door at the rear of the plane. He went down on his hip, and they slid the last four feet on the metal floor and stopped at the edge of the door, using the seats as cover. When the Twin Otter bogged down and swerved hard in the heavier snow, they were thrown into the aisle. Donovan rolled them back toward the door as two more wild shots were fired from the cockpit.

"What are you doing?" Montero yelled.

"We're out of here! Empty your Glock into the left engine. Aim just behind the exhaust stack!"

Montero squeezed off the remaining rounds in her gun until there was nothing. Then holding her tight against his chest, Donovan pushed against the floor and rolled them both out of the plane.

They dropped from the Twin Otter and hit the surface of the lake, bounced, and then tumbled and rolled in the snow drifts. Donovan lost his grip on Montero. Snow filled his nose and ears as he spun sideways. He came to a stop on his stomach. He moved his arms and legs and carefully raised himself on all fours, shaking the snow from his face. He blinked his eyes to see the Twin Otter accelerating away from them.

A cloud of black smoke erupted from the left engine, followed by the disintegration of the cowling as the engine tore itself apart from the inside. The snow was peppered with shrapnel and debris as a dirty orange fire consumed the wing. With the right engine still at takeoff power, the Twin Otter careened hard to the left toward the shoreline, nearly digging a wingtip into the heavy snow. Lonny corrected, and the left wing lifted clear of the snow. The airplane wobbled, lifted off, and staggered into the air.

Donovan watched as Lonny immediately tried to bank away from the trees, but instead, the battered and weakened left wing snapped near the root, twisted, and fluttered into the air as the fuselage of the Twin Otter plummeted back to the surface of the lake. Parts began to shed from the impact, and the full thrust from the right engine powered what was left of the Twin Otter straight into the trees. The collision silenced the remaining engine and shredded the airframe, splintered trees, until finally, the mangled airplane came to a rest upside down, the tail section twisted at an odd angle. The sound of the crash combined with the snapping trees echoed back and forth across the lake, until the ruptured fuel tanks ignited with a whoosh and the wreck became an inferno.

"That's just great!" Donovan heard Montero behind him.

He turned to find her on her back, propped up on her elbows. No hat. Her goggles twisted around her neck. Snow packed in her hair and against her face, he could see rage and disbelief in her eyes.

"Good plan, Nash, let's blow up the only way we have to fly out of this godforsaken place! I could have neutralized her, and you could have gotten control of the plane. But no, let's shoot the engine and jump."

Donovan saw Montero's anger grow as she tried to peel away the ice frozen to her eyebrows.

"Would you please calm down?"

"I will not. In fact, I'm going to yell at you until we both freeze to death. And where did you get that Glock?"

"I found it near where I rescued Sofya. She had a gun when she fled the Boeing."

"Well, it doesn't matter much now, does it? We're never leaving this place."

Donovan heard the sound of a snowmobile engine. Someone from the cabin was coming to get them. "If you'll stop yelling at me, I can explain, we have a way out."

Montero staggered to her feet and began brushing the snow off her suit. "So what have you got in mind? Travel a hundred and fifty miles in a snowmobile, camp out, and live off the land? How very cable TV of you. Like I said, the plane was our way out."

Donovan stood as the snowmobile drew closer. Judging from the driver's parka, Michael was coming to their rescue. As he came to a stop, Donovan saw he was right. Michael pulled up the visor on his helmet and shut off the engine.

"Is everyone okay?"

Before Donovan could say a word, a muffled sound came from Donovan's parka. Michael and Montero both looked at him, confused.

"Uh-oh." Donovan reached into a side pocket and removed the portable radio that Montero had taken from Paul. It was still on and set to the suspicious frequency.

"Romeo Charlie Tango, come in, repeat coordinates, over."

"Oh shit, someone's close," Michael said as he warily scanned the sky. "We need to go, right now. It won't take them long to spot the smoke from the burning Twin Otter."

Montero also looked skyward while simultaneously unzipping a pocket high on her left shoulder. She pulled out another magazine for her Glock, and in seconds, she once again had a fully loaded pistol.

"Montero, get on. We need to get to the cabin." Donovan looked at Michael who would have heard by now from Jesse everything that had happened at the dive site. "We've got one chance to get out of here."

"You're still alive, so Janie's got to be a good teacher," Michael said as he cranked the snowmobile's engine and lowered his visor.

Montero opened her mouth and then promptly closed it. She cocked her head as if she hadn't heard him correctly. "He said *Janie*, right? As in our Janie, our helicopter pilot? Are you saying we have a helicopter?"

"Yes. We just don't have Janie," Donovan replied.

# CHAPTER TWENTY-EIGHT

LAUREN OPENED HER eyes. She was disoriented for a few seconds. As the sound of the turbine engines and the rotor registered, she realized she was with Trevor and Marta in the helicopter, headed for Berlin. She rubbed the last remnants of sleep from her eyes and looked out the front. The glow of a large city reflected against the base of the low clouds. Trevor kept the helicopter in perfect position one hundred feet above the road. As he'd explained earlier, if they did accidentally make an intermittent blip on someone's radar, they'd be assumed to be a truck or other vehicle. Using his night-vision goggles, he could easily avoid collisions with any obstacles. Lauren found the volume on her headphones and adjusted it upwards. Marta and Trevor paused their conversation.

"Did you have a good nap?" Marta asked.

"Not bad, what are we discussing?"

"I was asking Trevor how he knows exactly where this nightclub is located."

"We ran an operation out of here about a year and a half ago," Trevor replied. "An extraction similar to this one. Only the principal came along willingly, that time."

"Is there any intel from that past op we can use tonight?" Lauren asked.

"The club is on the top floor of the Constellation Hotel, which is one of a cluster of high-rise buildings built around the SONY center. Being downtown, the general noise level will help mask the sound of the helicopter. There is a landing zone on the roof of the Constellation, but the higher buildings nearby make the chances of someone spotting us a rather high probability."

"I'd like to come in from the roof," Marta said. "I have a feeling that Tatiana Reznik knows exactly who comes in the front door. What about a drop and go? You could retreat and come pick us up if we need you."

"That works, but the stealth aspect might be compromised," Trevor said.

"That might be impossible to avoid," Marta said. "How tight was security when you were here before?"

"Average and predictable," Trevor said. "They were not much more than amateurs, glorified bouncers really, guarding the front door, flirting, never expecting anyone to come in from above."

"Though, with Tatiana here, that might boost the talent level, or at least the overall numbers," Lauren said. "Trevor, what about the layout? Where are we likely to find her?"

"The club is on the fifteenth floor, there's another level above that, and then the roof. We had blueprints that showed the stairs to the roof. There were two large spaces on the upper level, but we were never inside. They could be offices, an apartment, or storage. Who knows, but I doubt Tatiana tends bar."

"Does she cultivate girls from the club?" Lauren asked. "Could the upstairs rooms be a private club?"

"I think the clientele is all wrong," Trevor said. "Adrenaline is true to its name. It's a high-energy club with typically moneyed, hipster twenty- and thirty-year-olds, dancing, drinking, doing drugs, and hooking up. Not what I would describe as a brothel."

"Loud and chaotic," Marta said. "I like it."

"Marta, make sure you have the two-way radio," Trevor said. "It should work in short-range situations."

"We'll need it. My cell phone shows no coverage at all," Marta said.

"The solar storm is playing havoc with the electrical grid." Lauren looked at her own phone and found no signal. "It could be a plus. Everyone we encounter is used to communicating via phone. If we can't use them, they can't either."

"Okay, I can see the buildings of downtown. We're going to come in fast," Trevor said. "I'm not actually going to land, but I'll hover low enough that the jump won't be more than a foot or two, then I'm out of there, but I won't go far. If you can't make it back to the roof for extraction, let me know. There is a big park a few blocks to the north. If you can make it there, I'll be able to see you via the infrared and guide you to an alternate pickup point."

Lauren looked over Trevor's shoulder at downtown Berlin. She double-checked her Glock and tested the weight of her ankle holster that held a small palm-sized Sig. Lauren had no idea how many weapons Marta typically carried, but she knew that Marta was most certainly going to be the most lethal person in the room.

Marta reached between the seats and squeezed Trevor's arm.

"Be safe," Trevor said. "We're there in three, two, one. Go!"

Lauren held on tightly as Trevor suddenly decelerated and brought them to a rock-solid hover above the roof. Marta slid open the door and jumped into the darkness, hit and rolled, and then was up, motioning for Lauren to follow. Buffeted by the air from the thundering rotor blades, Lauren jumped. As soon as she felt the impact, she, too, bent her knees and rolled away. Marta reached up and slammed the door shut, and Trevor climbed away. Lauren's eyes adjusted to the light from the surrounding buildings as she followed Marta toward a door.

Condensation from their breath clouded in the air as they waited, listening for any sound coming from the other side. Marta motioned for Lauren to back away, and with her silenced Makarov, she took aim, destroyed the lock, and pulled the door open. Lauren followed as they went down a set of metal stairs probably designed as a fire escape. She could feel a rhythmic pulse resonating through the handrail.

As they reached the bottom of the stairwell, Marta paused at another door where she lightly tested the knob and found it was unlocked. Wordlessly, Lauren moved to where she could open the door. She gripped the handle and when Marta nodded, Lauren pulled it open.

Marta, both hands on her Makarov, swept the empty hallway and then signaled Lauren that it was clear. Together they moved silently down the carpeted hallway, turned the corner, and hurried to the first door they found. It was locked.

Lauren moved to the next door. A click told them that it was open. Marta pushed inside. Lauren followed, closing the door as quietly as she could. The lights were on, and Lauren surveyed the large office. A desk and credenza filled an entire wall, and a large flat-screen monitor was mounted behind the desk. Two overstuffed chairs flanked a sofa on the opposite wall, which was decorated with three large paintings, each a detailed still life depicting rural European cottages from a century ago. Lauren decided that the room, while designed to radiate strength, had a decidedly feminine style.

Marta went straight to the desk to search through the few papers scattered there. Lauren continued to take in the room, and her trained eye was drawn to a security camera lodged high on the bookcase. Lauren touched Marta on the arm and pointed out the lens at the same time they both heard a sound from the hallway. Lauren was closest, and moved to be behind the door if it opened. Marta sat down in the plush desk chair and swiveled to face whoever was coming. Lauren heard voices and gripped her Glock tighter as the doorknob turned and the door swung open.

"Who in the hell are you?" an angry female voice called out as she and a man strode into the room. "What are you doing in here?"

Lauren pushed the door closed, bringing her pistol up as the latch clicked. An overly manicured woman, pushing sixty, spun around and glared at Lauren, her heavily made-up face the picture of outrage. The man with her was easily ten years older, with thinning strands of gray hair combed straight back from a narrow face. He seemed less startled than the woman, though his eyes were alert and calculating, which Lauren's mind judged far deadlier.

Marta stood and walked briskly around the desk until the barrel of her gun was leveled at the older woman's face.

"What do you want?" Tatiana said. "I'll have you both arrested."

As Marta pulled back the hammer of her Makarov, the click echoed through the room. "Tatiana, be quiet."

The woman bristled, clearly not missing the fact that she'd just been spoken to like an errant child.

"I'm going to say this once. Archangel sent me. Do as I say, or I will kill you both." Marta produced two thick tie-wraps and handed them to Lauren. "Both of you, put your hands behind your back."

They complied, and Lauren snugged the plastic tight. She quickly frisked them, finding a passport in the man's pocket. She flipped it open. A Russian diplomat.

"I'm Dmitri Sobolev, and as you can see, I have diplomatic immunity issued through the Russian embassy."

"Not tonight, you don't," Marta said. She turned her attention to Tatiana, hesitated, and once again locked eyes with Sobolev. "I've heard that name before. You're SVR, aren't you?"

"I'm a diplomat with the Russian embassy," he said. "My business is my own, and I won't be interrogated by some little—"

Marta cupped her hand and hit him across the cheek in such a way that the sound of the pop was as surprising as the sting. As his head turned from the blow, Lauren could see the man's expression—utter astonishment.

"The camera on the bookshelf," Lauren asked. "Who is watching?"

"This room?" Tatiana answered. "No one."

"The monitor," Lauren said. "I want to see the entire club, front entrance included."

"There's a remote on the credenza," Tatiana said. "I guess I'd want to watch my back, too, if I were wanted by Interpol for questioning about a mass murder."

Lauren ignored her, found the remote, and brought the monitor to life.

"As the proprietor of a popular club, I work closely with law enforcement to ensure that any unsavory types are ejected from the premises and the appropriate authorities notified. I assume everyone in Europe knows about you by now."

Lauren's attention was drawn to the monitor. The screen was divided into eight different camera views. Upper left showed street level, and Lauren watched as several men hurried across the polished floor, pushing through people waiting for the elevator. When her eyes came to the feed in the lower left corner, she saw the image of herself standing with a remote control in her hand and Marta behind her with a gun pointed at Dmitri.

"She lied; we're about to have company."

"How many?" Marta asked, keeping the barrel of her pistol pointed at both Dmitri Sobolev and Tatiana.

Lauren studied the individual screens until she found the one that gave her a view of where the elevator opened into the lobby of the club. "Six,"

"Dmitri, are those your people?" Marta asked.

The Russian shrugged.

Marta pulled the radio from her pocket. "Extraction in five minutes."

"Roger," Trevor responded.

Lauren watched the monitor. The men were less than a minute from a set of stairs that presumably led up to where they were standing.

"The roof," Marta said as she prodded Dmitri in the small of his back with her pistol. "Both of you keep moving or I'll put a bullet in your elbow."

Lauren opened the door as Marta escorted Tatiana and Dmitri toward the fire escape to the roof. Once in the hallway, Marta kept moving, and Lauren kept turning and looking behind them, unsure when and where the men would appear. They reached the door to the stairwell, and as they ascended, Lauren could hear the heavy thump of a helicopter's rotor.

Marta's radio crackled to life and Trevor spoke excitedly. Lauren couldn't hear what he was saying, but Marta stopped and snapped her head around, shooting Lauren a worried look.

"New plan," Marta said. "There's a police helicopter about to land on the roof. We exit out this door and everyone stays low and follows Lauren. I'm bringing up the rear. If either of you tries to escape or slow us down, I'll shoot you. Lauren, go out, turn left, and run in the opposite direction of the police helicopter. Our friend is watching for us. Ready?"

Lauren nodded and put her hands on the door handle.

"Go!" Marta cried as the door at the bottom of the stairs opened.

Lauren burst out into the night. Above her, a blue-, white-, and yellow-colored helicopter with POLIZEI written on the side was descending. Pelted by the rotor downwash, Lauren put her arm up to shield her eyes, ducked, pivoted to her left, and ran. She looked forward, but all she saw was the edge of the building and the sprawling lights of Berlin beyond.

As Lauren continued to close the distance to the edge, a dark shape began to rise above the side of the building. The silhouette of Trevor's helicopter blocked the lights behind it and hovered as close as he dared to the drop-off. Lauren kept running and realized that the door wasn't open. As she neared, Trevor inched the Dauphin toward her. Lauren grabbed the handle as she reached the side of the chopper. She threw the lever and slid the door open just as Marta arrived with the others. Tatiana went first, followed by Dmitri, and then Marta. Lauren was about to lift herself aboard when the spotlight from the police helicopter lit up the night. Lauren dropped to the ground, blinded, as Trevor peeled away and descended below the edge of the building for cover.

Lauren crawled to the precipice and looked down, fighting through the spots dancing before her eyes. Through the spinning disk of the rotor she could see Trevor, hands on the controls. He'd stripped off his night-vision goggles. Lauren glanced behind her— the police helicopter was hovering low enough that the men inside were jumping to the roof. She looked down and saw Marta in the open doorway of the helicopter; she had her arm outstretched, and was using her fingers to count down from five.

Lauren crouched like a sprinter, and as Marta lowered her last finger and made a fist, Lauren heard the rotor blades change pitch and they bit harder into the damp air, pulling the helicopter upward. Lauren timed her launch, and the second the spinning rotor blades were above her, she took two steps and pushed off into space just as the doorway appeared. She misjudged the distance and hit hard against the ledge of the door, frantically trying to grab hold of anything to stop her as she began to slide out. Marta grasped her by the arm and pulled as Trevor continued to climb. Without warning, he banked, and Lauren was able to kick her way inside. The moment Marta slammed the door shut, she turned and pointed her gun at Dmitri, who had started to move toward her. He backed down as Trevor sped away, diving below the tops of the buildings.

Gasping for a full breath, Lauren wrapped her arms around her torso and rolled onto her back, fighting for air. As the first shriek of precious oxygen inflated her lungs, she felt tears fill her eyes. The second and third breaths came easier, and she finally opened her eyes. Marta was leaning over her, and Lauren realized that her friend was holding her hand, squeezing. With Marta's help, Lauren was able to sit up. In the dim light, Lauren spotted Dmitri cross-legged on the floor. He looked disheveled, an expression of resignation etched on his lined face. Tatiana leaned against him. Though her eyes were closed, she was clearly in pain. Lauren saw blood on the floor next to her just as she noticed the wound in her upper arm.

"They shot her?" Lauren asked, still breathing fast.

"No, I did," Marta said. "She slowed down."

# CHAPTER TWENTY-NINE

"WE'LL NEED TO dump all of our equipment," Donovan called out as Michael maneuvered the snowmobile to the edge of the lake near the cabin and shut it down. "Montero, go get the team ready to travel."

Michael began to lift the duffel bags out of the sled and stack them in the snow.

Donovan looked across the lake. The sun was low in the sky and partially obscured by incoming clouds. The weather was changing, and he felt a new urgency. It was going to be risky enough to fly the helicopter to Churchill in the dark, but he'd counted on the Northern Lights to help light the way. If clouds rolled in, it would create an additional set of problems.

"We'll be airborne before that weather gets here," Michael said as if sensing Donovan's concerns. "It'll be easy—you've already soloed, and I've got like, an hour flying the Eco-Watch helicopters, plus I sat and watched Janie and Eric in the simulator when they were upgrading to the new 412."

"Is this entire hour you have flying helicopters in a simulator, by chance?"

"Pretty much," Michael said.

"What did you learn?"

"I learned firsthand that helicopters are unnatural, satanic machines, and they should be left to the truly touched to fly."

"Good to know," Donovan said as a small smile came to his face. If Michael could joke around, all wasn't lost. Donovan leaned down and discarded the dry suits, tanks, and accessories such as the masks, weights, and flippers. He rearranged the survival equipment and made sure that the AK-47 and the ammunition were within easy reach. As he finished, Sofya and Rick, fully bundled up against the cold, came through the door, followed by Jesse, who had a section of cardboard and duct tape in his hand. Montero brought up the rear, a backpack slung over her shoulder.

"I can drive," Rick said.

"Shotgun," Montero called out and straddled the seat, leaving room for Rick in front of her. "You know what, Sofya, I think there's room up here for three of us."

Donovan watched as Rick joined the group scrunched together on the seat of the snowmobile, then he and Michael and Jesse found places in the sled. In preparation for the icy blasts of cold air once they were under way, Donovan pulled his stocking hat down as far as he could and adjusted his goggles. Michael and Jesse did the same thing.

"Can all of you ride up there?" Michael called out.

Rick and Sofya had claimed the helmets and Montero adjusted her equipment. "We'll be fine," she said, turning to them. "This takes me back to being a teenager growing up in northern Illinois."

"Am I the only one who can't picture Montero as a teenager?" Michael said, his gloved hands trying in vain to pull the zipper of his snowsuit snug against his neck.

"I'll have you know, I was prom queen, once, for about five minutes," Montero said over her shoulder.

"I'm getting a clearer picture," Michael said. "Why only five minutes?"

"The prom king whispered something in my ear that I felt was extraordinarily crude and inappropriate, so I decked him. As I was waiting for my dad to come pick me up, they crowned some other girl as queen."

"Your dad had to come get you?" Donovan asked. "Where was your date?"

"The prom king *was* my date."

"There it is," Michael said. "That's the image I was looking for, thanks."

Rick brought the snowmobile to life, and moments later they swung out on the lake and began to build speed. The trip went by in silence, and Donovan, Michael, and Jesse all continuously scanned the horizon. There was a respite from the arctic blast as Rick slowed to funnel them through the channel. As they reached the end of the river and broke out onto the other side, Donovan could see their destination. In the waning light, the helicopter looked frozen and abandoned on the desolate lake.

When Rick stopped, he left the snowmobile far enough away so as not to be a problem when they took off. Montero was the first to climb out. She was looking up at the sky when Michael said, "I hear something."

"I hear it, too," she said. "Which way?"

Donovan heard the distinct sound of an airplane, one with a radial engine. The ebb and flow of the sounds told him it was maneuvering. A crisp staccato drumming reached them, and then paused before continuing.

"That's automatic weapons fire," Montero said. "The cabin. They've got to be firing at the cabin."

"Everyone, get in the helicopter!" Donovan called out.

"You guys get airborne," Montero said as she grabbed one of the helmets.

"Where are you going?" Donovan asked.

"If they catch us on the ground, we're done," she said. "I'm going to use the snowmobile to create a diversion and lead them away from here. I'm going to need to go fast. Can you get rid of that sled?"

"At least take the AK-47." Michael threw off the attachments that connected the sled to the snowmobile as Montero restarted the engine.

"The AK-47 is yours. I'm going to be busy driving," she said. "But I will take the radio. Call me when you're airborne, and I'll bring them back this way for an ambush."

"How are you going to hear the radio?" Donovan asked as he dialed in a common frequency, and showed it to Michael before placing it in Montero's gloved hand.

"The LCD lights up when there's an incoming call, right?" Montero asked.

"Yes, but how are you going to notice?" Michael asked.

Montero sat down and wedged the body of the radio under her thigh until only the LCD display was visible. She lowered her visor and hit the throttle. With very little weight aboard, the powerful machine kicked up a plume of snow as Montero gunned it, heading for the opening to the river.

Donovan ran to the helicopter. Sofya was already aboard and she helped Rick climb in as Jesse hastily used the duct tape and cardboard to try to cover the shattered side window in the cockpit. Donovan went straight for the pilot's seat, while Michael ran around to climb in the other side. Jesse finished his field repair and joined Sofya and Rick in the cabin.

Michael found the checklist and flipped through the laminated pages. In the calmness of the interior, Donovan's breath froze and almost obscured his goggles with each exhale. He pulled off his cumbersome gloves, and from memory, pushed in the two fire handles he'd pulled earlier, flipped on both battery switches, and let his thumb hover over the switch that would start the first engine.

"Hit it," Michael said as he scanned the checklist.

The turbine engine began to spool up, followed by a familiar thump that told Donovan the ignitors had started combustion. Overhead, the rotor began to spin and the cabin rocked as it gained speed. Donovan watched the engine instruments climb into the green and then stabilize. Without waiting for Michael, Donovan hit the switch to start the second engine. He listened as the same series of events took place while he fastened his seat harness and cinched it tight. He threw the switch to take the computers from ground idle to flight mode, and the engines and rotor accelerated. He slipped his gloves back on and gripped the rubber grips of the cyclic and collective. After a hurried scan of the engine panel, he checked the rotor speed and engine rpm, glanced at Michael who nodded that he was ready. Then he smoothly pulled on the collective, and the 212 lifted away from the ice.

As before, Donovan over-controlled, and the helicopter descended and banked both left and right as he fought the oscillations he'd created. As if he needed help, Michael casually pointed in the direction they had to fly. Donovan made the corrections and the 212 began to bank and move forward to parallel the shoreline. Donovan flew slightly below the tree line and in the general direction that Montero had headed.

"You're doing great!" Michael said above the rotor noise. "I know you're probably not taking requests, but the lower we fly, the harder we'll be to spot."

"Good to know." Donovan gripped the collective, trying to get a better feel of the controls. He eased forward on the cyclic and the 212 picked up speed. Donovan spotted the gap in the trees that marked the river. He banked right and then left before aiming straight for the mouth of the river. Light touches on the pedals kept the 212 pointed where he wanted to go, and he found a flicker of confidence as he eased the helicopter lower.

The relative ease of flying over the open lake disappeared the instant Donovan nestled the 212 against the treetops that lined each side of the river. He clenched his teeth as he made each exacting turn to keep them dead center above the frozen channel.

"If I know Montero, she'll lead them straight toward us," Michael said. "I need to be ready."

"Go!" Donovan said, afraid to take his eyes off his flying for even a second. Michael threw off his harness and climbed over the seat into the passenger compartment. Donovan eased up the collective and the helicopter climbed slightly, and then the channel forced him to make a hard turn to the right. Donovan heard the blades make a distinct thumping sound as they bit into the dense air and pulled the helicopter through the abrupt change in direction.

From memory, Donovan knew that up ahead there was a hard left, followed by an easy right, and then they'd be at the end of the channel. Michael had already set Montero's frequency in the 212's primary radio. All Donovan needed to do was press the push to talk button on the cyclic, and her radio would light up. He made the first turn, pressed the transmit button multiple times, and then focused on the next bend in the channel.

As he made the final turn, a small sliver of the frozen lake came into view. Out on the open ice, Montero was hunched low on the snowmobile and zigzagging in their general direction. Above her, and off to the right, was a de Havilland Beaver, flying low and slow. Orange muzzle flashes erupted from an open window, followed by miniature geysers in the snow marking the impacts threatening to intersect with Montero.

Donovan pulled to slow the helicopter, and then kicked hard on the pedal that swung them broadside to the oncoming airplane. A rush of cold air enveloped Donovan as behind him, Michael slid open the door. Coming fast, Montero peeled off to her left to avoid the gunfire from the Beaver at the same moment Michael opened up with the AK-47. Donovan winced at the loudness of the machine gun as Michael's aim sent heavy 7.62 rounds straight into the Beaver's engine. The surprised pilot, intent on watching Montero, made a panicked turn and tried to climb. Michael adjusted, and the bullets continued to stream into the Beaver, shattering the windscreen and pouring into the cockpit and cabin. Trailing smoke, the bush plane flashed over the top of them and was gone. Donovan pivoted the 212 to try to keep the damaged Beaver in sight. The airplane, engine pouring oily smoke, climbed nose high, slowed dramatically, and while still in a tight turn fell off on one wing and plummeted into the trees and exploded.

The smell of smoke filled the cabin as Donovan made a wide circle above the crash site before he banked to fly toward Montero, who stood on the ice next to the snowmobile. Donovan couldn't help but relish another wave of relief as the helicopter's skids touched down smoothly on the ice and Montero began running toward them.

Seconds later, with Montero aboard, Michael climbed back into the cockpit, and Donovan felt a heavy congratulatory slap on his shoulder.

"Nice job," Michael said as he slid into the copilot's seat and began to buckle his harness. "Though I was wrong and I owe you an apology."

"Wrong? About what?"

"We're not going to beat this weather. It's starting to snow."

Donovan looked out across the lake and was surprised at how fast the visibility had dropped. Snow swirled around the helicopter as he once again gripped the controls, held his breath, lifted the 212 into the sky, and set a rough heading toward Churchill.

# CHAPTER THIRTY

"Everyone stay sharp," Trevor called from the cockpit. "I can see two people waiting on the ground. One of them looks to be Henryk."

Having had the wind knocked out of her, Lauren was finally breathing without difficulty. The flight from Berlin to Brody, Poland, hadn't been long, only twenty minutes, but Trevor flew a circuitous route to confuse anyone who might be trying to track them on radar as they slipped across the border unseen. Marta spent part of the flight tending to Tatiana's gunshot wound, though it wasn't much more than a flesh wound. Judging from Tatiana's facial expressions, Marta made little effort to minimize her discomfort.

"Henryk and who else?" Lauren asked, concerned.

"Probably one of Henryk's men from Wroclaw." Marta gripped her Makarov and double-checked it as Trevor lowered the wheels for landing. With a gentle bump, they were down.

"Marta, you're not going to believe this," Trevor called out over his shoulder. "The second man is Kristof."

Lauren instantly looked at their prisoners. Dmitri remained neutral, as he had since they'd first met, but Tatiana looked absolutely terrified at the thought of Archangel waiting for her.

"What in the hell," Marta muttered as she slid the door open and jumped out into the night.

Lauren eased herself to her feet and stepped down to the frozen grass. Trevor shut down the engines, and in the near silence of the remote woodlands safe house, the only sound was the still-spinning rotor blades knifing through the air. Moments later, Trevor climbed down out of the cockpit and joined Lauren. With the helicopter shut down, they could easily hear Marta.

"What are you doing here? We had a deal, and yet you find it necessary to check yourself out of the clinic to come spy on me."

"The doctor diagnosed me with fatigue," Kristof said. "I caught a commercial flight out of Gatwick to Wroclaw. Henryk picked me up."

"Dad!" Marta pressed her palms together, as if praying. "If the doctors tell you you're suffering from fatigue, you have to rest."

"So what, I'm a little tired. I've been fleeing from assassins. That makes an old man tired. I did take a nap on the plane."

"How did you even know where we—" Marta started, but with one knowing glance at Henryk, she slumped in exasperation. "Never mind."

"Henryk is a good man." Kristof's voice softened. "When I managed to get a call through to him, he gave me the update on Tatiana Resnick. Where is she?"

"We have more than just Reznik," Marta said. "She was with a Russian diplomat, Dmitri Sobolev."

"Dmitri?" Kristof planted his cane and headed for the helicopter.

Lauren held out her arms and Kristof hugged her and kissed her on both cheeks. He gave Trevor a brief handshake. Trevor stepped aside as Kristof climbed aboard the helicopter.

"Hello, Kristof," Dmitri said.

"Is there a light?" Kristof said to anyone. Moments later a small dome light illuminated the interior. "Dmitri, you look like hell."

"Your little girl, she's good." Dmitri tried to smile. "You should be proud."

"I am." Kristof produced a pocket knife and sliced away the plastic strip holding Dmitri's wrists.

"You two know each other?" Marta asked.

"We have for years." Kristof reached out to help pull Dmitri up by the hand, and the men briefly hugged.

"You've lost weight," Kristof said as he held Dmitri by the shoulders and looked his old friend up and down. "You're not sick, are you?"

"No, just getting old. We're being rude. Will you please introduce me to your daughter? I've heard so much about her."

"Of course." Kristof held his hand out. "Kitten, this is Dmitri Sobolev, one of my oldest friends, and one of our long-time customers."

"So pleased to meet you," Dmitri said with a small smile. "You're just as brave as your father and infinitely more attractive."

"Thank you," Marta said as she accepted the handshake. "I'm sorry about—"

"No, don't worry." Dmitri massaged the skin on his face. "It was a very well-executed maneuver, timed perfectly. You caught me off guard and established your authority. Well done. Kristof, you should have seen her."

"I'm well aware of her ferocity," Kristof said, turning toward Lauren. "Dmitri, this is Dr. Lauren McKenna."

"Doctor, your reputation precedes you." Dmitri reached out and took Lauren's hand in both of his. "Both you and your husband have been unwavering allies on behalf of Russia. I thank you."

"This is Trevor," Kristof said, almost as an afterthought. "Now, back to business. Dmitri, what do you know about the men who attacked my chalet in Austria?"

"Not much more than you," Dmitri said, turning toward Tatiana. "From what I do know, she has the answers."

"Tatiana," Kristof said, his voice firm and direct. "We've never actually met, and if you haven't already surmised who I am, I'm Archangel. I'm going to give you this one opportunity to avoid a great deal of pain and suffering. I'm tired, angry, and impatient. If you make me interrogate you, I doubt you'll live to see morning."

"I don't know what it is you think I did." Tatiana's voice wavered with fear. "But I'm sure there's been some sort of misunderstanding that we can discuss."

"Henryk!" Kristof called out without breaking eye contact with Tatiana.

Lauren heard Henryk approach, and as she turned, she saw Viktor, their prisoner from the Wroclaw hospital, being pushed toward the helicopter.

"Viktor," Kristof said as he jerked the frightened man closer so that Tatiana could see his face. "Is this the woman you know as Tatiana Reznik?"

"Yes, sir," Viktor said.

"Would you remind Ms. Reznik what she told you when you were in Wroclaw?"

"That she'd make me rich if I killed you, that you were old and sick, and it would be easy."

Kristof pushed Viktor back into Henryk's arms, and Lauren watched as Henryk shoved the broken man away from the helicopter, and fired his gun harmlessly into the ground as he took Viktor to a garage. At the sound of the gunshot, Tatiana flinched, her face went white with fear, and she began stammering, trying to talk.

"Tatiana, you had your chance." Kristof held his index finger to his lips for her to be quiet. "I'm afraid it's going to be a very long night for you. When Henryk has finished with Viktor's body, he'll be back to take you to the shed."

"The house is this way." Marta gathered everyone and pointed toward the path that led to the house, leaving Henryk to do his job.

Lauren processed what she'd just seen, and understood that terror was a better inducement than pain. Tatiana now believed that Viktor was dead, killed by Archangel, and that she was being taken to a shed, which sounded menacing. Archangel's reputation, coupled with Marta's degree in psychology, was a father-daughter combination that Tatiana couldn't hope to overcome.

"Kristof, Tatiana is still useful to us," Dmitri said as they walked. "What's to become of her?"

"Come inside," Kristof replied. "We have much to discuss."

Lauren dropped back as they walked toward a quaint house with smoke drifting from the chimney and light spilling out from the windows of several rooms. The cottage was nestled amongst a cluster of large trees; all of the leaves that had fallen earlier in the season were still underfoot, making the footing spongy. Trevor held the door open as Dmitri and Kristof entered, followed by Marta and Lauren. She was pleasantly surprised by a fire burning in a cast-iron stove, bringing a great deal of warmth. Even better, Lauren smelled coffee. In the peaceful setting, she suddenly missed Abigail and Donovan terribly.

The momentary tranquility was destroyed as Kristof abruptly turned to Dmitri and backhanded him hard across the face. Lauren zeroed in on the Russian. She could see that he was in pain, and his Adams apple bobbed up and down as he swallowed nervously. Marta pulled out a chair from the table, and Kristof shoved Dmitri backwards until he sat heavily, sputtering and confused.

"Dmitri, you and I are beyond games," Kristof said, and he peeled off his heavy coat as if he were about to engage in heavy labor. "We have done business together for years, but this is beyond commerce, this is personal. Start talking and save us both the indignity of more violence."

"Kristof," Dmitri said, hesitating and wincing as Marta secured him to the chair with zip-ties pulled tightly around his wrists and ankles. "I summoned Tatiana to Berlin to ask her perhaps these very same questions. She has your answers. We need to be focused on her."

"We'll know shortly, won't we?" Kristof found some cups hanging on hooks beneath the cabinets and set four on the counter. He filled each cup from the pot before setting it back on the stove. "How is your daughter, Elena? Is she still studying at the University in Saint Petersburg?"

"Leave my family out of this," Dmitri growled.

"Ah, an option I wish I could have requested." Kristof raised the steaming cup to his lips, then with one quick snap of the wrist, sent the scalding coffee into Dmitri's lap. As Dmitri shrieked and writhed against the pain, Kristof continued. "There is no way Tatiana has the authority to assemble an SVR hit team to assault my house. A six-year-old girl who calls me uncle, and whom I love dearly, was caught in that crossfire."

Marta used her knife to slice away the fabric of Dmitri's coat and shirt, from the shoulder to his wrist, exposing the skin of his left arm. Marta slipped an object from her pocket, carefully unfolded the cloth covering the contents, and set everything on the table.

Lauren had seen it before—the prototype drug cocktail from Israel. Marta had brought it from Wroclaw.

Marta tied off Dmitri's arm with a rubber tube. She slapped the veins on the soft underside of his forearm until a bluish vein began to bulge. She held the syringe up to the light, making sure that Dmitri could clearly see the needle. Dmitri started to stammer a protest as Marta slid the needle into his vein.

"We'll leave you to think." Kristof poured himself another cup of coffee, blew on the contents, and then sipped. "Marta, shall we go look in on Tatiana?"

Kristof grabbed his coat, and they all funneled out of the kitchen. He stopped halfway between the cottage and the shed to say, "Marta, nicely done, as always."

"I see now that all of this was carefully choreographed," Lauren said. "Do you think Dmitri knows something? Is that why you gave him the serum?"

"Dmitri is an old man who has seen it all," Kristof said. "He'd take days to break. Tatiana is ruthless, but her weakness is holding on to what little vanity and stature she has left in the world."

"She's sitting in the shed right now, her arm hurts where I shot her, and she's staring at a stack of batteries and jumper cables coiled up to look like a snake," Marta explained. "Henryk is with her, and he's sharpening some gardening tools. His role is to ignore her, and he hasn't so much as even looked at her. I can't imagine what must be running through her head, especially with her thinking that Dmitri and Dad are in the house having drinks. Experience has shown that after sixty minutes, her fear will peak. She'll be a complete mess after that and ready to talk."

"Since there's an hour to kill," Lauren said, "is there Internet available here?"

"Not here," Marta said. "But the closest town, Brody, has Internet. It's only ten minutes away. I'll take you."

"I'm happy to drive," Trevor added.

"Trevor, why don't you stay here with me," Kristof said and then sipped again from his cup. "You and I should spend some time together."

Lauren and Marta headed toward the front of the cottage where the full-size Mercedes was parked. Lauren settled in the front passenger seat. When Marta started the car, she said, "How did you know everything was going down the way it did?"

"The instant Dad called me 'Kitten', an endearment I'm not very fond of, I knew that we were about to go on the offensive."

"What will happen to Dmitri and Tatiana?" Lauren spoke as she checked her phone for a usable signal. There was none.

"That depends on them," Marta said. "As a rule, Dad doesn't like to kill people. He'd rather send them back out into the world absolutely terrified of Archangel. He still calls it intimidation, but in reality, it's a form of corporate branding."

Lauren felt a hint of a smile reach her lips—global arms dealers employing the same marketing terms as McDonald's or Apple. "What about Trevor and your dad?"

"Oh, that? I'm afraid that's probably straight-up intimidation."

"I think Trevor can hold his own," Lauren said, followed by, "This is so frustrating." Lauren pocketed her useless phone. "I'm so used to having information at the push of a button. With everything so erratic, it could take days to reach someone. At least e-mails, once sent, keep trying to get through, and eventually they do. I'm hoping there are some messages waiting for us. It might help us with these interrogations."

"You don't seem as bothered as I thought you might be with our tactics," remarked Marta.

"This became very personal when people shot at my daughter, and it became even more real when confronted with that bastard at Stephanie's. No one was more surprised than I was when I lost my temper and took a knife to him. Torture, or the fear of being tortured, does have its place, like tossing a man from a helicopter to plunge three feet to his inevitable bloody nose."

"Exactly," Marta said. "But Dmitri and Tatiana are professionals. They might be harder to break."

"These people, whoever they are, keep attacking us, and we have no real idea why. I don't know exactly where my husband is—or my daughter. All I know is that I'll keep doing whatever it takes to try to keep my loved ones safe."

"Just keep that thought in mind."

# CHAPTER THIRTY-ONE

DARKNESS FELL QUICKLY. Donovan was flying the helicopter using mostly the instruments. The broken clouds above them couldn't filter out all of the light from the Northern Lights, so there was just enough illumination to discern between the lakes and trees that slipped past a thousand feet below them. Michael sat next to him, a chart open on his lap. The signal from the Churchill navigation station was just now showing signs of life.

Michael glanced behind them in the passenger compartment. "I think Rick and Jesse are asleep," he said. "Montero and Sofya are talking."

"Trust me, if they understood that I have to land this thing in the dark—at an actual airport—they'd be awake. Have you been able to determine if we have enough fuel to even make it to Churchill?"

"We have enough." Michael pointed at the fuel gauges, as well as the current fuel flows to both engines. "We also have a nice tailwind. If you need a break, we can switch on the autopilot."

"The what?"

"Right here." Michael pressed two buttons. "There, it's all coupled up. You can relax. If you want to turn, use the heading bug."

"That's not funny," Donovan said as he flexed his tortured hands. "When were you going to tell me?"

"I'm as new to this as you are. I'm navigating and calculating fuel. Plus, you need the practice. You have to land at night, remember.

Let's assume for a minute we survive our arrival in Churchill. What then?"

"I've been thinking about that," Donovan said. "While we're assuming things, are we to assume that no one has tampered with the *Galileo*? For all we know, we may be grounded."

"What are you two talking about?" Montero stuck her head in the cockpit. "Oh, wow, look at that."

Donovan glanced to the north. Through an opening in the overcast, the Northern Lights were undulating and dancing in the clear sky above. The shifting shades of green, pink, and purple were mesmerizing.

"I don't think I've ever seen them quite like this," Montero said. "I'm sorry, I didn't mean to interrupt."

"We were talking about landing in Churchill." Donovan turned in his seat to face Montero.

"Why isn't anyone flying?" Montero asked in a calm voice, her eyes darting anxiously around the cockpit.

"Turns out we have an autopilot," Donovan said.

"That's nice," Montero said with indifference, as if to say she was sorry she'd asked, and was now bored with the subject. "I thought you'd like to see the pictures we took today. We didn't want to say anything in front of Sofya, but we found what we were looking for. Michael and I both agree that it's hard to say if he jumped or was thrown from the Boeing, but the results are pretty much the same."

Donovan took the camera from Montero and focused on the first image. Despite the snow and the man's abrasions, Donovan could see he was youngish-looking, maybe thirty, clean shaven, with curly brown hair. In the next image, Montero had zoomed in on his blistered fingers. The burns appeared more concentrated than the injuries on other passengers on the Boeing. The next picture was of his left forearm, and an ornate, full-color, fire-breathing dragon coiling around the shattered limb.

"It's possible we can trace him through the tattoo," Montero said.

Donovan punched through the rest of the images before returning to the one showing his fingers.

"Yeah, that's the one that caught my attention as well," Montero said. "When I was still with the FBI in South Florida we'd see this from time to time when someone was tortured. They'd burn them, and if the subject lived, it would be a lasting reminder about failed loyalty."

"Why would anyone start a fire aboard an airplane in the first place?" Michael said. "That's just crazy."

"When are you going to show these to Sofya?" Donovan handed the camera to Montero.

"Based on my experience, it's all about timing and environment," she said.

"What type of a setting are we talking about?" Donovan asked. "Like a medical facility?"

"No, not at all," Montero said. "We're not going to know if we have a Gulfstream until we land, right?"

Donovan was glad that Montero understood that the Gulfstream had been sitting in a hangar with no more than the airport manager's word that it would be safe.

"If the *Galileo* is good to go," Montero continued. "How long does it take to fuel and file a flight plan for London?"

"London?" Michael asked.

"Everything we've seen in regard to the crashed Boeing points toward the Russians, including Sofya," Montero said. "At some point, we need to show her all of the evidence we collected, including the pictures of the guy who was tossed from the 737. We stand back and see if anything registers. I've seen this before, women who were brutalized, and remembered nothing from the attack. Once we made sure these women were safe, and convinced them that the people around them were going to protect them, we showed them crime scene photographs."

"Sounds harsh," Michael said. "What typically happens?"

"Sometimes nothing. Other times, everything comes rushing back, and it's very emotional. Usually, it's something in the middle, but Sofya needs to see everything. We still have unanswered questions, including files from the Boeing, and she's the only one among us who can translate Russian to English."

"You want to do this in the back of the Gulfstream on the way to connect with Lauren and Marta?"

"Yes," Montero said. "There's no one chasing us while we're aloft. That's the key element. Once we have her in safe surroundings, I think you and I can get through to her. Also, once we do this with Sofya, we'll have a clearer picture to take to William. You're meeting him at Stephanie's for New Year's, right? We collect as much data as we can and then give it to him in person."

"Wait, why do you think I can reach her?" Donovan asked.

"She's attached to you," Montero said. "She told me about what happened at the lake, how she took your gun and then used it to save you from being killed."

"Wait, Jesse told me you dropped all of those guys with the AK-47 he floated up to you," Michael said.

"All but one. I never saw him coming. He was out of my line of sight while I was busy taking care of his friends. She saved my life, though she seemed to lose herself for a few seconds afterward, as if she was just as surprised at what she did as I was."

"That could very well be the case. Fractions of memories seeping through when needed to act. In my opinion, she's attached to you, and sees you as a protector, or father figure. She trusts you, which is the first element in easing her back into her reality."

"I'm pretty sure I'm not qualified to be helping people regain their mental health," Donovan said. "Are you sure we're not doing more harm than good?"

"The memories are in there," Montero said, "and it's hard watching her struggle. I once had a psychiatrist explain it to me as pulling off a scab so the wound can heal properly. Sofya is already in pain—she's a lost soul. She feels responsible for the deaths of multiple people, and she doesn't know who they are, or why everything is happening. She's the biggest part of this mystery. We help her find the truth and then go wherever it takes us."

"Did Sofya tell you what I asked her after she saved me?" Donovan asked. "I asked her if she could have taken out all of the men from the helicopter."

"What did she say?" Montero asked.

"She said 'maybe.'"

"Nice to know she's on our side," Michael said. "And what if the *Galileo* has been sabotaged? What's our plan then? If Sofya is left to unravel on her own, is that better or worse?"

"I've been thinking about that, too," Montero said. "If the *Galileo* has been compromised, then we'll be running, and I think we're then forced to put Sofya's recovery on hold and do whatever it takes to get out of Canada and back to the States. I think Michael has a point—there's an optimum window for Sofya, and sooner might be better. Let's hope the *Galileo* is okay."

"There are a couple other points we need to keep in mind," Donovan said. "The Twin Otter and the Beaver both have Emergency Locator Transmitters. Someone is eventually going to hear the ELT signals and investigate. We also need to assume that there's someone waiting for this helicopter to arrive back in Thompson. We need to get out of Canada as soon as possible and let someone else deal with this mess."

"How much trouble are we really in?" Michael asked Montero.

"From a strictly law enforcement standpoint, plenty," Montero said. "The key to deflecting and minimizing our issues is to uncover the root cause of everything, going all the way back to when you two nearly collided with the Boeing. If we can present the Royal Canadian Mounted Police with valid reasons for doing what we did, namely self-defense, then maybe we can walk away. Doubtful, but that's the best scenario."

Michael looked at his watch, and then down at the instrument panel. "We'll know soon enough. The Churchill airport is dead ahead."

"Is there a control tower we have to talk to?" Donovan asked.

"No tower," Michael said. "It's dark. No one is expecting us. I say we just fly in like we own the place."

"I agree. Michael, the second we land, you take Montero and check out the *Galileo*," Donovan said. "I'm going to keep the helicopter running. If someone has disabled the Gulfstream, as fast as we can, we pump some fuel into this thing and get out of here."

"Got it," Michael said.

Donovan spotted lights dead ahead. He put his hands on the controls, memorizing the position of the switches for the landing lights. "Michael, turn off the autopilot. Montero, everyone in town is going to hear us arrive. If someone is waiting for us, it'll happen quickly."

"The airport is twelve o'clock and two miles," Michael said. "Do you have it in sight?"

Donovan spotted the green and white flash from the airport's rotating beacon. "I have it. I'm going to set us down right next to the hangar where we left the *Galileo*."

"Power of positive thinking," Michael said. "I like it."

Donovan silently thanked Michael for the sarcasm-wrapped challenge. As they neared the field, he slowed the helicopter, used his thumb to switch on the landing lights, and started a descent. He was fixed on his spot, and made slight corrections until the skids touched lightly on the ramp. He exhaled a long-held breath, but his relief was cut short by the sound of Montero's voice.

"Michael, let's go!" Montero pulled her door open and jumped from the helicopter, her Glock in her right hand, and Michael followed.

Donovan sat in the 212—his hands positioned on the controls—and waited.

# CHAPTER THIRTY-TWO

THEY WERE PARKED just outside of a hotel in the small town of Brody. Marta had rattled off a password from memory, and Lauren understood that Marta had probably piggybacked this signal before. Her laptop cycled through its security protocols, and Lauren discovered she had several messages. Even though the signal was strong, the Internet was slow. After what felt like forever, her e-mail finally opened. Lauren immediately searched for any messages from Montero or Donovan, and when she didn't find one, she clicked on the message sent by Reggie.

> L-
>
> *We've lost track of Kristof, though there are no signs of him being taken, so we're in the dark. I've enlisted everyone within my immediate reach to search the city. I'm left with the distinct possibility that someone may have breached our security and taken him. That said, as promised, I reached out to the American embassy, and though William VanGelder is currently unavailable, he issued instructions to immediately fly everyone affected to Iceland, where they will be absorbed into his own protection detail. This is easily accomplished, and arrangements are already in the works. If it's any solace, Iceland is a daunting fortress. We will continue to search for Kristof.*
>
> *—R*

"Damn it!" Lauren said under her breath as she dashed off a reply explaining that Kristof had indeed bolted, and that he was with them. Lauren hit send, and waited for confirmation that her message was on its way. She cringed when she pictured Abigail telling Grandpa William that she rode a horse faster than bullets, and she reached the obvious conclusion that William would be less than happy with them all.

"What is it?" Marta asked as she used her phone to pull up her own e-mail.

"A message from Reggie—it seems that your dad left without telling anyone."

"Welcome to my world." Marta shook her head with familiar resignation. "I suppose Reggie is frantic?"

"Of course he is." Lauren saw that her e-mail was finally on its way. "To the point where he reached out to William, and Stephanie and Abigail are being whisked off to Iceland to join him under his diplomatic protection."

"Ouch." Marta lowered her hands into her lap. "Though now at least we know where William is, and Iceland isn't a bad place to hide."

"That's exactly what Reggie said." Lauren continued scanning her list of incoming e-mails until she found one from Calvin.

*Strongly recommend refuge at nearest US embassy. We'll fly you back to the United States and sort out the charges against you from here. Calvin*

Lauren didn't reply and returned to the list of messages. There was nothing else that required her attention. Out of curiosity, she logged into a website that would give her the latest raw data from NASA's Solar Dynamics Observatory. She scanned the data and was staggered by what she read. Calvin had told her about the geo-magnetic storm in progress, as well as the large coronal mass ejec-tion, but the initial estimate of strength and duration had been incorrect. NOAA's space weather prediction models had crashed. Information coming from space-based satellites was unreliable and erratic. The French, British, and Russians had already lost commu-nication satellites to the bombardment of charged particles hurtling in from the sun at millions of miles per hour. Without the sophisti-cated instrumentation to measure the outflow from the sun, as well as the computer models to crunch the data, she feared that the as-trophysicists were now only guessing about this storm. As Lauren reached the end of the report, she did the math, then deciding she'd made a mistake, she did it again. To her dismay, the numbers were the same. The coming solar radiation was three times the strength of any storm ever recorded.

"Close your laptop," Marta said in a rush as headlights reflected off of her mirror and illuminated her eyes.

Lauren snapped the lid closed and sank in her seat, unsure what to expect.

A dark sedan drove past them, and Marta pretended as if she were talking on her phone. The car continued slowly up the street, and then made a right turn. The instant the sedan was out of sight, Marta threw their car into gear, and with the headlights still switched off, she made a U-turn, and then an immediate right and accelerated.

"Who is it?"

"I don't know, but the make and model matched the type used by ABW."

"Poland's internal security," Lauren said. "What would they be doing here?"

"I'm not sure it was them," Marta said as she switched on the headlights and pulled out on the main road that would take them in the general direction of the safe house. "Though, if they're here, it's because of you. The authorities know you arrived via private jet into Wroclaw. They're also investigating the assault and kidnapping at the University Hospital."

"Great."

"The bad news is someone probably photographed the helicopter," Marta said as she kept checking her rearview mirror for anyone following. "We're safe for the moment, but the only way out of Poland is via that helicopter, so when we leave, we need to be ready to abandon it as soon as we land."

"I had an e-mail from Calvin. He said to surrender myself at the closest embassy. Maybe he's right?"

"Perhaps, but I don't think that's your play quite yet."

"Why not?"

"Because the first thing they're going to do is pressure you about your activities and want to know who was with you."

# CHAPTER THIRTY-THREE

DONOVAN WATCHED AS Michael came out of the hangar and gave Donovan the all-clear signal. Relieved, he began to shut down the helicopter's engines. Once again, his impatience won out over the checklist, and he pulled the firewall shutoffs and switched off the battery. He bundled up and was the last one to run from the helicopter to the warmth of the hangar where Michael and Montero waited.

"The *Galileo* looks fine," Michael said.

"Mr. Nash," Russell called out. "You're not who I expected."

"Russell," Donovan said warmly. "I was hoping you'd be here. Thanks for taking such good care of our jet—turns out we've attracted some unwanted attention."

"People here in town been talking," Russell said. "Some say you're hunting gold, others say you already found it. It doesn't take much whispering to get people to thinking. Though you can trust me, no one has been anywhere near your Gulfstream."

"Can you please assure everyone in town that we're scientists?" Montero said. "Wait, do you think the charter operator in Thompson thought we'd found gold? Is that reason enough to show up and start shooting?"

"It can be," Russell said. "Can I ask what happened to the Twin Otter, and my snowmobile?"

"The Otter had a problem, and though your snowmobile is fine, it won't be coming back anytime soon, so I owe you ten thousand dollars," Donovan said. "We also need the Gulfstream fueled, add that to the bill."

"Yeah, sure," Russell said as if processing what he'd just heard. "So I shouldn't be expecting the Twin Otter?"

"They had mechanical problems. The Twin Otter is the operator's problem now," Michael said. "Russell, is there any way I can make a long-distance call? I need to file a flight plan."

"There's a landline on the desk in my office that's been working most of the day. Help yourself." Russell slipped his hat back on his head. "I'll go bring the tug around, and we'll get your airplane pulled outside and fueled."

"Donovan," Jesse said as Russell hurried toward the door. "I can't go with you. After diving as deep as I did today, and as fast as I came up to help Rick, I need to stay on the ground for a few days."

"How are you feeling?" Donovan had forgotten about the threat of Jesse getting the bends. "I'm serious, because if you don't feel good, we'll forget Europe and fly you to the nearest decompression chamber."

"I'm fine, thank you, but flying in a pressurized plane is out of the question."

"Where is the nearest decompression chamber?" Montero asked.

"Winnipeg," Jesse said. "But I'm fine, really."

Rick pounded down the stairs of the *Galileo* and hurried toward the group. "All the systems check out." He motioned over his shoulder to the Gulfstream. "She's good to go."

"Jesse needs to stay behind," Donovan said. "But I don't want to leave him alone."

"Unless you need me to help fly," Rick said, "I'll stay."

"Montero, what do you think?" Donovan said.

"I like the buddy system," she responded. "I say we ask Russell about chartering an unpressurized plane to fly you two as far as

Winnipeg. Jesse, that way you're close to the chamber if you develop any symptoms."

Outside, the sound of a diesel engine drew close and stopped just outside the main hangar doors. Russell let himself in the side entrance and immediately walked toward the group. "Let me know when you're ready, and we'll open the hangar doors."

"Russell," Montero called out. "We have a small problem. We think you might be able to help. We want to get Jesse and Rick to Winnipeg in an unpressurized plane. Jesse's been on a couple of deep dives, and we think it would make sense for him to get checked out. Can we charter something from you and get him to Winnipeg?"

"Once you're gone, I've got a Cessna that I use for charter," Russell said. "I can have the two of them in Winnipeg inside three hours. You're being smart. We had a guy here last summer, a scientist, who was diving out in the bay and got the bends. He kept trying to explain his symptoms away as something else—until he collapsed. He about didn't make it out of here alive."

"We agree," Donovan said. "And I appreciate all of your help with everything, especially with the safety of my people."

"We all look out for each other up here." Russell pulled his hat snug. "It's how we survive."

"I'll go file a flight plan," Michael said.

"Michael." Donovan grabbed his arm before Michael could walk off. "File the flight plan to Glasgow or Edinburgh. We'll divert to London once we're on the other side of the Atlantic. I don't want to attract a crowd."

"I like that plan, but I'll need Sofya's passport," Michael said.

"It's on the plane. I'll go get it," Donovan said as the huge metal doors parted and began to move apart. The wheels screeched and chirped against the cold metal rails, the shrill sounds echoing in the cavernous hangar.

As Donovan approached the *Galileo*, he heard a separate high-pitched scream and it sounded human. He broke out in a full run for the stairs as the scream reached a crescendo. When he got to the aircraft, he took the steps two at a time and swung down the aisle into the cabin. He found Sofya in a chair, bent over at the waist, her entire body trembling as she shrieked. On the floor was a camera. In the dim light, Donovan recognized the photo on the screen as the man that had been thrown from the Boeing.

"Sofya, I'm here," Donovan whispered as he moved in and wrapped his arms around her. She turned and clutched him around the neck. He rocked her back and forth, whispering, "We'll get through this, I promise."

Montero arrived next. She took in the scene before turning to warn the others off, as if deciding that Sofya had what she needed for the moment. Donovan could feel Sofya's body rock with silent sobs as Montero picked up the camera, shut it off, and put it back in her bag.

"I'm here as well," Montero said, placing her hand on Sofya's head. "What can we do? Tell us what would help you feel better."

"We can't help you unless you talk to us," Donovan added, but his effort to pull away was met with resistance. Outside he heard and then felt the tug hook up to the nose gear of the *Galileo*, signaling that Russell was ready to pull them outside.

"Sofya," Montero said. "Donovan needs to help get the *Galileo* ready to fly so he can get us away from this place. I'll sit with you as long as it takes, and Donovan will come back again once we're out of here. Would that be okay?"

Donovan heard the main cabin door close and seconds later, the *Galileo* began to move forward. Through the window he could see Rick standing at the wingtip, helping Russell ease the Gulfstream out into the darkness. Idling near the perimeter was a fuel truck.

"Sofya," Montero said. "Please talk to us. You know we care about you. Can you at least tell us what the man in the photo means to you? I promise you're not in danger. You've already seen how far we'll go to protect you."

Sofya sniffed as she pulled away from Donovan's shoulder. She released her hold on his neck, her breathing ragged and shallow. She quickly put her hands over her face, and in that second, Donovan saw in her eyes a lifetime of pain and anguish.

"Here," Montero said as she held out a handful of tissues. "Deep, regular breathing, Sofya. Try to find a safe place in your mind. None of this is your fault; you're a victim, not a criminal. Do you understand what I'm saying? You didn't do anything wrong."

Donovan furrowed his brow at Montero's words. In truth, the exact opposite might be the reality. As if reading his expression, Montero shot him a confident look that told him she knew what she was doing.

"They made me," Sofya blurted without warning, her voice sounding ragged and unsteady.

"Can you tell us who made you?" Montero asked. "What do you remember?"

Sofya squeezed her eyes shut, as if experiencing actual physical pain at the question. She tried to speak and then shook her head as more tears streamed from her eyes, and she buried her face in her hands.

Donovan felt the *Galileo* come to a stop. The main cabin door opened, and Rick, who had helped get the Gulfstream out of the hangar, rushed up the steps and slipped unobtrusively into the cockpit. Rick ran several checklists and started the *Galileo's* auxiliary power unit to provide not only electricity, but heat, in an effort to help Michael and Donovan get the Gulfstream airborne quicker. Donovan felt a rush of mixed emotions. Once they fueled, they'd be free to leave, and the prospect of leaving Canada was galvanizing. The most powerful motivation was the prospect of seeing Lauren and Abigail, yet at the thought of family, Donovan knew that William's words still lingered, and the reunion with his mentor was still hovering out there somewhere.

As Donovan stood to leave, Sofya reached out, clutched his hand, and looked up at him. "They're still going to try to kill all of us."

# CHAPTER THIRTY-FOUR

"THE LIGHT IN the shed is off," Marta said as she wheeled onto the property and parked the car. "I wonder what that means."

Lauren followed Marta into the house where Dmitri was still secured to the chair, his head slumped to the side. Kristof sat across the table from him, arms folded across his chest, red eyes amplifying the exhaustion carved on his face. Henryk and Trevor stood at the stove as Trevor poured hot coffee into three different cups.

"The lights are out in the shed," Marta said. She went to her father and gently placed the back of her hand on both of his cheeks, checking his temperature.

"Tatiana needed a break," Kristof said. "I asked her a few questions, and she seemed somewhat forthcoming, but I sensed she was still holding out on us, so I thought she might need a little more time to sit in the dark and contemplate her situation."

Marta momentarily locked eyes with Trevor, trying to gather any information on what he and her father may have discussed while she was gone.

"Kristof, what are Dmitri's politics?" Lauren asked. "You said you'd known him a long time, and that he'd been a customer."

"He started his intelligence career with the KGB, but he's all SVR now. As far as his politics go, he's what I would describe as *adaptable*, though he's a devout Russian. In terms of our business transactions, I'd call him an opportunist. These days he buys weapons, pays top dollar, and I don't ask who the end user is going to be."

"Marta," Lauren said. "Do you remember when we were interviewing Viktor in the helicopter, when he first told us about Tatiana?"

"Yes," Marta said as she looked toward her father. "He said that Tatiana hates you because you supply weapons to the people that would keep Mother Russia from being great again."

"Viktor said that?" Kristof asked with a frown.

"Is Tatiana a holdover, a hard-line communist from the old days?" Marta asked. "Is she involved in politics, or simply girls and trafficking?"

"I think we put that on our list of things to learn," Lauren said as Kristof shook his head that he had no idea. "My other question is why Dmitri, an SVR operative, would be meeting with Tatiana? What's the common thread?"

"Maybe it's exactly what Dmitri said he was doing," Marta offered. "Perhaps he sent for Tatiana to find out what was happening with the girl Donovan rescued—she's clearly a serious loose end for someone."

"Henryk," Lauren said. "You mentioned in Wroclaw that Tatiana had Russian protection for her trafficking young girls. Is it possible that Sofya is one of Tatiana's girls?"

"It's a place to start," Kristof said with a subtle nod of approval in Lauren's direction.

"Dad," Marta said. "Tatiana is clearly more afraid of you than anyone else. Walk in there and call her bluff. Tell her Dmitri is drunk and talking. She'll cave."

"You are the better poker player," Kristof said. "She knows I'm here. Go introduce yourself as the new Archangel, which should serve as a surprise. My only request is that I don't want Tatiana killed. I'm not sure what we'll get from her on this first pass. We may need to go at her again with the drugs."

"To what end?" Marta said as she cocked her head inquisitively.

"It would be nice if we were able to eventually dismantle a significant part of her business from what we learn here tonight," Kristof said. "At some point, we're going to need our friend Montero to deal with Interpol on our behalf. Tatiana's operation might be a significant bargaining chip."

At the mention of Montero, Lauren wished she could talk with Donovan. She'd been trying not to dwell on the fact that they hadn't spoken in what seemed like ages. She continued to picture Donovan, Montero, and Michael on a frozen lake in Manitoba, but in reality, she had no idea where they were.

"Right now, I need to brief everyone on what we now know from our trip to Brody," Marta said. "Lauren had an e-mail from Reggie, who explained that he was beside himself because Dad vanished without a word." She paused and shot her father a look of disapproval. "Because of that, Reggie initiated a call to the American State Department, and as a result, Abigail, Stephanie, and Reggie are headed to Iceland to join William VanGelder under the protective umbrella of diplomatic security."

"Lauren, I'm very sorry," Kristof said. He lowered his head. "My actions were thoughtless."

"Everyone is safe," Lauren said. "That's the main thing."

"We also know that the solar storm is going to get worse, so we're not going to have our usual channels of communication for the foreseeable future."

"Was there any news out of Berlin?" Trevor asked.

"Not Berlin, Wroclaw. As you were quick to point out, we were photographed leaving the hospital, which has upped the ante on Interpol's efforts to apprehend Lauren. Lauren is thought to be connected with the kidnapping there, as well as the mess in Innsbruck. She received an e-mail from the Defense Intelligence Agency, urging her to surrender herself at the nearest embassy."

"What about Hannah?" Kristof asked.

"Who's Hannah?" Trevor asked.

"The girl hired to take care of the horses at the chalet," Lauren said. "She was a witness to the fact that I wasn't involved in what took place."

"That's my question—where's Hannah?" Kristof repeated. "Why didn't Interpol interview her?"

"Because they don't know about her," Marta said with obvious irritation. "I dropped her off at the police station in Zirl, where her uncle is a constable. He must have decided to shield her from the investigation and insisted she remain quiet."

"Leave him to me," Kristof said. "He and I have had dealings in the past."

"When we were in Brody, we also spotted a car that could have been driven by the ABW, Poland's internal security. We left town without incident, but one never knows," Marta said. "Trevor, be ready, we may have to leave in a hurry. Any other questions?"

Lauren, along with everyone else, remained silent.

"Good," Marta said. "Now, let's go chat up Tatiana. Lauren, I want you to come with me. We'll be back shortly, and then we can start in on Dmitri."

As they walked from the house toward the shed, Lauren noticed that the visibility had dropped, and the air had grown damp, as if it were going to snow.

"I'm going to work through this interrogation as quickly as possible. I want Tatiana to get the impression that I have little time for her, and that I'd rather just shoot her and get on with my night."

"Do you have something in mind for me to do?"

"I want you to watch and listen," Marta said. "If you see or hear something we need to know more about, don't hesitate to act."

Lauren followed Marta into the shed and squinted as a switch was flipped, and a harsh light erupted from above. Tatiana appeared as Lauren had seen her earlier, though her eyes were far less fierce, as if their wattage been dialed way down.

"Tatiana." Marta walked behind the bound woman. Then she leaned in and whispered into her ear, "Kristof is busy and asked me to finish this up."

"Please, I need something to drink," Tatiana said.

"Answer my questions, and I'll make that happen." Marta pulled her phone from her pocket, pushed some buttons, and pulled up a photograph. She held the screen up so Tatiana could see. "We know her as Sofya. Tell me everything."

"I have nothing to do with her. She was taken from me."

"Everything," Marta repeated.

"Sofya was one of my girls. She worked at a club in Warsaw until some wealthy Russian became infatuated with her."

"You kidnapped her, forced her into sexual slavery?" Marta said. "And then gave her to some Russian?"

"I helped her, and then she was stolen from me," Tatiana said. "The Russian didn't pay anywhere near what she was worth, but he promised me favors to be named later. I got the feeling that he was not the type of man who reacted very well to being told no. So I let him take her."

"Who was this Russian?"

"I don't know. I never saw him before or again."

"How long ago was this?" Marta asked.

"Two years."

"Interpol," Marta said. "How was the news of Sofya's survival in North America discovered so quickly?"

"The SVR has someone on the inside," Tatiana said. "I was ordered to intercept a woman. Anna was her name. I was told she'd have details about Sofya with her."

"Did she?" Marta asked.

"Yes."

"Did she know she had the material on her?" Lauren asked.

"She maintained that the documents were planted on her, though I didn't believe her. When she was confronted with the possibility that the information came straight from that American FBI Agent, Veronica Montero, I knew she was making up lies."

"So you were there when she was killed?" Lauren asked.

"No." Tatiana shook her head. "I took the materials she had in her possession and went to deliver them as directed."

"So, you gave the order to have Anna killed?" Marta asked.

"No, I only collected the documents she carried."

"Anna wasn't lying about former FBI Agent Montero," Lauren said. "She's coming, and she's not happy. Right now, Dmitri is sipping Cognac with Archangel, explaining how you went off script, killed Anna so you could sell the information yourself. He's pushing for you to be executed immediately."

Tatiana's eyes flared just long enough for Lauren and Marta to understand that they'd struck a nerve.

"Montero is going to go after everyone involved," Lauren said. "As it stands now, you'll be Montero's solitary target. Everyone else walks. Unless you tell us who is actually responsible."

"Dmitri is who I report to, the rest are all former KGB," Tatiana said in a whisper, as if saying the words aloud were enough to end her. "They are each stationed at different embassies in Europe. Untouchable."

"You supply them with girls, don't you?" Lauren asked, then acted on a hunch. "In fact, you used to be one of those girls. The money, the parties and travel, how exciting it must have been for you, until they tossed you aside for younger and younger versions of who you used to be. Why would you take orders from the men who've used you so terribly?"

"If I were to try to quit, or run, they'd have me killed. I know far too much to be allowed to live. I control the girls, but Dmitri, along with the others, control the clubs."

"Who does Dmitri answer to in Moscow?"

"I don't know."

"You could bring him down as well," Marta said.

"If I could have taken them all down, I would have done it years ago."

"What if we make it possible?" Lauren asked. "What if we turn Montero and Interpol loose on them? You may go to jail, but you'll be alive."

"What would I have to do?"

Lauren tipped a bottle of water to Tatiana's lips and held it steady as the broken woman sipped. "You have to give us all of the information about your clubs, the girls, the trafficking, the books, the money, and the customers. Everything, and then maybe we can ensure you live to see the dawn."

# CHAPTER THIRTY-FIVE

DONOVAN PUSHED UP both throttles and the Gulfstream thundered down Churchill's longest runway. The dense, frigid air aided both the wings and the engines and the *Galileo*, despite being heavy with fuel, accelerated to flying speed quickly. He eased back on the controls and the nose came up, followed by the main wheels. When he raised the gear, all three struts tucked up into the airframe, and the sleek *Galileo* gathered even more speed.

As Donovan banked the Gulfstream toward their initial fix, the shimmering tendrils of the Northern Lights illuminated the vast expanse of Hudson Bay, frozen as far north as he could see. The Aurora Borealis was as vivid and alive as he'd ever seen it in his thirty years of flying. The fluttering colors reached to the horizon and the intensity ebbed and flowed as wave after wave of charged particles, ejected from the sun, collided with the atmosphere. He took a quick glance over his shoulder into the cabin. Montero sat holding hands with Sofya, talking, though their words were drowned out by the hum of the engines and the steady rush of the slipstream. Donovan turned, saw they were already through ten thousand feet, and lowered the nose to allow the speed to push up toward three hundred knots as the Gulfstream headed toward their assigned altitude of thirty-nine thousand feet.

"Was she able to tell you anything about the guy we found?" Michael asked.

"No, all she said was that they *made* her. We need to tread lightly and try to find out who *they* are."

"But she remembers him, they're connected, right? That's what set her off?" Michael asked.

"I don't know. Seeing the pictures Montero had taken may have initiated a flashback, an out-of-context memory that evoked her emotional response. Or, the reaction may have been to the larger picture, which we don't fully understand."

"So, the man we found in the forest, who fell, jumped, or was thrown from the Boeing, could be someone who threatened her, or hurt her, or helped her."

"One of the oldest parts of the brain controls the flight or fight response," Donovan said. "She may have been terrified and not knowing why made it even worse."

"What about the other pictures?" Michael asked. "The ones from inside the plane that you and Jesse took? What if she looked at them? Is it too soon? Or would it help her put everything together?"

"I'm going to defer to Montero," Donovan said as a seemingly random thought crossed his mind.

"What is it?" Michael asked. "You've got that look, you know, the one you get right before I have to save you."

"I gather you've seen all the pictures from inside the plane?"

"Yes, Jesse showed them to me."

"The man in the forest, what was he wearing?" Donovan asked.

Michael had to think about it for a moment. "His clothes were pretty shredded, but I'd say dark slacks and a sweater. Why?"

"What color?"

"Black, but everyone wears black."

"Hear me out," Donovan said as he formulated his thoughts.

"We know for sure that the pilots were killed after landing. The 737 was obviously under control through the entire approach and landing."

"Absolutely."

"Sofya was alive and escaped," Donovan said. "The man you and Montero found had evidence of burns, as did some of the people in the plane. In fact, we found evidence of a fairly severe fire. So much so, that the pilots had on their oxygen masks."

"Standard procedure for the crew." Michael shrugged. "If you get a fire warning, the first thing you do is put on your mask."

"How do you start a fire on an airplane? It wasn't an electrical fire; it didn't start somewhere below the floor, or behind a panel. It looked like a fire that was started in the forward salon. Almost everything is flame retardant. How was the fire started? Right now, if you wanted to start a fire in the passenger compartment, how would you make it happen?"

"There's no fuel, there's oxygen, a match or lighter provides the ignition, but as we both know, nothing much in an airplane burns very well."

"What does a corporate 737 have that the *Galileo* doesn't?"

"A full galley," Michael said instantly. "With a complete liquor cabinet, and alcohol does burn. Sofya had no burns, and she was wearing black slacks, a white blouse, and a black sweater. You're saying that Sofya was the flight attendant?"

"I'm just thinking out loud," Donovan said.

"She was the only one to make it out of the plane," Michael said. "A flight attendant would be able to keep it together long enough to evacuate the plane. Though, like any flight crew, it would be unlikely for her to evacuate the plane if any passengers were still alive. Maybe that's why she didn't wait for the passengers. She jumped out of the plane because there *was* someone with a gun shooting members of the flight crew."

"Or because she'd already killed everyone on board and knew the plane was sinking," Donovan said. "I went back to where I found her in the snow. It didn't occur to me until after we'd been inside the Boeing when I saw all the gunshot victims, but Jesse and I didn't find a weapon."

"You found one?"

"A Glock, and it had been fired."

"I remember the doctor at the emergency room in Minneapolis told you she suspected that Sofya was drugged. How does a drugged person do all of that, function in that environment, and still manage to evacuate and survive?"

"Coming up," Montero said as she appeared in the cockpit.

"We were just talking about Sofya," Michael said. "How is she?"

"She's sleeping for the moment, but she managed to tell me a few things." Montero took a deep breath and began. "She's very fragile and fragmented, but her memories are starting to push through. Nothing in any organized timeline. She told me she was taken, kidnapped while traveling in Poland years ago. She kept talking about *they*, and I don't believe that she doesn't know who *they* are. She claims they made her do *things*. I'm assuming they were sexual things, though she couldn't, or wouldn't, explain—and I didn't push the subject. Sexual slavery is typically brutal—violence is used as a weapon to control the women. It's possible she spent a great deal of her time in brothels, held as a captive, and probably drugged. We may never get to those memories."

"Is she withholding information?" Donovan asked. "Does she possess the capacity to lie to you?"

"I'm not sensing that," Montero continued. "I think she's seeing bits and pieces, like flashbulbs going off in her head. With each flash, she understands more about her past, but like I said, she's all over the place. Nothing is linear, so it's impossible to piece together anything coherent yet."

"Has she said anything about being on the plane?" Michael asked.

"It's hard to say. Again, she says 'they found out' without it being clear who *they* are," Montero said. "I did hear one name. Andrei.

It's possible he was the man Michael and I found in the woods. She managed to say something about him *leaving*. That's when she broke down again, hard, and then she finally went to sleep."

"We were talking earlier," Michael said. "The other images, the ones from inside the plane, what if we just go for it, and let her see them all, try to explain to her in order what we think happened."

"From a cop's standpoint, I don't like the part where we explain anything to anyone," Montero said. "I always want to hear it from the witness."

"You don't trust her either," Donovan said.

"It's not so much that," Montero said. "The Glock you found bothers me. I've also seen guilty people latch on to the first thing that makes them seem not guilty. For Sofya, I need to see it originate from within. That said, I'm not opposed to showing her the pictures, I just don't want to offer much narrative."

"I say give her an hour to sleep," Donovan said. "You might also take a nap yourself, then wake her up and start again."

Montero glanced at her watch. "What time are we going to land?"

"We're going to land at twenty after ten in the morning, London time, which is exactly five and a half hours from now."

"I'm not sure I can sleep. I thought I'd brew some coffee," Montero said. "It's going to be a long night."

"I'd love some," Donovan said. "Though in reality, it's going to be a very short night. Flying east at six hundred miles per hour, the sun is going to come up well before we get to England."

"Ugh." Montero shook her head in disgust. "I hate that part of international travel."

Donovan looked past Montero and noticed one of the science stations was lit up in the back of the *Galileo*. "Did you switch on the computers in back?"

"Yes, I thought I'd download everything from both cameras into the mainframe, just to have a backup. I also want to know if there's even the smallest window of opportunity to use the Internet or the satellite phone. God, what I'd give for thirty minutes online. I feel like I'm working blind."

"Get used to it." Michael pointed out the windshield at the raging Northern Lights. "This is the most intense solar storm I've ever seen, and it's forecast to get worse."

"How are you able to talk to air traffic control?"

"Right now we're over land. VHF radio works over short distances so we're able to communicate with ATC that way. Once we're out over the ocean, we'll try to talk via our HF radios, though we've already been warned that it's almost impossible at the moment."

"What do we do then?"

"It's like in the old days," Donovan said. "We tell ATC what time and what altitude we'll be over a known point, and they use that information to separate the traffic. Though as far north as we are, I can almost guarantee no one else is out here but us. Once we get within a couple of hundred miles of Ireland, we'll be able to talk to ATC again."

"Unless we have a problem before we get there," Montero added. "What happens if we have an emergency or something?"

"Then it's like it always is," Donovan said. "We're on our own."

"Great," Montero said and then turned away.

Donovan glanced at the instrument panel. He found that they'd picked up a tailwind and their ground speed was nearing six hundred fifty miles per hour. With the Aurora Borealis burning brightly above them, and the snow-covered ground visible below, he had the odd sensation that they were sandwiched in the only safe place available, positioned precisely between the frozen planet below and the raging solar storm above. He pictured how this scenery must have looked to his predecessors crossing the North Atlantic, first in wooden ships, and then in propeller airplanes like DC-3s and C-54s. As the captain of his own vessel crossing the ocean, he felt a kinship to all those who'd come before. The aroma of fresh coffee drifted forward, and he glanced over his shoulder, spotting Sofya sleeping curled up in a chair. All his thoughts vanished except her whispered warning.

# CHAPTER THIRTY-SIX

"Hi, Dmitri," Marta said after she pushed the audio button on the phone that she'd taken from Viktor that would record the conversation. The old man opened one drugged eye at a time. "Remember me? We met in Berlin, at your nightclub. Tatiana wanted me to say hello."

"Where am I?" Dmitri seemed distracted by his surroundings. When he inspected his bound hands, a look of confusion came over his face. He turned to look up at Marta and then at Lauren.

"Dmitri," Lauren said. "How do you feel?"

"I'm fine. What are we doing here?"

"We have a little problem. Our mutual friend in Moscow said you'd help us out," Lauren said.

"Okay," he said.

"It's Sofya," Lauren said as Marta held up one of the first pictures that Donovan had taken aboard the *Galileo*. "She's finally dead, and our people said that you'd know what to do next?"

"She's dead?" Dmitri studied the picture with hooded eyelids.

"Yes, you did want her dead, didn't you?"

"Gregori does. We need to tell Gregori."

"Tell me how to call Gregori, and we'll tell him the good news. You'll get all the credit instead of Tatiana."

"I never call him, he only calls me."

"I understand," Lauren said. "Before she died, Sofya tried to tell us her mission, but we're unclear. Gregori wanted us to try to insert another girl into place, one of ours. We're working with Tatiana to find another girl to put in Sofya's place, but we don't have much time."

"I don't think so." Dmitri shook his head. "That makes no sense. Sofya was a spy. We can't run a double agent without knowing who she worked for. Did you find out? Do you know if she'd uncovered the secret?"

"She wasn't clear," Marta said. "She told us a great deal before she died, and we think she works for the British, but she was all over the place in terms of what she knew."

"The British." Dmitri said the words with a snarl. "We'll see how smug those bastards are when the hammer and sickle is flying above Big Ben."

"I agree," Lauren replied with a conspiratorial grin. "Though if we could somehow pretend that Sofya was alive, and in Europe, we could see who tries to rescue her."

"There's no time." Dmitri shook his head and tried to bring his wrist up to check his watch, seemingly confused once again by his arm being bound. "I don't think anyone can stop Gregori now."

"Stop him from what?"

"Victory." Dmitri smiled as his head swayed from side to side and his eyelids seemed to grow heavy. "He will win, he always wins."

"How?" Lauren asked. "Sofya told us, but we didn't understand. How does he achieve victory?"

Dmitri opened his eyes and then his head lolled off to the side.

Lauren was about to throw the water in his face when she heard the unmistakable sound of Trevor spooling up the engines on the helicopter.

"We need to go," Marta said as she pulled out a knife and quickly sliced through Dmitri's bonds, releasing him. They pulled Dmitri to his feet and headed out the door, meeting Kristof on the lawn.

"Henryk spotted three cars coming fast. We need to hurry." Kristof spoke in the darkness. "We should leave Dmitri."

"No, he said there's a plan in the works that puts the Soviet flag flying above London," Marta said. "He also said that Sofya was a spy and someone named Gregori was in charge."

Kristof said nothing and hurried the best he could to the helicopter and slid open the door. Marta and Lauren tumbled Dmitri onto the floor.

"What about Henryk?" Marta asked as she helped her father aboard.

"He'll be fine," Kristof replied, winded. "He's taking Tatiana somewhere safe. We'll leave her henchman to try to explain what happened to them."

Seconds later, the rotor blades bit into the air and the Dauphin lifted free. Once they'd climbed above the trees, Trevor pivoted the helicopter and flew away from the headlights of the fast approaching vehicles.

"Where to?" Trevor shouted over his shoulder.

Kristof looked down at Dmitri—the Russian's eyes were closed as if sleeping. Kristof slapped him on each cheek until Dmitri finally opened his eyes. "It's Kristof. Can you hear me?"

Looking disoriented, Dmitri's eyes opened and jumped from face to face of the three people leaning over him.

"Dmitri," Kristof said loud enough for Dmitri to fix his focus in his direction. "Gregori Petrov wants me to kill you. I don't want to end you, my old friend. Why does he want you dead?"

Dmitri blinked heavily as tears formed in his eyes and started to roll down the wrinkled skin on his face. "I made mistakes. The girl may have been silenced too late. Death is inevitable. Gregori has big plans, and they never included me. I'm glad it's you who kills me, Kristof. I will see you soon, no?"

Lauren felt as if she'd heard the name Petrov before, and even though Dmitri was completely severed from reality, he'd uttered the one name that brought a brief flash of concern to Kristof's face.

Lauren pulled on a headset and the moment Marta put hers on, Lauren asked, "Who is this Petrov?"

"Gregori Petrov is a hard-line communist who publicly hated Gorbachev for giving in to the West," Kristof said. "Over the years, Petrov has capitalized on the collapse of the Soviet Union by assembling a massive fortune from oil leases he stole. From there, he acquired arms and aircraft manufacturing concerns—always weapons, always making more money, but his open contempt for the West was always present. Petrov is the one man in Russia who has both the hatred and the money to try to topple the Russian government."

"How long do the drugs we gave Dmitri last?" Lauren asked.

"He'll be this way for another two hours before they start to wear off," Marta said. "What are you thinking?"

"Remember the e-mail from Calvin, suggesting that I turn myself in to the nearest embassy?" She turned to face Kristof as he donned his own headset. "I'm thinking we go back to Berlin and turn Dmitri over. I'll go with him."

"What can the Americans do?" Marta asked.

"I'm not talking about them. If Dmitri knows of a plot to topple the Russian government," Lauren said, "who better to interrogate him than the Russians?"

"You've got to be kidding," Marta said. "We kidnapped a senior SVR agent, flew him out of Berlin, drugged him, and now you think the best plan is to deliver him back to the Russians? What are you going to say, 'Hey, you guys need to hear this'?"

"Yes," Lauren said. "I'll turn myself in with him and explain what has taken place. I don't think they have any reason to harm me, but you have to promise to alert William to where I am."

"Remember what Dmitri said when he met you," Kristof said. "He thanked you and Donovan for your peacekeeping efforts and thanked you on behalf of the Russian people. Even considering the source, the words contain an element of truth. I think this could work, and I'm coming with you."

"No!" Marta snapped, clearly angry. "Dad, they'll kill you. They might even kill Lauren. None of us are going to the Russian embassy, it's insane!"

"I have a few things the Russians want," Kristof said. "I also know all of the players and can probably expedite a few things that Lauren can't. If Petrov is the man behind all of this, then we need help. I won't deny that it's risky, but in a clever way, an arms dealer and a DIA analyst might have the best chance to put an end to all of this."

"It'll be the end all right," Marta said, but she shook her head as if in pure disbelief.

"What's Dmitri's reaction going to be when he finds he's in the Russian embassy?" Lauren asked. "And will they listen to us?"

"I don't know if the phone recorded anything once we got on the helicopter, but I have the dialogue from the house," Marta said. "It might help get them interested."

"Let's ask him," Lauren said as she reached down and gently slapped Dmitri's face until he opened his eyes. As before, he seemed to need a minute to orient himself. "Dmitri, we have some good news. We're taking you to the Russian embassy in Berlin—you'll be safe there."

"No!" Dmitri yelled and tried to sit up, his arms flailing as he struggled to raise himself up.

"Dmitri," Kristof said as Marta pinned his arms to the floor. "Why don't you want to go to the embassy?"

"I can't," Dmitri said, wild-eyed. "It's too dangerous."

"Dangerous, how?" Kristof asked. "Dmitri, what is so dangerous about the embassy?"

"War," Dmitri said as his eyes closed and his head slumped back and hit the floor.

Lauren felt Dmitri's pulse. His heart was beating, but it was weak. "He's alive, but he's an old man, I hope he'll hold together."

"I'm still flying in a great big circle, burning fuel," Trevor reminded them.

"I don't like Dmitri's choice of words." Lauren frowned. "*War* wasn't what I expected him to say."

Marta turned toward Trevor. "We need to fly to Berlin, to the Russian embassy. Do you know where it is?"

"They're all lined up in a row. It'd be hard to miss," Trevor said as he immediately banked to the northwest.

"How long until we're there?" Marta asked.

"Quick and dirty, drawing attention to ourselves, maybe thirty minutes," Trevor said. "If you want a little stealth and finesse, make it forty-five."

"I vote quick and dirty. We might as well let them know we're coming," Lauren said. "Though we still need to figure out what the two of you can do once you drop us off."

"I have an idea," Marta said. "Trevor, will you be able to let the three of them out on the roof of the Russian embassy, or are we going to have to use the hoist?"

"Rooftop," Trevor replied.

"What about this?" Marta said. "You drop me off in the park across from Tatiana's club. I'd love to get a better look around that place, and what better time than in the chaos after our earlier visit, especially when the same helicopter returns to the neighborhood. From there, it's what, maybe two or three minutes flying time to the Russian embassy. After that, Trevor, you fly straight to the British embassy and surrender."

"I like the plan right up until I surrender," Trevor said over his shoulder. "With my night-vision goggles, I can maneuver fast enough to make my escape, and then land somewhere and walk away. Kristof, I'm sorry in advance about ditching your chopper."

"Don't worry about the helicopter," Kristof replied as he patted his shirt pocket and produced a pen. "Does anyone have a piece of paper?"

"Here you go." Trevor handed a notepad over his shoulder.

Kristof balanced the pad on his knee and began to write, then glanced up at Lauren. "Come sit with me. I want to discuss some things with you before we arrive."

Lauren listened as Kristof leaned in and spoke directly into her ear. Dmitri still appeared unconscious, and Marta, who lived in a world of whispered secrets, seemed not to care.

"I wrote a number on this piece of paper," Kristof said. "It's the number of dollars I'll accept for my business. The quickest way to get the Russians to listen is for me to explain my past dealings with Dmitri, dealings that Moscow would love to stop but can't, unless they buy me out."

"Would you really do that?" Lauren asked. "What about Marta?"

"She's already a very wealthy woman. The amount she'd receive in the sale would almost triple that fortune," Kristof said. "Then maybe I'll feel better about her future. She can make her own decisions about her life, like I did, like we all did."

"What did you learn from your time with Trevor?" Lauren asked, both surprised and impressed with Kristof for finding such a bold solution for the questions that had been plaguing him about his daughter's future. Once again she understood why this man and Donovan were such close friends.

"He's a brave man, and he loves my daughter for who she is, not for the collection of lies and deceptions we're both forced to live. He explained that he'd wanted to talk to me for some time about his feelings for her, but was deferring to Marta as to when she thought the time was right. He's very perceptive as well as sensitive, and he suggested that with my health being a consideration, that for Marta's and my sake, sooner may be better than later."

"Is he right?"

"Hard to tell. I'm glad he found the courage to say what he did. If I can send my daughter off into the world with money, options, and a man she seems to care about, and who cares about her, then I could die a happy man."

"Don't die yet," Lauren said. "There are other girls who love and need you, and could benefit from your wisdom."

"Abigail." Kristof smiled at the thought.

"And me."

"Everyone hang on," Trevor said. "It's time to start down, after which we're going to be evasive and fly really fast."

Trevor dropped the helicopter down on the deck, his night-vision goggles allowing him to thread below the tops of trees, over power lines, between chimneys, confusing any radar operator that tried to lock in on them. When they reached the taller buildings, he flew the Dauphin toward central Berlin like he was on a giant slalom course. Marta leaned forward, kissed Trevor on the cheek, then pulled on her hat and gloves and crouched near the door.

Lauren held on as they burst from the forest of buildings and Trevor banked steeply over the park while slowing. He descended rapidly into a clearing surrounded by trees, checked his descent until he was hovering only three feet above the ground. In a blast of noise and cold air, Marta jumped to the ground. Kristof left the door open as Trevor powered upward and out of the park, pivoting the machine sharply and then roaring forward as they headed toward Embassy Row.

Lauren moved to Dmitri's left side; Kristof was on the right.

"This needs to be quick. Be ready," Trevor shouted.

Lauren watched out the open door as the trees of the park vanished. They crossed a boulevard with light traffic, and then below them was the Holocaust memorial, the rows of huge monoliths a tribute to the millions of departed souls. Seconds later, Trevor brought the Dauphin to a motionless hover over a stained and cracked roof, with ducts and vents dotting the surface. Lauren ignored the brutal cold from the rotor wash and jumped out, holding onto Dmitri. Kristof followed, and together they lowered the drugged Russian to the concrete as Trevor climbed and banked away. The sound of the rotor blades faded, replaced by the shouts of armed men pointing automatic weapons, motioning for them to lay on their stomachs and put their arms behind them.

Lauren felt herself being searched and she winced at the rough pat-down as she was relieved of her passport as well as the phone containing Dmitri's interview and the images of Sofya. Moments later, both she and Kristof were dragged to their feet, and as they were marched toward a hatch, two soldiers rushed past with a stretcher for Dmitri. As Lauren was propelled forward toward a narrow stairwell, she squinted at the harsh light as she began a descent into the bowels of the Russian embassy.

# CHAPTER THIRTY-SEVEN

"DONOVAN, SHE'S AWAKE," Montero said softly from the galley space. "I think you should come back and sit with her."

"You have the airplane," Donovan said to Michael as he released his harness, stepped out of the cockpit, stretched, and went to Sofya.

Montero led the way. Sofya was sitting up, her legs tucked underneath her. As he neared, he saw that her eyes were red, and overall, she looked raw, fragile, and damaged.

"How are you doing?" Donovan said as he took a seat across the aisle. "Did a nap help?"

"Yes," Sofya said. "Maybe. I don't know."

"I can't even pretend to comprehend what you must be going through." Donovan turned in his seat, leaned across the aisle. "I'm ready to listen, I want to know what you know, and I'll do whatever I can to find a way to help you. First and foremost, I need to understand why we're still in danger. Who is trying to kill us and how can we stop them?"

Sofya put a hand over her mouth and remained silent.

"Do you remember anything?"

"Andrei," Sofya said. She reached out and took Donovan's hand as the first fresh tear rolled down her cheek. "He was my partner, actually more than my partner. We were going to be married."

"I'm listening." Donovan put his hand over hers. "Is Andrei the man Michael and Montero found in the forest?"

"Yes, he and I are—were—operatives for the Russian government," Sofya said as she fought her tears. "The SVR likes teams that operate as a couple; it draws less attention to our activities and movements. Andrei and I were working undercover when everything went wrong."

Donovan, still holding her hand, squeezed it, hoping to keep her talking. Montero came forward, stopped and listened, not wanting to interrupt.

"If you want to help me, then you need to know that I can't ever go back," Sofya said, her eyes shifting from wounded to deadly serious. "I need you to tell my handlers I died in the plane crash, because I would rather die than go back. For years after I was kidnapped, I was tortured, and raped. At some point, I was taken by the SVR and ordered to do whatever they wanted. It was either submit to them and become an agent, or they would send me back to the sex clubs where I know I would have eventually died."

"Whatever it takes," Montero said. "I promise you'll never have to go back to that life."

"I promise as well," Donovan said. "Between the two of us we have the resources to help you live whatever life you might choose, but we need to ensure that we all survive. Can you help us understand who wants all of us dead?"

"His name is Gregori Petrov; he's our enemy."

"I know who he is," Donovan said and his eyes flared in anger. "He's one of the richest and most corrupt men in Russia, and he made that fortune on the backs and lives of the less fortunate. Was the Boeing his?"

"Yes. We were trying to understand what he was doing, why he was making these flights. I trained as a flight attendant and Andrei as a steward, though there is a huge hole in the events, and then I remember when they started torturing Andrei. After that, I see just darkness, fragments of what happened, a jumble I don't understand. I'm sorry."

"Was Petrov ever on the airplane? Did you ever meet him?" Montero asked.

"No," Sofya said. Her eyes fluttered briefly and she stared up at the ceiling as if in thought, and then her gaze dropped to her lap. "But Petrov's son and the son's wife were aboard, traveling under another name. They're in their fifties. I remember from the briefings."

"So they were on holiday?" Donovan asked.

"No, everyone was very serious. There was a bodyguard, as well as another man, and a woman who seemed in charge of the trip. Everyone seemed afraid to be around them."

"Sofya," Montero said as she knelt down in the aisle. "There are more pictures, images that Donovan and Jesse took inside the Boeing. Do you feel up to looking at them? They might help you fill in the black spaces."

"Are they terrible?" Sofya asked as her eyes danced between Donovan and Montero, as if pleading for help, to not have to see horrific things ever again.

"There are some pictures of people who have died," Montero said. "They can't hurt you. All they can do is help you remember. Think of them as a harmless clues left behind by the universe to help you piece your life together."

Sofya swallowed and then nodded as she pulled her hands out of Donovan's and crossed her arms defensively across her chest while Montero opened the laptop.

"Just so you know, these are arranged in the order Jesse took them, so they start in the main salon, work aft to the main stateroom, and then forward to the galley and cockpit. If you need me to slow down, go back, or stop, let me know, okay?" Montero set the laptop on the desktop and positioned the screen so all three of them could see the images. "Are you ready?"

Sofya nodded.

Montero brought up the first image of the Boeing, shot from above, showing the airplane sitting on the sandy bottom, its nose pointed up into the air as if struggling to leave its watery tomb. The second was taken from the wing. The hole in the fuselage where the over wing exit had been opened was clearly visible.

Donovan looked at the computer, then at Sofya, trying to gauge her reaction. So far, her face seemed locked in a wince of anticipated pain and remained unchanged through the next four exterior shots. Jesse hadn't taken another picture until he and Donovan had shed their tanks and entered the cabin. The instant the view of the flooded salon filled the screen, Sofya's head jerked backward, startled. She closed her eyes and tears trickled down from both eyes. Montero waited until Sofya could continue, and Donovan was relieved that the next several images showed nothing but the empty passageway leading to the stateroom.

Donovan knew what was coming, and as the picture of the dead man and woman appeared on the screen, Sofya flinched as if remembering and then turned away. Montero stopped and waited.

"You're being very brave looking at these," Donovan said, and Sofya managed to turn back to look at the young woman in the hallway.

"Can you tell us who these two people are?" Montero asked.

"It's the man everyone was afraid of, Konstantine, and his assistant, her name was Jaqueline."

"Do you know how they died?" Donovan asked, knowing what the next image was going to show.

"I killed them," Sofya said softly.

Donovan looked into Sofya's eyes. The soft light from the computer combined with the Northern Lights spilling in through the window created an otherworldly glow. From the matter-of-fact way she said the words, he understood that she had no regrets.

Montero hurried through the next dozen pictures and slowed as Jesse entered the main salon and she stopped at the shot of the open briefcase with the gold coins.

Sofya leaned forward as if studying each coin, then turned to Donovan. "Did you take pictures of the papers that were inside the bag?"

Surprised by the request, Donovan had to stop and think. "No pictures, but we have the papers themselves, they're in the baggage compartment. I think Jesse put everything we found in a blue duffel bag. They're probably still half soaked and frozen."

"You two keep going. I'll go find them." Montero jumped up and hurried toward the rear of the plane.

"Okay, you're doing great," Donovan said. He steeled himself for the next series of pictures as he pushed the button that advanced to the fire damage he'd found in the salon. "This is what I don't understand. Why was there a fire?"

Sofya's body began to shake, and she lowered her face into her hands. Donovan reached out and put his hand on her back to comfort her.

"They were torturing Andrei!" Sofya said as she cried. "They caught him going through the briefcase. They were burning him with a cigar lighter—it was like a tiny blowtorch. He was screaming. I couldn't take it anymore and I made them stop."

"You did the right thing," Donovan said. In his peripheral vision, he caught Montero coming up the aisle, and as before, she stopped in the darkness close enough to listen but not so close as to interrupt.

"They were burning Andrei, so I grabbed two bottles of vodka. I broke them on the table. As I'd planned, the alcohol ignited and the men caught on fire, one man, the bodyguard, was shouting, then clothing, magazines, and blankets caught on fire. The smoke was bad, and the plane began to descend."

"Did you know we were there?" Donovan asked.

"No, not until I was out on the wing."

Sitting in the semi-darkened cabin, Donovan allowed himself a small smile. She'd just given him the first inkling that she was filling in the gaps after the landing. "What happened then?"

"Konstantine, who was in the stateroom, rushed forward and grabbed Andrei who was still in shock, reeling from the burns on his hands and neck. I tried to save him by using the broken bottlenecks as weapons, but I had no chance. Someone hit me from behind, and I went down to my knees. Konstantine yelled that I wasn't to be killed, only put out of commission, and as someone held me, Petrov's daughter-in-law jabbed me in the shoulder with a hypodermic needle. I think that's when I went berserk. A woman named Tatiana, this horrible woman who was in charge of the girls at a club, used to drug me before she let the men at me. I learned to use my adrenaline to fight off the drugs as long as I could."

"That ability probably saved your life," Donovan said.

"I screamed at Konstantine as he held Andrei. The cabin was filling with smoke, and then Konstantine pulled open the emergency exit, gave me a sick twisted grin, and threw Andrei out into space. He was gone and I lost it. I threw off Petrov's son who was holding me, picked up the shattered bottlenecks, and threw them at Konstantine, cutting him deeply on his arm, and he retreated. I turned and kicked Petrov's son in the groin, and then without warning, the airplane touched down. The reverse thrust threw all of us off balance, and we were tossed across the salon."

"Why do you think the pilots landed?"

"I think with the heavy smoke and all of the screaming, they thought the entire cabin was on fire and that they'd lose control of the plane and everyone would die."

"Who had the gun?" Donovan asked.

"The woman, Petrov's daughter-in-law, completely panicked. I doubt she even knew where we were. I think she wanted to kill everyone who knew she and her husband were on board. Once we were stopped, I heard two shots from the cockpit. When she stepped out of the cockpit, I was waiting. I grabbed the pistol and hit her hard in the throat and stomach until she released the gun. I pointed it at her and pulled the trigger. I felt nothing, no anger, no remorse, just overwhelming grief for Andrei. Next, I killed her husband, who was still on the floor holding his balls. Then, I shot their badly burned bodyguard. After that, I ran back toward the stateroom and met Jaqueline coming out the door. She had no time to react, and I shot her, too. I remember the look of shock and denial on Konstantine's face when I pointed the gun at him. He was pitiful. He begged like a weakling to live, offering me money, freedom. I shot him twice, once to inflict great pain, the other to multiply that pain and to summon his death."

"Then what happened?"

"I heard the sound of the cracking ice. I ran to the exit and threw myself out on the wing, but I could feel the drugs starting to take effect. It was so cold, and all I could think about was to get away from the sinking plane and the people inside. I jumped. The icy water felt like an electric shock; it drove me to climb out and keep running, but I grew so weary my legs wouldn't push through the snow. I fell. I was only going to lie there a moment and rest before getting up again. The next thing I remember is you picking me up from the snow. I thought you were an angel. I think maybe you still are."

"What you did was so courageous," Montero said. "I'm in awe of what you did to survive."

Sofya started to say something, then started to unravel. She'd recounted the events, and now the emotions caught up. She let out an involuntary moan and closed her eyes. She rocked back and forth as sobs wracked her body. She cried out to Andrei in painful, gasping spasms. Over and over she told him she was sorry.

Donovan set aside the computer and gathered her in his arms, rocking her as she cried. She was inconsolable, and he knew there were no words. The least he could do was let her know she wasn't alone. He knew all too well the depth of her pain and the agony she felt, and would always feel. The guilt and anguish might diminish eventually, but it would never leave—it's impossible, the wounds run too deep. Dying was easy; surviving was the hardest part.

Montero went forward to the galley and returned with a mug and a small box of tissues.

"Sofya, I brought you some tea," she said, and even though Donovan pulled away, Sofya kept rocking back and forth. "I know it hurts, but this is not over, and we can't lose you to your grief. You need to help us stop the people who hurt you and took Andrei's life, starting with the Tatiana woman. I promise, when this is over, I'll take you to Florida, or wherever you want, and I'll introduce you to people who can help."

"We can't change what happened," Donovan added. "But we can make sure that there is no one left who wants to hurt us. But to do that, we need your help. Montero found those papers, and we need you to help us read through them, to see if they can help. Can you do that?"

Sofya stopped rocking and wiped at her eyes. She started to talk several times, but her voice failed and the tears continued. Montero pressed the cup of tea into her hands and Sofya sipped. Then she opened her eyes and blinked; for the moment, she seemed to be pulling it together.

Donovan stepped away as Montero set the stack of documents on the workstation. He watched Montero peel off several of the sheets to discover that the papers beneath were soaked and fused together.

"My suitcase," Montero told Donovan. "In the side pocket is my hairdryer—can you go get it for us?"

Donovan hurried down the aisle, switched on the light, found the blow dryer, and headed forward. When he came back, Sofya was holding the first page, reading out loud, translating the Russian to English, while Montero, pen in hand, was taking notes. Donovan slid into the science station across the aisle and plugged in the dryer. Montero handed him the stack of soggy pages and Donovan went to work. As each page succumbed to the blast of heat and could be safely peeled away from the others, he'd hand it across the aisle to Montero, who would lean in as Sofya began to read. He finally decided to aim the blast of heated air at the side of the entire stack and move the nozzle back and forth. The hot air coupled with nearly zero humidity in the cabin was working, and he began separating the stack into smaller and smaller piles until he was working well ahead of Montero and Sofya. When he was finished, he switched off the dryer and motioned to Montero that he was going to the cockpit.

"Are you okay?" Michael asked as Donovan sat down and buckled into his seat. "I could only hear parts of what was said, but it sounded difficult. Was Sofya able to help?"

"Yes. Give me a minute to process everything." Donovan scanned the instruments and discovered that they'd already crossed a huge portion of Canada and would reach the east coast of Baffin Island in a matter of minutes. "Sofya is a Russian spy. Her fiancé was the man you found in the woods. He was thrown from the 737 after his cover was blown. He was tortured, burned with a butane lighter, and she stopped them. She killed everyone on the 737 except the flight crew, and I don't blame her. They're going through the documents now. Maybe we'll learn more."

"Is she going to be okay?" Michael asked.

"I told her I'd do whatever I could to keep her safe," Donovan said. He looked over at his friend. "Help me keep my word, and let's not let anything happen to her."

"You got it," Michael said.

Donovan looked outside, and as far as he could see were the undulating ripples of the Aurora Borealis, the glow from the Northern Lights overpowering the stars. Below them, snow covered the land and the North Atlantic appeared on the horizon as a vast expanse of black. Lauren and Abigail were on the other side of the ocean, as well as a host of people who wanted them all dead. In the back of the plane a Russian spy and a former FBI agent were trying to understand how to stop the killing. He glanced at their ground speed, which was still over six hundred miles per hour, and as they roared through the night sky eight miles above the earth, Donovan had the brief sensation that they were all hurtling toward an uncertain fate.

# CHAPTER THIRTY-EIGHT

ONCE INSIDE THE Russian embassy, Lauren had been immediately separated from Kristof. Even though she sat in what appeared to be an unused office, she had no illusion that it was anything other than a holding cell. Lauren crossed her arms; they'd taken her coat and the room held a chill. As she sat in the bare room, she could finally feel her fatigue closing in on her. She had no idea if it would take them twenty minutes or twenty hours to come for her.

No sooner had Lauren closed her eyes than a man wearing a suit opened the door.

"Dr. McKenna. Come with me." He spoke in perfect English.

She followed him down the narrow hallway until they came to an elevator. It opened immediately, and they stepped inside. There were a series of buttons, but the man with her inserted a keycard instead of pressing a floor. An unmarked light illuminated, the doors closed, and Lauren felt the car descend. There was no real sensation of how far they'd gone down, but when the elevator opened, two armed soldiers stood on either side of a heavy steel door. Another swipe of a keycard and the door swung open. She walked into a control center not unlike the one where she worked at the Defense Intelligence Agency.

She was surprised by how many people were on duty. She spotted a dozen men and women sitting at workstations, many using multiple monitors. There was a low murmur of hushed conversations. What words she heard were unintelligible. Several people glanced up at her before going back to what they were doing.

"To your right, the first office," her escort said.

Lauren did as she was told, and when the door swung open, she found an older man sitting at a desk. Thinning gray hair was parted into a comb-over. His jacket hung on a coat rack and he was wearing a long-sleeved shirt that strained across his belly, the sleeves rolled to the elbows and a tie loosened at the neck. He removed his reading glasses and stood as the door behind her closed.

"I'm Dr. Lauren McKenna," Lauren said as she held out her hand in an effort to appear forthright and unafraid. Unexpectedly, the man stood and reached out and shook her hand.

"I'm the senior diplomatic attaché on duty. You may call me Nikolai," he said as he eased back down in his chair, leaving Lauren standing. "I know who you are, though I'm more familiar with your CIA code name, Pegasus. You're nothing if not intelligent, but I have yet to figure out what exactly it is you think you're doing. Start with what kind of drug you've given Dmitri."

"It's classified," Lauren said. "All I can tell you is it's a prototype developed by Mossad."

"You're an analyst with the DIA. You're also highly placed within Eco-Watch, due to the fact that your husband is the Director of Operations. You seem to be at the center of a great many—let's call them interesting events, shall we? Tonight you kidnapped a high-ranking member of the Russian government, drugged him, interrogated him, and then you personally deliver him back to our embassy, accompanied by an extremely dangerous man we know as Archangel. Have I missed anything?"

"The woman, Sofya," Lauren said. "You left her out of your summary."

"Where did you get the pictures of her? It appears she's dead."

"Only unconscious. She's alive and safe for the moment."

"Dmitri's interrogation tape." Nikolai interlaced his fingers and then stretched them as he spoke. "We know you're there. Who is the other woman?"

"Classified."

"Very well, let's say for the moment I have a vague idea why you're here. Why are you with Archangel?"

"His name is Kristof, and he's a friend of mine."

"He has no phone, no passport, no identification."

"Yet you still know who he is." Lauren remembered her conversation with Kristof in the helicopter. "Are you sure he didn't arrive with anything else? He told me he had something you wanted."

"The single piece of paper?"

"With a number written on it?" Lauren asked.

"Yes, and nearly illegible, I have no idea what it means."

"Well, he did write it while riding in the helicopter. The number is thirty million, and it's the price in dollars for what it is you want."

"That's preposterous," Nikolai said through a forced laugh. "I could kill him and take what I want."

"That would be an ill-advised move," Lauren said evenly. "You know he's sick, right? He has a succession plan in place, has had for years. You'd gain nothing, and the new leader would seek revenge."

"A valid point," Nikolai said. "What else compelled you to arrive on my roof?"

"There was another interrogation earlier tonight. Tatiana Reznik spoke freely about the SVR, Sofya, and Dmitri. That tape is in the hands of someone who will release it to Moscow, as well as the world media if anything happens to Kristof or me. I can promise you won't like what Tatiana had to say, and neither will Moscow. Nikolai, I'm not here to threaten you. I'm here to get you to listen, to help me figure out what is happening so we can work together to stop it."

"You have no leverage. You're a fugitive. Interpol desperately wants to talk to you."

"We both know I didn't have anything to do with the attack in Innsbruck. But there have been attacks in Minnesota, London, and Prague, carried out by Russians." Lauren placed both hands on the desktop and leaned in toward Nikolai. "I don't think you sent those men to kill my friends, but I do think you need to find out who did, and why. You also need to find out who wants Sofya dead. I'm assuming she's one of yours?"

"That's classified."

"Thank you. At least we're being honest. She's SVR, same as you, and I have her."

"We demand her immediate release," Nikolai said effortlessly. "She is a Russian citizen."

"Nikolai, please don't start posturing. I think there's something about to happen somewhere in the world that will do harm to both of our countries. We found Sofya on a frozen lake in the Arctic, and the moment we asked Interpol to help in identifying her, people started dying. Dmitri used the word 'war'. That's why I'm here. Our governments, our countries, are not at war, but I think someone else might want us to be."

"What if our countries are at war?" Nikolai said, as he put his hands on his desk and stood to face Lauren.

"If I thought that were even remotely true, I wouldn't have come here," Lauren said without blinking. "The second I think it is true, I'll come across this desk and kill you before your men can stop me."

Nikolai's eyes flared in surprise and then he stared at her, as if assessing the chances that she might be capable of her threat. Then a smile came to his fleshy face. "I've heard the stories. You and your husband have done much for our country. The business last year in Slovakia, I was involved in that operation. You and your group of friends were impressive, though I never believed the entire story. After meeting you today, I'm far more apt to believe what I've heard."

"I'm done with the CIA. I'm really more of a stay-at-home mom these days," Lauren said as she backed off, and smiled sweetly to hide the fact that she had no clue how to kill anyone barehanded. "If you know about Slovakia, you know a small group of people risked everything to avert what would have been a disaster. Is it asking too much for your help in return?"

"We both know the risks of dealing in maybes and innuendo. Both of our governments get dozens of threats every day. Sometimes we even threaten ourselves so we can display our readiness to those who might be watching. It's a bit insane, I know, but it's how the system of checks and balances works. You brought me a rambling interview, given by a drugged, or perhaps just a drunken, old man. One who is clearly under duress."

"I'm well aware of what I delivered, which is exactly why I'm here. The drugs we gave him should last at least another hour." Lauren watched as Nikolai's eyes narrowed as he processed the implications. "Make it count."

Nikolai reached for the phone, waited for someone to answer, and began speaking in Russian. The conversation was entirely one-sided and after a minute, he hung up and leaned back. "What can I do to make you more comfortable? This may take some time."

"I want to see Kristof. He needs a doctor. It would be tragic if he passed away while enjoying your hospitality."

Nikolai was about to reply when his phone rang. He swept it to his ear, listened, and then grunted something in Russian.

"Follow me," Nikolai said as he hurried Lauren out of the room.

She followed him around the open-sided corridor that bordered the operations center. Maybe it was just her imagination, but there seemed to be more activity than before. When Nikolai opened a heavy door, Lauren passed into a semi-darkened space. She understood that the only light came from a window that was one-way glass. Kristof and Dmitri were seated at a table in the room under observation. Another man, someone much younger, faced them.

Lauren realized she and Nikolai weren't alone. Two other men stood off to one side, watching. One wore a crisp military uniform, the other was a civilian who appeared somewhat unkempt, unshaven, with a yet-to-be-knotted tie looped around his neck.

"Dr. McKenna, there will be no introductions," Nikolai said quietly. "Everyone is well aware of who you are, and would prefer to remain unknown to you."

"What's going on?" Lauren asked. "Why is Kristof being interviewed with Dmitri?"

"It was Kristof's idea," the unkempt man said as he flipped up his collar and began tying his tie. "The man conducting the interview is asking a set of questions that Kristof devised. Kristof's deception has convinced Dmitri that they are both prisoners, and Kristof is selling Dmitri out for leniency."

"What have you learned so far?" Nikolai asked. "And why did you send for us?"

"We already know that Kristof sold several shipments of AK-47s to Dmitri, along with a large consignment of ammunition. Dmitri then asked that the contraband be smuggled to Moscow."

"Where the AK-47s were probably stolen from in the first place," Nikolai said.

"That's the thing—Kristof is giving us an inside look into his operation. Archangel's empire is far more complex and far-reaching than we ever anticipated."

Lauren smiled to herself in the darkness. Kristof was breaking Dmitri, as well as marketing his business at the same time. "Where in Moscow did Kristof smuggle the guns? I mean, why would Dmitri buy guns he already has access to?"

"Just listen."

"Kristof," the interrogator asked. "Where did your organization deliver these guns?"

"I'll tell you," Kristof said. "And when I do, you'll understand that my friend Dmitri thought he was doing the right thing."

"Explain," the interrogator said, as if growing irritated.

"Dmitri told me that the order came from a senior officer within the SVR," Kristof continued. "I assumed it was yet another ill-conceived attempt by the SVR to buy guns from me and then track my sources. Prepared for this, my people subcontracted with locals, and then watched as the guns were ultimately delivered to a hangar at the Vnukovo airport, and not the SVR."

"Wait, what? That's not where I was instructed to send the weapons," Dmitri sputtered.

Lauren turned to Nikolai. "Where did Sofya leave Moscow from?"

"We suspect Vnukovo airport, from one of the private jet terminals."

"Dmitri," Kristof said. "We still have time to get out of Berlin, but you have to tell them what you told me earlier, about the coming war. We'll make our deal and get out before it's too late."

"What war?" the interrogator asked, his voice even and calm.

"Gregori Petrov's war," Dmitri said. "I think he's been buying weapons to start a war."

"The AK-47s are hardly enough to start a war," Kristof said. "What else have you tried to locate for him?"

"Tell me and I will suggest amnesty instead of charging you with treason and conspiracy," the interrogator said hungrily. "Better to live out your days on a pension, than be hung as a traitor."

"Months ago he started looking for a nuclear weapon, and then, just as quickly, he stopped asking," Dmitri said. "I received word that he'd found one."

"And he's going to detonate it today?" Kristof asked. "How would you know that?"

"There were whispers. I was warned to avoid any large city today, so we need to go."

"Do you at least have a target, a time, or a delivery system?" Kristof asked.

"No, only that Gregori wanted the spectacle to be in the daylight. He wanted people to see what had happened."

"The airplane in Canada," Lauren said as she spun to face Nikolai. "Is it carrying a nuclear weapon? Did Sofya bring it down because she knew?"

"I don't know," Nikolai said. He turned to the men in the room. "Find out the whereabouts of Gregori Petrov, as well as all of his family members. I also want the locations of all of Dmitri's known acquaintances."

"Can you help me locate my husband?" Lauren asked. "I need to know if he's still in Canada. He's traveling in an Eco-Watch Gulfstream."

"This way," Nikolai said. "Anything that involves a satellite or cell phone has been severely affected by the storm, but I think the land-line links will get us what we want."

Lauren fell in beside Nikolai as he escorted her through a door and into the operations center. They went straight to an empty workstation where he typed in a password and waited. Lauren noticed the large monitors were from the same high-quality man-ufacturer preferred by the DIA. A search page finally materialized, and Nikolai typed in more commands until an outline of Canada filled the screen.

"What's his call sign?"

"Eco-Watch zero one," Lauren said, and moments after Nikolai entered the data, a page for the *Galileo* appeared. As English was the international language used by the aviation industry, she could read what was on the screen.

"There we are—Eco-Watch zero one left Churchill earlier today."

"That's them." Lauren felt an enormous wave of relief as she seized on the fact that they weren't in Canada. "Where are they now?"

"The flight plan is to Edinburgh, Scotland." Nikolai scrolled east-ward until the icon of the *Galileo* illuminated on the big screen. "They're here, flying over Greenland."

Lauren could see the small white aircraft icon, and when Nikolai placed the mouse pointer over the airplane, an abbreviated data block appeared. The information for the *Galileo* showed their origin and destination, and that they were flying at thirty-nine-thousand feet. Lauren couldn't help but notice that in the broad expanse of sky depicted, there were only two other aircraft icons. "What's this airplane here?"

Nikolai swung his pointer up and tagged the target. "It's a Gulfstream, en route from Luton, England, to Keflavik, Iceland. The registration number is G-CGEL."

Lauren recognized the registration as the chartered Gulfstream on standby for Abigail, Stephanie, and Reggie. "How long until they land?"

"They're scheduled to arrive in forty-five minutes. Why?"

"This other aircraft up here to the northeast." Lauren pointed. "Who's that?"

"Hmm," Nikolai said as he studied the data block. "It's tagged as a Russian Federation Tupolev 214. It's using a call sign that marks it as a diplomatic flight."

"Landing at Keflavik?"

"Yes," Nikolai said as his eyes narrowed. "In one hour."

Lauren put a hand over her mouth and nose as if to suppress a cry for help as all of the possibilities seemed to hit her at once. She stepped back from the screen and turned to Nikolai. "I think there's a diplomatic summit taking place in Iceland. American Ambassador William VanGelder is already on the ground, waiting. Nikolai, what if there is a delegation of diplomats in Iceland, and there's a bomb aboard the Tupolev?"

Nikolai's eyes flared and he set his jaw. Instantly, he began to speak in Russian to the analysts in the room. He seemed to assign a specific task to each and receive a short reply in return. As Lauren watched the process, she saw the determined expression on Nikolai's face turn to one of frustration.

"What is it?" Lauren asked. "Tell me what's happening."

"I'm told the entire island of Iceland is experiencing a complete blackout due to the storm. We're unable to contact anyone on the ground there. We have no clear picture of what is happening."

"As a precaution, call air traffic control, have them turn the Tupolev around," Lauren said. "Petrov wouldn't detonate a bomb in Moscow."

"We don't know that there is a bomb, and if there is, we have no way to know how it might be detonated. An altitude sensor, a switch connected to the landing gear, it could be anything."

"Call the crew, have them search the plane," Lauren said.

"With the storm there is no HF or satellite communication. We can't talk to anyone, warn anyone. As it stands, we're powerless."

"Call the British," Lauren said, knowing she was clutching at empty ideas. "Have them scramble fighters and shoot the damn thing down! Don't let Petrov start a nuclear war."

"Royal Air Force jets intercepting and downing a Russian diplomatic flight would do exactly what you're trying to avoid," Nikolai said. "I feel like Petrov has used the storm to his advantage, and played this perfectly. Whatever is going to happen, we're powerless to stop it."

Lauren felt nauseous; she pressed her fingers to her temples and started to pace. She thought of the DIA, but even if she could reach Calvin, he would face the same obstacles that the Russians did. There were probably trunk cables on the ocean floor that ran from Iceland to Europe, but without any power they were ultimately useless. At some point, there needed to be electricity. She mentally raced through every form of known communication that could reach Iceland. She sensed the tiny spark of an idea, paused, and then slowly turned to look up at the oversized monitor. The icon that was the *Galileo* was pushing eastward and Lauren's eyes flared wide as she put it all together. She estimated the distances involved, quickly did the math, and then turned toward Nikolai.

"Dr. McKenna?" Nikolai must have sensed the shift in her mood.

"Nikolai, please tell me you have a submarine close enough to make direct radio contact with the Eco-Watch Gulfstream."

"All of our submarine movements are classified, and even if we did have one in place, our naval communications are done via satellite."

"No, they're not," Lauren said. "Before satellites, we, you, all of the superpowers used VLF communication as the primary method of communicating over long distances. The Very Low Frequency transmissions travel great distances by bouncing the signal between the ocean floor and the ionosphere. The solar storm will cause some decay in the transmission, but the majority of the signal is within our atmosphere—below the events taking place in space. We can use your antenna in Murmansk, it's the closest. In fact, we don't care who intercepts the message. Send an uncoded, plain-language priority broadcast for any submarine in the North Atlantic within three hundred miles of Iceland to attempt contact with Eco-Watch zero one on the emergency aviation frequency. They can do that, right?"

"Yes, the submarine only has to be in range of the jet. If so, it's a simple process for the submarine to float a VHF antenna to the surface and make the broadcast," Nikolai said as a subordinate handed him a sheet of paper. "You are correct. We've just confirmed that there is a classified high-level summit scheduled to begin in Iceland—today."

"What's the meeting about?"

"To discuss a plan that would accelerate the nuclear disarmament between the United States and Russia."

"Oh, God," Lauren said and rushed to the desk, grabbed a pen and a sheet of paper, and began to write furiously. When she finished, she handed it to Nikolai. "Send this message, exactly as I wrote it, and if we're lucky, the Eco-Watch Gulfstream can land in Iceland before the Tupolev and send out a warning."

Nikolai turned to look at the screen, frowned, and then reached for a calculator.

"I already did the math," Lauren said. "If everything remains the same, the Eco-Watch Gulfstream will land eleven minutes before the Tupolev—which is an eternity if you can reach a shelter. Nikolai, you have to send this. If nothing else, it will show the world we tried to stop what's happening. If you have the means to reach out to the Russian President, I suggest you do it as fast as possible, and maybe prevent an even bigger nuclear exchange."

"Stay here," Nikolai said as he walked to another station and picked up a phone.

# CHAPTER THIRTY-NINE

"MICHAEL, I NEED to get up and stretch. Do you want some more coffee?" Donovan asked as he began to unbuckle. The orange glow of the sun coming up over the Atlantic Ocean always had the same effect on him. His body felt as if it were nearing midnight, yet the dawn gave irrefutable proof to the contrary, and the contradiction always threatened to multiply his fatigue.

"I'm good," Michael said after he checked his cup.

Donovan stood and stretched; his old injuries seemed to tighten and resist as he did. He put his hands on the backs of both seats and pushed hard against his hamstrings.

"Eco-Watch zero one." A strong male voice poured from the cockpit speakers. "I repeat, Eco-Watch zero one, how do you read? Please respond."

Donovan instantly slid back into the captain's seat. He fastened his harness at the same time Michael picked up the microphone. The radio call had come in on the emergency VHF frequency every aircraft monitored while out over the Atlantic Ocean. It was unusual for someone to use Eco-Watch's call sign and not identify themselves. Montero had heard the call as well and hurried forward.

"This is Eco-Watch zero one, we copy," Michael said into the microphone. "Identify yourself and send your message."

"Roger, Eco-Watch zero one. Please switch to your company frequency."

Michael quickly spun in the private frequency that Eco-Watch was licensed to use as an operational channel. The possibility of anyone else in the area listening in on the forthcoming conversation had just dropped to nearly zero.

"What's going on?" Montero asked. "Who knows our frequency?"

"Not many," Donovan replied as Michael dialed it in the radio.

"Eco-Watch zero one is up," Michael transmitted.

"Eco-Watch, this is Commander Mitchell Trask aboard the United States Navy attack submarine *Minnesota*. How do you read? I have an urgent relay for you from Pegasus."

"We read you loud and clear. Send the message." Michael shot a concerned look toward Donovan and Montero and then picked up a pen, ready to write.

"Pegasus says: there is an unconfirmed possibility of private sector Russian attack on a diplomatic summit in Iceland. William, Stephanie, and Abigail are on-site. Unable to send direct warning due to total Icelandic power failure. Approaching Tupolev 214 contains delegation from Russia, and is most likely unaware that a possible bomb is aboard. Suggest you divert and initiate early warning, and evacuation if possible. Calculations suggest you'll arrive eleven minutes before the Tupolev."

"Captain Trask, is this for real?" Michael asked as he finished copying the message verbatim. "How did you get this?"

"That's not relevant," Trask replied. "We did confirm that Pegasus is one of ours, and we do know that this message went out as a plain-language transmission from the Russian long-range communication station in Murmansk. We think Pegasus and the Russian government are working together."

"Can you shed any light on the power situation in Iceland?" Michael asked.

"Negative," Trask said. "Though I can confirm the existence of the summit, but that's the extent of the information I can pass on until secure satellite communication is reestablished."

Donovan picked up his microphone. "Captain Trask, this is Captain Nash. If at all possible, can you send a return message to Pegasus?"

"Negative," Trask replied. "Good luck, Captain Nash, *Minnesota* out."

Donovan was about to ask Michael to plug in a direct course for Iceland when Michael, already ahead of him, pressed a button. The course needle swung to the left, and the display told them that the straight-line distance to the airport in Keflavik was eighty miles.

Michael switched frequencies on the VHF radio. "I can hear the tower talking to traffic."

"Don't contact anyone yet," Donovan said as he eyed their altitude, speed, and fuel. "We need a plan."

"This is crazy. I mean, how are we going to play this? I don't think we just call them up and tell them, 'Hey, we're Eco-Watch, and FYI, there's a possible bomb on its way. Oh, and it might be nuclear.'"

"You're right." Donovan looked down as the *Galileo* settled into its new course. At their present speed, they were fifteen minutes from Iceland. "We're going to declare an emergency and get on the ground as quickly as possible. The priority here is to warn these people without panicking either the population or the people aboard the Tupolev. Lauren's message was very clear about this being an unconfirmed possibility."

"There's also William's warning about us not screwing up his deliberations with the Russians," Michael said. "Montero, what do you think?"

Donovan turned and discovered that Montero was gone. He turned further, and spotted her in the cabin. Moments later she returned with Sofya. Both women squeezed into the small space where all four of them could talk.

"When I told Sofya about the message from the submarine, she remembered something. Sofya, tell them what you just told me."

"When Andrei and I were trying to infiltrate Petrov's organization, we were once called for an interview with the entity that handles many of the VIP flights out of Sheremetyevo Airport in Moscow. One of their divisions oversees the diplomatic flights for the government. When we were at the facility, we saw ground crew we recognized from Petrov's operation. I just read a note on Petrov's calendar about Sheremetyevo in reference to a Tupolev. It seemed odd about twenty minutes ago, but now it seems obvious. I also came across another hastily written note that didn't make sense until just now. It was a brief paragraph about air versus land, and the kill radius related to both. It makes sense if you apply it to a nuclear detonation."

"Sofya," Montero asked. "Do you think Petrov's people had access to this Tupelov that's flying into Keflavik?"

"Absolutely," Sofya said.

"Okay," Donovan said. "I've heard enough. In a few minutes, we're going to declare an emergency, which will give us priority handling. There's no power on the island, but the airport will have backup generators for essential items. This is going to go down fast, and once we arrive, I have no idea what's going to happen."

"Meaning, we may arrive just in time to get vaporized?" Michael said.

"I think we'll have a fair idea of the Tupolev's position before then," Donovan said. "And let me be clear, there is no way we allow this airplane to be within the blast zone. I'm serious, Michael, promise me you'll get this airplane safely airborne long before the Tupolev arrives. The three of you will not die on this particular mountain. You leave—even if I'm not aboard. Do you understand?"

"What are you talking about?" Montero asked.

"You heard the message. William, Stephanie, and Abigail are down there. I'm not leaving without my family, and you are not to stay long enough to get blown up. Michael, make the call to Keflavik," Donovan said as he put his hands on the throttles. "Let's don't get them all worked up. Tell them we have something nonlethal. What was it you used in Minneapolis?"

"A pressurization leak, that'll work," Michael said as he pressed the button and began transmitting. "Mayday, Mayday, Mayday. Keflavik tower, Eco-Watch zero one, declaring an emergency."

"Eco-Watch zero one, this is Keflavik, say your position and the nature of your emergency."

"We're seventy-five miles southwest, descending out of thirty-nine thousand feet. We're losing pressure in the aircraft cabin."

"Keflavik tower, I copy. You are cleared direct to the airport, plan runway one one, descend and maintain three thousand feet. The clouds are scattered at five thousand, the wind is zero eight zero at ten knots. Our radar is down, report five miles out, and when you can, please advise number of souls and fuel on board, and if you will require assistance upon arrival."

"Four souls, and our fuel will be thirteen thousand pounds on landing. No assistance will be required," Michael replied.

Donovan continued the descent, making sure the air-speed needle was pegged against the red line. With only eleven minutes to work with, every second mattered. The sense of speed grew as they plummeted toward the top of the cloud deck. The Gulfstream shuddered as they entered the opaque gray world inside the precipitation. The wings flexed as the *Galileo* rode out the turbulence and continued hurtling downward toward the ocean.

"Montero!" Donovan called out without taking his eyes from the instruments.

"I'm here," she said from behind him.

"The visibility is good, so we're going to break out of the clouds shortly and have a good view of the airport before we land. Go to science station two, power it up, and use the *Galileo's* primary optics to scan the airport. Try to find out what's going on there before we land."

"I know how to manually use the imager, but that's about it," Montero said. "If you need anything more, I'm not that person."

"Manual is fine," Donovan said. "I want to know what airplanes are on the ramp, and where. Usually when a dignitary arrives, there are people waiting, politicians, VIPs; we need to get to them as fast as possible."

"Got it," Montero said, and she hurried aft.

"Eco-Watch zero one, this is Keflavik tower. Be advised there will be a Gulfstream landing ahead of you, and will not be a factor. Say your distance from the airport."

"Eco-Watch zero one is eighteen miles out," Michael replied.

"Ask him if there is any other traffic," Donovan said, and as Michael made the transmission, they burst from the base of the cloud deck. Below them were the choppy waters of the North Atlantic. Ahead, just visible in the marine haze, was Iceland, and after several seconds of searching, Donovan picked up the runway.

"The only other traffic is an inbound Tupolev 214, approximately sixty miles east, no factor."

"That's him," Donovan said.

"Keflavik tower this is Gulfstream Charlie Golf Echo Lima turning final for runway one one."

"Roger Echo Lima, this is Keflavik tower, you are cleared to land runway one one. Be advised we have another Gulfstream landing behind you with an emergency in progress."

Donovan spotted the other Gulfstream far ahead, no more than a white speck. It landed and cleared the runway to the right.

"Eco-Watch zero one, this is Keflavik tower, you are number one for the airport. I have you in sight, cleared to land on runway one one. Wind is zero eight zero at twelve knots."

"Michael, give me twenty degrees of flaps, standby on the gear." Donovan felt the *Galileo* slow dramatically and he adjusted the power and made a smooth turn that lined them up for the runway. "Gear down, full flaps, final checklist."

Michael went through the electronic list and confirmed all of the systems were set for landing.

"Donovan!" Montero cried out from the back of the *Galileo*. "I just saw them! Stephanie, Abigail, and a man I didn't recognize just got off the Gulfstream and climbed into a maroon SUV. They drove away, and I don't know how to lock the camera on them. They're leaving!"

"Michael, flaps to twenty, we're going around," Donovan said as he pushed the throttles to the stop. "Gear up."

"What shall I tell the tower?" Michael said.

"Nothing. In fact, turn the volume down. They're not going to like what I'm about to do." Donovan leveled the *Galileo* and flew down the runway at a hundred feet going two hundred knots. As the airport spread out below him, he spotted two Icelandic airliners parked at the main terminal. Off to the right was the transient ramp and he banked to pass low overhead.

"That parked Boeing 757 belongs to the Air Force's Special Air Mission wing," Michael said as they flashed past. "It's probably William's ride."

"What else?" Donovan said as he focused his eyes out ahead of the *Galileo*, trying to spot and follow the access road leading away from the airport.

"There was a space next to the 757 that's empty, and I think you're right, there was a group of vehicles and people. It looks exactly like a diplomatic greeting party waiting for the Tupolev."

"I trust everyone on the ground saw us?"

"Oh they saw us all right, and then right afterwards, they heard us."

"Montero, do you have Abigail and Stephanie?"

"I will in a second," she said.

Montero pressed powerful binoculars to her eyes as they flashed over snow-covered roofs of what looked like apartment buildings.

"Three storage tanks straight ahead—do you see them?" Montero said. "There's an SUV just beyond—that's the vehicle which pulled away from the chartered Gulfstream. They just made a right turn onto the highway headed northeast, accelerating."

Donovan had very little time to maneuver. He banked the Gulfstream directly over the top of the SUV Montero swore held his daughter, and then seconds later the *Galileo* roared out over the harbor. He spotted the breakwater and using it for reference, made a steep turn, picked up the speeding SUV, and pointed the *Galileo* to cross right in front of the vehicle. He held fifty feet and two hundred knots. As the Gulfstream roared across the highway, less than ten car lengths from the front of the SUV, he pulled up and swung back around in a tight left turn. The maroon SUV swerved to the inside lane and slowed. From there, the driver made an abrupt turn onto the median and stopped. As the *Galileo* flashed over once again, he saw Abigail waving from an open window. Donovan rocked the wings and pulled up as the SUV bolted forward, finished the U-turn, accelerated, and headed back toward the airport.

"Now what?" Montero asked.

"Now we land," Donovan said.

"Which runway are you using?" Michael asked.

"Gear down," Donovan said as he continued his turn toward the airport. "I'm thinking a short approach to runway one one. We'll make that turnoff at the end, and from there it'll be a short taxi to where we saw those people waiting."

"Checklist complete down to the final flaps," Michael said as the landing gear swung down and locked into place.

"Full flaps," Donovan said as he added power and banked hard to make the steep ninety-degree turn to final. The Gulfstream slowed to approach speed as Donovan leveled the wings. He brought the throttles to idle and the tires lightly kissed the runway. In a flurry of practiced motion, he pulled out the spoilers and deployed the thrust reversers as he eased forward on the controls until he felt the soft rumble of the nose tires. He took the final turnoff, and as Michael reconfigured the airplane for their immediate departure, Donovan added power and quick-taxied toward the assemblage of people.

As he swung around to park the *Galileo*, he discovered that already, half a dozen official vehicles were speeding down the ramp to intercept them. Breaking free from the small gathering was a familiar face. William VanGelder, impeccably dressed, was running toward the Gulfstream. Even from this distance Donovan could see the concern on William's face. Donovan felt the deep fear that his failure meant everyone only had minutes to live.

"Keep both engines running," Donovan said to Michael as he jumped out of the seat and hurried toward the door, only to find Montero already lowering the airstair. Donovan turned back toward Michael. "How much time have I got?"

"The Tupolev will be here in eight minutes."

Donovan stood at the top of the stairs and scanned the ramp. There were nearly twenty people, including William. The chartered Gulfstream was parked on one side, and William's 757 on the other. A quick glance told him the 757 was buttoned up for the night, and of no use in an evacuation. Three cars lurched to a stop, blocking the Gulfstream, and men wielding automatic weapons aimed their guns at Donovan as he hurried down the steps to meet William.

"What in the hell are you doing here?" William yelled above the steady whine of the idling engines.

"We only have a few minutes. We think the incoming Russian Tupolev has a bomb aboard—there's a chance it's nuclear. As soon as Stephanie and Abigail get here, we need to leave," Donovan said as two armed men closed in on them.

"They've already left to drive into town," William said, his eyes becoming frantic.

"I think my low pass managed to turn them around."

"Keep your hands where I can see them! I'm Special Agent Robertson, and I need you to step away from the Ambassador."

"Wayne, it's okay," William said. "This is Donovan Nash. He has information about a credible threat. The Russians might be flying in a bomb."

"Nuclear?" Robertson asked.

"There is a high probability. I need you to allow me to fly the Ambassador out of here, as well as all the other people we can," Donovan said as he saw the Gulfstream that had brought Stephanie and Abigail from Europe flash its taxi lights, followed by their right engine spooling up in preparation for departure.

"Donovan," Montero yelled as she came rushing down the steps. "Michael explained to the other Gulfstream crew what was happening, and they're going to follow us out of here. Get as many people as you can into their airplane. We're leaving in four minutes."

"Is that Veronica Montero?" Robertson asked.

"Yes," William said. "And I suggest we all do as she says."

"Move those cars, split these people up," Robertson radioed his men and then turned to Donovan. "How many people can you take?"

"As many as I need to," Donovan said. "But I need your help finding my family. They're in a maroon SUV. They have to be close. They just landed and got off the other Gulfstream, but they're headed back this way."

"I remember them," Robertson said and started talking into his radio.

"I should have let them stay here at the airport," William said, lowering his head. "But Stephanie was exhausted, and I figured Abigail would be bored to death waiting for me, so I sent them to the hotel. Oh, dear God."

Donovan watched as Robertson and his men worked quickly. Montero joined the fray, the cars were moved, and eleven people split and ran toward the other Gulfstream.

"Three minutes!" Montero yelled as she ran toward the Eco-Watch jet and followed William up the stairs of the *Galileo* along with seven others.

The other Gulfstream had started its second engine and closed the door. The pilot flashed the taxi lights again, indicating that he was ready to roll. Donovan stood aside and motioned for Robertson to go ahead and board the *Galileo*.

"We have them!" Robertson called out as he put his hand to his earpiece. "They'll be here in thirty seconds!"

A rush of relief left Donovan's body as he hurried to the foot of the steps. "Michael, they're coming!"

"We have room for maybe five more at the most," Montero said. "I've got Sofya on the jump seat. I'll sit with her once we go, but all of the other seats are taken and people are going to be crowded on the floor."

Donovan caught a flash of motion in his peripheral vision, and found an official car careening around a hangar, lights flashing, and the maroon SUV in close pursuit. Both the car and the SUV screeched to a stop just outside the wingtip, and everyone piled out and ran toward the Gulfstream.

"Donovan, including the driver of the SUV, and the security agent who escorted them, there's seven people," Montero said. "I'm not sure everyone will fit."

"Daddy!" Abigail cried out as Stephanie hurried toward the stairs with Reggie close behind.

Donovan hugged his daughter. "I love you, sweetheart, go with Stephanie, Daddy has to fly."

"Go!" Robertson yelled as he herded the driver of the SUV, as well as his colleague, the woman who was driving the Secret Service car, up the stairs.

When they'd all squeezed in and Montero had closed the door, Donovan slid into his seat. That's when he discovered that Robertson had not boarded the Gulfstream. Looking out the window, he saw that Robertson had climbed into his vehicle and was swinging around to escort the two Gulfstream jets out to the runway.

Donovan released the brakes, and the *Galileo* began to roll as he fastened his harness. The instant he was strapped in, he pushed up the throttles and the Gulfstream powered down the taxiway faster than he'd ever taxied in his life. Robertson led the way. He kept his lights flashing, raced ahead, and turned two official airport cars off the taxiway so the jets had a clear path to the runway. Robertson finally pulled aside and let the *Galileo* race past him, and in the process, Robertson offered a solemn salute.

"Michael, where's the Tupolev?" Donovan asked as he returned the salute.

"He just turned a five-mile final," Michael said. "He'll be here in less than three minutes. The checklist is done, we're ready to roll. Which runway are we using?"

"I want to get as far away from the Tupolev as possible," Donovan said as he slowed just enough to round a corner. "How much runway do I have from this intersection?"

"Enough, hit it!"

Donovan pushed the throttles forward, and as the Gulfstream accelerated, he stole a glance to the west and spotted the lights from the Tupolev. The *Galileo* reached takeoff speed, and Donovan pulled back on the controls. The jet lifted free from the ground, and he called for Michael to raise the gear and then the flaps. He lowered the nose and leveled off at five hundred feet to let the Gulfstream accelerate.

"Montero," Donovan said. "Have everyone in back close the window shades and shut their eyes. If that thing goes off, it'll be bright."

Donovan turned to Michael. "Did the other Gulfstream make it?"

"Yes, they're behind us, low and to the right."

Donovan focused on the instrument panel and felt the airplane rumble as the *Galileo* thundered low across the nearly flat ground, the volcanic rocks blurring as they streaked past. Donovan had no idea how far was going to be far enough. Each agonizing tick of the clock offered a tantalizing glimmer of hope that they might escape. Moments later the world went completely white as the unearthly brightness from the nuclear detonation flooded the *Galileo's* cockpit.

# CHAPTER FORTY

LAUREN THOUGHT SHE might be sick, but she kept pacing back and forth behind the people working at their consoles. What was done was done. Nikolai would only tell her that there was confirmation that her message had been successfully relayed to the Eco-Watch jet via an American submarine. There was no other information. All Lauren knew was that Donovan had received the message that William, Stephanie, and Abigail were in Iceland, and there was a possible nuclear threat. She had no doubt that he and Michael had immediately turned for Iceland and that they'd be on the ground at Keflavik by now.

Her throat tightened again, and she fought the fear that built in her stomach. Would Donovan get to them in time, or had she sent her husband to be killed along with their daughter? The thought brought tears to Lauren's eyes, and she was almost glad she couldn't see the hands of the clock moving toward the Tupolev's estimated touchdown. With no satellite data, there was no real-time information, nothing to alert Lauren to what was happening, and if the worst took place, she would have no immediate knowledge as to who survived. All she could do was wait. She wiped her eyes and found Nikolai hanging up a phone and starting across the room toward her.

"Dr. McKenna," Nikolai said as he neared. "I need you to come with me."

"Where are we going?" Lauren asked.

"Not here." Nikolai held out an arm inviting Lauren toward the hallway.

They walked and Lauren felt even more isolated. At least in the control room there was the constant murmur of voices and the clicking of keyboards, normal actions. She felt like she'd know if something happened by the activity level, or maybe even facial expressions. Now she had nothing. They pushed through heavy metal doors, past a guard, then around a corner to an elevator. Nikolai grasped her upper arm as he pushed the button. The door opened slowly.

"I've spoken to Moscow," Nikolai said once inside the empty car. Pushing an unmarked button, he continued, "I spoke directly with the President. He knows of your efforts."

"What does that mean? What's happening?" Lauren asked.

"He didn't share his thoughts, but if you'll pardon a term from the height of the cold war, I think it's possible we could be only *seconds to midnight.*"

Lauren understood. Nikolai had referenced the doomsday clock—a hypothetical representation of how close the world was to global Armageddon. In her lifetime she'd seen as few as three minutes, and as many as sixteen.

"Seconds?" Lauren asked. "What's happening? Where's Kristof?"

"He's waiting for you."

"That's it?" Lauren said as the elevator doors opened and she found two armed guards waiting for her. She stepped out, turned, and stared at Nikolai angrily.

"Our countries may soon be at war. I hope not, but it's best for both of us if you are not in this building," Nikolai said and respectfully shook Lauren's hand. "Until next time."

Lauren was escorted to a point where a door buzzed and she was led out and deposited on the sidewalk. It was daylight, a dreary, rainy day, and the traffic noise seemed harsh after the quiet hum of the control room.

"I see they kicked you out as well," Kristof said as he walked toward her.

Lauren stopped and then opened the piece of paper that Nikolai had passed to her when they shook hands:

*Confirmed nuclear detonation in Iceland*

"What is it?" Kristof said as he moved closer.

"A nuclear bomb went off in Iceland. I have to get to the American embassy." Lauren fought her tears to look beyond Kristof, trying to get her bearings.

"Oh, dear God," Kristof said after he glanced at the paper in her hand. He lowered his head as the full gravity of the words seemed to come to him in stages. He staggered as if wounded and reached out for Lauren and hugged her, seemingly as much for him as for her.

"Which way?" Lauren asked between the sobs that shook her body. "I have to get there so I can find out what—"

"It's this way." Kristof wiped the tears that had formed in his own eyes and held her arm tightly. As they began to walk, other pedestrians moved and swerved to get around them.

"I found Donovan," Lauren said. "He was flying to Europe, and I was able to get a message to him to fly to Iceland. He had eleven minutes to get in and out. Oh, God, what was I thinking? Kristof, I may have killed my husband and daughter; I may have killed them all."

"You're the most analytical and levelheaded person I've ever met. Don't unravel yet, you still have work to do."

"What work?" Lauren asked as she fought to collect herself. As she did, she knew Kristof was right, the day was far from over.

"What are you going to tell the people at the embassy? It'll be the CIA, I assume?" Kristof asked. "You know I can't go in there to be with you."

"I know. Did Nikolai take you up on your offer?" Lauren wiped her eyes as she remembered Kristof's bargaining chip to get them into the Russian embassy.

"Yes," Kristof said as he kissed Lauren on both cheeks, then pointed up the block. "The American embassy is across the street; the entrance is around the corner. Now, if you'll excuse me, I'm going to go find Marta. One more thing—know that if I had eleven minutes to risk it all, Donovan Nash is the man I'd want making the most of that time."

Lauren nodded against a rush of new tears as she said good-bye, crossed the street, and continued walking. Kristof was right, his words kept echoing in her head, and she held on to them fiercely. She dabbed her tears, squared her shoulders, and with singular determination, she approached the embassy, and went up to the first uniformed United States Marine she saw. "I'm Dr. Lauren McKenna. I need to talk to the senior CIA specialist on duty."

The Marine keyed the microphone on his radio. "She's here."

# CHAPTER FORTY-ONE

DONOVAN RECOILED AGAINST the bright spots dancing in his vision, blinking and shaking his head as he escaped the imprint from the flash. He gripped the controls even harder as the *Galileo* approached the coast. His electronic flight instruments and radios flickered twice and then blinked out. Donovan had no choice but to do this by feel. He spotted a yellow lighthouse and knew they were close to where the ground abruptly dropped off and met the wild water of the North Atlantic.

The instant the land fell away beneath him, Donovan yanked back on the throttles and turned hard, putting them into a sixty-degree bank. He flew the Gulfstream down toward the water, leveling off, and moving in as close to the bluff as he dared. Below them a mixture of black sand and breaking surf seemed to reach up for the *Galileo's* belly.

Above and to his left, at the top of the cliff, he saw the billowing debris that marked the leading edge of the shock wave expanding out into the air above them. The *Galileo* rocked and shuddered as it collided with the violent outer edge of the bomb-induced turbulence. Donovan heard screams from the back as he battled to keep the aircraft level. He held their position like a surfer riding inside a massive curl. Donovan knew they'd all die instantly if he flew into the pressure wave overhead. He couldn't afford even one small mistake. Ahead and to their right, he could see the effects of the blast wave as it caved downward and whipped the ocean into a white-capped frenzy. He and Michael both watched as the powerful surge pushed out to sea, where it finally faded from view.

With the initial shock wave past them, Donovan added power, raised the nose of the *Galileo*, and began to climb. As they roared above the terrain, he spotted the unmistakable shape of the mushroom cloud billowing up from where the airport used to be. He thought of Agent Robertson, and the first stab of grief overcame all his adrenaline. He scanned the sky and then turned to Michael. "Where's the other Gulfstream? I don't see them."

Michael turned, and after a moment, a sigh of relief escaped him. "Unbelievable. I'm not sure how, but they're still back there. We should buy those guys a case of whiskey, and then we should all sit down and nobody leaves until every drop is gone. You know, if we're not in prison for all of the laws we've broken over the last few days."

"Deal," Donovan said, happy for Michael's humor. A flicker caught his eye as one of his primary instrument displays lit up and began running through its initial start sequence, followed by a second tube and then the radio panel.

"The electromagnetic pulse knocked most of the stuff offline," Michael said as he began resetting frequencies. "Who knew it would come back?"

"Eco-Watch Gulfstream, are you there?"

Michael picked up the microphone. "Affirmative."

"We're still with you, and we can't thank you chaps enough for what you did back there. Hell of a thing. There's a very thankful group of passengers aboard, not to mention the crew. We don't have enough fuel to go off island, so we're going to land at an airport north of the glacier."

"We copy," Michael replied. "We're headed to Ireland or Scotland."

"Earlier we gave our card to Ms. VanGelder. Next time you're in London, give us a ring—the drinks are on us."

"You bet. Eco-Watch out." Michael stowed the microphone and turned to Donovan. "Where are we going?"

"I like your idea about Scotland, but first let's find out if anyone's hurt. Can you take the airplane for a minute?"

"Sure." Michael took the controls and adjusted the power and the trim as the *Galileo* continued to climb.

Donovan turned in his seat and found Sofya sitting wide-eyed in the jump seat, her cheeks streaked with recent tears. He leaned in and kissed her on the forehead. He couldn't imagine what she must be thinking, what anyone in the back was thinking. Montero was already up in the aisle, and he could hear her asking about injuries. Donovan heard William's baritone, and once Montero moved further aft, he spotted his oldest and dearest friend. Abigail was on his lap and they were holding hands.

"She's adorable," Sofya said. "I'm glad you were able to save her."

Donovan turned his attention to Sofya. "We saved her. None of this could have happened if it weren't for you."

"What happens now?" she asked.

"Whatever it is, you're with us. Every promise we made to you, we'll keep," Donovan said. "If I were you, I'd let Montero take the lead for a while. She's good at what she does, and she'll get you to the people she trusts. She'll give you the time to figure out what you want to do with the rest of your life."

Montero stepped past the people and worked her way back toward the cockpit. "Okay, we've got a total of sixteen people on board. I have no idea who some of them are, but there are no injuries. Reggie is with us, calming some of the more anxious passengers."

"I've never met the man, but I know he's one of Abigail's favorites. Ask him to come up and say hello when he can."

"I'll do that," Montero replied. "Meantime, the one question everyone is asking is: Where are we going?"

"Michael and I are thinking Scotland?"

Michael looked up from the data he'd entered into the FMS. "All the systems have come back online, autopilot included. We've got the fuel, so if they don't mind being cramped up in back, we can land in Edinburgh in an hour and a half."

"Run that past William," Donovan told Montero. "For the moment, we're headed to Edinburgh."

Montero left and seconds later she returned. "I think you need to check with the guys out there."

Donovan turned and found a Typhoon fighter in close formation, positioned just off the left wing. "Michael, do you have a fighter on your side?"

"No," he said. "I don't see anyone. What do you see, and what are they flying?"

"It's a solitary RAF Typhoon," Donovan said. He felt someone else squeeze in and replace Montero; a man whom he guessed was Reggie. Though they'd talked on the phone and had many mutual friends, they'd never met in person. Donovan reached around and the two men shook hands.

"Mr. Nash, I'm Reggie. Nice to meet you." The former SAS commando then turned to Michael. "You must be Mr. Ross. Abigail does go on about the two of you."

"Reggie, nice to have you aboard," Donovan said, "and thanks for getting everyone back to the plane." Then he pointed out the window. "Any idea what he wants?"

"They usually come in twos. The other guy is probably behind us," Michael said as he dialed 121.5 into the primary radio and brought the microphone to his mouth. "Eco-Watch zero one calling Typhoon flight."

"Eco-Watch zero one," the reply sounded from the speakers. "This is Venom leader, how do you read?"

"Loud and clear," Michael said.

"Roger, can you confirm that you have Ambassador VanGelder aboard?"

"That's affirmative, we have Ambassador VanGelder, as well as fifteen other souls on board, no injuries, our destination is Edinburgh," Michael said.

"Venom one, I copy. Slight change of plans, we're here to escort Ambassador VanGelder at best speed directly to the Faroe Islands. They have power and functioning landlines. Fly your present heading and say requested altitude."

"Tell him we'll level off at flight level three five zero," Donovan said. As Michael entered the coordinates, he saw that their new destination was less than three hundred miles away.

"Looks like we're not going to Scotland just yet," Reggie said with a shrug.

"Why isn't Lauren with you?" Donovan asked. "How is it you ended up in Iceland without her?"

"Communication has been spotty at best," Reggie said. "When Kristof vanished, I made the call, at Dr. McKenna's insistence, to contact William, and request that he fold the three of us under his diplomatic security."

"Kristof is missing?" Donovan asked.

"Was. He wandered off, it seems, without telling anyone. I made the only assumption I could at the time, that something had happened to him, and I pulled Stephanie and Abigail out of England."

"Good work, but that still doesn't answer my question. Where's my wife?"

"Last I heard, which was through an e-mail, was that she's in Poland with Marta, Trevor, and Kristof."

Donovan was relieved at the news about Kristof, but instantly concerned about Lauren and the others. "What are they doing in Poland?"

"Finding out who is behind all of this. They had a lead; a man involved in the abduction of the woman from Interpol was captured."

"Captured by Archangel?" Michael asked.

"Uh, no." Reggie hesitated as if confused. "I'm sorry, is there a player in this I'm not familiar with?"

"Never mind," Michael said and looked away, disappointed.

"Anyway," Reggie said. "I'm assuming they're still in Poland. We'll know more, I'm sure, once we land."

Donovan spotted tiny legs walking up the aisle behind them.

"Daddy," Abigail called out.

"Ah, fatherhood calls," Reggie said as he stepped aside and helped Abigail move up near her father. "We'll all talk later. Thanks again."

Donovan slid his seat back, put an arm around Abigail, and pulled her into his lap. Abigail rewarded him with a hug and a kiss on the cheek.

"Daddy, you surprised me. You and Michael flew over low enough for me to wave to you. Did you see me? I didn't even know you were coming. No one told me. Then we drove really fast. Did we fly faster than a bomb? I can't wait to tell Mommy. You know, Mommy and I rode a horse faster than bullets, but the *Galileo* is even faster. The horse, his name is Zephyr, was really fast though, and I know we just had Christmas, but for my birthday can I get Zephyr as a present? I think Zephyr and Halley would be great friends, and they'd keep each other company."

Donovan smiled, hugged his daughter, and kissed her on top of her head. "We'll see."

"Is there room for one more up here?" William asked as he came forward.

"Sure." Donovan reached out and was more than a little surprised when William closed the gap, hugged him fiercely, and kissed him on the cheek.

"I'm sorry about our last conversation. I was—" William said and then leaned down and wrapped his arms around Abigail as well. "I'm sorry I was so shortsighted. I love both of you more than anything."

"We love you, too, Grandpa," Abigail said.

"Thank you, Abigail," William said as he kissed Abigail's cheek.

"We're being escorted to the Faroe Islands; I don't think our day is over yet," Donovan said. "Montero has calculated we're in trouble across half the globe, and that was before Iceland."

"Do you have any idea who orchestrated everything that's happened?" William asked.

"Tell him," Donovan said to Sofya who was still sitting in the jump seat.

"Gregori Petrov."

William casually put his hands over Abigail's ears. "That son of a bitch is a dead man."

# CHAPTER FORTY-TWO

LAUREN FOLLOWED THE Marine and was quickly handed off to a man in a suit waiting on the other side of a door. Not a word was spoken as she was escorted into a conference room and offered a seat next to a man at the head of the long table, who held a phone to his ear.

"Yes, sir. She just walked in," he said, and handed Lauren the phone. "It's for you. It's the President of the United States."

Lauren took the phone, cleared her throat. "This is Dr. Lauren McKenna."

"Dr. McKenna, this is the President. Are you okay?"

"I'm fine, thank you."

"I need some information. I have confirmation that a nuclear device has been detonated in Iceland. I also have intelligence that you were in the Russian embassy, and a Russian submarine communication system was used to send a message to divert a U.S. registered Gulfstream to Iceland prior to the explosion. Is any of that true?"

"It's all true."

"Dr. McKenna, I'm about ten minutes away from another phone conversation with the Russian President. We've averted a full-out nuclear war, but I need to understand what the hell you were doing, and why he asked me to thank you."

"Did that Gulfstream manage to leave Iceland?"

"We don't know, though if it did avoid the explosion, who would be on this airplane?"

"Hopefully, Ambassador VanGelder, as well as other members of his staff and members of my family," Lauren said. "The Russians and I couldn't stop the events in Iceland from happening, but we came upon the idea of diverting the Gulfstream as a way to minimize the casualties. We also hoped to evacuate key personnel. I trust you've been informed that myself, as well as certain members of the SVR, believe that Gregori Petrov was behind the attack."

"We're aware of Petrov's actions. He's being sought as we speak. I'll ask again, why did the Russian President want me to thank you?"

"Can you imagine what may have happened if the bomb went off without any warning? My friends and I uncovered the plot that could have thrust our countries into another cold war, or worse. The Russian President owes me; you both do. I hope you can leverage what's happened into something diplomatically beneficial." Lauren looked down as a sheet of paper was slid onto the tabletop in front of her.

*Eco-Watch jet on the ground in the Faroe Islands. Communications via land line will be established shortly. They are being instructed to call here.*

"With all due respect," Lauren said. "I need to go."

"Why?" the President asked. "What's happened?"

"The Gulfstream is on the ground in the Faroe Islands," Lauren said just as the phone on the table rang and was instantly answered by one of the communication specialists who nodded that the call was for her. "Mr. President, I have a call I need to take."

"Tell them to patch it into here," the President said.

Lauren relayed the information and the rising static told her a connection had been made. "Hello? Donovan?"

"Lauren, it's William. Donovan and Abigail will be in shortly. Where in the hell are you? What's going on in Russia?"

"William, the President of the United Sates is also on the line," Lauren said as she blinked at the tears forming in her eyes. "You two talk, I want to be free when my husband and daughter call. Mr. President, it's been a long day. Any chance you could get me out of Berlin to go be with my family?"

"I'll take care of it, and thank you, Dr. McKenna. I look forward to meeting you soon."

Lauren handed the phone to the man in the suit, and she was escorted by a young woman into a nearby office. On the desk sat coffee service and a plate of Danish. Lauren sat down for the first time in what felt like hours, and moments later the phone rang. The woman answered, handed the receiver to Lauren, and stepped out of the room.

"Lauren?" Donovan asked. "Are you there?"

"I'm here," Lauren said as tears broke free from her eyes and tumbled down her cheeks. "Are you okay? How's Abigail?"

"We're fine," Donovan said. "You're amazing, and the message from the submarine, that was genius."

"I'm glad it worked." Lauren didn't want to know how many of the eleven minutes Donovan and her daughter actually needed.

"Here," Donovan said. "Someone wants to talk to you."

"Mommy, you should have seen us. Daddy flew really low. Aunt Veronica wasn't scared at all, but I think Grandpa was a little afraid, so I sat on his lap and held his hand. Where are you?"

Lauren struggled to find her voice. "I'm in Germany right now, so we both still have some traveling to do, but I'll see you soon, sweetheart. We might be a day late, but we're all going to celebrate New Year's at Aunt Stephanie's house, okay?"

"Okay, Daddy wants to talk to you again."

"Hey," Donovan said. "I'm standing here next to William, and it seems the President wants to talk to me. Though I did overhear that he cleared the way for us to leave and fly to London as soon as William talks with someone in Moscow. Apparently, you're being flown directly from Berlin to London via State Department jet. I'll see you in a few hours. How about I buy you dinner tonight?"

"I'd love that more than you'll ever know. Do me a favor—play nice with the President. Tell Abigail I love her, and I'll see you both soon."

# EPILOGUE

"She's finally asleep," Lauren said as she walked out onto the patio where William and Donovan were watching the Northern Lights. Donovan put his arm around her to try to keep her warm in the chilly night air. "I don't know if we're going to be able to send Abigail back to school. All she talks about is riding horses, bullets, and flying faster than a bomb."

"There's always homeschooling," Donovan said.

"Honey, that's so sweet of you to offer to leave Eco-Watch to stay home and teach your daughter. We'll tell her in the morning."

"Very funny," Donovan said. "Does that have anything to do with the President asking me if the White House could borrow you for a few years? What's that about?"

"Oh, probably nothing." Lauren laughed. "That's about political favors and making things happen, like using a State Department jet to fly me to London and then getting Michael home to his family. We both know that anything they might offer would pale in comparison to what I do now."

"Which is what exactly?" Donovan teased.

"Being married to one of the most wonderful men in the world and raising our daughter. Who, by the way, told me that you two have already decided on her next birthday present? A horse named Zephyr is coming to live with us. Does that ring a bell?"

"It was something she blew past me in the heat of the moment. I told her we'd think about it. Why does she always take that as a yes?" Donovan shrugged it off and then briefly wondered the best way to transport a horse across the Atlantic Ocean to Virginia. He turned to William. "I've been meaning to ask you, did Robertson, the agent who stayed behind and marshaled us out to the runway, survive?"

"He didn't," William said. "The Secretary of State told me that Agent Robertson used his tactical frequencies to spread the word and help a great many people seek shelter before the bomb detonated. He's a big reason there were less than five hundred casualties."

"He made some things happen for us that would have been difficult otherwise," Donovan said. "Let's make sure that his family is taken care of. Okay?"

"Absolutely," William said. "In my conversations with Washington today, I was told the bomb was relatively small, a crude copy of a North Korean design using radioactive material manufactured in Russia. It was small as far as nuclear devices go, though if the same bomb had gone off in the heart of Washington, D.C., they estimate over eighty-five thousand fatalities, and another two hundred thousand injured. It's still a terrible tragedy, but thankfully, Iceland isn't densely populated. Plus, the airport sits out on a peninsula, and Reykjavik is situated miles away, far outside the bomb's blast radius."

"What about the Boeing?"

"Now that the connection between Iceland, Russia, and the Boeing has been confirmed, the Canadian authorities were happy to allow a joint Canadian/American salvage effort. Any evidence of wrongdoing by Eco-Watch in Canada will be dismissed. The RCMP has already arrested the head of the charter operation in

Thompson. I understand he's being charged with conspiracy and held without bail until a full investigation can be made."

"I spoke with Jesse Burke today. He and Rick are finally both back home," Donovan said. "He did a great job in Manitoba, so I took the liberty of promoting him to Eco-Watch senior diver."

"That's fine," William said. "Though maybe I should ask why?"

"So you and I could ensure he's one of the men on the team who are going back to raise the 737. He seems focused and ready to get back to work. I think he's turned a corner."

"You guys are going to freeze out here," Stephanie called from the door. "Uncle William, please come inside."

Donovan led Lauren back into the parlor of Stephanie's house. He reached out and took her hand and they sat close on the sofa, soaking up the heat from the crackling fireplace. Across from them, William took a seat between Kristof and Stephanie. They were all still full from dinner, and slowly working their way through Stephanie's wine cellar.

"Everything is perfect," William said. "Stephanie, thank you for still having us over tonight even after everything that has happened."

"I'm thrilled we're all still here to enjoy this," Stephanie said. "But please, Lauren, keep talking."

"Where were we?" William asked. "Lauren, you were telling us what happened when you left the Russian embassy."

"Thrown out was more like it," Lauren said. "As soon as the VLF message was sent, Nikolai couldn't get Kristof and me out of there fast enough."

"He couldn't very well have Archangel and a DIA analyst in his operations room at what might be the beginning of a nuclear war, could he?" William said. "Though of all the phone calls I've taken in the last twenty-four hours, the most surprising one was from the

Austrian President. Imagine my surprise when he profoundly apologized for the police work that made Lauren a suspect in the attack on Kristof's residence."

"I have officially been cleared of any wrongdoing. Though to be accurate," Lauren said, "it was Kristof and Montero who made a deal with Interpol that erased all of the misunderstanding."

"Where are Marta and Montero?" Donovan checked his watch. "They're going to be late."

"I think they're here now," Stephanie said as headlights flashed across the patio.

Donovan stood. Even though the house was fully protected by diplomatic security service agents, he still felt the need to be prepared. He heard the slamming of car doors and smiled inwardly when he counted four of them.

"We're here," Montero said as she opened the door.

"We're all in the parlor," Stephanie said, jumping up. "Here, I'll take your coats."

"We brought a few extra people. I hope you don't mind." Montero strolled into the parlor followed by Marta, Trevor, and Sofya.

"Oh my God!" Lauren jumped to her feet and hugged Montero and Trevor. She turned to Sofya. "I'm Lauren, Donovan's wife. Sofya, I'm so happy to finally get to meet you."

"It's good to meet you as well," Sofya said quietly. "Everyone has been so kind."

"We all owe you a huge debt," Stephanie said as she came over. "I'm Stephanie, William's niece. Can I get you some wine?"

"Do you know what I'd really like?" Sofya said. "Is there any vodka?"

"I know where it is," Donovan volunteered, and then turned to the others. "Anyone besides Sofya and me switching to the hard stuff?"

Montero and Trevor both raised their hands.

"Everyone, sit," Stephanie said and headed for the kitchen. "I'll bring everything out."

"So, what have we missed?" Marta asked as she leaned down and gave Kristof a kiss on the cheek.

"Never mind that," Lauren said. "Why don't you bring us up to speed about the gorgeous diamond ring on your finger?"

Donovan watched Kristof light up as Marta smiled and held up her brand-new engagement ring. Trevor leaned in and he and Kristof shook hands. The two men shared a knowing glance, telling Donovan this engagement wasn't a surprise to anyone but Marta.

Marta and Trevor kissed, as Lauren and Montero moved in to take a closer look at the ring.

"Congratulations," Donovan said as he hugged Marta and shook Trevor's hand.

"I was so shocked," Marta said as she brushed a tear away. "I didn't know he and Dad had talked. We were in the park in Berlin, the sun was just coming up and he proposed. Turns out he'd had the ring for weeks."

"Always prepared." Trevor smiled and intertwined his fingers with Marta's.

Donovan turned away and saw Sofya standing alone, away from the happiness, looking lost and very alone. Donovan moved in at the same time as Montero did, and joined her just as Stephanie showed up with the drinks.

"I heard the news," Stephanie said. "Here's champagne and glasses. We need a toast."

Kristof and Trevor opened two bottles, filled the glasses, and passed them out.

"To Marta and Trevor." Kristof raised his glass. "May you find a lifetime of happiness together and enjoy your retirement. As of today, we're both technically out of a job."

"What?" Marta looked stunned. She scanned the eyes of her friends as if to uncover the joke, and ended up looking back at her father. "You quit?"

"No." Kristof smiled and then dug in his trouser pocket until he found a receipt of deposit and handed it to Marta. "I sold the business. The money was deposited yesterday, and I put this amount in your personal account."

Marta's eyes grew wide and she quickly stuffed the paper in her pocket.

"I transferred the business and the inventory to the new owner, who is Russian. It was pretty much all of their arms and equipment anyway. I gave everyone in our employ a severance check and a letter of recommendation. I'm officially retired. As for you two, call it an engagement present."

"I couldn't be any happier for all of you," Donovan said. "Kristof, I think you're going to like retirement. I also have one small announcement to make, and then I think I'll switch to whiskey, and we'll turn the floor over to Montero," Donovan said and then smiled at Sofya. "Sofya, yesterday I had a moment to talk with both William and the President of the United States. You've been granted diplomatic asylum in the United States, Montero is your official sponsor, and we will all participate in your transition. If you'll have us, we're your new family."

"I don't know what to say," Sofya said as tears of joy formed. "Thank you all so much."

Montero hugged Sofya and they each downed a shot of vodka, then Montero glanced at her watch. "Thanks to Sofya, there is something else we managed to put together on short notice. In fact, the first reports should be coming in on the BBC."

Stephanie found the remote and switched on the television. There was a commercial, so she muted the set. Moments later a BBC reporter appeared, and Stephanie turned up the volume.

"We have a developing story that was first reported from Prague. Similar reports filtered in today from Rotterdam, Warsaw, and Berlin. In all four cities, an unknown group of people raided and shut down several nightclubs. Sources tell us the clubs involved were thought to have been engaged in sex trafficking and prostitution. There have been no reports of violence. Witnesses told us that immigration officials descended on the establishments and led women into waiting buses. No word yet on where they were taken, or what will happen to the clubs' owners and customers. We'll have more on this story at the top of the hour."

"Where are they being taken?" William asked.

"They'll be flown to different locations provided by Montero through a deal she worked out with Interpol," Trevor said. "The simultaneous raids on the clubs were carried out by Interpol in conjunction with local police. With assistance from Reggie and the guys, too."

"You put all of this together in less than twenty-four hours?" Lauren asked Montero.

"It's a plan that's been in my mind for a while now, and after meeting Sofya, and then thanks to Marta and Lauren, once I was in a room with a woman named Tatiana, it didn't take long until I had the information and leverage I needed. I brought in Interpol, who were eager to act. When Reggie and Trevor and their former SAS connections volunteered to help, it was a slam dunk. The latest estimate is that we're going to rescue as many as three hundred young women, and I hope this is just the beginning."

"What's going to happen to Tatiana?" Kristof asked.

"She helped Interpol, as well as the Russian government," Montero said. "She'll live, but she'll never see the outside of a prison cell again."

"I'm so proud and happy for everyone," Stephanie said as she switched off the television. "I'm sorry, but I'm the hostess, and I don't want to sit here glued to the telly. I rarely get to see all of you as it is. Now, who needs their drink refreshed?"

"You're right." Lauren held out her glass as she turned to Kristof. "You know, if memory serves me correctly, the last time we were all sitting here, you were in the middle of telling us a story. Something about a young Donovan Nash, high winds, and a large sheet of cardboard? You never had a chance to finish. What happened?"

Donovan groaned and reached for his glass.

"Aha!" Kristof smiled. "Yes, thank you for the reminder. I believe it was summer vacation, August probably, and Donovan and I were in Virginia. I think he was maybe in sixth grade. Anyway, it was a really windy day, howling at least forty miles per hour out of the south, maybe more. For days we'd been threatening to sneak off to a house under construction down the road, and check it out, so we finally did. Donovan discovered this big section of cardboard that had been removed from a furnace, or a hot water heater, something else equally sizable. Anyway, I remember the second he saw it, he had this idea, and he surveyed the site, and explained that if we cut handholds into the cardboard, he'd be able to hold on and jump from the top of one of the towering piles of dirt. Once he did that, he described how he'd use the high winds to his advantage, and he'd fly."

"Oh God, this is where I always start to lose it." Stephanie put her hand to her mouth and began to laugh silently as her eyes filled with tears.

"In theory, it wasn't a bad idea." Kristof began to chuckle as he continued. "Initially, the fierce gusts kept ripping the cardboard from Donovan's hands. Though once we found the ball of heavy twine, all of our engineering problems were seemingly solved. We went back up to the top of the dirt hill, and using the twine, I bound Donovan's hands tightly to the handholds. I remember the look in his eyes. He was fearless, and with no chance of the wind ripping the cardboard away, he simply turned into a huge gust and launched himself off the hill. I'm not sure exactly what happened, but it looked like some sort of cardboard pterodactyl cartwheeling out of control, ending at the bottom of the hill in an explosion of dirt."

"But I flew," Donovan said, his voice barely carrying above the laughter.

"There may have been a few seconds of flight," Kristof managed to say as he wiped tears from his eyes. "All I know is you also crashed. But I've never in my life seen anyone covered with that much blood and dirt who was still smiling as much as you were that day."

William raised his glass. "To that boy and his wings, and may he always remain fearless."